OUT OF THE ORDINARY

OUT OF THE ORDINARY

FM Alexander's early life: a novel

Kate Jenkins

EQUINE
PRESS

Kate Jenkins is a writer living in Hobart Tasmania. She is a long-time practitioner of the Alexander Technique and the author of *Twice no one dies* and *A certain kind of justice*, crime novels set in Togo, West Africa, where she worked for many years.

Published by Equine Press 2024

Book design and production by Lachlan McLaine

A catalogue record for this book is available from the National Library of Australia

ISBN 978 0 9942 6045 1

Frederick Matthias Alexander
Table Cape 1869 – London 1955

Founder of the Alexander Technique,
an educational process of behaviour, human movement,
and breathing, recognised worldwide.

Acknowledged as one of the '200 people
who made Australia great'.

(From a plaque at Table Cape, Tasmania)

Part 1

Wynyard, Tasmania

1879 to 1885

1

Monday, 3 February 1879

In the little rock-edged bay Robert was alone with the seagulls. He picked up another shell. There must have been a sea creature, a soft-bodied mollusc, that had fashioned it into a home, but now the shell was empty, split in two and washed clean by the sea. He held the smooth hollow of its underside on the tips of his fingers, and with his thumb traced the tiny ridges that fanned out in half-moons, the colour changing from grey through an earthy palette to dull gold.

This one he would keep. It spoke to him of patient endeavour, of triumphs from small beginnings, and gave him heart. He slipped the shell into his pocket and stood on the wet sand, looking out over Bass Strait. Up there was a vast continent. Less than a day's sailing he was told. After the long voyage from Scotland and the confusion of the arrival in Tasmania, it was enough to be here at last in Wynyard.

The sun was yet to rise, and the water was calm, almost green, the waves no more than languid swells that toppled on the sand without fuss and spread in lacy ripples. Further out and high overhead, long scraps of clouds were turning shades of pink and coral.

Robert tried and failed to imagine where Scotland might be from where he stood. It would already be dark over there he supposed, and still cold and wintry. He pushed the thought away; there was no point dwelling on the past. He traced the outline of the shell in his pocket and watched the clouds change colour. The town itself had been something of a disappointment, remote and undeveloped in a way he couldn't have imagined back home. But the shoreline, the seascape! It was quite wonderful.

He walked back over the dunes and followed the path along the river to his house. The school had provided him with a modest timber bungalow, much like most of the other houses in the town as far as he could see, and it was comfortable enough. By the time he knocked the sand off his boots, Mrs Harris had laid breakfast on the table in the front room. He'd spent more time than he intended at the beach, and he ate quickly then hurried to his bedroom to get ready.

Washed and shaved, wearing the suit he'd bought in London, he inspected himself in the wardrobe mirror. Surely that wasn't a mark on his jacket! Peering closer, he held the lapel up to the light and brushed it with his fingertips just in case. Not that the children were likely to notice, but it was his first day at the school and he wanted everything to be perfect. His first day as a teacher at any school for that matter. How would they be, these children?

He licked one finger and smoothed his moustache, then he took a last look, silently wished himself good luck, and let himself into the hallway. Mrs Harris was polishing the brass knob on the sitting room door, and when he walked past she stood up and looked at him appraisingly, one hand on the small of her back.

'Don't you look the gentleman,' she said.

'I aim to make a good impression, Mrs Harris. Lead by example. "Clothes do maketh the man", they say.'

Mrs Harris looked confused.

'Shakespeare,' he explained. 'Hamlet.'

Mrs Harris nodded, but he could see she was none the wiser.

'There's those that say getting educated is a waste of time,' she said, 'but I tell them that if God hadn't meant us to read, he wouldn't have written everything in a book.'

Robert smiled to himself.

'Very wise, Mrs Harris. In this day and age, all children should have the right to a good education.'

Robert took his hat off the peg, and using the round mirror set in the hall stand, he twisted it so that it sat straight, then he picked up his leather satchel and opened the front door.

Mrs Harris had followed him down the hallway and was watching him approvingly.

'Now you just enjoy your first day at the school Mr Robertson. No need to worry about anything here. I'll stay on for an hour or two and make sure everything is in order. It's my daughter Rose who will see to your evening meal.'

'You're too kind, Mrs Harris.'

'Good luck sir. I'm sure the children will think themselves fortunate to have you as their teacher. If they don't, they should.'

Robert took a left turn onto Goldie Street, then almost immediately another left turn off the macadam and onto the dirt road that led straight to the school. Half cleared fields came to the edge of the dirt, and rambling bushes grew under and around the post-and-rail fences that marked the allotments. There was an occasional timber house where gardens had been planted, but to Robert it all looked sprawling and untidy. He wondered if his pupils would be like that too.

He could feel the early morning sun on his back and a chorus of bird song rolled out from a stand of river gums. Curious, he thought, how these awkward looking birds could make such a sound; a melodious, sweet warble that spilled out and wrapped itself around him. Nothing like the magpies back home. Not much here was like Scotland.

Nevertheless, there was something he liked about the generosity of the landscape. He took a deep breath and picked up a hint of sea salt and the elusive, sweet–sharp smell of the eucalypts. It was the right decision to come to Tasmania, he was sure of it. If you couldn't make a fresh start here, then you couldn't do it anywhere. Look at the way the men had cleared the land! They'd started farms, built everything from scratch: mills, shops, hotels, houses, and roads. Everything was evolving.

He turned left into Hogg Street and crossed the road to the school. Function had triumphed over charm, and Robert stopped and looked up at the plain timber façade, the four windows seeming to stare down at him. Some of the smaller panes were cracked and he made a mental note to get them repaired. Any gravitas in these children's education was going to come from himself, not from solemn stone buildings with lofty rooms and ancient timbers like the schools he was used to.

All the better, he reminded himself, fresh new minds to be fired.

He walked around to the other side of the building where a covered verandah had recently been added. Some children were playing a game in the far corner of the yard under the peppermint tree. Marbles, he guessed, from the way they were kneeling on the ground. They didn't take any notice of him, and he continued up the wooden stairs, unlocked the door and went into the classroom.

For a minute he stood looking around the empty room. It had been cloudy yesterday when he'd come here to work, and the room had felt painfully bare and unpleasant. This morning the desks on the northern side were pooled with sun that streamed through the windows, and the glowing timber gave the whole room a softer feel. It could be worse, he thought, a lot worse.

A blackboard covered the front wall. It was bare except for the date in the top left-hand corner: Monday, February 3, 1879. In front was a solid oak table, and in one corner a glass-fronted cabinet housed samples of rocks and fossils. Tucked into the opposite corner was a hat stand. He realised he was still wearing his hat and went over and hung it on a hook.

Sitting at the table, he pushed the box of books to one side and opened the attendance roll. He picked up the book on the top of the pile and copied the first name from the roll on to the cover. Then he did the same to each of the books in turn, ticking the names off as he did so. It had been an extravagance, buying these little reward books. They were a happy reminder of his own school days, and his hope was they would be the same for these children.

He'd just put the last book on the finished pile when there was a knock and a tall young woman appeared in the doorway. When she saw Robert she hesitated, and he waved her in. She removed her wide-brimmed hat and hung it on the stand, then patted her hair back in place.

Robert pushed his chair back and went over to greet her.

'You must be Mrs Roebuck.'

'Yes. Isabelle Roebuck. Your assistant teacher.'

'Pleased to meet you Mrs Roebuck. From what I hear, I'm going to need your assistance.'

Isabelle laughed.

'Yes. They're quite a handful.' She looked at the clock. 'Do you think I should bring them in?'

Where had that time gone? Five minutes to nine already.

'Yes. Thank you.'

Robert stood in front of the desk and Mrs Roebuck went over and opened the door. There was a sudden noise of loud chatter, but it died away as she stood waiting for silence.

'Girls up the front, boys up the back. And bring the little ones here. They can wait with me.'

Robert watched the children file into the room. They filled the whole seven rows of wooden desks, so by his calculation there were almost fifty students. Mrs Roebuck settled the new five-year-olds in the front row, and there was the sound of scraping chairs and excited whisperings as the other children chose a desk. Before long, most of them were sitting quietly, eyes ahead, watching Robert.

Most, but not all.

In the row of desks at the very back of the room, four or five boys were still not settled. They'd come in talking to each other and passing something that looked like scraps of paper. Now they were sitting at their desks, shuffling and talking, passing something between them, half aware of Robert standing there, but more interested in a fair-headed boy who was sitting at the desk at the end of the row. He looked younger than the boys around him, not more than ten, Robert guessed, and although the older boys were at least pretending to face the front, this boy took no notice of anything except whatever it was he was doing.

Robert stood and watched.

Unhurried, the fair-headed boy pushed something under his desk and only then gave his attention to Robert.

The silence in the classroom stretched like a slingshot.

Robert let it continue. His work in the courts back in Scotland was unorthodox training for a schoolmaster, but he had learned something about control. When every child was desperate for him to break the silence he walked up to the blackboard and wrote his name.

Then he turned back to the room.

'Good morning class.'

Mrs Roebuck made a palm up gesture and the children shuffled to their feet.

'Good morning Mr Robertson.'

It was said hesitantly, trailing into murmurs when it came to the unfamiliar name. There was more shuffling and scraping of chairs while they sat down again. Robert put the chalk back on the desk and walked up the centre aisle. He took his time and looked carefully at every child, though it was clear to all of them where he was heading.

The fair-headed boy looked down at the scratches and ink marks on his desk, as if by doing that he wouldn't be noticed. Robert stopped in front of him and stood there.

Finally the boy raised his head and stared up at Robert.

'Sir?'

Robert's instinct told him there was a well-worn path with this boy. People he'd met in Wynyard had been quick to tell him that his predecessor didn't spare the strap, and Robert guessed that's what the other children were expecting to happen. Well, if he was here to test his own ideas about teaching, this was an excellent place to start.

Robert leaned down slowly, a hand on either side of the desk so his face was inches from the boy's. The boy met his look with steady blue eyes.

There was something Robert saw there that helped him decide. It was hard to explain, even to himself, but Robert felt that an understanding of some sort passed between them. He straightened up and walked to the front of the class then turned around and spoke directly to the boy.

'You can be the first to write your name on the board.'

Robert held out a stick of white chalk. The boy stood up reluctantly and walked up the aisle. He took the chalk and went to the blackboard, reached up as high as he could and wrote: Frederick Matthias Alexander. His letters were neatly formed and surprisingly straight. He put the chalk with the other pieces in the box and started to return to his seat, but Robert hadn't finished.

'And now could you give us a short description of the enterprise you were engaged in when you arrived.'

The boy looked at him.

'Enterprise?'

'Pieces of paper,' Robert prompted.

'Oh that. It's horses sir.'

'Horses?'

'At the beach on Saturday. There's going to be a big race – eight horses. I'm running a book on it. The long odds are on Robin, but I think he's got a good chance if it rains on Friday.'

'Robin?'

'It's my pa's horse sir.'

'And do you think it might rain on Friday?'

'My pa says there's a good chance.'

Robert had to hold back a smile.

'Let's hope he's right. I'm told we need the rain. Meanwhile, you, Mr Alexander, can wait behind during the morning break. Now sit down and pay attention.'

★

When the bell rang for the morning recess, Robert waited until the last child had left the classroom, then he went over and closed the door. The last to leave were the boys who'd been sitting up the back and one of them spat on his hand and rubbed it on his pants, then grinned at Fred, who ignored him.

There was a long flexible cane hanging by a strap over near the hat stand. Robert had no idea how he would bring himself to use it if it became necessary.

'Come here Mr Alexander. There's the matter of your punishment.'

Fred did as he was told and stood facing Robert in front of the table, his hands behind his back.

'Do you know why you come to school?' Robert asked.

'To learn facts.'

'Yes. But that is only one part of it. You are coming to school to learn discipline, respect, and right behaviour. You will stay behind during the break and write for me an essay explaining why running a betting scheme during class time does not conform to those three things. Repeat them to me.'

'Discipline, behaviour and…. I can't remember. I don't mind getting the cane sir.'

'Punishment, Mr Alexander, is intended to teach you not to do something by making you do the very thing that you don't like. Discipline, right behaviour, and respect. Go and write those words in your essay book immediately.'

'It's too hard.'

'And add to that a fourth one. Reasons why you must not argue with the teacher.'

The boy sighed and trudged back up to his desk. Robert wondered if he was being weak in refusing to cane the children. He would do what he could to discipline this boy, but discipline was one thing, and breaking the spirit another, and that Robert had no wish to do.

2

That evening

There was still an hour at least before Rose would arrive with his evening meal, and Robert was working at the table in the front room, determined to finish the lessons for tomorrow before she came. He could hear his mother's voice saying he should keep the parlour, as she would call it, for guests, but what a waste that would be. It was the best room in the house, with good-sized windows on two sides. When he was seated at the table he looked onto a thick stand of peppermint gums and blackwood trees; if he stood, he could see the river and the wharf.

The sun was about to set and the light was heavy and golden. It was pouring in through the western window and dust particles followed it across the room. Robert looked up from his books and noticed how the shaft of light played on the photo of Emma. It put him in mind of ancient Celts, who built their stone monoliths so the sun would fall in precise locations. He marked his place in the book and went over to the mantelpiece to have a closer look.

The photo was in a wide leather frame richly decorated with gold brocade. The picture itself was much smaller than the frame, and the oval shape softened the lines of Emma's face and shoulders. Her head was tilted to one side and she had that familiar smile, as if she was thinking to herself 'Come now – is that really what you think?'

When she'd presented the photo to him, not long after their engagement, he'd had no idea how much it would come to mean to him. It was as if she was looking straight at him. Her thick copper-coloured hair was secured loosely with a clasp, and, exactly as he remembered her, some curls had escaped and wisped around her ears. The colour of the sepia photo was deepened by the shaft of light and Robert stood for a while looking at it, his hands in his pockets, his thoughts back in Scotland.

When she'd broken off the engagement it had been as if he changed from a boy to a man in the time it took her to tell him. He tried not to think about that time, but the memories appeared unbidden. The pubs, the drinks, the larks, as he and his friends called them.

Then the night it went too far, and he ended up in the police cell. With distance, it was easier to understand her determination to end their engagement. 'I'll change', he had said, and meant it. 'I've already changed. Just give me another chance.' Now, Robert wanted very much to rid himself of the urge to drink. The rational side of him didn't believe in the devil, yet how else could he explain the way that drink took hold of him, changed him into a person he didn't want to be?

She still loved him, he felt sure of that, and if he could show her he'd changed, they might still have a life together. That was his understanding. He brushed some dust off the photo with his handkerchief and was winding the clock when there was a knock on the door. His first thought was that Rose was early with his dinner, but it was too confident and loud to be her. There was a sound of footsteps and when he looked round, the fair-haired boy from school was standing at the entrance to the room. Alexander, that was his name. But what was he doing here?

The boy's trousers were rolled up to mid-calf and he was carrying something in his hand. He seemed perfectly at ease.

'The door was open Mr Robertson sir.'

Robert wasn't sure what he should do. He couldn't imagine anyone letting themselves into the house back in Stirling, let alone a young lad who had been in trouble at school today.

'Mr Alexander. What brings you here?'

'I was over on the beach and I found these.'

The boy kept one hand cupped, and with the other hand he carefully opened the wet cloth that was holding three dirty looking shells. Robert peered down at them. Now he could see they were some sort of crustacean.

'Oysters?'

'Yes. They're fresh off the rocks. I thought you might like them.'

An apology? Again, the boy had grabbed his interest and Robert forgot about feeling cross.

'I've never had fresh oysters off the rocks like that. How do I open them?'

The boy looked pleased.

'I can do that for you.'

He wrapped the oysters back up, but he didn't move. Instead, he looked up at Robert, still standing in front of the mantelpiece, his back to it now.

'Where are you from, Mr Robertson? Not the seaside?'

Had the boy seen him with the photo? Through the window perhaps? Were there other sea creatures that would appear from a pocket? Robert moved towards the door.

'Come on Mr Alexander. The scullery's the best place for those oysters.'

'Most people call me Fred, sir. Except my ma and pa. They call me Frederick, or when they're really angry, Frederick Matthias. But I like people calling me Fred. Who's that sir?'

Fred pointed at the photo of Emma and instead of following Robert, he went closer to the mantelpiece and peered up at it.

'Is she your mother sir?'

There was something in the contrast between the bold manner of the boy and his naivety that Robert found poignant and interesting. He came back to the fireplace and took Emma's photo off the mantelpiece so Fred could see it better.

'You mean this one? No, she's not my mother.'

He pointed to the right of the mantelpiece where a serious, upright woman was photographed sitting on a straight-backed chair, an equally serious man next to her, his hand on her shoulder in a possessive gesture.

'That's my mother.'

'Does she miss you? My mother says she wouldn't know what to do without me. Is that one your missus? Do you miss her too?'

'You ask a lot of questions, Fred.'

'Yes sir. It's because I want to know the answers.'

He looked so earnest, one hand still clasping the oysters in the sodden handkerchief, skinny ankles sticking out from the rolled trousers, the shoes scuffed and worn, big enough for him to grow into. Robert put the photo of Emma back on the mantelpiece.

'No. She's not my missus.'

'Is she your sweetheart?'

'Not now. And I daresay my mother does miss me in her own way.'

Fred started to ask another question, but Robert had had enough, and he took the boy by the shoulders and propelled him towards the scullery.

'No more questions, Fred.'

'Just one?'

'Very well. Just one.'

'Mother wants to know if you would come to roast dinner on Sunday.'

So that was why he was here. The cheekiness of it made Robert laugh.

'Tell your mother I am honoured to accept.'

3

The following Sunday, 9 February 1879

Robert felt comfortable in the charming little church. After the first hymn, Reverend Brown started on the sermon and Robert lapsed into daydreaming. He imagined the sort of house that he and Emma might live in if she changed her mind, if he could entice her to this remote little settlement. A house across from the beach at least two storeys high, maybe three. He liked the way people used verandahs here, and his would be wide and grand. The house would be brick or stone, with French windows opening onto the verandah and dormer windows upstairs. His mind was happily wandering through the house, when he realised Reverend Brown had stopped talking and a visiting minister was being introduced.

Robert watched Reverend Brown step down from pulpit. People shuffled their feet and shifted around on the hard pews. The new minister took his place at the pulpit and spread his notes on the lectern, then waited while everyone settled.

It might have been a glimpse of the communion wine that set him off, or perhaps the time of day (it was getting towards noon), but quite unbidden, the thought of a glass of whisky hit Robert and he had a sudden craving for a drink. His mind jumped in the way he found so tiresome but couldn't seem to control: just one won't hurt…you never stop at one…you promised Emma…but she would never know…

The minister, who'd been introduced as Reverend Palfreyman, took hold of the front of the lectern and looked straight at Robert, at least that's how it felt.

'My text today is from Proverbs 20:1 Wine is a mocker, strong drink is raging, and whosoever is deceived thereby is not wise.'

His voice was strong and intelligent, more academic than clerical, as if he might be giving a lecture at a university. The sermon was nicely developed, referring to a scientific examination of alcohol and alluding to some disturbingly pertinent comments on the way strong drink affected the mind and the body.

It touched something deep within Robert, as if the minister was speaking directly to him. This was what he'd been looking for: something spiritual, someone greater than himself to say, 'Come on Robert, we can do this together.' He felt lighthearted. People had told him the change had to come from within himself, and now it had.

Robert watched Reverend Palfreyman intently, his mind racing now with ideas of how to act on his resolve. Mrs Roebuck had been talking to him about the temperance movement that was catching on in this area and that seemed a good starting point. As the headmaster of a state school, he had standing in this community, so why not start his own society?

When the last hymn had been sung, Robert made sure he was at the end of the line of people waiting to shake hands with the ministers, and when it was his turn, he was surprised at the way Reverend Palfreyman greeted him, as if he already knew him.

'Mr Robertson, is it? The new headmaster? I saw you looking at me when I started my sermon.'

'I wonder if we could have a word in private,' Robert suggested.

By way of reply, Reverend Palfreyman held his arm out in a gesture for them both to go back into the church, away from the chatting groups of churchgoers who were clustered around the porch.

Robert slid into one of the pews at the back of the church, leaving a space for the minister to sit beside him. The stained-glass windows at the end of the chancel were lit from behind and, though he knew better, it felt to him as if a personal God was watching over him.

Reverend Palfreyman seemed to guess what he was thinking, because he looked at the windows and then at Robert.

'Surprising, aren't they? Every time I take the service here, I'm struck by how close the spirit of God seems to be in this little church. Anyway, in what way can I be of assistance, Mr Robertson?'

'I know I can count on your discretion, Reverend Palfreyman.' The minister nodded, and Robert continued. 'You were correct in the remark you made to me outside. The topic of your sermon did have personal resonance for me. I have made up my mind to abstain completely from alcohol, and during your excellent talk I came to the conclusion that my contribution to the community here might be to start a temperance society of some sort. I hope it's not impertinent, but I thought you might be of a like mind, that we could work together to establish such a society.'

Robert knew he sounded stilted and formal, and wondered what the minister would make of him. Twice he'd paused, expecting some response, but Reverend Palfreyman had listened in silence. Now he turned to Robert and smiled.

'My own thoughts have been turning towards doing just such a thing, but something has held me back. Now I realise that I've been waiting for the right person to work with, and God has sent you.'

An elderly woman came in and saw them, then excused herself and went out again.

'I have my flock to take care of now.' The minister nodded in the direction of the woman. 'But let's meet up and make a plan.'

They shook hands, and before he released his grip, the reverend gave Robert's hand a hearty pump.

'You've come to the right place, Mr Robertson. The hardest part is already behind you.'

4

Coming from the darkness of the church into the sunlight blinded Robert for an instant, and he squinted and put his hand up to shield his eyes.

'Over here Mr Robertson.'

Robert heard the voice before he made out Fred Alexander, waving his arm over his head and calling out to him. The group of people Fred was standing with spanned at least three generations. Fred introduced his mother first, and Robert hoped he didn't look as surprised as he felt when she turned out to be the pretty, youthful looking woman who Robert had thought might be Fred's sister. The more matronly woman standing next to her was one of Fred's aunties.

He felt at a distinct disadvantage when it came to names. The ones who weren't Mrs or Miss Alexander were introduced as Mrs something else who used to be an Alexander, and was a cousin or sister or aunt. Then there were the children who had clustered together and stood in a group looking bored, occasionally pushing each other and giggling at something whispered. Robert couldn't remember the names of the other Alexanders who were in his class, so he was relieved when Fred took it on himself to point them out.

'The tall one, that's my brother Arthur. He's a year younger than me, but he's bigger and plays cricket. The one in the hat with the yellow bows is my sister Agnes. She's seven, and that's my cousin...'

Robert would never remember them all and was relieved when Mrs Alexander cut him off before he had a chance to go through the whole group.

'Go and fetch your father, Frederick. And tell the others that we're leaving now.'

The men were in a separate group, and Robert watched Fred go up to a compact, fair-haired, lightly bearded man who was emphasising something he'd said with an upraised arm and cautionary finger. He turned around impatiently when he noticed Fred standing next to him, and the resemblance between them was evident: the fair hair, high forehead, and long straight nose. But there it ended. Mr Alexander's face held judgement in long brows ready to frown, and challenge in the tilt of his chin, whereas Fred was more like his mother, with a mouth that looked ready to smile.

It was a short walk back to the Alexanders' house; nothing was too far from anything else in Wynyard. The morning showers had settled the dust on the roads and the air had a welcoming after-rain freshness about it.

Mrs Alexander walked alongside Robert and she was almost as full of questions as her son.

'Tell me about the old country Mr Robertson. Where is your home back there? What do you think of Wynyard? Is it very different? Of course it is. Do tell me about your town.'

It was hard to know where to start. Robert looked around at the vacant blocks, the untidiness of it all. As he talked about the medieval castle in Stirling, and the river Forth that snaked its way through rows of neat brick houses, all alike with their tiled roofs and bay windows, the tidy grass walks along the banks of the river, the paved streets, he wondered that two places could be quite so different.

'I do so want to go to the Old Country one of these days,' Mrs Alexander sighed.

'Were you born over there, Mrs Alexander?'

'No. I was born in Launceston. But England feels like my real home.'

Robert thought he understood. There was something raw and unfinished about Wynyard, and yet the long stretch of blue sea with its white sandy beaches and charming rocky headlands was as beautiful as any landscape he'd seen.

They were walking past a corner block, tidier than the others, with a good crop of grass on it. There was an iron trough under a peppermint tree and a group of horses was standing in the shade, flicking their tails and watching them.

Fred came running alongside his mother and called out to Robert.

'Come and see our horses. I'll show you which one is Robin.'

'There's no time for that now Frederick,' his mother told him, and sure enough, the house was right there. A short brick path led to the verandah and the open front door. A young girl came out to meet them, holding the hand of a toddler.

'My niece Mary-Anne helps out on Sundays,' Mrs Alexander explained to Robert. 'And this is Richard. He's been helping Mary-Anne look after his baby sister Amy, haven't you Richard?'

The little boy sucked his thumb and nodded gravely but said nothing.

'Take Mr Robertson through to the dining room Mary-Anne.'

Mary-Anne picked up Richard and balanced him on her hip, then she led the way down a long hallway. The house was much like the one Robert was living in, big enough for him but not so large for a family like the Alexanders. Single storey of course, like most of the houses in Wynyard. Rooms went off on either side of the hallway and Robert followed Mary-Anne through to a dark room on the right. The table was almost as big as the room, with plates and cutlery stacked at one end next to a cruet set, and a mixed assortment of chairs on either side.

Mary-Anne busied herself lifting the reluctant Richard into a highchair, then she asked Robert to keep an eye on him and hurried out to the kitchen. Robert was wondering what to do, when Mr Alexander strode into the room and seated himself at the head of the table.

'Sit anywhere,' he said to Robert, not unfriendly, but blunt, with no more than a nod.

But while Robert was still trying to decide where to sit, the room was filled with children, led by a chattering Fred. He scooted around the other side of the table, followed by a small boy with a round, angelic looking face.

'Over here Mr Robertson,' Fred called out.

Robert squeezed into the space left for him between Fred and his brother, who was introduced to him as Albert. Arthur sat on the other side of the table, at his father's left hand, and then Richard, who had found a spoon and was banging it on the arm of the highchair. Agnes was next to him, and now that he had a better look, Robert recognised her as one of the quiet girls in his class, and he caught her eye and smiled. She gave him a shy smile that showed her missing front teeth, then acting more like a little mother than a seven-year-old, she managed to get the spoon off her brother.

When Mary-Anne put a steaming leg of ham in front of Mr Alexander, Robert realised how hungry he was and any doubts he may have had about the invitation were gone, as Mrs Alexander and Mary-Anne filled the table with dishes of baked vegetables and peas and a large gravy boat of what looked like parsley sauce.

Mrs Alexander sat at the end of the table next to Agnes. Her hair was loosely pulled back into a simple knot on the back of her neck and Robert still found it hard to believe she had six children. Had he been asked, he would have put her age around twenty. A dimple appeared at either side of her mouth as she smiled at Robert.

'Welcome to our table, Mr Robertson.'

Robert was about to reply when Mr Alexander cleared his throat and made a downward gesture with his hand. All the heads were dutifully bowed and the bountiful mercy of God was expounded on and earnestly thanked.

When he was finished, Mr Alexander pushed his chair back and stood over the ham. He looked perfectly at ease now and he smiled at Robert as he pulled the knife back and forth over the sharpening stone, then tested the blade with his finger.

'See this? It's the best blade in the district. One I made at the forge. Anyone can roast a joint, but the secret is in the carving.'

Maybe it was the carving, like Mr Alexander said, but Robert guessed that Mrs Alexander was also a very good cook. Unlike the roast dinners back in Stirling, this food set off an explosion of taste buds, and everything – ham, vegetables, sauce – had succulence and flavour that he wasn't used to.

'This is the best roast I've had in my life,' he announced happily to the table at large.

Albert and Agnes looked at each other and giggled at the new teacher who talked in a funny way and was so excited about vegetables and ham.

Fred frowned at them.

'It comes from my Uncle Martin's farm,' he said, sounding rather adult and serious. 'Do you know the Cape?'

'You mean the point across the river I can see from my house?'

'No, that's the bluff.'

'Fossil Bluff,' Mrs Alexander added.

'Past that, there's the Cape. You can't see it from here, but my uncles own all the land up there and there are miles and miles of things growing and gardens and animals. Everything. And it was me who rode up there today and brought the potatoes and the pumpkin, and cream, and my pa helped to kill the pig…'

Mr Alexander looked up from his almost finished meal.

'That's enough. The teacher doesn't want one of your speeches about it.'

'Let him be, Johnny,' Mrs Alexander looked fondly at Fred.

Such a torrent of words. Maybe that was why the other Alexanders were so quiet. Arthur didn't look happy at school and he didn't look happy now. Agnes was ignoring Fred and fussing over Richard, cutting up his meat and keeping the area around him clean. Albert looked like he wanted to say something, and Robert turned to the round-faced little boy beside him.

'Do you help too, Albert?'

The dark head nodded and the knife and fork were laid on his plate. He looked up at Robert.

'Ma has the vegetable patch and I help her. Every day.'

Robert looked at Mrs Alexander, who nodded and smiled.

'And what did you do today?'

'Those beans I picked.' He pointed to the pool of bright green peas on Robert's plate. And me and Agnes shelled them too.'

'Peas,' Fred said. 'Not beans.'

Albert blushed and looked down at his plate and Fred kept talking.

'He gets beans and peas mixed up.'

'And you never get anything wrong!' Arthur almost shouted.

Fred looked at Arthur with an annoying smirk.

'Well I'm not the one who thought the capital of England was Melbourne.'

The frown between Mr Alexander's eyebrows deepened and his knife and fork were suspended on either side of his plate. He didn't shout, but there was no doubting that he meant what he said.

'Enough. There'll be no pudding and a thrashing for you Frederick if you don't stop right now.'

Fred bit back whatever he was going to say and turned back to his food. By the end of the meal Robert had learned a lot about the racing scene here, and how Wynyard needed a proper racecourse. There didn't seem to be much that Mr Alexander didn't know about horses. However, he also made it clear what he thought about books. 'Rubbish. A waste of time.'

Robert thought of passing on Mrs Harris' idea about God's wish to have people read the Bible, but there was a gruffness about John Alexander that made him think better of it.

After two helpings of raspberry trifle Robert asked Mr Alexander about his forge and the smithy. It was as if Mr Alexander had been waiting for that cue, and without even a word to his wife, he stood up and waved in the direction of Robert.

'Come on son. I'll show you the forge. I'm thinking you won't have seen much of that, being a letters man and all.'

Robert noticed that Mrs Alexander frowned, but she said nothing.

Mr Alexander strode up the hall and out the gate and was silent during the short walk across the yard to the smithy. They stopped in front of a large timber and corrugated iron shed, and Robert stood to one side as Mr Alexander pulled back one of the heavy wooden doors, kicked a stone in front of it, did the same with the other door then went into the dark interior and pulled a black cloth off a window in the far wall.

'Stops it from getting too hot,' he explained.

Once his eyes adjusted to the light Robert saw a dusty, timber-lined workplace. Cluttered, yes, but in a purposeful way. There was a high brick chimney and open fireplace in one corner and a set of shoulder-high leather bellows facing into it. Horseshoes were hanging from poles along one wall, racks and racks of them, and Robert went over and examined them.

'Am I right in thinking these are all different?'

Mr Alexander came over and took down two horseshoes. He held one out.

'Run your hand over the inside of this one.'

Robert did what he was asked.

'Now this.'

And yes, there was a difference. Small, but he could feel it and see it, the slight difference in the holes, the thickness, the shape.

He handed the shoes to Mr Alexander, who hung them back over the rack.

'It's an art. Even the same horse might need slightly different shoes. Depends.'

'How do you know?'

Mr Alexander almost smiled.

'The horses tell me.'

On the other side of the smithy most of the floor space was covered with heavy looking farm equipment and tools of all types.

Robert went over and squatted down in front of a ploughshare.

'Did you make this plough Mr Alexander?'

'Everything here.' Mr Alexander ran his hand along the handles of the ploughshare. 'That's for the Rylands' farm.' Then he pointed to a finely worked fireguard and a set of shovels and pokers. 'Those are for the Courthouse Hotel.' Stepping around the clutter, he went over to a half-broken cupboard that leaned against the wall and pulled out a bottle. 'Speaking of hotels,' he said, 'I'm thirsty. How about you?' He turned the label towards Robert. It said, 'Jamaican Rum'.

Robert hesitated before answering, but Mr Alexander didn't notice and went ahead and poured a good amount into two enamel mugs he took from the cupboard. He held one out to Robert, and there was nothing he could do but accept it.

Then Mr Alexander pulled out a couple of wooden crates. He handed one to Robert then he brought the bottle and the other crate and put them on the ground in front of one of the doors. Robert followed Mr Alexander's lead and sat cautiously on the crate.

The smithy tossed back the rum in his mug, wiped his mouth with his hand then poured himself another one.

To his own surprise, Robert cradled the mug in his hands, not tempted by the rum. It felt wonderful, as if he'd been freed from an iron trap that had had him in its grip. There was no doubt that something in his mind had changed in church this morning, no doubt at all.

Mr Alexander pointed to Robert's mug.

'Out with it son,' he said. 'You haven't touched a drop and I can see there's something on your mind.'

The informality of the situation lowered Robert's guard, and his instinct told him that Mr Alexander had grappled with the same problems as himself. In any event, for the second time that day, Robert was talking about himself. He started with his life in Stirling – the drinking, his arrest, Emma's ultimatum – and ended with his resolution in church this morning and his conversation with Reverend Palfreyman.

'I can't say I'll never be tempted again,' Robert finished. 'It's the very fact that I might be tempted that leads me to believe that total abstinence is the only solution. Reverend Palfreyman and I are going to call a meeting in Wynyard in the next month or so, to see what interest there is in forming a society.'

Mr Alexander finished his rum and shook the dregs out on to the grass.

'God works in mysterious ways,' he said. 'That might be why a man like you ends up in a place like this. Lord knows I shouldn't be drinking on the sabbath, and I don't need Betsy to tell me that I'm a better man without this.' He pointed to the bottle of rum. 'That society of yours could be just what I need.'

5

Two months later, Saturday, 29 March 1879

Robert slackened the reins and sat back in the saddle. The grey mare slowed to a walk and picked her way through saltbush and pink flowering pigface that covered the track over the sand dunes. It was a path she'd followed often, and now they were off the road and away from the other horses Robert relaxed and allowed her to walk at her own pace.

After only a couple of months it felt normal to be riding to the beach. Or riding to the Cape. Riding everywhere. It only needed a day of rain and the unsealed roads – that was most of them – turned into muddy bogs that you could sink into up to your knees. Robert rode to school on those days and he left Misty to graze with the other horses in the paddock next door. She was called Misty because of her colour, but she was tranquil too, like her name.

It was thanks to Johnny Alexander that he had a horse. And to give him his due, thanks to sharp-eyed Fred, who had seen Robert picking his way along the dirt road to school after the first heavy rainfall.

Never one to keep his opinions to himself, Fred had come up to Robert while he was using the foot-scraper to get the mud off his boots. Rain was falling, light but steady, and the thought of a wet day with fifty children and no shelter-shed had done nothing to put Robert in a good mood.

'You need a horse Mr Robertson.'

No good morning or excuse me. The child was incorrigible.

'And I suppose you're going to tell me from where I should get one?'

Fred wasn't put off. He probably didn't even notice Robert's bad temper, and he went on, earnest and enthusiastic as usual.

'You can get one from my pa. He hires out horses and carriages. I'll tell him.'

And that same afternoon Johnny Alexander had set him up with Misty.

Now it was the last Saturday in March and Robert took up the reins again as Misty trotted down to the beach. The tide was out and on the wide stretch of damp sand men were preparing for the first race. Jockeys were riding their horses to the far end of the beach where posts had been set up for the starting line and it seemed that most of the town were here on the beach to watch.

Robert dismounted and walked Misty along the soft dry sand close to the dunes until he was on the edge of the crowd. He'd never seen anything like it. Children were building sandcastles and digging with little spades, their parents standing in groups chatting, or sitting on rugs spread out on the sand. Some men were riding and others were leading horses around. There were even two carriages right there on the beach, the horses unhitched and tethered to a post. It was so warm today that, like many of the other men here, Robert had come without a jacket. With his sleeves rolled up and wearing his new cabbage tree hat, he felt like a different person. He dismounted and tied Misty with the other horses then looked around for a familiar face.

'Over here, Mr Robertson. Come and see.'

From behind a wobbly table that supported a rough looking wooden box, Fred Alexander was waving both his arms and calling out to him.

The usual group of boys was milling around in front of the table and when he got close to it, Robert saw that Fred had made a sort of cabinet out of the box and was using it to run 'a book' as he called it on the races. Fred pointed to the back of the box and Robert bent down and peered inside. There were lots of little things wrapped in wax paper with a twist at either end.

'Sweets?' he asked.'

Agnes came running across from where she'd been sitting on a rug with her mother. There was a hooded basket next to Mrs Alexander – the new baby, Robert guessed.

Agnes was almost as excited as Fred.

'They're toffees. I made them myself.'

'Do you want to place a bet Mr Robertson?' Fred asked.

Robert shook his head.

'No thank you Fred. I'll go and keep your mother company.'

'Come on Mr Robertson. I'll take you over to her,' Agnes said.

Mrs Alexander was sitting on a picnic rug. Next to her was a wicker basket and she was squinting against the sun from under a wide brimmed hat watching Richard and Albert, who were further down the beach, digging in the sand. Robert squatted down next to the basket and was charmed to see tiny baby Amy sound asleep, shaded by a cloth thrown over the hood. He looked across at Mrs Alexander and smiled, and she motioned for him to join her on the rug.

Robert did as she suggested and sat next to her on the edge of the rug.

'You must think us very rough, Mr Robertson, but the beach is the only place for us to race until we can get our own racecourse.'

Surprising, yes, but certainly not rough, Robert thought. No, there was a great deal to like about the degree of informality here, the determination of these people to find pleasure in simple things.

'Quite the contrary, Mrs Alexander. It's a real pleasure to enjoy the outdoors on such a splendid day.'

'I hope you're happy with Misty, Mr Robertson. Mr Alexander and I thought her temperament would be suited to a...' she searched for the right word, and Robert filled it in for her.

'A novice rider. Yes, thank you. Misty has made my life so much easier. And speaking of horses, Fred's been telling me about your skills as a horsewoman.'

Mrs Alexander shook her head but looked pleased at the same time.

'I'm afraid it's taking him a long time to learn to think before he speaks. What's Frederick been telling you now?'

'He said that people called you the lady with the magic hands and that you used to strap him to your back and ride miles through the bush to tend women in childbirth.'

Mrs Alexander relaxed and nodded.

'Dr Wilson gave me some training and sometimes needs must. It can be hard for women in the remote areas and if I can help them, I do. Fancy Frederick remembering about those times.'

She shook her head in a way that suggested pride in her first born, which led Robert to ask another question.

'I'm not sure if this is a delicate topic, Mrs Alexander, but what are your thoughts on Fred's...shall we say enterprise in regard to horse racing.'

There was no hiding the flush that rushed onto Mrs Alexander's cheeks and she reached up a hand and brushed at her face as if she could make it disappear. Had he been too blunt? But she answered with the same directness as before.

'To be honest with you Mr Robertson, it's a sore point between my husband and myself. God fearing man though he is, Mr Alexander won't hear a word against the horse betting. "It's gambling," I tell him, but his whole family is mad about racing and it's like a force of nature: you have to live with it. I was brought up with a different set of beliefs and wonder if they aren't paving a road to that other place.'

Robert nodded sympathetically. He wasn't sure where he stood on the matter of wagering and hell.

'At least where Fred's concerned there's no money that changes hands,' Mrs Alexander said. 'We only allow Frederick to pretend. Sometimes the betting is on marbles or eggs. Today he's using toffees that Agnes made.'

'He's a smart young lad with a good head for numbers.'

'We're lucky to have good teachers.'

'It's not every family that takes advantage of that.'

'No. But my parents made sure that I could read and write, and I know the world it opens up. None of my children will miss that opportunity, no matter what it takes.'

Mrs Alexander looked across at Robert and paused for a

moment, deciding whether to speak or not. When she did, she looked away from Robert, staring out over the ocean.

'My husband told me of your plans to start a temperance group. It would mean a lot to me if he decided to join. I would prefer he didn't bet on the horses, but his wagering does no real harm. Strong drink, however, can turn a good man into someone else.'

Robert looked at her sympathetically, so close were her words to his own thoughts. She was still looking out over the sparkling sea and if she noticed, she gave no sign of it.

'Total abstinence is what we're going to put to the meeting next Thursday night,' he said. 'It's hard to know what sort of support we can expect.'

Mrs Alexander turned away from the sea and looked at Robert.

'My husband seems to have taken a shine to you Mr Robertson. It's not every teacher who has his approval. I think you can be sure to see him at your meeting next week.'

'That's excellent news. I look forward to it. And yourself?'

'Yes, I'll be there to lend my support and swell the crowd. It's a chance not to be missed.'

People were gathering down the beach, ready for the start of the first race and Mrs Alexander pointed to where the horses were lined up, far along the other end of the beach.

'Perhaps you could give me a hand up, Mr Robertson. I don't want to miss the race. Look after the baby,' she said to Agnes, then she took Robert's hand and despite her long skirt sprung lightly to her feet and they followed the others down to the wet sand.

★

That evening Robert sat at a table on the verandah of his house and tried to bring to life for Emma the day at the races. The sun was setting behind Fossil Bluff and the light was fading, but he liked to stay outside as long as he could and watch the changing colours in the billowing clouds.

Dearest Emma,

All day I was thinking 'if only Emma could be here' and 'I must tell Emma this' and 'Emma would really like that'. I think this is the place to make a go of it, as they say here. As each day passes, I'm more and more sure of it. These giant skies and vast oceans right on my front door are such that open the mind and the heart to life's possibilities, and the daily kindnesses from these hard-working people continue.

I have fallen into the habit of 'dropping in' to the hospitable Alexanders (Betsy and Johnny) and I think you would enjoy the informality here. I know what you must be thinking, and you are correct. When I first arrived here, I missed the traditions of dress and address that I'd grown up with in Stirling. But I'm learning as well as teaching, and now I understand that there can be different paths to right behaviour.

Gone is my regret of being sent to such a raw and isolated place. Were I to be amongst the folk in Hobart or Launceston, no doubt I would still be dressing for dinner and being reminded of my standing in the social hierarchy. Here it's a wonderful freedom, and not least, I'm sure, because of the unfortunate circumstances that brought many of them here and which they have worked hard to overcome.

But what about the races you ask? A more beautiful setting can hardly be imagined, the 'track' being the hard wet sand on the long stretch of beach in front of the settlement. The sea that lands gently on the shore is the southernmost part of what they call Bass Strait that runs between the south of the mainland and the north of Tasmania. After the rough passage to Devonport, I was surprised to find that the water all along this stretch of coast is almost without waves and most often is a lovely turquoise colour. The beaches are wide and made entirely of white sand that is so fine it squeaks under one's feet.

The day could hardly have been better and such that you would give much for in Stirling. Late March though it is, in this upside down world, we are in autumn, though there's little sign of it in the trees. There was barely a cloud and just a light breeze and where all the people came from, I can't imagine. The race caller, Mr Dowling, (a very decent man and a free settler) explained to me that they come from as far as Stanley to the west and Burnie to the east. If you could see what passes for roads here, you would share my amazement. In fact there's little more than a dirt track between here and Stanley and the folks from there travel by boat. According to Mr Dowling there are settlers all through the hinterland, clearing trees and cultivating the earth. One day this will be all tamed and civilised, but, dear Emma, I think I'm lucky to be here in the early days and to see history in the making.

Every second person at the races was the parent of one of my pupils, and half those were related to young Fred. Can you imagine that they even had a race for the women, and I discovered that Fred was right: his mother came out well in front. Not only is she an excellent cook, but a fine horsewoman as well.

I'm sorry not to be more eloquent and wish I had the words to bring this place alive for you. Should the receiving of my letters cause you any grief, or if you think that might be so, then although it will be like cutting off my better half, you only have to say the word and they will end. As you can see, I am making an independent, sober life here and my hope is that time heals all wounds.

Meanwhile, I am your devoted friend,
Robert

6

Eight months later, Thursday, 18 December 1879

River Cottage
Goldie Street,
Wynyard

Dearest Emma,

Can you believe that it's coming up to a year since I've been in this rather idyllic part of the world? I was more than happy when you said how much you would like to see it for yourself, and I'm sure that you would feel as I do, that what is lacking in convenience and sophistication is amply made up for by the friendliness of the townsfolk and the natural beauty of the setting.

As I write this, you must be very busy preparing for Christmas and I can imagine the smell of ginger and cinnamon and cloves drifting from the larder, feel the frost in the air and see the secret buying and hiding of presents in that busy house of yours. I think of you at the piano, singing in harmony with your sisters as you do so well. Christmas carols, if I'm not mistaken!

It's almost midnight here and the fire is not lit. We are starting to get a taste of summer weather, and it's hard for me to believe that it is really going to be December 25 in less than a week. At school I have the children doing the usual activities, singing carols, making nativity scenes, putting on a little play about the three wise men and that sort of thing. We do it, but it's not with the same spirit as back home, and the children seem to feel there's something lacking too. At least we've been doing readings of the wonderful A Christmas Carol and they like that.

I've not long been back from the Good Templar meeting, and I hope it doesn't seem too self-congratulatory when I tell you what a success my Better Late Than Never Lodge has been. Were tonight's meeting to be the last, I would still count it a resounding success when I consider the number who have taken the pledge already. As we're coming into the holiday period, the thoughts of many of the men in this town are towards stocking their homes with strong liquor, and my neighbour Mr Pearce at the Court House Hotel has been busier than usual, offering any number of Christmas specials, which I took him to task for. 'Think of their families,' I urged him, but he said 'Think of the men who have worked all year without a break. Not every man who drinks is a home wrecker.' Of course he has point, but my thoughts are with the families where that is not the case.

I fear there may be more differences between Mr Pearce and myself in the coming year, as I have pledged to work towards the discontinuation of the sale of liquor in the town. However, he's not at heart a bad man, and he is married to the sister of Mrs Alexander who, as you know, has been so hospitable to me, which makes things a little awkward.

I'm sure I told you that she and her husband have turned out to be staunch supporters of the cause. Johnny Alexander has needed a lot of support to help him keep to his pledge, but tonight I think he turned the corner. It must have been Mrs Alexander who helped him, since like so many here Johnny can't read, but he stood in front of the crowd (there were more there tonight than at any other meeting, almost sixty) and he recited a very wry ballad that you might have heard. It's called the Teetotal Mill. When Johnny recited the verse about the husband and wife, the truth of it must have struck home. This is the part I'm referring to and it's very touching:

> 'The next that went in was a man and his wife
> Many long years they'd been living in strife
> He had beat and abused and swear he would kill
> But his heart took a turn in the teetotal mill'.

You see what I mean!

There was one awkward moment with a certain Mr Ridge. Our chairman considered he had taken more time than his due and cut short a long recitation. We were all taken by surprise when said Mr Ridge turned on his heel and rudely left the Assembly Room. It may be a sign of things to come, as we have the Band of Hope here as well now, and in such a small community it's very hard to keep harmony in a non-sectarian group. But as I said, so much good has been done already, and not least for my own self. Mrs Alexander senior – Aunty Joe as she asked me to call her – has offered to help fund a coffee palace in Wynyard and that will give the group a more lively place to socialise, so there's progress there too.

There's the clock striking midnight and it's time for bed. I think that you of all people can understand how much satisfaction I get from having founded this little temperance group. It seems so different from my former self, but in the most positive way. My better self can have free rein now, and to be able to bring so many along with me I consider a small achievement.

I will be thinking of you on Christmas Day, and I hope that you spare a thought for me.

Ever yours,
Robert

7

Two years later, Tuesday, 22 March 1881

Robert was trying to concentrate. Pen in hand, he was working at a makeshift desk in the shed he used as his office. At his request, a window had been added, but there were gaps between the frame and the glass and when the wind was coming from the west it made a sound like a human voice pretending to be a ghost. It was doing it now and didn't help his nerves.

It had been late yesterday afternoon when Mr Dowling had come to his house and announced that Governor Lefroy himself was planning to visit the school the next day.

The Premier, the Governor, and their entourage had arrived in the late afternoon and the people of Table Cape produced an impressive escort to welcome them. Robert saw the men on their horses heading out past his place, then two or three hours later, back again, leading the visitors with great formality to Pearce's Courthouse Hotel next door. It wasn't long after that when Mr Dowling had called in and passed on the news about the governor's plan to visit the school.

Sir John Lefroy, newly appointed Governor of Tasmania, was a name Robert recognised from articles he'd read in the *Scientific American*. He was well known for his work on magnetic observations and meteorology, and apparently he also took a particular interest in education. There wasn't much time to prepare, but Robert was confident that he could show his school off at its very best.

This morning Robert had picked out pupils – two from each age group – to give recitations from the Reading Book, and he'd rehearsed them until they were word perfect. These children might not be sophisticated, but they had energy and enthusiasm and Robert hoped the governor would be impressed.

Now he was using his penmanship to finish the programme. Robert blew on the ink to dry it more quickly, then carefully blotted it and held it up for inspection. The border decorations that Mrs Roebuck had done in the morning looked professional, with elaborate curlicues interspersed with tiny drawings of some native animals. Robert was adding the names and the titles, and there was just one to go. He put the stiff parchment on the table, carefully removed excess ink from his pen and wrote: Frederick Alexander, *After Blenheim* by Robert Southey. The governor could hardly fail to be impressed with the boy's recitation. He had talent, there was no doubt about that.

The whistling noise rose to a shriek and suddenly the door swung open and crashed against the bookshelf. The whole shed shook, and Robert put the pen back in the stand and went over to close it. He was just in time to see Fred Alexander launch himself at John McKenzie, swinging his fists and yelling something that the wind blew away. Branches were whipping back and forth and some of the children were running over to watch the fight; others were joining in.

Mrs Roebuck was already there, and she had separated the boys by the time Robert reached them. They were all yelling at the same time, but Robert's voice cut through the din.

'You are not savages so stop behaving like them. The Governor of Tasmania will be here in twenty minutes, and you know what I expect from you. You, Mr Alexander, tidy yourself up then stand against the wall and don't move an inch.'

Fred's face was red and twisted in anger and he muttered under his breath as he walked away.

'Tell them to leave my sister alone.'

Robert grabbed at his hat as another gust whipped across the playground.

'What is it this time?' he asked Mrs Roebuck.

'It was over Agnes. She was turning one end of the jump rope when Sarah McKenzie fell over and started crying. Sarah's friends blamed Agnes for making the rope too high, and when Agnes went to the toilet, they followed her and called out names. Fred heard them and decided to take it out on Sarah's brother.'

Frederick Alexander! If only he could control that temper and stop the eternal questioning, teaching would be so much easier. But then Fred was the sort of boy one wanted to teach, because he caught on so fast and had a real thirst for knowledge. It wasn't easy to know what to do.

'At least he knows not to hit girls,' Robert said.

Mrs Roebuck looked up at the branches tossing as if possessed.

'I think it's the wind. It always has this effect.'

'Just when we want everything to be perfect! Let's hope they settle down before the governor arrives.'

And once the children had filed back into the classroom and were out of the wind, they did calm down. The exact time of the visit wasn't known, so Robert started with a Geography lesson. Using green for the outline and blue for the water, he quickly drew a map of Great Britain on the blackboard. He drew the border between England and Scotland last, using a thick line of brown chalk for Hadrian's Wall, then he asked his usual question.

'And what is the most important town in Great Britain?'

All the little ones raised their hands and Robert picked a boy in the front row.

'It's Stirling sir.'

The expected laugh came from the older students and Robert drew a castle in the Scottish part.

'Very good. Thank you.'

There was a knock at the door and without waiting for a reply, a man in a stiff white collar and knee-high black boots marched across the room and stood next to Robert. He didn't salute, but it seemed that he might.

'His Excellency has arrived.' He glanced at the children. 'Rough looking lot aren't they,' he said, then the man turned on his polished heel and stalked back out the door, leaving it open.

Almost immediately, a tall, dignified man appeared in the doorway, a walking stick tucked under one arm,

Robert made a polite bow.

'Please come in Your Excellency. The children are expecting you.'

Sir John Lefroy acknowledged the greeting with a nod and a smile, then he walked across to the front of the desk, taking some of his weight with the walking stick,

Prompted by Mrs Roebuck, the children stood at their desks. They tried not to stare, but it was as if a rare and exotic specimen had appeared in the classroom. Governor Lefroy's long jacket, pinched in at the waist, made him seem even taller than his already considerable height, and his flowing grey hair was startling, the side whiskers so long they came all the way to the top of his collar, and his drooping moustache entirely covered his upper lip.

'Good afternoon children.'

'Good afternoon Your Excellency.' Some of the youngsters trailed off at the end, but the older ones spoke briskly and in unison. Robert allowed himself to relax.

Sir John must have noticed the map of Great Britain as he came in, because he half turned and pointed to it with his stick.

'Can anyone tell me about that castle in Scotland?'

Almost all the hands went up and the governor picked a little girl who was biting her lip trying not to call it out.

'It's in Stirling where Mr Robertson lives when he's not here. And it's very big and further than anywhere here.'

The older students exchanged looks and some of them laughed, but Sir John nodded seriously, pleased with the answer. He rested some of his weight against the master's desk and looked very much at ease.

'How do you think Mr Robertson communicates with people he knows in Stirling?'

Hands went up and suggestions were made, involving letters sent by ships or trains or horses.

'And if the message is urgent?' Sir John prompted, and finally one of the older girls thought of the telegraph, and the way dots and dashes were used to send important messages.

'Yes. The telegraph is fast. But now I'm going to tell you something very wonderful. There's a man who lives in the

United States of America.' Sir John pointed his stick far to the left of the map on the board, 'His name is Alexander Graham Bell, and he has made a scientific discovery that means one day Mr Robertson will be able to talk directly to his people over there in Stirling.'

Sir John paused for effect, and the whole classroom was caught up in the drama of the story and sat waiting to hear what came next.

'You're wondering how? Then I'll tell you. It's very like the telegraph. You take a transmitter and a receiver and connect them with electricity. The difference is that when someone speaks into the instrument at one end, a person many miles away is able to hear them.'

While he was speaking, a hand had shot up in the back row, and now it pushed even further up and waved around.

Sir John pointed at Fred, whose hand it was.

'Young man. You have a question.'

'How do you know it works?'

'Just two weeks ago, from the office in Hobart, I myself spoke to a person who was in Launceston.'

Fred's hand was up again.

'Where does the voice go? How does it get in?'

Robert knew what was coming. An endless string of questions from a boy who questioned everything, even the books themselves. Nothing would stop him. The other children were used to it, but some of them shuffled awkwardly, embarrassed by Fred's rudeness. Robert knew he didn't do it to be cheeky, but that didn't make it any easier to accept. The boy, when he was like this, had no consideration of other people, of rules, or of punishment.

Sir John, master of military discipline and training as he was, was not at all put out, and seemed to welcome the questions.

'I can see that you have an enquiring mind young man. Very good. Now I want you to do something for me. Put your fingers on the front of your throat and say 'ah'.'

Fred did so.

'What did you notice?'

Fred tried two more times, feeling with great concentration.

'Movement. And a different sort of sound.'

'Precisely. Well done. Vibrations of the vocal cords over the larynx. Now everyone try.'

The room filled with the noise of 'ahs' until Sir John held his hand up and the class fell silent.

'Mr Bell has discovered a way to pick up those vibrations and to use a copper wire to carry them long distances. Then using a microphone, the person at the other end gets a translation of the sounds and hears what was said at the same time as it was spoken.'

Fred's hand shot up again, then without waiting to be asked, desperate to be heard, Fred called out.

'But what's a microphone? How does it work?'

The rudeness was unforgiveable and in a moment of complete silence, Fred realised he'd gone too far, and he dropped his arm and looked down at the desk. But it was too late.

Mr Robertson didn't raise his voice, but it was hard and final.

'Mr Alexander will leave the classroom immediately and wait in my office.'

At first it seemed that he might refuse, and Robert held his breath, but then the boy slowly got to his feet and walked down the aisle and out the door, his face flushed with anger.

*

When Robert finally got back to his office, Fred was slumped in the visitor's chair, looking sorry for himself. He didn't bother to stand when Robert entered the shed and Robert, exhausted after the day, ignored the rudeness and sat behind the desk, his chin on his hands, looking at Fred's sullen face and thinking about what Sir John had said to him.

'That boy,' the Governor had said, as Robert waited with him for the carriage to arrive. 'A fine enquiring mind, would you say?'

Robert nodded hesitantly.

'Enquiring, yes.'

Sir John noticed the omission of 'fine' and smiled at Robert.

'Feed the mind, Mr Robertson, then let it go after the ideas. You could make a scientist of the boy, and science is the future.

Your classroom may not, however, be the best place for such a mind.'

The carriage arrived and Sir John climbed onto the padded seats, then leaned down towards where Robert was still standing.

'You're a smart man. You'll find a way.'

From outside the office came the sound of children laughing as they left the classroom. Robert pushed himself back in the chair and folded his arms, his mind made up.

'You're a lucky boy Frederick Alexander.'

'But I missed the Governor's talk, and I didn't get to recite *After Blenheim* even though I learned it specially and I'm the best. And I should have got one of the governor's prizes, but I didn't.'

Robert waited.

'Because?'

'Because I was asking questions.'

Robert leaned forward now, and spoke slowly so there could be no misunderstanding.

'No Fred. Because you were impossibly ill mannered. You showed no regard for the others in the class. You disgraced yourself and embarrassed me in front of the governor. I am no longer willing to have you in the classroom. There are formalities I'll have to follow, but from today you are expelled.'

'But I'm the best in the class.'

'No Fred. You're the worst in the class. You think only about yourself and whatever ideas entertain you. You're the most selfish, the worst tempered and the most arrogant student in the class. Outside the classroom you know how to behave. It's time for you to learn to think about other people, and to understand that there are very, very intelligent men who know a great deal more than you can imagine, and you will need to find your place within that.'

'It's not fair. Nothing is ever fair.'

'However,' Robert continued, ignoring him, 'you are lucky, because from next week you will take lessons with me in the evenings. What you do during the day will depend on what your parents decide.'

Robert saw Fred's face turn white. He was finally lost for words.

'Report to my house on Monday at 6.00 pm. Bring your notebook and your pen and ink. You're dismissed.'

Robert waited until he couldn't hear Fred's footsteps then he went and stood at the door of the office. The wind had dropped and he walked over to the stand of eucalypts. He picked up some branches that had broken off and threw them in the heap next to the woodpile; then he stood in the sun, looking at the peaceful schoolyard, and thinking back over the day.

Despite everything, the governor's visit had gone well. Very well. 'Your students have shown themselves to be equal to the best in any school in the country,' Governor Lefroy had told him. And that was without Fred's recitation, which was going to be the highlight of the afternoon.

Frederick Alexander! The relief Robert felt made him realise how much the situation had been troubling him. It had been like an ill-fitting shoe; after a time you got used to it, but the discomfort was always there. And finally he'd found the confidence to follow through on an idea he'd had for some time. Some people would see it as irregular, but there was no doubt it would be better for the class, and Robert's instinct told him the boy would flourish too.

8

Seven months later, October 1881

Johnny Alexander swung himself on to the top rail of the horse yard. He took the bridle off the post and threw it to Fred, who caught it and walked over to the horses grazing on the short grass near the water trough. Long rays of early sun lit the dew that was thick on the grass, but there was no warmth yet and Johnny pulled his hat down and held both ends of his jacket tightly around himself.

He watched Fred as he approached the horses.

Titania. What sort of name was that for a horse? He suspected that his son had chosen it on purpose, just to annoy him. All he heard about these days was Shakespeare and poetry and Johnny wondered what good it was ever going to do for anyone.

A pretty chestnut mare went over and rubbed her nose in Fred's pockets and Johnny watched him pull out a piece of carrot and hold it out to the horse. Whatever name she had, the horse was a good one. Give her a couple of years and with the right training she could be a winner. At least that was something the boy could do – he understood horses.

The last few months had been nothing like Johnny had expected. Of course, he gave the lad a good belting over that business with the governor, but in one way he didn't mind that Fred had been expelled from school. The boy was twelve already, and what was the point in keeping children at school until they were fifteen? A lot of nonsense. At Frederick's age, he'd been working a full day in the forge, learning the smithy trade, working on the farm in his spare time and in the hotel on top of that. The oldest boy should follow his father, but that had been a disaster from the start. Frederick could barely last a couple of hours in the smithy before he'd start coughing and feeling poorly. Or so he said.

What was it with that boy? Right from the start he'd been difficult, different. And weak. Johnny thought back on the first few weeks when his firstborn seemed fit to die. And as far as he could see, that's when it all started. Betsy fussing over him, insisting that he be fed goat's milk, feeding him with a dropper like a poddy calf. Of course he wanted the baby to live, but only if God wanted it. God had his reasons for giving life and taking it away.

Now Johnny wondered if the boy's mother was ever going to let him grow up. No matter what Frederick did, she could never see any wrong in him, and the boy used her to get his own way. 'He's not well, let him be,' she'd say. But was there really anything wrong with him? More like excuses to get out of doing things he didn't want to do. Look at him now. Up early every morning, waiting for the chance to work with the horses. You couldn't fault him. When it came to what he wanted to do, there was nothing wrong with him at all.

Fred patted Titania's nose with one hand and slipped the bridle on with the other. He checked in her mouth to make sure the bit was comfortable then walked her across to where his father was sitting.

Fred stroked the horse's flank and looked up at his father.

'What do you think?' he asked.

'Not bad. Let's see how you've been going with head work. Everything is about the head. If you can't help her to hold her head right, she'll never make a racehorse. And more than that, she'll never be comfortable. Show me head up.'

Fred made a slight movement of the bridle and Titania's head straightened, perfectly balanced on either side.

'Good. Now head down.'

Another tug on the bridle.

'Very good, son. Remember to always check across the ears and never force. Saddle up. We'll see how she goes on the beach.'

Johnny vaulted down from the railing and lifted each of Titania's hooves. The shoes were holding well and the extra thickness at the back had done the trick with keeping her head straight. Not even the best training in the world would make up for shoddy horseshoes.

They rode their horses side by side at a walking pace, along Dodgin Street, past the teacher's house and along Goldie Street, then across the bridge and over the sand dunes to the beach. There was still a bite to the air and little clouds of steam puffed from the horses' nostrils.

The tide was halfway out and a wide swathe of wet sand showed the high-water mark. They cantered to the point and back, and then took the horses for shorter gallops. It was good for Robin to have a companion horse, and Titania had taken to the beach so quickly that they ended with a long walk in the shallow water.

'It strengthens the hind muscles,' he told Fred. 'And look at the way your horse is so straight in the head. That's because she's lifting her hooves out of the water. Do you see?'

To give the horses a rest after all the exercise, they dismounted and led them slowly back over the dunes. It was working out well, these mornings when Fred helped with the horses. Perhaps this son of his would make something of himself after all. He was a hard worker, you had to give him that, and despite the loss of his best horse, the carriage rental business was running like clockwork since Fred was helping with the books.

There was a rustle in amongst the spiky grass and Fred, who was walking ahead, held Titania still and motioned to his father to do the same.

'Look.' He pointed to where a small bird had pushed under a clump of saltbush. 'It's a curlew. If it wasn't for the black beak, I would never have spotted it. It's exactly the colour of the dunes.'

Johnny came and stood next to Fred.

'Under that saltbush,' Fred said. 'Lucky I saw it – Titania nearly stepped on it.'

Johnny looked where Fred was pointing and picked out the little bird, holding itself perfectly still so as not to be seen.

'You did well to spot it,' he said. 'There are lots of people older than you who don't see what's right under their feet. You know what I always say. Look close enough and there's more to learn from the things around us than in all those books of yours.'

His son looked at him and nodded, then he loosened the reins and walked on over the sand dunes.

9

Nearly two years later, February 1883

Fred dismounted, careful not to spill anything from the basket of things he'd brought from Uncle Martin's place. He lifted the chain off the gatepost and followed Titania through the opening. It was only when he closed the gate and leaned over the top rail to put the chain back that he noticed the time. Most of the paddock was in shadow and the sun was sitting just above the purple haze of the mountains in the west.

Where did the time go?

It had been a long day up on the Cape, and it was another half an hour before Fred had finished washing and grooming Titania. He hung the bridle on the nail in the stall then picked up the basket and walked across the paddock, climbed through the fence, and let himself into the house by the back door.

Agnes was helping his mother clear the table, scraping the plates into a bowl and stacking them in a pile at the far end.

'You're late again,' she said without looking up.

Fred ignored her – she was so bossy these days, just like Aunty Joe. He pushed the rest of the dirty plates to one side and started pulling things out of the basket and piling them on to the table.

'Butter. Cheese. Lemons. Bay leaves. Potatoes.'

His mother picked each of them off the table and inspected them.

'Lovely.'

She brushed some dry leaves off the back of Fred's vest.

'You'd better have something to eat before you go to your lesson. How were things up on the Cape?'

'Uncle Martin says that there will be a side of lamb for us tomorrow, and there are still plenty of cherries on the tree that will go to waste if we don't take them. I helped him in the dairy and he asked me to exercise his horses. And look what I found for you.'

Fred pulled a stone out of his pocket and held it out. His mother took it from his hand and went over to the window to look at it more closely.

It was almost perfectly square and pure white. She put it on the sideboard in a glass dish that was half-filled with other stones.

'Thank you.'

'There's something else,' Fred said to his mother. 'Close your eyes.'

Agnes took away the last of the dirty plates and rolled her eyes at him. He shrugged and followed her out to the scullery. A bunch of yellow and white roses was in a bucket of water just outside the back door where he'd hidden them. Fred picked them up, careful to use the hessian strip that was tied around the stems and took them into where his mother was waiting.

'Open your eyes.'

His mother opened her eyes and wasn't as surprised as he'd been expecting her to be. She took them from him and held them up to her nose.

'Thank you, Frederick. They're lovely. I could smell them as soon as you came into the room,' she laughed. 'Agnes, smell these.'

Agnes had started washing the dishes and came back in from the scullery, wiping her hands on her apron.

She had to admit that the roses smelt very good.

'And this is for you.'

Fred pulled a glossy brown and white cowrie shell out of his other pocket and handed it to Agnes.

She took the shell and ran her hand over the shiny round surface, then polished it some more with her apron.

'Oh Fred! It's beautiful.'

Fred spoke in a gentleman's voice and swept a mock bow, taking off an imaginary hat.

'I'd feign give you the world.'

Agnes laughed and pushed him.

'You're silly.' She pressed the shell against her ear. 'I can hear the sea. Where did you find it?'

'I took the horses down to Fossil Beach and had a bit of a wander. Mr Robertson wanted me to bring back some things for the lesson tonight. Did you know that you can see fossils that are millions of years old?'

But Agnes didn't hear him. She was stroking the shiny surface of the shell as if she thought it might come alive.

His mother had arranged the roses in the tall vase, and she came back from the scullery carrying them carefully, then stopped and looked around.

'Where should I put these? Here or in the front room?'

Fred picked up the cruet set and set it down at the end of the table. He patted the space in the middle.

'Right here Ma. Then we can see them every day.'

The clock chimed seven and Fred quickly rolled down the sleeves of his shirt.

'Time to go.'

'You must have something to eat. Mr Robertson will understand if you're a bit late.'

'I've eaten. Aunt Maria invited me for tea.'

'Don't forget your jacket.'

'But it's too hot for a jacket.'

'You can't go to Mr Robertson's without a jacket Frederick, no matter what you think.'

It was a conversation they had often.

Fred took his jacket off the peg in the hallway and put it on as he hurried out the front door. Trees cast long shadows over the road, and he was glad of the jacket as picked his way between the potholes and ruts left by the logging drays.

Mr Robertson was sitting at the little table on the verandah, and when Fred unlatched the gate he looked up from the book he was reading.

'I'm sorry I'm late. Uncle Martin had a lot for me to do today.'

Robert put a leather marker in his book and stood up.

'With all there is to learn, a few minutes here and there won't make any difference.'

Fred laughed.

'Unless you're betting on a horse.'

'Come inside and sit down. Is there anything to report from the Cape?'

'It was glorious up there. The crops are doing much better this year, Uncle Martin said, and I helped him work the horses. I rode one of them down to Fossil Beach and had a good look this time. I could see what that article was saying about the geological layers. Look what I found.'

Fred pulled a fossilised shell out of his pocket and handed it to Robert.

'Interesting. That looks like a bryozoan. Another journal came today. I'll pass it on when I've read it. And something else came in the mail.'

They took their usual seats at the table in the front room and Robert pointed to a brown parchment envelope.

'Open it.'

Fred took the letter out of the envelope and read through it, then handed it to Robert.

'Is that the mathematics test you were worried about?'

'That's the one. I knew it was beyond the pupils in the class, but it seems you did well. And that means the powers that be are happy with my teaching.' Robert smiled. 'There's no need for them to know where we have our lessons.'

If it would help Mr Robertson, that was enough for Fred, and his mother would be happy. Personally, Fred didn't think much of examinations, and had not much idea why they were thought of as so important. One knew things, or one didn't.

Robert reached to the end of the table where there was a pile of leather-covered books. He pulled out a large volume from the bottom and talked to Fred as he flicked through the pages.

'Did you learn that soliloquy I wrote out for you?'

By way of answer, Fred got to his feet and stood behind his chair, his hands resting on the back of it.

'Friends, Romans, countrymen, lend me your ears...'

Robert started to follow him, running his finger down the open page of the book, ready to correct, but Fred was reciting the piece so well that Robert found he was enjoying the performance for its own sake.

'...Bear with me: My heart is in the coffin there with Caesar, and I must pause till it come back to me.'

Robert clapped and Fred made a deep ironic bow, one hand across his waist, the other by his side as Robert had shown him.

'Well done, Fred. You know you really do have a gift for recitation. There's a career in that too these days,' Robert paused, 'though maybe not here.'

'How many mistakes did I make?'

'Hardly any, and one didn't notice because of the energy you put into it. And the phrasing was very good too.'

Robert walked across to the empty fireplace and stood with his hands folded behind his back, as if it was winter and he was warming them by the fire.

'There's something else I have to tell you Fred.'

'What have I done?'

'Nothing. Not everything is about you.' Robert's smile took the sting out of the words. 'I've been granted six months leave to visit my parents in Stirling. I'll be leaving in April and returning in October. '

In what way was this not about him? Would he have to go back to school? This was all about him. Fred sat back down, and Mr Robertson came and sat opposite him.

'What will that mean for me?' Fred asked.

'I've thought about that. There's a teacher coming from Launceston to take the class while I'm away, a Mr Delmar. I suggest that you consider taking on the role of unpaid assistant to him. If after the six months you prove your ability, then I am sure I would be able to have you appointed to the position of paid teaching assistant.'

Fred could feel walls closing around him.

'Teaching assistant? Like Mrs Roebuck?'

'Yes. Look Fred, I can see this is rather sudden, but you're fourteen years old now, and frankly, there isn't a lot more that I can teach you. Your father told me again at the Good Templar's meeting this week how worried he is...'

Fred interrupted.

'He has Arthur helping him in the forge now. And I'm doing the other work with the horses and transport business.'

'He's thinking about paid work, contributing to the family.'

'Pa wouldn't want me to be a teacher anyway.'

'Once you're being paid, surely he'll think differently. It's not easy for him.'

Fred wondered if his father would ever see merit in learning, no matter how much money he made from it, but he supposed Mr Robertson was right about getting work, and why not teaching?

'I'll do it then.'

'Good lad. It will make me feel better about taking leave. Providing you keep that temper of yours in check, of course.'

'I'll try. It's just that people can be so unfair and stupid.' Fred complained, then he noticed that Mr Robertson was looking at him and shaking his head. 'But I'm sure I can keep my temper in check,' he added. 'You'll see.'

'I know you'll try, and that's all that any of us can do. Now let's see those fossils.'

10

Five months later, 22 August 1883

It was low tide, and Fred walked carefully on the slippery rocks, keeping an eye out for the next wave and peering into the rock pools, looking for something of interest; a sea anemone he could poke his stick into, an oyster, an interesting shell.

It was late winter and still too cold to think of taking off his boots and paddling, let alone swimming. Clouds that had come in from the west earlier in the day were low in the sky and sucked the colour from the sea. A strong wind was pushing rough waves that ground on to the sand and left ugly foam along the edges.

The day at school had been much like other days, and it went quickly. Mr Robertson had been right. Fred liked the fact he knew things the others didn't, and he rather enjoyed the challenge of finding a way to help the pupils understand, though sometimes he felt like throwing things at the really slow stubborn ones who didn't even try. However, life was dull with Mr Robertson away. Mr Delmar was well-liked, but once school was out, he was off with his family or rowing on the river. Fred never asked, but it didn't seem as if he was interested in literature or new ideas and Fred missed the weekend expeditions with Mr Robertson; no one to hunt with now, or go fossicking with, and fishing wasn't the same when it was just Albert tagging along.

Without his evening lessons to look forward to, Fred had taken to walking on the beach in the late afternoon. His mother encouraged him; it was the best way to prevent his illness Dr Wilson had said. Fresh air and exercise. The others could help mother for an hour or so without him having to keep an eye on things. Since baby Horace had arrived in April, he'd taken Amy and May off her hands for a couple of hours every day.

By herself, Amy was easy and fun; she was only four, but she had no fear and tried to copy everything he did. May was the opposite. She was two years old and nothing was ever right with her. Fred knew she would probably grow out of it, but he was tired of her tantrums and her stubborn refusal to be the least bit obliging.

He continued back along the beach, digging his boots into his own prints in the sand, and stopping to pick up and inspect a stone, or a shell or a sponge. He'd decided to surprise Mr Robertson by memorising something from every single play that Shakespeare wrote and this week it was Macbeth. The gloom and the wind were a perfect backdrop and Fred stood for a minute facing the sea and tried to project his voice over the waves. 'Methought I heard a voice cry "Sleep no more! Macbeth does murder sleep," the innocent sleep, sleep that knits up the ravelled sleeve of care.'

He turned back to the beach and bent close to the sand, looking around until he found a flat, smooth little stone and sent it skipping across the water. Three skips. Not bad considering the choppy waves. He sent a few more after it, but three was the best he could manage.

Was that a voice he could hear?

He dropped the pebbles and walked along the beach towards the track over the dunes. It was too dark to see who it was, but he could make out a figure running towards him. As the person got closer, Fred realised it was Arthur.

Fred walked more quickly, and saw that Arthur wasn't acting like Arthur at all. He was running and shouting and waving his arms. And finally, Fred could make out what he was saying.

'It's father. You have to come now. It's father.'

Arthur stopped and bent forwards, his hands on his hips, panting and trying to catch his breath. From his bent position he looked up at Fred and took a deep breath, then another one before he could speak.

'Father's had an accident.'

'Is it bad? What happened?

Arthur's breathing calmed down and he explained to Fred as they walked fast back along the track.

'He was riding Peter out to the Calders' place to look at one of their horses that had gone lame. The Calder boy came to tell us just now. He wasn't sure exactly how it happened, but a tree came down and Peter fell on father. They thought he was dead, but he wasn't, and they've taken him on the dray back to the Calders' place.'

'That place way out near the quarry?'

'Yes. Mother's riding out there now. She's gone already. She said you're to take care of things. Aunty Joe's coming too.'

His father? Other people had accidents with horses, not his father.

Arthur was quiet for a minute, then he gave Fred a frightened look.

'What if he dies?'

Fred put an arm on Arthur's shoulder.

'He won't die. Mother will know what to do.'

Fred was less confident than he tried to sound. His mother had the healing touch, everyone knew that, and Dr Wilson would do what he could, but Peter was a big, heavy horse and if it happened like Arthur had said...

At the front gate the boys could hear baby Horace crying and on top of that May was having one of her tantrums and Richard was trying to hit Albert who was running up and down the long hallway and staying just out of reach.

Fred could see why he was needed.

'You go and close up the smithy Arthur. I'll help out here.'

Arthur started back up the path, his head down, hands deep in his pockets.

'Hey Arthur,' Fred called after him.

Arthur looked back over his shoulder, his face pinched and worried looking.

'You know how strong father is. He'll pull through. And he's got God on his side too.'

Life at home had changed for the better after his father had taken the pledge of abstinence. There were extra prayers and church going, but that was a fair exchange for less anger and fewer arguments.

With Aunty Joe here, there would be even more prayers, he thought, and he was right. After they got the little ones settled, she led the rest of them in a long prayer time. It didn't always happen, but this time Fred got some comfort from the prayers. It seemed like the right sort of thing to be doing, and there was time to think. Fred couldn't believe in God the way his father and Aunty Joe did, but he badly wanted there to be a powerful force for good and he closed his eyes and put his heart into the prayers, hoping his father would recover.

Then Dr Wilson arrived with more news. Over a drink of hot milk, the tired doctor explained that their father's body took the whole weight of the horse when it was knocked by the branch coming down on him.

'It's serious, but your father should pull through. And you know your ma is the best in the district when it comes to nursing.'

'What about Peter?' Fred asked.

'I'm sorry, but we had to put him down Fred.'

Agnes started crying and Fred felt cold and sick. He watched Aunty Joe go across to Agnes and rub her back as the sobbing continued. Peter was more than a horse; he'd been part of the family. They'd all learned to ride on him. He was the strong, reliable, sure-footed Peter.

It was already well past midnight by the time Fred crept into bed beside Albert and Richard. Even then he lay wide awake in the darkness, thinking of his mother up in the hills at the Calders' house, straining to imagine how it must be for her and for his father, thinking about them as if it would make sure that his father would survive. When he finally fell asleep the roosters were crowing and birds were chirping in the tree outside the bedroom window.

He heard sounds in the bedroom, but they seemed distant and not enough to pull him out of his deep sleep. Time passed and he felt a hand on his forehead. It seemed his eyelids were glued together, but he forced them open, a little bit to start with and then the whole way.

First he saw the familiar blue dress with the calico pinny over it. Then as he turned his head, his mother's face, calm as always.

Fred sat up and took in the empty bed, the daylight showing through the drawn curtains. Then it came flooding back.

'Father?'

'In a bad way but alive. They're bringing him down in the dray later today. What about you Fred?'

Fred pulled the blanket tight around himself.

'I couldn't sleep for worry, but I'm better now. And mother…'

'What is it?'

'I've been thinking that if father can't work, I should start earning some money. Maybe they need someone at the mill.'

His mother brushed his forehead with the back of her hand.

'You stay with your teaching Fred. The family will help us over this, and they need you at the school. It's like Mr Robertson said. You'll get the job after he comes back. But you'll have to look lively and get up there. It's after eight o'clock.'

His mother closed the door behind her, and Fred scrambled out of bed and pulled on his trousers and a warm shirt and vest. He drew the curtains back and looked at the bright day outside. Of course his father would recover.

11

Two months later, Wednesday, 3 October 1883

Betsy Alexander put the last of the chicken and egg pies on the improvised table set up on the sand, then she took a minute to look around. The first week in October could just as easily be windy and wet, but today really was the most perfect weather.

It was a rare event for a school holiday to be declared like this, but when the weather was so nice, the secretary of the Mothers' Club, Mrs Peart, had come up with the idea of a welcome back picnic for Mr Robertson and his new wife and it would double as a farewell to Mr Delmar, the substitute teacher. The rest of the Mothers' Club were all for it, and they had prevailed over the men on the school Board, so here they all were.

It had taken all morning to get things ready but now it was coming together. At first nobody had been able to agree on where to hold the picnic, but in the end they'd compromised. This place was a bit further from the town, but there was plenty of room for the horses and traps, and the beach was right there, without having to walk across the dunes. The boobialla trees held the sandy bank in place with their roots, and branches of the sprawling trees spread over the beach, giving enough shade for those who needed it.

Already there was so much food you could barely see the white cloths on the trestle tables: tarts and pies, cakes and sandwiches, legs of ham and loaves of bread. Women were still coming with their baskets of food and Betsy left them to it and joined Agnes and Albert on the picnic rug. Betsy smiled to herself when she saw the way they were stretched out on the rug with baby Horace between them, sitting up as straight as you please and only five months old. The children had made a sort of cage between their feet and their heads, and little Horrie was sucking on a dry crust and laughing his gurgling laugh every time Albert pointed to the seagulls.

Betsy sat on a sunny corner of the rug, hugged her skirt around her knees and felt the warm spring sun soak into her. She let herself relax and enjoyed the rare chance to do nothing except admire the clear green water with its gentle swells and scalloped lines of tiny bubbles on the wet sand.

For now at least everyone in the family was happily entertaining themselves. Johnny was finally able to walk again after that terrible accident. He still used a stick for support and was leaning on it now, but he looked happy enough, talking horses with Mr Dowling and some other men. They weren't moving too far away from the food, and like the seagulls further down the beach, they were keeping a close eye on it.

Arthur and Richard were playing beach cricket with some other boys down at the water's edge, a safe distance away from the chatting groups of parents.

To the left of the main group, Mr Robertson and his new wife Emma were talking to Mr Delmar. Fred was there too, chatting to them and supervising Amy, who was trying to teach two-year-old May how to build a sandcastle. May was having more fun knocking it down than building it up, but Amy had such a placid temperament that she didn't seem to mind. It was funny the way it had worked out with the children, but Amy was always happy when she was somewhere near Fred, whereas Richard wanted to be with Arthur. There was no point wondering why – it was just how it was.

Mr Delmar was such a kind, hardworking young man that he'd completely won her and everyone else over during the six months he'd run the school while Mr Robertson had been in Scotland. Of course they wanted to welcome Mr Robertson back too, and meet his new wife, but they especially wanted Mr Delmar to know how much good feeling there was towards him, and what good wishes they wanted to send him away with.

The way he had saved that little girl from drowning in the river on Saturday had only added to the occasion. Mr Delmar didn't say, but Betsy had heard that his watch had been ruined when he went in the water after the little girl fell off the bridge and that Mr Stutterd had organised a new one for him.

As for Mr Robertson, her fears that he might settle back in Scotland had not been realised, and Betsy was relieved and happy that he'd decided to bring his new bride back to Wynyard. The way he'd taken Frederick under his wing and tutored him was something so special that Betsy knew she would always be in his debt. And without Mr Robertson, would Johnny ever have been able to turn his life around the way he had? Some were wont to criticise Mr Robertson's Better Late Than Never Lodge and the hard line he took against alcohol, but Betsy knew that for some people total abstinence was the only thing that worked.

Looking at Frederick chatting to the teachers, one eye on Amy and May, Betsy felt proud of him. He was looking so grown up these days. Since he'd started the assistant teaching there had been all sorts of small changes, and some not so small. Who would have thought he'd be fussy about the cut of his jackets and the colour of his vests? He seemed a bit calmer, too. He could still talk the leg off a chair, but it was more considered.

Horace had lost interest in the seagulls and was making funny noises with his lips, then he stretched out his little arms towards her and said something that sounded like 'mama'.

'Listen Ma. Horrie is talking, aren't you Horrie?' Albert said and he tickled the baby on the chest as he'd seen the others do.

Horace ignored him and kept reaching across Agnes' legs towards Betsy who picked him up and sat him on her outstretched skirt then jiggled him up and down a few times. A shadow blocked the sun and she looked up to see Frederick and Mr and Mrs Robertson standing in front of her.

'I've come to meet the new little Alexander,' Mr Robertson announced.

Albert and Agnes made room and Fred joined his mother on the mat. Emma chose to stand, and Robert, having started to sit down, changed his mind and stood with her. Despite the wide-brimmed hat that she was wearing, Emma's cheeks were red, and Betsy hoped it was just the warm day and not sunburn.

'I've been telling Mr and Mrs Robertson how strong Horace is,' Fred said. 'Look.'

Fred held his finger out towards Horace and after a few tries, the baby grabbed the finger and held it with his tiny hand. He did his funny chuckling laugh and tried to put the finger in his mouth.

'See,' Fred said, then he replaced his finger with the crust.

But Mr Robertson wasn't looking at Horace. He was listening to something that Emma was saying, then he put a hand on her waist and led her to a place where the shade was deep, and some folding chairs had been set up.

'It won't be easy for Mrs Robertson,' Betsy said to Fred. 'Not with her fair skin and fine clothes. But at least she's here and it's not every woman who would make the voyage out. Mr Robertson is a very lucky man.'

12

A week later, 11 October 1883

The bedroom was so dark that even when Fred opened his eyes the room was black. He had no idea what time it was; he'd been asleep and then the crying had woken him. Now he was lying awake, praying as hard as he could that the noise would stop.

'Is he going to die?' Albert whispered.

Fred could barely make out Albert's face, even though they were lying so close together. On the other side of the bed Richard was sound asleep, but Fred had sensed that Albert was awake.

They were all used to babies crying during the night. Fred had seen and heard the arrival of six babies already, Horace was the seventh. This crying was different though, so high and piercing and frightened, the only thing the poor little chap could do to tell them how bad he felt. Even so, it was hard not to get angry when it went on and on and on. Fred just wanted it to stop so everything could go back to how it was. He whispered to Albert, glad it was dark so his little brother couldn't see him.

'No. He won't die. You know mother is so clever. Remember how she saved me from dying.'

'I'm glad she did,' Albert whispered.

Quite soon Albert fell back to sleep, but Fred lay stretched on his back, every fibre and nerve straining in the darkness.

Despite what he said, Fred was frightened. There was nothing comforting about the sound of their mother walking up and down the hallway, or the image of Horace's little face all screwed up in pain with the angry red splotches all around his eyes. Sometimes it was father's walk – heavy, light, heavy, light – as he put all the weight on his good leg. Fred couldn't make out much of what they were saying but the voices had an urgency that rose and fell under the high-pitched wailing. Doors opened and closed, and Fred recognised Doctor Wilson's voice.

'Is there nothing you can give him?' he heard his mother ask.

The doctor's reply was drowned out by crying that was almost a scream.

Then the crying stopped and Fred drifted off to sleep.

It came from the sea, a giant wall of water and it filled the house, was far bigger than the house. They were all trapped in it, but he could breathe, and he fought his way through. He had to save everyone, and he kept reaching for them, but they disappeared and he had to get to the top, but the water kept going over and over him like a mountain.

Fred jolted awake and looked around. There was no water; he wasn't drowning. This darkness had an early morning, less dark feel to it. It was time to get up.

His mother was in the kitchen heating goat's milk on the stove. Her face was an ashy colour and there were dark marks like bruises under her eyes. When she spoke, her voice was low and scratchy, and she had to clear her throat before any sound came out at all.

'See that the others get their proper breakfast Fred. Agnes knows how to make the porridge and you can help her get the little ones dressed.'

Then she hurried with the milk back into the bedroom from where Fred could hear his father calling out something.

May was the only one who was oblivious to the situation. She put up her usual struggle about not eating porridge and refused to let Agnes get the knots out of her hair. The other children whispered to each other and kept looking at the door of Ma and Pa's bedroom where Horace was. Aunty Joe arrived to take care of May and Amy, and Fred walked with the others across to the school.

The warm spring days they'd had last weekend had been pushed away by a westerly that brought heavy clouds and scudding showers and they pushed miserably against the wind, pulling their hats down against the rain.

It should have been a relief to be in the classroom, doing something to take his mind off what was happening at home, but nothing went right. How could these children be so stupid? What was so hard in memorising a few times tables? Fred got so angry with one boy that the lad ended up in tears. Mr Robertson wasn't happy and gave Fred a dressing down that was humiliating and frustrating. Why did people get so upset when he lost his temper? It's not as if he was going to hurt them. Fred wanted to tell Mr Robertson about Horace, but the opportunity passed, and anyway one part of him was still sure that his mother would make things right again.

But when Fred and the others arrived back home there was no point in hoping any longer. Their father was on the verandah to meet them. He looked different, smaller, and he shook his head and looked at them so intently that they knew what had happened without a word being said and when he turned and walked into the front parlour they followed.

The drapes were always kept closed in this room, and dressed head to toe in black, Aunty Joe loomed out of the cold darkness. She was standing with her arms folded in front of the unlit fireplace, and Pa went in and stood beside her. It didn't seem right to sit down, so the children grouped themselves silently in front of them. Fred hadn't noticed Amy curled into the corner of the old sofa, but now she came over and tugged at his hand. He gave it a squeeze, as much to comfort himself as to comfort her. Only bad news was going to come from the sombre gloom of this room. And where was Ma?

It was Aunty Joe who broke the news.

Their mother was sleeping and not to be disturbed. Their little brother Horace had passed away at 2 o'clock this afternoon, may God rest his soul. The Lord giveth and the Lord taketh away. Ours not to ask why, but to accept the Almighty's plan and they must understand that He had one for everyone, no matter how small. The children were to remember that their baby brother had gone to a better place.

Fred wished he could believe what his aunty was saying, but he couldn't. His father looked anything but happy that Horace was in that better place. Quite the opposite.

Agnes started to cry, taking in great gasps of air between sobs. Arthur put his arm around her, and she used the back of her hand to wipe away the tears and looked up at him.

'But he was so sweet,' she managed to say and then started crying again.

'Will Horrie be coming back?' Amy asked Fred.

It was Richard who answered while Fred was still choosing his words. A superior seven-year-old who knew things that his little sister didn't.

'Of course not, silly.'

And Amy started crying too.

'Where do you think a better place is?' Albert asked no one in particular.

Fred fought against a powerful urge to be by himself, to get away from all the sadness and find a place to be alone with his feelings. A year ago, even six months ago, that is what he would have done, but now he pushed that feeling aside and tried to think how he could help the others. It was too much for the younger ones to take in, and they couldn't be expected to sit silently in the grieving house, especially when Ma needed to sleep.

'Horace is in a special place where he's feeling no pain, Albert,' Fred said. Then deliberately ignoring whatever it was his aunty started to say, he went across to Arthur and Agnes. 'Why don't we have a game of cricket? Ma likes us to play outside. Then we can pick some vegetables for tea and see if we can find some eggs.'

Aunty Joe shook her head and started to say something, but his father cut her off.

'Let them be,' he said. 'They're better outside.'

'I'll get the kit out,' Arthur said.

Fred nodded at Arthur.

'Good idea. Out, the rest of you. Out, out.' Then he went over to where May was earnestly stacking and unstacking empty cans. He picked her up with one arm and took the cans in the other hand.

'You too. You can play with these outside.'

Now that Arthur was a member of the Wynyard Cricket Club, he had proper stumps and a willow bat. They were usually out of bounds, but today he was prepared to let the others use them.

The clouds were still heavy out to sea, but the sky in the west had cleared and the sun was breaking through in patches. They didn't notice Aunty Joe watching them through the kitchen window or Father O'Callaghan who had come to visit and stood beside her.

Her lips were pressed tightly together, and she shook her head as she spoke.

'It would never happen in the old country, Father. If it were up to me, I'd have them in their rooms praying for the soul of that poor babe. But their mother lets them run wild. "It's healthy," she says.'

Father O'Callaghan put a hand on Aunty Joe's shoulder.

'There now Josephine. We'll all miss the dear little fellow and sometimes we can't help thinking that God has made a mistake. He'll understand you wanting to have a bit of a cry.'

Aunty Joe used the edge of her pinny and wiped around her eyes. The priest watched Arthur, his arms around Amy, helping her to hold the bat. Together they sent the ball flying off into the corner where a few hens were scratching under the pepper tree.

He opened the window and called out. 'Good shot.' Then he turned to Aunty Joe. 'Don't forget what Jesus said. From the lips of children the Lord calls forth his Praise.'

Aunty Joe let her pinny drop and smoothed it down with practised hands.

'I hope you're right Father. There may be hope for them yet.'

*

That night Fred lay awake again. It was too hard to keep trying to believe in God. He could never have the steady belief of his mother, or understand how his father could talk as if God was a real person, a magical being who saw everything they did and punished and rewarded and made plans for them.

If God was good, why would he make a little baby suffer like Horrie did? And what about Ma? She was always helping to keep other babies alive, so why would God make her own baby die? Fred had been doing his best to believe, and he prayed every night, but it made no difference. The rest of them could believe what they wanted, but they couldn't make him accept that a merciful God would do such terrible things. As far as he could see, it was other people who made good things happen. Fred wasn't sure how he would do it, but he wanted to be one of those people.

13

Two years later, 9 November 1885

When Fred left the Robertsons' cottage the night was clear, the new moon a sliver in the west, the sky glowing with stars. There was a frosty feel to the air, and he pushed his hands deep into his pockets and walked fast. He felt the edges of the envelope in his pocket and thought back over the past hour.

Mrs Robertson had shown him through to the sitting room. She was always friendly, but tonight she seemed especially pleased to see him.

'Come though, come through,' she said. 'He's been waiting for you.'

Mr Robertson was standing in front of the fire in the sitting room, both hands behind his back, and there was something in the slight lift of his eyebrows and a half smile that suggested he had news to tell.

It was Fred's habit to take in an armful of wood and he'd done so that night. He unloaded it into the basket by the side of the hearth and brushed little chips and bits of bark off his jacket. Then instead of going over to the table, where he could see the collected works of Shakespeare open, ready for the reading they had planned, he stayed where he was, certain that something was in the air.

Mr Robertson did the slight rock on to his toes that had earned him the nickname 'twinkle toes'.

'Something came in the mail today,' he said.

It was what they'd been waiting for, it had to be. Fred had almost given up hope and resigned himself to another year as a teacher's assistant.

'What did he say? Is it good news?'

Robert smiled and handed him a heavy cream parchment envelope.

'Have a look for yourself.'

The letter was to the point. Considering Mr Frederick Alexander's examination results and good reports on his teaching practice from Mr Rule and Mr Robertson, Mr Richard Hamilton is honoured to offer the said Mr Alexander a place in the teacher training class of 1886. Further details in due time etc., etc.

It was hard for Fred to take it in. The training would mean he could be a real teacher, with his own school and a house, like Mr Robertson. He'd find some clerical work in Hobart, support himself for the year. His life would change. Nobody he knew had done anything like this. Boys like him took up a trade, worked on the farm or at the mill. January was still two months away. How could he find the patience to wait? He wanted to pack up and leave tonight.

He flourished the letter triumphantly.

'Some have greatness thrust upon them,' he cried out dramatically, then laughed. Robert laughed too and shook Fred's hand.

'Congratulations Fred. This is a big opportunity for you and well deserved.'

'Thank you, Mr Robertson. It's all because of you. I won't let you down.'

★

He turned the corner into Hogg Street and took the short cut across the horse paddock and past the vegetable garden. His mother would be pleased for him, he knew that, they'd already discussed it. But his father? There was only one way to find out. He let himself in the back door and went straight to the kitchen where his parents were sitting in front of the fire in the stove. The fire door and the oven door were both open and the room, lit by the oil lamp and the glow from the fire, was warm and welcoming. His father was snoring, and his mother was pulling a needle in and out of something white, leaning into the light as she checked that the thread wasn't knotting. He gave the letter to his mother, who read it, then read it again. Fred hadn't tried to hide his excitement and the look she gave him was what he'd expected and hoped for.

'Oh Fred. This is such good news. This is your big chance.'

'Yes. And with this training, I'll have my own school and a good salary and a house to live in.' Fred spoke quietly, almost a whisper, trying not to disturb his father, but the sound, soft as it was, was enough to rouse him.

His father sat up and looked at them. He saw the letter in his wife's hand and pointed to it.

'What are the two of you up to now?'

'It's good news,' Fred said, and started to explain.

'It's an offer for Frederick to advance himself,' his mother cut in. 'From Mr Hamilton in Hobart.'

'Hobart! What's that?' he said, pointing to the letter. 'Read it to me!'

Fred took the letter from his mother and did as he was asked. When he finished there was silence and his father sat looking at him, trying to take it in.

'It's just for a year,' Fred started to explain, 'and it means I can be a proper teacher.'

His father cut him off.

'I know what it means. I don't know what you are thinking! Both of you.'

He slapped one hand on his thigh then stood up.

'I've had enough of this. We'll discuss this man to man in the front room.'

Fred followed him down the hallway and they stood awkwardly in front of the unlit fireplace. The only light in the room came from the hallway, and away from the cosy warmth of the fire in the kitchen the cold ate at his heart.

The discussion was one-sided, with his father doing most of the talking. Fred wondered if he hadn't taken a drink despite his pledge, he seemed so worked up. Every time Fred tried to explain what a great opportunity this was, the good money for a Class 1 teacher, the work he would do in Hobart while he was training, his father cut him off. Refused to listen.

The training was out of the question. What could Fred have been thinking of? Next January he would be seventeen years old. He wasn't a boy. It had been a bad year, with the big slump in Victoria and money was getting tighter and tighter.

'What you have to do, Frederick, is to get a proper job,' his father said. 'Playing around with teaching might make you feel good but it's now we need the money. What do you think we're supposed to do with you away getting more educated? You need to find a job and find it fast. Without Arthur to keep things going, where would we be? I've had enough of your fancy ideas. If all that learning is worth anything, you will make your education do what it's meant to do. Earn money. You will discover that in life, it's the money you make that counts. The rest is doing God's work and sowing seed to be fruitful and multiply as He wants.'

There was no point in further argument and in fact Fred was only half listening. His father would never understand. He didn't seem to want to understand. Fred felt sorry for that excited boy who had walked home with his big ideas. More than that he felt sorry for Mr Robertson who had worked hard to give Fred the best possible start. How was he going to break the news?

Suddenly his father had changed from talking about God's will to something else.

'And there's no point running to your mother,' his father said. 'I've made up my mind.'

The thought had been in Fred's mind but now that option was gone.

It was so unfair. Nothing he did would ever please his father. Well, if it was going to be like that, so be it. There were things of the mind and spirit that his father would never understand, but that was not a reason to give up on them.

He had to get away. Leave Wynyard. He would show his father that he wasn't a child any longer to be pushed around.

'I'll get a job in Mt Bischoff,' he said. 'I can stay with Uncle James and Aunt Jane and help out in the hotel while I'm looking for a job.'

'Wynyard's not good enough for you then.'

'You want me to make money. Well, I've read the ads for work up there, and they pay better than anything around here.'

His father shrugged.

'It's what your Uncle James said when he was down last time. "Riches to be had," was how he put it. "Ten times the size of Wynyard and still growing". I'll give you one month to find work up there. After that you can get your hands dirty right here, like everyone else. Get your mother to arrange it for you.'

His father walked out the door and slammed it behind him. Fred heard the front door open and shut and footsteps going up the path and out the gate. The temperance hotel would still be open, and for that matter, the Courthouse Hotel as well. His father could complain about him to his mates down there. The house felt lighter with him gone and Fred hurried down the corridor to join his mother in the warmth of the kitchen.

Part 2

Waratah

1886 to 1889

14

Two weeks later, 24 November 1885

Fred put his elbow on the window ledge and leaned his face on his hand, so close to the glass that his breath clouded it like mist. The train lurched as it turned to the right and he caught the book that had been sitting unread on his lap, closed it, and tucked it between his leg and the side of the carriage.

For miles and miles they'd been travelling through dense stands of myrtle and blackwood. Now, as the train straightened, there was a clearing and a river that tumbled around moss-covered boulders then spread wide and clear over sand and pebbles.

The train slowed again and the clickety-clack took on a lighter, hollow sound as they crossed the bridge. Fred caught a glimpse of white frothing water, dark rocks, and green leaves dappled by the sun that bounced off the stream. There was a flash of blue and a splash.

The train kept its steady pace. Fred wanted it to stop, to go back. There was so much promise in that one glimpse, and he might not see it again. He looked back, straining to take it all in, but they were travelling between wooded hills and the moment had passed.

Opposite him, the red-haired man in the checked jacket spoke for the first time since they had left Burnie nearly two hours ago.

'Kingfisher.'

Fred wasn't sure what he meant.

'Pardon?'

'The blue flash. What you saw.'

'Some sort of bird?' Fred guessed. 'We went by so fast.'

The man smiled, pleased with himself.

'Azure kingfisher, to be precise. Little things they are, but I've seen one take on a snake this long.' He held his hands wide. 'And nothing like them for catching fish. One minute they're bobbing away on their branch and then down they go.'

That both of them had shared a glimpse of the little blue kingfisher gave them the sort of temporary closeness that only happens on a train. It was new to Fred, but the man seemed used to it.

He'd come from Melbourne, he told Fred. He wished he'd been around for the gold rush. That was the ticket, striking it rich. Imagine that. Anyway, people were talking about Mt Bischoff and the riches to be found in these mountains. Biggest tin mine the world, so they said. Fancy that. Technical stuff was his line of business, on the engineering side, and he was sure there'd be opportunities for him there.

'And what's your line of work?' he asked Fred.

Teaching assistant seemed inadequate in these circumstances and Fred searched in his mind for something more impressive. He thought of the work he did to help his father.

'Business accounting and helping run a carriage hire operation.'

'And what's that you're reading?'

'Poetry. Ballads.'

Fred took the book out and held it so the man opposite could read the cover.

'The *Collected Poems of Lord Tennyson*,' the man said. 'Too high-brow for me, I'm afraid.'

The man gave Fred a sharp look, as if he hadn't really seen him properly before, and then went back to staring out the window. Fred did the same, and they both lapsed back into silence.

It felt as if a long time had passed since he'd left home this morning, but it was only a few hours. They'd set off early while the tide was low and travelled along the beach for the first leg of the trip, Fred, his mother, and Albert, squeezed into the front of the buggy, his luggage taking up the other seat. The salt-smell on the wide, empty beach was sharp in the pre-dawn darkness and when the sun finally appeared over the horizon it made golden pathways over the sea. Ma had declared it a good omen and Fred was happy to agree. It was a tangible image of what he felt but couldn't express.

And already the adventure had started. Steaming along in the train with its upholstered seats, wood panels and wrought iron luggage racks, surrounded by strangers, it all held the promise of something very different.

As soon as he'd made the decision to find work at Mt Bischoff, life in Wynyard had changed for him. Things kept happening that made him want to get away and he'd ended up dragging himself through every day, just waiting until he could leave.

It had been humiliating, having to break the news to Mr Robertson that he wouldn't be following him into the teaching profession after all, and it didn't help that Mr Robertson had been even more upset than he was. There was nothing that Fred could say that hadn't already been said, and they'd sat by the fire in silence, absorbing the finality of the decision.

And a few days after that, Fred had been shocked by something one of his pupils had said to him. For as long as he could remember he'd felt secure and certain about his place in the community and the world. Before he died, Grandfather Matthias had been a big man in the Table Cape area. He had owned practically the whole of the Cape and half of Wynyard and Fred in turn had a feeling of ownership, of birthright to all that and, without thinking about it, a sense of importance.

But apparently, there was another way of looking at his family, and by extension, himself. The girl hadn't said it to be cruel, or at least Fred didn't think so, because she was one of his best students, a questioning type, a bit like himself. She just wanted to know.

'What's it like being from a family of convicts?' she'd asked.

Fred had pretended not to mind. 'I wouldn't know,' he'd said, and changed the subject. When he told his parents, neither of them would talk about it. 'Just ignore it,' Ma had said. 'It doesn't mean anything.' But on the weekend he'd ridden over to Burnie to see Nan Lewis. He'd always been close to her and felt he could ask her anything.

'Yes. Her Majesty's Government transported me here,' she told him, 'but I'm not ashamed and you shouldn't be either. The times were hard and I did what I could to help the family. The person you become is what counts. You should be proud of what we've all made of ourselves. A proper chance, that's all we needed. But one thing, Fred. This is something we don't talk about. Not because we're ashamed. Your great uncles were real heroes in some people's eyes. But when other people find out, they put you down. You come from landed folk on your father's side and on your mother's…well you could say her father's a magistrate.'

Fred had started to object. If there was nothing to be ashamed of, then why hide it.

'But…'

That was as far as he got. Nan Lewis interrupted him, an edge to her voice.

'No buts this time Fred. It's not just about you, it's about all of us. You're a smart lad and a bit different. Around here everyone knows you. Heaven knows you're related to most of them. Young people think they know everything, but you don't know people like I do. You'll do nothing but harm if you go around telling the truth. Nothing but harm.' She closed her mouth around the words with a finality that even Fred couldn't argue against.

'You can trust me, Nan.'

Fred leaned back against the headrest and gave himself over to daydreaming. Where would he be in ten years' time? He was sixteen now, so he'd be twenty-six. What would he be doing? He wouldn't be in Wynyard. Maybe he'd make lots of money from mining like his grandfather did and live in Scotland in a big two-storey house made of stone, with turrets and attic windows and French doors, like the photos he'd seen of Mr

Roberson's house in Stirling. Mr and Mrs Robertson would live just up the road and there would be concerts in the evening and he would wear a dinner suit with tails and a high collar and recite Shakespeare so well that he would make people cry.

He felt something touch his sleeve. The woman next to him was patting him on the arm and saying something.

'Here, have one of these. That'll cheer you up.'

She took a cloth off a basket and held it out in front of him. Fred's first thought was to correct her. No. He didn't need cheering up. Couldn't a chap have a bit of a think without someone wanting to cheer him up! But the plump nest of scones was not to be resisted.

The woman shook the box enticingly.

'Here. Take one. Mind you, get the whole thing now. There's jam and butter on them.'

Fred carefully removed a scone and thanked her before devouring it.

'Elevenses. Thank you.' The man in the checked suit demolished his scone in two bites. 'Perfect timing. I must say.' He brushed the crumbs off his hands and checked his fob watch. 'We should be there before long.'

It was as he said. Dense forest gave way to scattered trees and the train whistled twice before it crossed another bridge. People's descriptions had not prepared Fred for what he saw. The land dropped away as if a giant axe had been driven straight through the steep wooded hills.

'Waratah Gorge,' the man opposite told him. 'Splendid wouldn't you say? Takes you by surprise. No doubt about that.'

No reply seemed called for, so Fred nodded acknowledgement, then suddenly they were pulling into the station and his fellow passengers were gathering up their things and helping each other get luggage down off the racks.

Fred caught sight of himself in the mirror at the end of the carriage, and he pulled his jacket down and straightened his collar, then carefully readjusted his hat. First impressions were very important, something Mr Robertson always said. Yes, he'd been talking about performing, but wasn't this going to be a sort of performance? Young man looking for work. Fred smiled to himself as he pulled his bags from the luggage rack. This was going to be an adventure.

15

Fred swung himself on to the platform, then he reached back in for his luggage. When he turned around he saw a familiar figure waving to him from the other end of the station.

Aunt Jane. Other passengers were being claimed by people who had come to meet the train, and she pushed her way through the crowd, holding the front of her skirt with both hands. Fred left his luggage where it was and went to meet her.

'Aunty Jane!'

'Fred! You made it! I was hoping I had the right day.' She gave him a hug then stepped back and looked him up and down. 'You've grown again,' she said approvingly, as if Fred had accomplished something special. 'Welcome to Mt Bischoff.' She looked past him to his luggage. 'You might need some help with that.' she said, and she waved to one of the boys who were standing next to wheelbarrows on the edge of the platform.

'Here's a penny to take these to Pearce's Hotel, Jimmy,' she told the lad, 'and another penny to carry them upstairs.'

'Good as done Mrs Pearce.' The boy pocketed the pennies, loaded the luggage into the wheelbarrow and the three of them set off, following the straggling line of new arrivals along the main road in the direction of the mountain.

'I see you've packed for all eventualities,' Aunt Jane said. 'Am I right in thinking that your mother had a hand in it.'

Fred laughed. 'Yes. Had it been left to me, the trunk would have been enough! The duffel bag is mostly full of things for you, Aunt Jane. Bolts of fabrics and some fresh things from the farm as well. Ma said she'd got everything you wanted except for the blue checked ribbons which were all too wide'.

'It's good of you to bring them. Look, Fred.' Aunt Jane stopped and Fred followed suit. On their right, a wooden footbridge crossed a fast-flowing stream surrounded by a grassy meadow. A short distance to the left, the land suddenly disappeared into a deep gorge and the stream became a waterfall that sprayed out over boulders before it too disappeared into the chasm.

'Yes,' Fred said. 'I saw it from the train. It's such a surprise, a waterfall in the town like that.'

'Extraordinary, isn't it?' They started walking again, past an untidy collection of large wooden sheds that came right to the edge of the road. 'Listen to that noise!

Fred realised the noise had been there all along; a rhythmic thudding, clanking sound that got louder the closer they got to the hotel.

'It's the processing sheds for the tin,' Aunt Jane explained. 'The stampers make that thumping noise and the waterwheels that run the electricity make the grinding and slushing.'

The road they were walking on ran parallel to the gorge, but the scrubby bush and ugly bare trunks of ring-barked trees hid all signs of the valley. Fred wondered how a landscape could change so dramatically. What a strange town!

Jimmy had stopped in front of a sizeable two-storey building fronted by colonnaded verandahs on both levels. It was painted a cream colour, with dark green trimming around big windows, rather like the Courthouse Hotel in Wynyard. *Pearce's Hotel* was written in stylish black lettering under the gabled roof.

'Here we are,' Aunt Jane announced.

The boy heaved the trunk out of the wheelbarrow and rested it on his shoulder and Fred took out the duffel bag. Aunt Jane held the door open and directed Jimmy up the stairs to room five.

'The duffel bag can go over there,' she told Fred, pointing to a table under the staircase. 'That's our family quarters there,' she said, and indicated a dark hallway, then she led the way up two flights of stairs. On the landing she turned to the right again and opened the second door on the left.

Jimmy had deposited the trunk on the bed and Aunt Jane gave him another penny then closed the door after him.

Fred took in the spacious room. 'Is this all this for me?'

Aunt Jane laughed. 'Yes – it's all yours. No cousins that you need to share with. But you're lucky to have this room. Mr Smith from the mining office was staying here until last week, but his contract finished and he's moved on.'

'Ma said you'd have some work for me to do while I'm here.'

'She's right. There's always more than enough work to do in a big hotel like this Fred. Your uncle could do with another pair of hands at the bar, especially when it gets busy around knock off time. That's if that teacher of yours hasn't turned you against such a thing.'

'Mr Robertson? No. He cautions me about sobriety, him and mother both, but I haven't taken the pledge and don't intend to.'

'That's alright then. But it's not only the work in the bar. There's always wood that has to be cut and stacked. You can imagine with all these rooms and with cold weather up here in the mountains…'

'I'll do it. You can count on me.'

'Good. You can help me out too. I was very pleased when your mother wrote and told me you were coming here – an extra pair of hands, I thought. But it wasn't just that. It's nice for the children to have their big cousin to stay – they're quite excited. You'll meet them when you come down for luncheon. That's in half an hour, so I'll leave you to get unpacked.'

Fred waited until she closed the door behind her. He bounced on the bed a couple of times then he went over to the window, pulled the drapes back, pushed the window up as high as it went and leaned out.

The noise of the machines was suddenly louder. He took in a deep breath of air and picked up the hint of something that was unpleasantly like the smell left by the nightman when he went passed their house. It was faint and might have been from the mine works, but it wasn't fresh like the sea air at home, and he pulled his head and shoulders back into the room and closed the window. He could still hear the machines, but now the noise was muffled.

The wooden sill doubled as a window seat, and he perched himself on it and peered out through the glass. To his left, he could see most of the main street and behind it the looming presence of Mt Bischoff. From this distance the mountain looked like a child's drawing, a triangular shape that stood out from the hills around it. Then Fred realised what it was. It was as if the mountain had been carved like a statue. The shape of the other hills was softened and coloured by forests that formed a green carpet over the land, but Mt Bischoff was bare, except for a tuft of trees on the very top.

When he leaned against the glass and looked down, he could see a post office and a chemist then a general store and what looked as if it must be a barber shop, judging by the neatly trimmed men coming out of it.

There were more people down on the street than you would see in a week in Wynyard! Mostly men, but some women too, going in and out of the general store with parcels and loaded baskets. Men in suits and serious looking hats were chatting in small groups, some of them with box files under their arms, or holding small leather cases. Weaving their way amongst them, workmen pushed laden carts, and others were digging with shovels on the side of the road.

Across the road from the shops, a miniature train was coming along tracks that Fred had noticed earlier. As the train passed by the hotel, he could see that it was made up of iron buckets on wheels, each of them loaded with rocks. The engine disappeared around the back of the big shed and there was a crunching noise. The stamping sheds, Fred guessed.

He dragged himself away from the window and took out his new watch. Fifteen minutes before luncheon.

There were three places to put things: the wardrobe, the washstand and the desk, and Fred had found somewhere for most of his things by the time he heard the dinner gong. He was more than ready for something to eat, and he left his photos and books on the bed and hurried down the stairs to the living quarters that Aunt Jane had pointed out.

She had been right about his cousins. They were peeping out of the door of the dining room, and when they saw Fred walking along the hallway towards them, they ran back inside the room, giggling and pushing each other. When Fred followed them in, they were standing next to Aunt Jane, looking up at him from bent heads.

'They're not really shy,' Aunt Jane laughed. 'It's a pretence.' She put a hand on the blonde curls of the little girl. 'This is Harriet, she's four, and Mattie is five. Say hello to your cousin Fred.'

Mattie looked up at Fred but stayed close to his mother.

'Hello cousin Fred.'

Fred laughed and took his hand.

'Pleased to meet you, Mattie. You can just call me Fred.' He squatted down in front of Harriet. 'Hello Harriet.'

She covered her eyes with one hand and giggled, then she quickly pulled her hand away.

'Surprise,' she said with a big smile, and Fred laughed and stood up again.

'I want to sit next to cousin Fred,' Mattie announced.

'Me too,' Harriet said, and reached up and held his hand.

Fred looked at Aunt Jane, an eyebrow raised.

'If you don't mind…' she said and smiled at Fred. 'I warned you,' she added. 'You're a novelty for them.'

They went across to the table and Aunt Jane was rearranging the table settings when Uncle James came through the door that connected with the kitchen. He shook Fred's hand and then looked him up and down approvingly in much the same way as his aunt had done.

'Welcome to Waratah.' he said. How was the journey? I don't know about you, but I'm starving. Let's eat.'

Fred didn't mind having his little cousins competing for his attention, but by the time the pudding was served it had worn thin, and it was a relief when a competent looking woman, introduced as Miss Wilson, whisked the children away with quiet authority.

Uncle James leaned back in his chair and folded his arms.

'Now Fred, tell me about your plans. Your aunt said you might be looking for work.'

'Yes. I'm here to look for a permanent job. Something with decent pay.'

'Well, it doesn't hurt to aim high, and there are opportunities here. What sort of work?'

'I've been helping father run the carriage hire business, in fact running the business side of things. I can do bookkeeping, and I'm good with numbers, so maybe something in that line. Aunt Jane said that I can help around the hotel while I'm looking. I want to earn my keep.'

'Your aunt is right. It's a busy hotel. But why don't you take a couple of days to have a look around first?'

'Thanks uncle, but I really am ready to start whenever you are. I'm not used to having spare time.'

'Well, if you really think so, now is as good a time as any. I could do with an extra pair of hands in the bar.'

'Are you sure that's a good idea?' Aunt Jane asked.

His uncle acknowledged what she said and turned back to Fred. 'There's not much to it, but that teetotal family of yours probably hasn't prepared you for a room full of thirsty miners. Will that be a problem?'

Fred thought of the framed pledges of total abstinence that hung over the fireplace in the parlour and what his mother had said to him before he left. 'Promise me you'll stay away from intoxicating liquor Fred,' she'd said. 'Remember how your father was before he took the pledge. I know I can trust you.' 'Of course you can trust me Ma,' Fred had said. He hadn't promised, and he didn't think he needed to promise. He'd never been tempted. He loved his mother more than anyone, but he meant to live his own life and make his own decisions.

'Not at all,' he said to his uncle, as he followed him through the kitchen and into the public bar, 'and I'm a quick learner.'

The public bar was a good-sized room in the front corner of the hotel and there were big windows on the two outside walls. In the corner of those walls a fireplace made a triangular shape and on the wall above it was a framed photo that took up the entire space.

Uncle James saw Fred looking at it.

'Do you recognise him? That's Philosopher Smith. He's the one who found the tin on Mt Bischoff. Without him there wouldn't be any of this.' He waved his arm in the direction of the mountain and the sheds.

'He doesn't look like a miner.'

The man had a good-humoured face, his eyes screwed up a little, as if he was holding back a smile. Although his full, soft beard was grey, almost white, and long enough to sit on his chest, his face was unlined, and he had a pipe loosely clamped in his mouth.

'Is he rich?'

'He's been well rewarded, but he's not a greedy man. One reason he's so well respected and renowned. But enough of that. Serving behind the bar isn't going to make you famous, but you have to start somewhere. Let's go and meet John; my barman and my right-hand man.'

Two men, each with a foot resting on the brass foot rail, were leaning against the polished blackwood bar that ran the length of the room. They were talking to a placid looking sandy-haired man who was half listening to them as he polished the glass doors on the drink cabinets, turning towards the men every so often to make a comment.

Uncle James lifted the hinged entry to the bar and motioned to the barman.

'There's someone I want you to meet, John.'

The man came over to where Fred was standing with his uncle in front of the beer taps.

'This is Mr John Spencer, Fred,' his uncle said. 'John manages the bar for me, and you'll be helping him. I've got plenty to organise. There's a meeting of the hospital committee at six, then after that a group of twenty in the banquet room for a farewell dinner, so I'll be glad of your help.' His uncle put a hand on Fred's shoulder. 'Are you sure you're comfortable doing this? You don't have to, you know.'

Fred wondered why there was so much fuss about him working in the bar. It couldn't be too difficult and just because he was serving drink didn't mean he would be consuming it.

'Perfectly alright.'

'Good. It gets crowded in here, but by and large we don't have trouble. Mr Kayser runs a tight ship, and the men want to keep their jobs.'

'You get your larrikins, though,' John Spencer said. 'And the ones who don't want to pay. It's those passing through that cause the problems. I think we get men who come here to kill themselves with drink.'

Uncle James laughed.

'Come on John, you'll put the lad off. Just make sure you teach him well.'

Pulling the beers was a lot harder than Fred had imagined and there were only so many times he could waste the beer with a bad pour.

'Watch what I do,' John said. He pulled a glass down from the overhead rack and held it up to the light. 'It has to be clean,' he explained. 'Any dirt and you won't get a head at all.'

'Head?' Fred asked.

John looked worried for the first time.

'You really don't know?'

'No. But keep going, I'll do what you say.'

'Right.' John took the pint glass by the base and put it under the tap. 'Now see here, you've got to put the nozzle right at the bottom of the glass to get a good pour. Then all you have to do is pull the handle steady like. It'll take a couple of pulls, mind you.'

Fred had come closer and was trying to get a good look at what the barman was doing. It looked easy enough, and John handed him a pint with just a finger width of creamy foam on top.

'That's the head,' he told Fred. 'That's what it should look like.' Then he noticed that Fred wasn't drinking it. 'Okay – give it to me. 'One going spare,' he said to the men who were still at the bar, and he put the beer in front of them. 'Now you try,' he said to Fred.

The first few that Fred poured were mostly froth and he had to tip them out and start again, but then he realised there was certain rhythm to it and John pronounced the fifth one perfect. Measuring the spirits should have been straightforward, but John explained that there was an extra trick of giving the right quantity to certain customers.

''There's no way I can teach you that. You'll get used to it,' he told Fred. 'Start with the measure and then use your judgement.'

At four o'clock the noise of a hooter blared across the town.

'They'll be here soon. It might be a good idea to stick to collecting and washing glasses for the first few nights – leave the pouring to me.'

'I've got the hang of it,' Fred said.

John Spencer looked doubtful, but he shrugged. 'Up to you.'

As it turned out, the rush hour went smoothly enough. Uncle James came in to help for a while, and a lot of the men had only two or three drinks then left.

But that still left a noisy crowd of men who stayed on and got steadily more and more drunk. The oil lamps were lit and outside the street was dark. Then it started to rain, and there was even less reason for the men to leave.

Most of them took no notice of Fred as he collected glasses and cleared the worst of the mess – they were too busy arguing and joking amongst themselves. But there was one miner, a heavily bearded, stocky man with a loud voice, who stood out from the others. He was with a group of miners who were gathered around the narrow bench that ran along the wall between the window and the fireplace. Fred would have preferred to avoid that group, but the clutter of glasses and mugs on the table in front of them really needed to be cleared.

'Do you mind if I take these?' Fred asked.

One of the men waved his hand indicating that he should go ahead, and Fred started to gather up the glasses when there was a loud voice that came from behind him. He turned around and saw the aggressive, drunk miner pointing at him.

'Oi, listen up boys,' the man said. Then he put on a posh accent, mimicking Fred. 'Do you mind if I finally get round to taking these glasses?'

It wasn't a very good imitation of Fred's accent, and Fred ignored him. He continued picking up the glasses then took them into the scullery. After that, he came out to the bar and turned towards some men in suits who had been waiting to be served.

John was busy up the other end, serving some businessmen who'd come for the Specimen Reef meeting.

But the miner who'd made fun of him was spoiling for a fight and he had followed Fred over to the bar. He pushed in front of the other men and crashed his empty glass on the counter.

'A pint and a rum,' he said. 'And make it quick.'

Fred wasn't sure what to do. He should serve the men who'd been waiting, but he recognised the sour anger of the man, so he decided to serve him first. He took a pint glass down from the rack and as soon as he started to pour the ale he knew it was going to be a disaster. He hadn't put the nozzle down far enough, and there was more froth than beer. To buy time, Fred left the beer on the counter and took down a tumbler and a bottle of rum. He poured two measures into the bottom of the glass then turned back to the glass of ale. It was still full of froth and the only thing was to start again.

Before he could do anything, the man scooped up a handful

of the foam and flicked it at Fred's face then followed it with the rum.

'Ya little poofter,' the man sneered at Fred. 'Go back to ya mother.'

Fred wiped the foam off his face. There were things he could have done to save the situation, but they were the things he didn't do. Instead, he picked up the frothy glass of ale and threw the rest of it at the miner.

'And you can go to hell,' he shouted.

It could have been worse. The miner tried to take a swing at Fred, but the other men at the bar restrained him. Fred himself had his fists clenched, ready to fight. He wanted to fight.

Then John came over and gave Fred a look. Not sympathetic, not judgemental, just a look. 'You'd better go and clean yourself up,' he said. 'And make yourself scarce. Oh, and tell Mr Pearce I need some help in here.'

Then he poured a tumbler full of rum and pulled a perfect pint of ale.

'On the house,' he said.

The miner shook off the two men who were restraining him and took the tumbler of rum and tossed it down in one gulp, then put it down again. John filled it up, and only then the man took the two glasses back over to the table where his friends were watching to see what would happen.

'What you won't do to get a free drink,' one of them laughed.

'I thought he was going to go for you for a minute there,' the other one said.

'Shut your trap,' the miner growled, but his friends took no notice.

★

Later that night, after Fred checked that the horses were settled and did a few other things to help his uncle close the hotel for the night, he sat on the window seat in his room and stared out at the darkness. Rain was falling steadily, making light tapping noises on the glass, but it didn't drown out the grinding thumps from the stamping machines.

What a day! Was it only this morning that he'd left the railway station at Emu Bay? It felt like a week had passed. There was something calming about the noise of the rain on the window and Fred thought about what Aunt Jane had said to him.

After the incident in the public bar, Fred had taken the quickest way out through the kitchen door. He hadn't needed to say anything. His uncle had taken one look and reacted just like John Spencer.

'I suppose I'd better take myself into the bar,' he'd said. Fred had felt so hot and swollen with anger and shame that he couldn't do anything but nod and rush past him up to his room. He'd poured some water from the jug and wiped the sticky, smelly beer off his face and was sitting on his bed, angry and miserable and wondering what to do with himself when there was a knock on the door. It was Aunt Jane.

'Your uncle told me about what happened,' she said. 'I'm sorry things got off to a bad start.'

'Should I go back down?' Fred asked her.

'Not yet. I think you need to pull yourself together. Let's go onto the balcony.'

They went out of his room and along the hallway though a door that opened on to a wide covered verandah with an iron-lace railing. There was a break in the rain, but the night was still dark and the sky was dense with heavy clouds.

'Look down there, Fred,' Aunt Jane had said, and she pointed to the valley. It was like nothing Fred had ever seen. Rows and rows of lights were shining in the darkness.

'Electric lights,' his aunt said. 'They're in the sheds so the machines can work all night.'

'Electric?' Fred had never seen anything like it.

'Yes. Quite wonderful, don't you think? You'll find a lot of things that are different up here Fred. There's a harsh edge to things. Some of it is splendid and quite beautiful, like those lights. But you feel as if your time is not your own. The miners especially are driven like machines.'

'That man in the bar had the brain of a machine.'

'He was drunk. Not that it excuses his behaviour, but he's just a man working hard and letting off steam.' Aunt Jane looked across at Fred. 'Don't take this the wrong way Fred, but your uncle and I think it's best that you don't work in the bar.'

He'd hardly had a chance to show what he could do! He was about to protest, to plead his case, but his aunt continued.

'I know you work hard, but you don't have the temperament to work in the bar. That temper of yours – I don't know what to say. Betsy tells me it's getting better, but you've got a way to go yet. A public bar is never going to come up to your standards. You don't suffer fools gladly and you want everything to be fair. Well, in the bar, like in life, that's not always the case. The difference is that in the bar, you're serving customers and Uncle James and I rely on their goodwill to make a living.'

'I'm sorry Aunt Jane. I didn't think…'

'We took a risk coming up here and you were probably too young to realise that your Mr Robertson and the Alexanders and their temperance movement drove us away.' Aunt Jane shook her head. 'Anyway, building this hotel when there were two here already was a huge risk, and you have no idea how hard your uncle worked to make it a success.' Then she sighed and gave Fred a smile. 'That's in the past now. I know you wouldn't want to make things hard for us, so here's our idea. You've got a good head for numbers.'

Fred nodded.

'You can do the accounts for us. Enter the figures every day and do the reckoning each week. Your uncle James has got so many things on the go he finds it hard to get around to the bookkeeping.'

The pattering of the rain grew louder and Fred rested his head on the wall behind him, stretched his legs along the wide sill and closed his eyes. In the end, he thought, things had turned out for the best. There were other ways of helping around the hotel, and he knew now that he would much rather balance books than serve behind the bar. The sound of the rain and the rhythmic thump of the machines made a sort of tune and the next thing he knew, his head hit the window and his eyes shot open.

Feeling groggy and only half awake, he left his clothes in a pile on the chair, pulled on his nightshirt and crawled under the quilt. The clanking and thumping continued, but he was oblivious to it.

<h1 style="text-align:center">17</h1>

A couple of weeks later, Thursday, 10 December 1885

Every table in the dining room at Pearce's Hotel was occupied. Not that Thursday was any more special than other nights; it had been busy like this every evening since Fred had been in Waratah.

The reason was simple. Pearce's Hotel offered a three-course meal every evening at seven, except on Sundays. For the first couple of days, Fred had missed his midday dinner and he'd gone to the kitchen, hoping for some slices of ham, or cold roast potatoes, but it wasn't like home and a piece of dry bread was all that the cook would give him. Now the evening meal was routine, and he made sure he ate a good breakfast to get him through the day. c

Behind him there was a steady hum of chatter coming from the other diners. He was sitting at a table for two that was pushed against the wall close to the fireplace. It had been the only vacant table the first night when he came down for dinner, and it suited him to be a little apart from the others. Now he pushed the cutlery to one side and opened the ledger that he'd collected before dinner. He started to put the new slips in order while he waited for his meal. Once he'd eaten, he would take the accounts up to his room and make the entries there.

What an interesting day it had been. Fred had given Aunt Jane a hand with Mattie and Harriet during the morning, then Uncle James had introduced him to one of his friends, Mr Duncanson, who had offered to show him around the mine. They rode on the running board of the little train that ran between the mountain and the town, then walked the rest of the way to the rock wall they called the 'Red Face'. It was the part of the mountain that had already been cut back to expose the tin bearing ore and Mr Duncanson had taken him to inspect the washing cradles that were sloshing back and forth, getting the worst of the dirt and debris off the rocks. There was a tap on his shoulder and Fred had looked up to see his bird-watching companion from the train.

'This is Mr O'Dowd, one of our assistant engineers,' Mr Duncanson said.

'We meet again,' Fred said. 'I guess there are no kingfishers up here Mr O'Dowd.'

They both laughed and shook hands.

'You know each other then?' Mr Duncanson asked.

'In a manner of speaking. We shared a carriage on the trip up here. Any work yet?' Mr O'Dowd asked Fred.

'Not yet. But if you hear of anything let me know. I'm staying at Pearce's Hotel.'

'Accounting, isn't it?' Mr O'Dowd asked.

'That's it,' Fred said, impressed that the man had remembered. 'I'm helping my uncle with the books at the hotel meanwhile.'

Mr Duncanson was staying on at the Red Face and before they parted company, he shook Fred's hand.

'Like I've been telling you, Mr Alexander, the Mt Bischoff Mining Company is going from strength to strength and there's a good chance we might need more accountants. I'll mention it to Mr Horne.'

So far looking for work had been a frustrating part of Fred's visit. Everyone said there was work in Waratah and on his second day here, he'd gone to the Mt Bischoff Tin Mining Company offices, expecting to walk into a job. But when he said he didn't want to work at the mine face, they weren't interested. Uncle James always seemed to be too busy to sit down and talk about it, and a good two weeks had gone past with Fred no closer to finding employment.

Fred was just putting the last slip in the pile when he looked up to see a man with his hand on the back of the chair opposite.

'Mind if I join you?' the man asked.

'No. I mean yes. Yes, of course.' Fred closed the ledger and exchanged it for his cutlery.

He was a dapper looking, youngish man, clean-shaven, with neatly styled gingery hair and a jacket cut fashionably wide with long lapels. He adjusted the table settings to suit himself then held out his hand.

'Frederick Horne. It's young Mr Alexander isn't it? Your uncle tells me you're helping him with his bookkeeping.'

Could this be Mr Horne himself? Fred took the offered hand.

'I'm Frederick Alexander, and I'm very pleased to meet you.'

'Most people call me Frank.'

'And most people call me Fred.'

Frank Horne released his firm grip and relaxed back into his chair. He had an open manner, a lack of formality, and Fred liked him immediately.

Frank Horne looked around the crowded dining room and nodded towards a group of men seated at the round table.

'That's Mr Kayser over there. He manages the Mt Bischoff mine, but I suppose you know that.'

Fred turned to get a better look. He saw a solidly built man in a fitted jacket, fair skinned and neatly bearded, and recognised him as someone he'd seen just this afternoon. He was no taller than any of the other men at the table, shorter than some, but his back was rigid, and he had the sort of authority about him that Fred associated with the district inspector.

Fred turned back to Frank Horne.

'I didn't know that was his name, but I saw him this afternoon.'

'He's my boss. Everyone's boss.'

Of course, he should have guessed as much, Fred thought. The accent. His aunt and uncle had told Fred about the German mine manager, but Fred hadn't put the two things together.

'My uncle told me he's German. I saw him this afternoon, but I didn't realise that's who he was.'

Frank had brought a bottle of red wine to the table, and he poured himself a glass. He held the bottle up in front of Fred, who shook his head.

'Come on Mr Alexander. I know you have a story to tell. Everyone here has a Kayser story, but it doesn't mean that he isn't a respected manager. People say that without him the mine would only be worth half its current value.'

'Remember, you asked me to tell you the story, Mr Horne.'

Fred leaned forward and lowered his voice, conscious that Mr Kayser was just a few tables away.

'I was on my way to the post office to check for mail and there was a group of three or four men just off the train, walking along the road in front of me. Mr Kayser – I know that's who it was now – came out of the post office and I saw one of the men go up to him and ask him something like "who should we see for work at Mt Bischoff?" Then Mr Kayser said in a voice loud enough so even I could hear it "Young man, I am the Bischoff!"'

Frank leaned back and laughed, and Fred joined in. It really had been the oddest thing.

'Well, that's all you need to know to get on here. Mr Kayser is the Mount Bischoff manager and Waratah is only here because of the mine, so you could equally say that Mr Kayser is Waratah too. Keep on the right side of him and you can't go wrong.'

'I am the Bischoff. Did I get that wrong?'

'No – perfectly correct. You have a good ear for accents – have you "trod the boards" as they say?'

Fred thought about the school performances and the two recitals he'd taken part in at the Wynyard community hall.

'A bit here and there. Shakespeare mostly,' he said cautiously.

It was certainly true that he could declaim great chunks of the bard, but opportunities for real theatre were lacking in Wynyard.

'Stick around here and you'll get plenty of chances to strut your stuff. There are plans in the wings to start a theatre company. Mark my words, Mr Alexander, this is a great place to be right now. Our Mr Kayser might be like his namesake, the Kaiser, but he's a man who understands community. So long as he's the chairman of every club, and you agree with everything he says, he'll support all manner of things.'

'Did you say you work for Mr Kayser, Mr Horne?

'Have done for five years now and no complaints. I started as an assistant accountant and it's Mr Kayser who made me the head accountant. That's not bad for a man who's just had his twenty-sixth birthday. There are opportunities here you'd be hard put to find in another place. Not just for work, but socially too.'

'Uncle James told me about the cricket club.'

'Yes, he's the president. You're lucky to be living at the hotel. I thought I'd stay for a couple of weeks when I first arrived, and I'm still here five years later. There's no better place in Waratah.'

'My uncle thinks it's a place with prospects. Waratah, that is.'

Frank gave a wry sort of laugh.

'He has a point, but you need to be prepared to take huge risks. A couple of years ago in '83 it was really something. There were big specimens of gold from Mt Lyell not far from here, and people were off their chunks about it. No one could talk about anything else, and every second person was either setting up a new mining section or buying into one. I bought in as well, in fact I had shares in your uncle's South Specimen Reef mine. It's one of the best hopes, but if you ask me, there's not enough gold there. It's all very well to go deeper and deeper into the mine, but I hear that it's only showing bits and pieces of pyrite.'

'I don't I understand anything much about mining, but I'm interested in finding work up here.'

'You're looking for work?' Mr Horne asked.

'Yes. In fact, Mr Duncanson mentioned your name to me today. He told me there might be an opening for an accountant and that you would be the one to know.'

'He's right.' Mr Horne inclined his head towards the account book. 'It looks like you have some experience in that area.'

'I've done some bookkeeping for a small business. I'm a fast learner and have a good head for numbers, so I'm sure I could pick up accounting without any trouble.'

'I don't have any openings at the moment, but something might be coming up in the next week or two. How long are you planning to stay here?'

'Until I get a job,' Fred said. There was no point thinking about his father's stipulation of one month. The work would come, he just had to wait.

18

Ten days later, Monday, 21 December 1885.

Despite what he'd said to Frank, Fred was expected back in Wynyard for Christmas and if he didn't have work by then, he wasn't sure what he would do, or where he would go. Fred tried to concentrate on the receipts he was sorting through, but his mind kept wandering. The ledger was open in front of him, and he'd ordered his dinner, but all he could think about was how much he didn't want to go back to Wynyard.

He'd been offered a job with the pharmacist and maybe he should have accepted it. But £1.50 a week wasn't much more than he'd been getting as an assistant teacher, so what was the point of that? He wished now that he had told the pharmacist how unacceptable that wage was before he expressed an interest. That would have saved some unpleasantness, but how was he to know?

The timing was the problem. If he could stay on until he got work, he was sure that something would turn up before long. But the ultimatum that his father had given him was to find work before Christmas. Wednesday was when his ticket was booked on the train to Burnie and his mother had sent a telegram telling him that she would be at the station to meet him. That was still two days away. He just had to look harder. He would go back around to all the businesses and convince someone to take him on. Otherwise, he didn't want to think about what it would be like over Christmas.

He went back to sorting through the pieces of paper and receipts in the ledger and was trying to make sense of a scribbled note that he could only half read, when Frank Horne sat down opposite him.

He was holding a bottle of porter and he held it out towards Fred. 'Still not taking a drop?' he asked.

Fred shook his head and pointed to his glass of water.

'Thank you, but Adam's ale is strong enough for me.'

Frank poured himself a glass and put the bottle in the middle of the table.

'Not even to celebrate?' he asked Fred.

'To celebrate what?'

'Finding work.'

'You have something for me? Work?'

Frank Horne nodded. 'It's what you've been waiting for. Young Mr Newton, our junior accountant, has just told me that he won't be back after Christmas. Something to do with a young lady, and a position in Launceston. So how would you like a job as junior accountant Fred Alexander?'

He'd like it very much, Fred thought, but he'd learned his lesson with the pharmacist.

'It's exactly what I've been looking for,' he acknowledged. 'Can I ask how much it pays?'

'£2.20 per week on a monthly contract.'

Fred did a quick calculation. That was more than he'd been getting as a teaching assistant, but not as much as the teaching salary he'd been aiming for. It was his father's voice he heard. 'Never sell yourself short.' And it was his father to whom he had to prove himself.

'I could do it for £2.50 a week,' Fred said.

Frank rubbed the back of his neck and looked at Fred.

'£2.50?' he said. 'That's what you think you're worth?'

'Yes. That's what I'm worth.'

'Luckily for you, I like a man who knows what he's worth,' Frank said, and he reached across and held out his hand. 'The job is yours if you want it. You'll be employed as a casual for the first year of your contract, and you'll be required to study accounting at night and work a full day. Are you prepared to do that?'

Fred took Frank's hand, and they shook on it. 'I'm more than happy to do the night study, Mr Horne, I'll make sure you don't regret it,' he said.

He hadn't thought about the study requirement, but then that surely was a bonus. Putting a few numbers into a ledger didn't make him an accountant, no matter what he told people.

Emily, the dark-haired maid who reminded Fred of his sister Agnes, came up to their table and picked up the empty plates.

'You're leaving on Thursday then?' she asked Fred.

'Even sooner, it's Wednesday. But I'll be back. As it happens, you're the first one to know that Mr Horne has just offered me a job in the accounting office.'

Emily clasped her hands together.

'Well that is very good news. Congratulations.'

'Yes it is, Emily. Very good news,' Fred said. 'I'll expect you to treat me like a gentleman now.'

Emily laughed. 'You and your nonsense.'

Frank took a sip of his beer and nodded in the direction of Emily, who was expertly picking her way between the tables, her long skirt swishing a counterpoint to each turn.

'She's right you know Fred. We'll all be happy that you can stay on. There's no getting out of it now. The Athletics Club needs a new secretary, and you're it.'

It wasn't the right time to confess his lack of interest in athletics, so Fred raised his glass of water and held it out towards Frank.

'Here's to that.'

19

A month later, Monday, 25 January 1886

Fred was standing at the window in his room in the hotel, looking at the grey mist and low clouds that hugged the hillsides and made Mt Bischoff barely visible. He'd felt disappointed when he pulled the curtains back and saw just another dull, damp day. It reminded him of what Mrs Robertson had asked him when he was back home for Christmas: what would he miss about Wynyard? Apart from Mr Robertson, nothing had come to mind – all he could think of then was the excitement of starting a new job.

Well, now he would be able to tell her he missed the sunny days and the beaches. That reminded Fred of the other thing Mrs Robertson had said, about not belonging. It would take time, of course it would, everyone said so, but he felt as if he hardly knew the other men in the office. The two clerks were much the same age as he was, but they seemed so silly. They were always whispering things to each other and working out ways to meet 'the ladies'. And the two senior accountants, Mr Gonders and Mr Tyson, tried their best to find the most trivial sort of work for him to do, as if he was just another clerk. Frank Horne was different, a good friend as well as his boss, and the two other junior accountants seemed like decent chaps.

At least the office was spacious, and it felt good, sitting at the big, solid desk on a high stool, ledgers and papers spread out in front of him, working on figures for the famous Mt Bischoff Tin Mining Company.

It was the way time dragged that Fred couldn't get used to. By lunch time he had entered all the figures, checked the balance, filed the invoices. No matter how slowly he tried to go, the afternoons went on and on. He tried to make the work spin out and look busy, but whoever he'd replaced must have been the slowest worker under the sun! The younger men just laughed at him. Not Mr Gonders and Mr Tyson though. Fred had never seen either of them smile, not once. Frank Horne understood, and he encouraged Fred to ask questions. In the last couple of days, Frank had been getting him to check the salary records and even trusted him to handle the money.

'Work hard and show a little patience, Fred,' Uncle James had told him. 'You've only been in the job for a few weeks.' Uncle James was probably right, but Fred's patience was wearing thin.

Fred shook himself out of his bad mood and went over to the washstand. He poured out some water into the bowl and splashed his face with it, then he changed into his work suit and walked along to Frank Horne's room. It was three weeks since Fred had started work, and the two of them had fallen into the habit of eating breakfast together. Being an early riser, Fred was always the first up. Frank was the opposite, and some mornings he wasn't even awake when Fred knocked on his door, so this morning he wasn't surprised when there was no answer.

He knocked again, a couple of harder raps with his knuckles. Still no answer. Fred put his ear against the door and listened hard for a reply. A half grunted 'won't be a minute' or 'come in' would have been enough, but he could hear nothing.

Fred pushed the door and then he heard a rasping sound. He walked across to the bed. There was no need to touch Frank's brow to see that he was running a fever. Frank must have heard him come in because he managed to push himself up on the pillows and started to say something that was lost in a painful round of coughing and the struggle to breathe.

Fred had helped his mother nurse people enough times to recognise pneumonia when he saw it. There had been stories all week of people going down with it – the damp weather, people said. He poured a glass of water for Frank and helped him take a few sips. The coughing calmed and Frank managed to talk, though the hoarse whisper was a pathetic substitute for his usual voice.

'Not sure I'm fit for work today, Fred. Let Mr Kayser know, can you?'

'Of course. And I'm going right now to get some help for you. Aunt Jane will know what to do, and I'll send someone to get Dr Kennedy.'

Frank seemed to be protesting, but it was lost in his laboured breath and a deep cough that was painful to listen to.

20

An hour later Fred was standing in front of a heavy wooden door. On the frosted glass inset was written *Mr H.W.F. Kayser esq. Manager, Mount Bischoff Tin Mining Company.*

Fred tugged on his waistcoat and brushed the front of his jacket, then he knocked on the door. There was an impatient '*ja*' and Fred removed his hat and entered the room.

A very large desk took up much of the office, but Mr Kayser wasn't sitting at it. He was standing in front of a wall of books, his head bent over a leather-bound journal that he'd just pulled from a row of identical volumes. He turned around as Fred hesitated just inside the room.

'Come in, come in.'

Mr Kayser put the journal on the desk then seated himself in the high-backed chair and looked up at Fred.

There was a visitor's chair in front of the desk, and Fred stood next to it.

'Good morning Mr Kayser. I have a message from Mr Horne.'

'Ah. You're the new man. Mr...'

'Alexander, sir. Frederick Alexander. The thing is that Mr Horne is very ill. It looks like pneumonia.'

'Very ill?'

'Yes Mr Kayser. When I went to get Mr Horne for breakfast this morning, he could hardly breathe and he was very feverish...'

Mr Kayser held up a hand as if warding off the disease itself.

'Enough.'

Mr Kayser took each end of his moustache between his thumb and finger and rolled it back and forth. Then he pushed his chin forward and looked up at Fred, his eyebrows pulled so forbiddingly tight that Fred wondered if he'd done something wrong.

'Sit down, sit down. You work in the office, Mr Alexander. Tell me how I can run the biggest tin mine in the world with my chief accountant sick.'

Fred did as he was asked and gave scarcely any thought to what he said next, it seemed so obvious.

'I can help, Mr Kayser,' he said. 'Mr Horne has been taking me through everything. I've a good head for numbers and I'm a very hard worker.'

Fred had only a vague idea what the extra work would entail, but he felt sure there was nothing he couldn't do if he put his mind to it.

Mr Kayser took his time answering. Fred started to say more, thought better of it, then sat back in the chair and waited.

'Wages? What do you know about them?'

'Nearly everything Mr Kayser. I've been helping Mr Horne prepare the wages for Friday.'

'Friday this week? '

'Yes Mr Kayser. They're almost ready. And I've worked in the counting house too.'

'You are being very busy, young Mr Alexander.'

'I prefer to be busy, sir.'

'Yes, yes. Very good. Even so….' Mr Kayser opened his diary and ran his hand down the page, then looked back up at Fred. 'Profit and loss? What do you know about all of that? This is not easy work, Mr Alexander. I have to report to the directors next Saturday. That means I have to have the half yearly report with the balance sheet, statement of accounts, profit and loss and distribution by Friday morning.'

'Mr Horne has taken me through the process.' It wasn't true, but Fred assumed it would be simply a matter of calculation.

'You're lodging at Pearce's Hotel? Or?'

'Yes sir. Mr Pearce is my uncle.'

'So you get what you need from Mr Horne as necessary. And you are having some good men in the office who can help you. You must do vhat you can and don't be afraid to ask for help.'

'Thank you, sir.'

Just like that! Fred could hardly believe it. Frank would be off work for a week at least. This was a chance not to be missed. Fred wasn't sure what to do now, but he got to his feet and took his hat off the hat stand. He was halfway out the door when a shout came from Mr Kayser.

'Report to me every day until Mr Horne is back at work.'

'Here sir?'

'Here or somewhere. You vill find me.'

'Yes Mr Kayser.'

Fred continued out the door then closed it behind him. Firmly. Harder, perhaps, than he needed to.

He could feel a hot flush on his cheeks. 'You vill find me.' He was accepting who knew what sort of extra work, no mention of pay, and all he got was 'You must do vhat you can' and 'You vill find me.' The curt way the man spoke! Frank had warned him about Mr Kayser. Even in his miserable feverish condition, in short bursts of shallow breaths, Frank had thought to caution him. 'Don't mind the Kaiser, Fred. His bark is worse than his bite.'

Fred didn't stay angry for long, and as he walked back up the road to the accounting office, he was already thinking about how he was going to manage all the work. Only three weeks since he started, and he was trusted to manage the accounts for the Mt Bischoff Tin Mining Company. Now that was something he could write home about!

He took out the keys Frank had given him and opened the door to the head accountant's office, the next room along from where Fred and the others had their desks. Everything was how Frank had left it, the ledgers and files neatly shelved in the secretaire, custom-made with nooks and drawers and shelves and slits that make it possible to keep every record, every transaction, every stray bill of sale or invoice or even an informal note in its right place. Frank Horne was meticulous, always working late, and Fred wondered where he got his energy from; there wasn't a sports club or a social event or a meeting of some sort that he didn't have a role in.

'Start with the wages', is what Frank had told him, so Fred ran a finger along the labelled pigeonholes until he found what he was looking for. He pulled out everything he could find that had anything to do with wages and company accounts and put them in a pile on the desk. Then he seated himself in front of them and not yet knowing what he was looking for, opened the top ledger.

21

A week later, Thursday, 4 February 1886

Fred rubbed his eyes and blinked a few times then he opened them as wide as they would go and held them like that before relaxing them. He blinked again. The hollow feeling in the back of his eyes was still there, but the little black marks stopped swimming on the page and became numbers again.

He turned the switch on the side of the table lamp and coaxed the wick up until the pool of light brightened and expanded to cover most of the desk. Outside the circle of light his room was pitch black. He'd heard the last of the guests going to their rooms hours ago and now the only noise was the stamping machine and its rhythmic thudding. He'd grown used to it, but with everything else so silent it was hard to ignore, and it added to a sense of urgency that was getting close to panic.

He put the ruler under the entries on the first line across both pages of the ledger and forced himself to start again.

There had to be an explanation, something he'd missed, something he'd entered incorrectly. How could the difference be so big? It was over £3,000 and it had to come from somewhere. If he'd started earlier, at the beginning of the week, then he wouldn't be sitting here in the middle of the night having just discovered that all the calculations and entries he'd finally got round to doing today just didn't add up.

But how could he have started earlier? By the time he'd finished his own work and then did as much of Frank's work as he could manage, even working sixteen hours a day it was a struggle to get through it all. So far he'd managed to take care of the essential work, but this week there was the extra pressure of the shareholders' meeting that was taking place in Launceston on Saturday.

Mr Kayser had been asking him for the final accounts statement since Tuesday. He had to present them on Saturday, he'd told Fred. He had the ongoing, daily updates for the past six months, but for the directors and the shareholders at the meeting, he must have the balance sheet and the accounts statement, with copies for the four directors and himself.

'They're almost finished,' Fred had told him on Tuesday. Then, 'I'm getting them cross-checked,' he'd reassured him on Wednesday. Mr Kayser trusted him, which only served to make Fred feel worse about lying to him.

Now it was Thursday night. Friday morning, strictly speaking, and he was still working on the accounts.

Fred tried to concentrate on the ledger, but his mind kept going off in other directions. What if he really couldn't work it out? Would he lose his job? Fred suddenly had an almost overwhelming desire to put his head on the desk and sleep, but he forced himself to stand up and walk over to the window. The curtains were still open, and he pushed the window up and stuck his head out. A strong southerly wind pushed scudding clouds over a full moon, and across the road the battery machines thudded and clanked from behind the rows of electric lights.

He let the wind play around his face, then he closed the window and sat back down at the desk. With a ruler firmly against the pages of the ledger he ran his eye over every entry. When he got to the bottom of the page, he could feel exhaustion taking over again and he leaned back in his chair and closed his eyes. Numbers kept swirling around under his eyelids. His brain must have been working though because suddenly he saw the problem. Depreciation. Was that 10% last year or 20%? He was fairly sure it was 20%, but this year he'd used 10%. That must be it.

Now he didn't feel tired – he felt alert, excited as he ran the ruler down until he found what he was looking for.

Sure enough. 20% is what it should be. 10% was the calculation he'd actually used. He must have mixed it up with the bonuses. No wonder the figures were out by so much. He re-calculated and changed the numbers. It looked a mess, but it would have to do. Then he went back over the columns and made the new additions and subtractions.

The numbers at the bottom of each column were the same.

He'd done it!

22

The following Monday, 8 February 1886

On Monday morning Frank Horne was well enough to go back to work, and Fred walked with him to the office.

'Mr Kayser said the Saturday meeting went very well,' Frank told him. 'I don't know how you did it all, Fred. Not just the things for the meeting, but the books. Some of the finer details are missing, but you've kept it all up-to-date. The salaries, the profits and losses, the exports, everything. I can't thank you enough.'

'It might sound odd, Frank, but I rather enjoyed doing it. Though not on Thursday night when I couldn't get anything to balance.'

'There's always an explanation, Fred. You just have to keep looking.'

It sounded like good advice; advice that seemed familiar. Where had he heard it before? Who did it remind him of? Then an image of his father came to mind, his father bent over a horse's hoof, hammering on a horseshoe, the bellows gasping like a giant toad at the back of the smithy, sending out sparks from fire. 'If you look hard enough, Frederick, you'll find there's a reason for everything. And the solution might be a hair's breadth shaved off a horseshoe.'

'I'll remember that Frank. Did Mr Kayser say anything about me?'

'No, Fred. You know what he's like. He probably has no idea how much you took on, but I'll make sure he knows.'

*

Frank must have been as good as his word. Later that morning, Fred was sitting at his desk in the office, trying to concentrate on an entry that needed checking. After being so busy for the past two weeks, it was hard to fit back into the normal office routine and it was a relief when Mr Kayser's messenger came into the office. The two of them had had quite a lot to do with each other over these last two weeks so the clerk went straight over to where Fred was sitting at his desk.

'Mr Kayser wants to see you right now,' he said.

Fred marked the place in the accounts book and buttoned the top of his jacket then walked the short distance to Mr Kayser's office. Why did Mr Kayser want to see him? Had he made a mistake after all? There was only one way to find out, and Fred gave two firm knocks on the door.

Mr Kayser's usual '*ja*', sounded almost welcoming and Fred let himself in to the office then closed the door behind him and went over to the desk. Mr Kayser indicated he should sit down, then got straight to the point.

'How old are you, Mr Alexander?' he asked.

'I had my seventeenth birthday on the 20th of last month, sir.'

Mr Kayser shook his head, not in a negative way, but disbelieving.

'You are an exceptional young man, Mr Alexander. I believe you have a great future ahead of you with the Mt Bischoff Tin Mining Company. A person who is willing to undertake such responsibility and work such long hours is not easy to find. Mr Horne is impressed too by your ability to keep control of the accounts, and he is most grateful for your work. But I'm sure he will tell you that himself.'

'I was happy to be able to help out, Mr Kayser. It's the least I could do for Mr Horne. And for the company,' he added.

'For which the company is grateful. So much so that I have decided to make you a permanent official of the Mr Bischoff Tin Mining Company. It's a little unusual, but I have also sought and been granted the directors' permission to include you amongst the company officials who will receive a 10% bonus to mark the 100th issue of dividends.'

It was the last thing Fred was expecting. When he was entering the very large figures for bonuses it had never crossed his mind to think that he might be a lucky recipient. There had been plenty of times he had resented the rude way that Mr Kayser treated him, but except for these past two days, the truth was that Fred had enjoyed having the extra work.

'In addition, in line with your new permanent position, you will have an increase in salary to £3.50 per week.'

Already that was more than he would earn as a teacher.

'Thank you, Mr Kayser. You can be sure that I'll work the best I can for the company.'

Fred stood up to leave.

'By the way,' Mr Kayser added. 'The directors have agreed to fund a formal dinner to celebrate the awarding of the bonuses as part of the 100th dividend celebrations. I'm still making the arrangements, but of course you must attend. Now, I'm leaving you to discuss things further with Mr Horne.'

When Fred walked out of the office he felt as if his life was really starting. A job with prospects. Good money. And a formal dinner! That would be a first! What would he wear? He must write to Mr Robertson and tell him that all the boring work on bookkeeping had been worthwhile after all. And his mother. He'd write to her today. Of course she would be proud of him. He could already imagine what she would tell everyone. And how could his father not be impressed?

23

Two weeks later, Saturday, 20 February 1886

'You look nice,' Harriet said. 'Can I go too?'

'Of course you can't silly,' Mattie said. 'Are you going to a ball?'

'Not a ball, a dinner,' Fred told him. 'An important dinner.'

'Like mummy and daddy.' Harriet took hold of her mother's hand and looked up at her, not sure if she was right.

'Yes Harriet,' Aunt Jane said. 'We go to quite a few balls,' she explained to Fred. 'It's one of the nice things about living here – there's always something going on.'

Fred peered at himself in the mirror over the fireplace and pushed at the white bow tie so that it was perfectly straight, then he turned back to face Aunt Jane.

'What do you think?'

She cast a critical eye over him. 'Turn around.' She went over and gave a sharp tug across the back of his shoulders, then she stepped back again. 'That's better. They've done a good job, the tailors. It fits well and looks very elegant.'

That's exactly what Fred thought too, but it was nice to have a second opinion. He liked the slim black trousers and the way the jacket cut into his waist, with the long tails at the back. It had taken three weeks and cost him nearly half his bonus, but it was worth it. The only thing he didn't like was the stiff white collar that poked into his chin, and he wriggled his neck from side to side, trying to make it more comfortable.

Aunty Jane laughed.

'You'll get used to it. What you need to do is to pull those shoulders back and stand up straight. Then you won't notice it.'

Fred took her advice and found that she was right.

119

'Time to go,' he said. 'Goodnight Harriet, goodnight Mattie. Be good.'

'Enjoy yourself Fred,' Aunt Jane said. 'I still can hardly believe that you've been invited. After only two months up here. You've done well for yourself.'

It felt a bit odd walking past all the familiar shops in his new suit, but once in the banquet room, he didn't give it a thought. Most of the other men were wearing similar evening dress, and the room itself was rather grand. Not in size, although it was roomy enough, but in the matter of décor it was quite unlike anything Fred had seen. Apart from the lacquered forest green ceiling, the whole room was covered with exotic wallpaper in deep greens and charcoal grey with dusky pink flowers trailing through it, the graceful curving shapes dancing around each other. At one end of the room there was a very large, framed mirror over a roomy fireplace and at the other end an elaborate mahogany sideboard. In the corner near the fireplace a grey-haired, elegant looking man was playing the piano.

Just inside the doorway, a waiter was standing with a tray of drinks and Fred helped himself to a lemonade then went across to where Frank was arranging gilt-edged name cards around the large oval table.

'Do you want some help?'

Frank held up a hand with two cards in it.

'Thanks Fred, but these are the last two. Did you see where I've put you?' Frank pointed to one end of the table. 'Up there. You're between me and Mr Kayser.'

Fred wasn't sure what to think about that. He could see the names of his colleagues at the other end of the table.

'Was that your idea?'

'No. It was Mr Kayser's idea. You're something of a special guest, being so young and so new.'

'Well, I'd rather be up there with you than between Mr Gonders and Mr Tyson. I can never think of anything to say to them.'

'They're very solid men, honest accountants, but a bit set in their ways, I grant you that.'

Fred waved a hand to include the room itself and the tastefully decorated table with its tall candelabras and elegant frosted glass vases, filled with red waratah and white lilies.

'This doesn't feel like being in Mt Bischoff,' he said. 'Or even in Tasmania. It's so…different.'

'There was an Italian interior decorator working in Waratah a few years back. Mr Kayser came to an arrangement with the hotel to have a room fitted up especially for formal occasions like this.' He pointed towards the ceiling. 'The chandeliers came from Venice.'

Fred looked up at the clusters of delicate little glass bowls and realised that each was a flower-shape in a soft opaque pink that exactly matched the wallpaper.

'The lights are beautiful,' he said. 'Venice, you say. Maybe I'll go there one day.'

Frank laughed and put the last card in place, then pointed up to where Mr Hill was showing Mr Kayser to his seat.

'It looks like we're about to start. Come on.'

Mr Kayser turned out to be a good dinner companion. He had well-polished stories about the early days of the Mt Bischoff mine, and Fred listened and laughed at the right time. The beef consommé was followed by fried whitebait and curried lobster, saddle of lamb and braised ham and Fred was feeling so full that he wondered where he would fit the dessert. But when the time came, he didn't have any trouble finishing off a compote of pears with port wine jelly and whipped cream.

Each time the waiter came around with the wine, Mr Kayser tried to persuade Fred to try some of the 'wonderful Rhine Riesling – the best in the world', but each time Fred put his hand over the empty wine glass and said 'Not for me, thank you.'

By the time the dessert plates were cleared the noise level in the room was so loud that Mr Hill, the chairman for the evening, had trouble getting the men's attention, and it took several taps with his fork against the side of his wine glass before the chatter gradually stopped and everyone looked in his direction. He made a short speech of welcome and congratulations, then he sat down and Frank stood up.

'Please charge your glasses for a toast to the Mt Bischoff Tin Mining Company,' he announced.

There was shuffling as the men got to their feet. Two waiters with bottles of champagne moved around both sides of the table, filling the champagne flutes.

When the waiter came to Fred, he did what he'd been doing all night. He put his hand over the top of the glass.

'Not for me, thank you,' he said.

But Mr Kayser leaned towards him.

'You must,' he said, 'I order you to make the toast in champagne.'

Mr Kayser was smiling when he said it, but he was so easily offended that Fred wasn't sure what to do. His mother would make no exceptions, he knew that. She'd see it as a weakness, just like she did with his father. 'Never be like that, Frederick,' she would say, 'it's pathetic to see grown men who can't say no to a drink.'

He kept his hand over his glass. Surely Mr Kayser would understand. He was notorious for his disapproval of 'the drinking man'! And yet there he was, happily allowing his glass to be re-filled.

'I don't think I should, Mr Kayser,' he said. 'I've never taken an alcoholic drink in my life, and I fear that I might be under the table, as they say, if I start now.'

'Well, if you do land under the table, I will carry you to your hotel myself,' Mr Kayser smiled. 'Remember, it's an order.'

'Very well. If it's an order,' Fred took his hand off the champagne flute. He watched the waiter fill his glass, the explosion of little bubbles, the way the foam almost spilled over the rim.

'Be upstanding and raise your glasses,' Frank Horne was saying. 'To the Mt Bischoff Tin Mining Company.' Fred joined in with the other men and raised his glass. 'To the Mt Bischoff Tin Mining Company,'

He took a sip. It tasted sour, and he sucked his lips in and tried not to show anything, but Mr Kayser noticed.

'A few more toasts and you'll be used to it,' he told Fred.

He was right. Fred lost count of the number of toasts, and replies to toasts, but by the time they finished, he was on his third glass of champagne and wondered how he would have been able to sit through all those speeches without it. Nothing had happened. He was steady on his feet and felt sure he was twice as sharp as usual. So much for all those warnings!

Later, they all retired to a smaller, adjoining room where everything was in dark brown leather – two big chesterfields, ample lounge chairs, buttoned tub chairs – and looked like Fred's idea of a London gentlemen's club. There was port and brandy on offer, and cigars were handed around. Fred had lost the inclination to refuse anything, and he selected one of the largest cigars to go with his brandy.

They hadn't been there long when Mr Kayser stubbed out his cigar and got to his feet.

'This is a vonderful evening,' he said. 'But you know, my wife…' He laughed and the men joined in. They did know his wife and the strict house that she ran. But they also knew that it was a signal that the formal part of the evening was over. 'I trust you vill continue to enjoy yourselves,' he said. 'And I don't vant to see any of this left in the morning.' He swept his arm towards the mirror-backed sideboard where there were bottles of wine, champagne, port, whisky, and brandy, some full, others at various stages of emptiness.

Now they had permission to leave, most of the men declared it a night, until there were only four of them left; Fred and Frank Horne plus Tom Patterson and Jimmy Reid, the other two junior accountants from the office.

Fred settled back in one of the giant leather armchairs, both legs stretched out in front of him and crossed at the ankles, a freshly lit cigar in one hand and a glass of brandy in the other.

'What do you think?' he asked the others. 'Should I become a politician?

'Or a mining magnate,' Tom suggested.

'Whad'youreallywanna do?' Jimmy asked him. He struggled to say the words clearly and tried a second time. 'What do you really want to do?'

Fred was sure his own power of speech was as sharp as always and he sat up and pulled himself forward, so that he was on the edge of the seat. He flourished the hand with the cigar in it and struck a pose.

'A famous actor,' Fred said, 'what do you think?'

The other men all laughed as he wanted them to.

''Give us a taste of what you can do,' Frank suggested.

Fred put the hand holding his glass of brandy across his chest and declaimed theatrically:

'O that this too too solid flesh would melt,

Thaw, and resolve itself into a dew!

Or that the Everlasting had not fix'd

His canon 'gainst self-slaughter!'

Then seeing that the others were rather enjoying it, he got to his feet and paced back and forth, using both hands, still holding the cigar and the brandy glass, to emphasise each phrase,

'O God! God!

How weary, stale, flat, and unprofitable

Seem to me all the uses of this world!'

He made a sweeping bow as the men laughed and applauded, then he dropped back into the armchair.

Suddenly Jimmy made an exaggerated shushing sound, his finger held melodramatically in front of his mouth. When the laughter subsided somewhat, he held up an empty wine bottle and tapped it with a silver corkscrew.

'Iveannounzement t'make,' he slurred. 'The bottlesrempty.' He pulled the corkscrew across the row of empty bottles, and along with the others Fred laughed until tears were coming out of his eyes.

'Lezgo' Jimmy said. He moved away from the sideboard and instead of the step he intended to take, he somehow ended up on the floor.

Frank got on one side of him and Fred on the other and between them they pulled him to his feet. With one arm around each of their shoulders, Jimmy dragged them first one way and then the other.

'Home James,' he said, and his laugh set the others off again.

'Right,' Frank said. 'Let's get you home. Steady on the stairs now.'

Fred was surprised to find that Jimmy was almost a dead weight, but they made it down the stairs and on to Main Road where the going was easier.

'I know where he lives,' Tom said, and he led the way along Main Street. Every few steps he made a little sideways lurch and then corrected himself and behind him Jimmy pulled Frank and Fred from one side of the road to the other.

'Splendid chaps,' he would say, and then laugh to himself. 'Home James.'

It was a relief to find that Jimmy had a room on the ground floor of the boarding house, and they managed to deposit him on his bed without too much fuss.

The fresh air and the effort of getting Jimmy back home had helped to sober them up, but none of them was ready to call it a night.

'Look at that,' Frank said. He was standing still, looking up at the sky that had turned a deep pre-dawn blue. Hanging just above the mountain, the moon was almost full, glowing white, and looked bigger than it should be. 'Here's an idea. Let's walk up Mt Bischoff, right to the top, and watch the sunrise. What do you say?'

Half an hour later the three of them were standing at the top of Mt Bischoff. As far as you could see, there were folds and folds of dark, forested hills broken only by the rocky tors of distant mountain ranges. Below them moonlight lit the grey lichen on the mountainside so it looked like snow.

'Can you see that range way over there?' Frank asked them, pointing to the west. 'That's the Heemskirk Range, and the peak you can see on the north end is Mt Agnew. That's where we thought the next big tin mine was going to be.' Then he turned in the opposite direction, and pointed to the east, 'You can't really make it out, but over there is Cradle Mountain.'

As they watched, the clouds over the far ranges turned a delicate colour, not pink and not orange, but something in between. There were no words equal to the spectacle, and the three of them watched in silence as the colour deepened and spread to the higher clouds.

Then with a burst of deep gold, the sun appeared.

'I think it's telling us it's time to go,' Frank said. 'We don't want the miners to find us here.' Fred felt like staying on, to have it to himself for a bit longer, but he laughed along with the others and followed them down the road to the sleeping town.

24

A few hours later, Sunday, 21 February 1886

It took all Fred's willpower to drag himself out of the oblivion of sleep, and even then he was only half awake. Someone had been knocking on the door, he knew that much. If they had been trying to rouse him they were only half successful, because he sank back on to the pillow, pulled the eiderdown over his head, and closed his eyes.

Not long after that, just when he'd fallen back to sleep, there was knocking again. Then he remembered. It was Sunday.

The knocking stopped and he heard light footsteps that came to the side of his bed, close to where his head was buried under the eiderdown.

'Fred? Are you awake? The service starts in half an hour.'

Aunt Jane. Fred took long, deep breaths and stayed very still. It didn't take much to feign sleep. His eyes might as well have been glued together, and his head felt as if it its entire contents had been replaced with something that didn't belong there.

Then he heard his uncle's voice from outside the room.

'Leave him be, Jane. I hear they made a night of it at the dinner last night.'

There was the sound of footsteps crossing the room, then of the door being closed.

The effort of feigning sleep had the effect of waking him up. He waited until he heard the front door closing, then rolled onto his back and opened his eyes. He blinked and squinted and closed them again. The curtains were open – that must have been Aunt Jane – and the sun seemed far too bright. Using the palms of his hands he rubbed his eyes then cautiously opened them again and sat up.

It was only then that he realised he was still wearing his dinner shirt, complete with cuff links, and his dress trousers. Of course, the dinner last night. Would Aunt Jane have seen? He stood up and winced at the stabbing pain in his head. His mouth felt as if it was coated in fur and he poured himself a glass of water, drank it down, then poured another one.

What should he do? If he hurried he could make it in time for church – that would be the right thing to do. But now he realised there was a sour feeling in his stomach. How would he be able to sit there for two hours? The bed looked tempting.

He went over and opened the window then he leaned his elbows on the sill and looked around. There was some warmth in the sun, and the clouds over the mountains looked as if they might stay there. A walk was what he needed. That and something to eat. Breakfast would have finished but Mrs Waring would be at church, and he could help himself to something from the kitchen. If he left now, he'd easily be back before Sunday lunch.

★

Fifteen minutes later he let himself out the front door and stood in the middle of the road. With everyone in church or at home, there was not a single person in sight. The sun lit up the windows of the quiet machinery sheds and played with the water tumbling over the falls. There was something eerie about such complete stillness, as if the town had been suddenly deserted.

The silence was broken by the sound of voices singing. It was too faint to make out the hymn, but it reminded Fred that he shouldn't waste time and he headed past the hotel and out to the open country south of the town.

There were no more than a few streets in Waratah, and he was soon following a rough track through gorse-strewn button grass and lichen covered rocks. Small earth-trodden trails branched off the main path, leading to outcrops of granite rocks with their clinging shrubs and windswept trees, favourite places for picnics. Beyond the high plains, wooded hills rolled on and on to the horizon.

He walked for nearly an hour, following animal tracks, and finally reached the rocky outcrop where he liked to sit. It faced away from Mt Bischoff, across to the hazy blue of the Western Ranges, over wilderness that Fred had no wish to explore, but that was fresh and unspoiled. The rocks had soaked up the sun and he spread his jacket on the bottom stone then leaned back into the warmth of the one behind.

He closed his eyes and lay there, the sun making his eyelids seem translucent, half asleep yet conscious of the spikey smell of the gorse and the twittering of the busy ground parrots. He went back over the dinner and thought about what he would write to his mother. She would love to hear about the table with the fancy place cards, the silverware, and candelabra. And he could tell her that he'd been asked to sit right next to Mr Kayser, and the way he'd shared stories about the early days of the mine.

What about the champagne? Would he tell her about that? No. No matter how he put it, she would be disappointed in him. He was glad he'd shown the other men that he wasn't a boy, that he could hold his own, and on such a high-class occasion too, but his mother was so set against alcohol, she wouldn't understand.

But that didn't change how he felt. Last night was a turning point that he wouldn't go back from; he knew he belonged in a world far different from what Wynyard had to offer. And climbing up Mr Bischoff this morning! When had he ever had so much fun? Never. He would never forget it.

Suddenly he sat up and opened his eyes. What if Aunt Jane noticed his clothes this morning? He could feel his face getting hot. Would she tell his mother? How could he face Aunt Jane again?

Like a curtain dropping, the warm sun was replaced by a shadow. He looked up and saw that dark banks of clouds now covered half of the sky. His jacket was warm from the sun and the heat from his body, and he pulled it out from under him and put it on. As he got to his feet, a gust of wind whirled around him, and the rocky tor felt exposed and unfriendly.

Fred wished he had thought to bring some water. Even a few sips would help to wash away the sourness in his stomach. He checked his watch. Ten past midday already. Now he was going to be late for Sunday dinner as well.

He headed back the way he had come. After a while, a few heavy drops of rain goaded him into a fast walk and the wind picked up so that he had to lean forward and push against the gusts. With the wind came heavier rain and he hugged his jacket around himself with both hands and broke into an awkward run. It was as if there had never been the sun and the peace. He couldn't get used to the way the weather here could change in an instant. And why did it have to rain almost every day?

He hurried along, his only thought now to get back to the hotel and a hot meal.

25

When Fred got back to the hotel he took off his wet jacket and stamped and slapped as much water off himself as he could, then he changed his boots and put on the spare jacket that he kept on the peg in the front hallway. As he walked through the empty saloon bar, the smell of stale yeast and cigarette smoke crawled out of the rug, and his stomach lurched.

The door opposite the bar led in one direction to the family's private quarters and in the other to the stairs that went up to the guest rooms. He hesitated. Could he face his aunt and uncle like this? He caught the smell of roast lamb and realised of course he could. He continued down the hall to the dining room and opened the door.

At one end of the table, Uncle James was carving a steaming leg of lamb and Aunt Jane was facing him at the other end. Harriet and Mattie were looking earnest and small, perched on cushions that helped them to see over the table. Emily was moving behind them, spooning roast potatoes and pumpkin on to their plates. There was a place setting for Fred opposite the children.

'Cousin Fred,' Mattie called out. 'Why are you wet?'

Harriet giggled and pointed at the water that was running down the side of Fred's face, so he got out his handkerchief and wiped it off.

Fred's mouth watered from the smell of the lamb, as his uncle took each slice with the carving fork and laid it on a white oval plate. Then Uncle James put the carving knife down and covered the meat with a silver salver. He looked at Fred unsmiling, his whole forehead furrowed.

'What have you got to say for yourself? You had your aunt worried sick about you Fred.'

'I'm sorry Aunt Jane, I didn't realise you'd be worried.

'Well I was. It's not like you at all Fred. What was I supposed to think when we came home from church, and you had disappeared without so much as a note? On a Sunday!'

There was a long pause. Fred had said he was sorry, what else could he do? What was she expecting him to say?

'I really am sorry. I overslept this morning, and when I woke up you were all at church.'

'Well,' Aunt Jane said. Her voice was like his mother's got sometimes when she was angry. It was a cold, grating sound that went through your insides like a saw. 'It wasn't for want of trying to wake you. I went in twice, but your uncle said to leave you alone.'

His uncle shrugged.

'The lad needs to have a chance to spread his wings now he's away from those abstainers down in Wynyard.'

Encouraged by the support, Fred pressed his advantage.

'Mr Kayser's banquet went on until all hours,' he told his aunt. 'Mr Horne insisted we walk up the mountain to see the sun rise.' It couldn't be bad if Aunt Jane's favourite lodger, Mr Horne, was behind it. 'After all the rain we've been having, when I saw that it was a sunny morning, I just had to get out in it, so I went for a walk up to the rocky point.'

But Aunt Jane made a dismissive 'pff' sound.

'The demon drink, your mother would say,' she said.

Uncle James smiled at her, inviting peace.

'Yes, she would. But Betsy doesn't have to know,' Uncle James said. 'It would only upset her. The important thing, Fred, is that you learn from it.'

'You're right uncle. It was great fun, and I'm relieved that I didn't disgrace myself, but if I'd known how I would feel this morning…'

Uncle James cut him off. 'Moderation in all things Fred, remember that. And over-indulgence is not an acceptable reason to miss the Sunday service. Now sit down so we can start eating before the food gets cold. Why don't you say grace?'

They all clasped their hands and bowed their heads.

'For what we are about to receive, may the Lord make us truly thankful, amen.'

Emily came around and added the lamb to the vegetables and they helped themselves to the gravy from the jug that was passed around. They must have all been as hungry as Fred was, because at first there was only the sound of eating. Even Mattie and Harriet were quiet.

Then Uncle James looked over at Fred, an eyebrow raised in a way that his uncle had when there was an amusing story to tell.

'You missed out on some excitement at church this morning Fred,' he said. 'Mr Kayser walked out and took his whole family with him. He took exception to the minister's sermon.'

'The text was the money in the temple,' Aunt Jane explained. 'Mr Kayser took it personally. The way Reverend Jackson told it, we should have enough money and not more. It was about the sin of greed, and you know what all the talk is about how much money the mine makes at the expense of the workers. You would know if was true or not, I suppose, now you're doing the accounts.'

'Well, I don't know about other mines and what they pay, but it's all done very correctly, though the men don't like having the money deducted for the hospital. It does seem a lot to take out of £2.50 a week.'

'Whether Reverend Jackson is right or wrong,' Uncle James said, 'he should have more sense than to preach about it. That's if he wants to hold down his appointment. I won't be surprised if we get a new minister after this.'

Aunt Jane called Emily to collect the plates then nodded her agreement.

'New preachers, new doctors! He's not a bad man, Mr Kayser, but I wish he would let some things alone.'

'I could have built another hotel in the time it took to get the billiard room up and running. All that paperwork just to be able to hit a few balls around on a table!' Uncle James laughed. 'But we got there in the end.'

'I know what everyone says about him,' Fred said, 'but he's been good to me. It's my chance to get on in the world.'

'What's the world? Can I get in the world too?' Mattie asked, and Fred realised how serious he must have sounded. He smiled at Mattie and tried to explain. It was harder than he thought it would be.

'The world is all the different countries and oceans that are part of where we live Mattie.'

Mattie still looked confused, but the lemon pudding was being served and he soon forgot. When plates were scraped clean and removed, Uncle James got up and walked over to the window that looked out over the meadows that surrounded the dam on the far side of the railway bridge. He opened one of the windows and leaned out, closed it and sat back down again.

'The rain's stopped and in five minutes the sun will be out again. Let's go for a walk to the horse paddock before it starts to rain again. I want to see how those new macadam streets have stood up to the rain. You come too Fred. There's something I want to show you.'

Uncle James was right about the weather, and half an hour later they left the hotel and walked over to the cleared land that ran back from the dammed part of the river.

There was grass right to the edge of the water, and willows. A little island had stunted myrtles and wattles growing on it, and the channel between that and the knotted roots of the trees that fringed the bank was a favourite place for platypus.

'Shh,' Fred said to the children, 'we might see a platypus.'

Mattie and Harriet followed him down to the water's edge and the three of them peered down into the water. Fred didn't expect to see one, not at this time in the afternoon, but a long duck bill shot out from a hole in the bank, and he just had time to see a sleek dark blob and a flash of orange that might have been a webbed foot, before the platypus sensed their presence and ducked back in the hole.

'I saw it,' Mattie said.

Harriet didn't want to be outdone.

'So did I,' she said.

Fred knew how that was going to end, so he pointed over to the far end of the paddock where his uncle and aunt were leaning on the fence, looking at the horses that were gathered around the water trough under the black gums.

'I'll race you,' he said, and the three of them ran across the paddock.

Fred joined his aunt and uncle at the fence. He recognised the two mares with foals, half grown now, and the two work horses that had been brought over from the stables at the hotel to range free for a while. There was another horse that he hadn't seen before, a rather fine-looking chestnut filly with a straight back and long legs. She was standing apart from the other horses, ears on alert, watching everything.

It reminded Fred of their horse paddock down in Wynyard, and the early mornings with his father.

'Penny for them,' Uncle James said.

Fred was startled and turned towards his uncle.

'Oh, sorry. I was thinking about how much I miss working with horses.'

'Johnny Alexander is the best teacher you could have when it comes to horses.'

'Yes. I was thinking about that too. The way Pa can make the perfect shoe for a horse is like getting the books to balance. It's all about attention to detail.'

'So young and so wise,' Uncle James laughed. 'What do you think of the new mare?'

Fred held out some scraps of carrot and let her come over to him. She nuzzled his hand, and he felt the soft moistness of her nose.

Uncle James ran a hand down the horse's flank. 'I bought her from Mr Davis – you might have come across him at the races in Wynyard. He brought her over with some other horses from Latrobe. Money's a bit tight and he figured on getting a decent price for them here. She's called Estelle. I'm happy to keep her, but I thought you might be interested.'

Fred had another look at the horse, noted her straight back and the strength in the hocks.

'She looks like she could run a bit, but she's still young. Two years old?'

'Not yet. One year and three months. Which means she'll be ready to race by the end of the year.'

'Is there anywhere to race up here?'

'The committee's going to meet next month and make a decision. We've found a place that should be perfect for the racecourse, so we just need to persuade Mr Kayser.'

'That's the first I've heard of it. Where do you have in mind?'

'It's a little way out of town – about six miles along the VDLC train tracks. Apparently we can use the Forty-Mile Camp stables for the two days of the races, so that should clinch it.'

'I could train her myself – make a racehorse out of her. Maybe a winner. What do you think?'

'Good idea. She's young, but you could give her a go.'

'How much do you want for her?'

'I paid £5/3s for her. Why don't we say £5 and you can give me a hand with my other horses to pay off the shillings. I had you in mind when I bought her, but as I say, I'm happy to keep her. You might like some time to think about it.'

But Fred didn't want to waste time thinking about it. It was perfect timing. The bonus, the raise. His own racehorse.

'I wouldn't be able to give you the full amount until after my next pay. That's nearly two weeks away.'

'Fortunately I don't have to rely on horse trading for a living! Consider her yours.'

The mare had turned away from them and was nibbling on a patch of fresh grass.

'What did you say her name was?" Fred asked.

'Estelle.'

Fred made a clucking noise with his tongue and held out his hand again. This time it was empty, but Estelle nuzzled it anyway and Fred climbed through the fence and stood next to her. His own horse. He would make her into the greatest racehorse ever.

26

A week later, Tuesday, 2 March 1886

Fred pushed against the wind that blew off the mountain straight down Main Street. He had his hat over his eyes and his head down, but he could still feel the icy rain hitting his face. Sleet, and summer was barely over!

He had almost decided to go straight back to the hotel after work but decided on the spur of the moment to go up to the post office and check for mail. Mrs Cole was in the back room, keeping warm no doubt, and he rang the little bell and waited. He noticed water dripping into a bucket in the corner and wondered what it must be like for her to work in such a cold, damp space. No wonder she stayed out the back when she could.

'Not much mail today,' she told him, and she reached into the pigeonhole and handed him a letter in a cream parchment envelope. 'It's from Mr Robertson – that's the schoolteacher isn't it?'

'Is there anything you don't know Mrs Cole?' Fred asked, and they both laughed.

Mrs Cole tapped her forehead. 'If it goes in there, it stays in there,' she said. 'Mind how you go now, it's not fit for a dog out there!'

Fred made a mental note to be careful what he told Mrs Cole, but he thanked her and hurried back to his room, impatient to read the letter.

Emily had kept the fire in his room alight, and he stirred the glowing embers, added some kindling and a couple of the smaller pieces of wood, then leaned against the mantelpiece and opened the letter. The wet wool of his jacket started to heat up, and it gave out a steamy smell, earthy and unpleasant, as if a sheep had wandered into his room. He put the letter on the mantelpiece, took his jacket off and changed into a flannel shirt, then went back to the fire and picked up the letter again.

River Cottage,
Goldie Street
Wynyard
24th February

My Dear Fred,

Congratulations on the elevation to your new post with the Mt Bischoff Company. As you say, the work on bookkeeping and mathematics, about which you were so reluctant, has borne fruit, and I couldn't be happier for you. It is not the path that we expected you to take, but you're still young and there is nothing to stop you making another change when you are ready. I've said it many times and will say it again. You have a fine sensitivity to great literature and the ability to interpret it for others, and I do hope that you continue to develop this talent of yours.

Now to my news. I am happy to tell you that in August of this year, God willing, I'm to become a father. It's a role that I look forward to with much pleasure. However, it has for me an unwanted consequence. There is no easy way to convey this: Emma and I are leaving for Scotland on March 3, sailing from Hobart to Sydney on the SS Mangana and from there to Plymouth in the Samuel Plimsoll, and on to Stirling by train and coach.

The reason for our sudden departure is that Emma cannot contemplate starting a family so far away from where she still calls home. We're taking the voyage back to Scotland while she is in good health, with an arrival scheduled for a good two months before the birth, even taking into account the possibility of inclement weather on the voyage.

You will understand more than most just how reluctant I am to leave my position at the school, and the Table Cape area. I've been able to make a wonderful life here, and only the day before Emma shared her news with me, I had negotiated to buy a plot of land on which I intended to build that house I have talked about so much. Now, even my most optimistic self must acknowledge that sadly it will never see the light of day.

My own opinion is that Wynyard is an ideal place in which to raise a family, and in regard to the birth of the child, I have never had reason to doubt the competence of good Dr Wilson. In fact, your mother herself is so experienced in these matters that I would happily put my trust in her, and her alone. However, Emma does not share my confidence, nor does she share my great love of this part of the world, and as you know, Emma's happiness means everything to me. So we are to leave. It's a sudden turn of events, but I'm doing everything I can to ensure that the voyage will be as comfortable as possible, and I have reserved first class accommodation. It is unlikely that I will be travelling again for many years, though already I'm imagining what it might be like to visit here with a son, or a daughter.

When we had that evening together over Christmas, it felt to me that you were part of our family, and my thoughts were entirely on making my home here in Wynyard. So much good has happened to me in this little town, and I include in that my friendship with you. Watching you grow from the frustrated youngster you were to such a steady, hardworking, artistic young man, has been a great pleasure. At the risk of sounding immodest, I also feel that I have been able to be of assistance to many of my fellow townsfolk, and for that opportunity I will always be grateful.

There is much to do before we leave, so I will close here, but be assured I will write again when we are settled in a home in Scotland.

Meanwhile, I am your affectionate friend,
Robert Robertson

PS. Until I have arranged our accommodation, you can write to me c/- my parents at 51 Forth Street, Stirling, Scotland.

Fred wasn't sure what to think. He felt let down. Why was it always about Emma? Why couldn't they stay in Wynyard? What of all Mr Robertson's plans? To think that he finally negotiated to buy some land and now he was leaving! Without Mr Robertson there, Wynyard wouldn't be the same place.

That was one thing, but surely it would be grand to live in the old city of Stirling, with its ancient castle, and gas lights and beautiful old houses and parks. Sometimes Fred dreamed that he might live there one day.

It felt like losing someone, knowing you would never see them again. Fred folded the letter, went over to the desk, and put it in the box with the others. The weekend would be soon enough for a reply. There was no chance of getting a letter to Mr Robertson before he sailed for Scotland. No, he'd wait a few days, then send it to Stirling. He felt like going out for a ride and he went across to the window to check the weather. The rain was still coming down, swirling around as a gust of wind swept along the valley. A ride was out then.

Too early for dinner, and anyway, he wasn't hungry. Billiards? He wasn't in the mood. He went back to the desk, picked up *The Collected Works of Shakespeare* and sat back in front of the fire. There were still bookmarks there from the time that Mr Robertson had gone back to visit Stirling, and Fred had set himself the goal of learning a monologue from every play. He smiled to himself at the thought of the optimistic boy who had no real idea how many plays Shakespeare had written.

He chose one of the marks at random and found himself looking at a speech by Coriolanus. It made no sense as it was, and he turned back to the beginning of the play. Ancient Rome was as good a place as any to escape to.

27

One month later, Saturday, 10 April 1886

It was a few minutes after two o'clock on Saturday afternoon and like most of the Bischoff Mine workers, the accounting office had closed for the weekend. The custom was to gather at the post office and make plans for the afternoon, and Fred was there with Frank Horne, Jimmy Reid, and Tom Patterson. The tailor's shop was a few doors up the street, and their friend Albie Lyle had taken a smoko and come over to join them.

'It's all very well for you,' he told the others. 'Some of us have to work!'

People were jammed onto the verandah of the post office and crowded onto the road in front of it. A man pushing a pie cart jolted Frank as he squeezed through, and they moved further to the edge of the road and out of the shade of the buildings.

The sun made a brief appearance from behind the clouds, and Fred leaned back, his arms outstretched.

'Ah. The sun vieweth the world,' he declaimed dramatically.

'Well if it's not Fred Alexander!'

The voice came from behind him, and he swung around to see who it was. It took him a few seconds to recognise his first schoolteacher, Mr Seagrave. It had been a battle between them from Fred's first day at school, but that had been years ago. Now Mr Seagrave had the look of a man who had prospered, and he was not alone. A young woman was resting her gloved hand on his folded arm.

'The same,' Fred said, and made a half bow. He smiled at the young lady and raised an eyebrow. He didn't want her to think he was seriously deferential.

Frank moved to one side and made room for the newcomers in the circle of men.

'Good afternoon Mr Seagrave. I didn't know you two were acquainted. But I haven't had the pleasure...' Frank let his voice trail off.

'I'm sorry. Let me introduce Miss Elizabeth Ashton' Mr Seagrave said. 'Miss Ashton is my niece, and she and her sister have recently started work as assistants at Mrs Dobson's new school. You haven't met before?'

Fred, along with the other men, avoided obvious glances, but at the same time they were all aware of the young woman's tiny waist. Her hair was brown and thick, swept up under a wide-brimmed straw hat and the blouse she was wearing was crisp and white with little frills at her neck and wrists. Between the sensible grey skirt and the blouse, she had tied a wide black sash that was utilitarian but nevertheless showed off her neat figure.

In the next few minutes Fred found out that Mr Seagrave managed the National Bank, chaired the School Board, was an agent of the Mutual Fire Insurance Company, a Justice of the Peace, and a keen supporter of Mr Kayser.

From Miss Ashton, they heard that she had a sister called Annie, her family belonged to the Congregational church community, and that apart from the weather here – so much colder and wetter than Burnie – it was a fine town to live in, with all the concerts and dances, and the splendid library in the Mechanics' Institute that had as good a selection of reading matter as might be found anywhere in Tasmania.

'I'm always happy to hear good words about our Institute,' Frank said. 'We need all the subscribers we can get.'

'I don't know what I would do without the reading room,' Miss Ashton said. 'Did you know that they're taking in the *Scientific American* now?'

'Is that the sort of thing young ladies like to read these days?' There was a suggestion of disapproval in Jimmy's remark, and Mr Seagrave put a protective arm on Miss Ashton's shoulders.

'My niece is an accomplished pianist and does splendid water colours,' Mr Seagrave said, 'but she is also a teacher with an inquiring mind and a thirst for knowledge.'

'I make use of the library when I get a chance, Miss Ashton,' Fred said. 'I'm surprised I haven't seen you in the reading room.'

'My guess is that we'll be running into each other all the time now.' Miss Ashton said. 'My mother says that's how it is in Waratah. You don't know of someone's existence one day, the next day you meet, and suddenly the two of you seem to be in all the same places.'

'It's like words,' Fred said. 'You come across a new word in your reading and then the next thing you know, you're sure to see it and hear it again and again.'

The other men murmured politely, but Miss Ashton gave Fred an interested look, and smiled at him.

'Exactly,' she said, 'I know what you mean.'

'By the way,' Mr Seagrave said, 'before I forget. I'm looking for an agent for the insurance business I run for the Mt Bischoff Tin Mining Company. I thought one of you accounting chaps might be interested.'

'I am,' Fred said. He looked around at the other men but no one else showed any signs of taking up the offer.

'Excellent. Come and see me in my office. Just ask any of the assistants in the National Bank and they'll show you where to go.'

Before Fred had a chance to say anything, Frank interrupted them.

'Rain.' He held out his hand and then they all noticed it. The drops were intermittent for the moment, but it was more than a drizzle, and no one was left in doubt as to how the afternoon would turn out.

'I don't go anywhere without this,' Miss Ashton said, and coaxed open a green silk umbrella which she held over her head. 'I'm told we need the rain here for the mines, so there's no point complaining about it.' She held the umbrella high enough to include Mr Seagrave under it, or at least part of Mr Seagrave, but he shook his head and stepped to one side.

'Thank you, my dear, but I'll take my chances with the rain.' He pulled his hat a little further forward and held his hand out to Fred. 'It's a pleasure to meet you again under these changed circumstances, Fred. I'll look forward to seeing you at the bank.' And then to the group in general, 'I hope the weather doesn't spoil your plans for the afternoon my friends.'

Frank watched them leave and then turned back to the other men. The drops of rain were more frequent now, and the heavy dark clouds that hung over the mountain completely blotted out the sun.

'Well it doesn't look as if it's an afternoon for football after all,' Frank said to the group of men. 'What do you say?'

Albie and Jimmy had made up their minds and they said goodbye and headed up the road. The crowd that had been here only half an hour ago had almost disappeared, and apart from some men waiting on the verandah of the barber shop, only the three of them were left in the street.

'You're right Frank,' Tom said. 'No footie this afternoon. It might be a better afternoon for billiards.'

Fred agreed. He was always ready for a game of billiards, and the three of them hurried along the road, hats pulled down against the heavy drops of rain, jackets clutched around them.

They took the path by the side of the hotel that took them straight to the billiard room.

'We're in luck,' Frank said. 'Not a soul here.'

'The two of you go first,' Tom said. 'I'll fetch us some drinks from the bar.'

Frank handed Fred a cue and then picked up the cue balls.

'Yellow or white?'

'White.'

'First to twenty?'

'That suits me. Let's shoot for break.'

Tom came back with a jug of beer and three glasses. He poured himself a glass and stood by the side of the table, watching the game.

'So, what do you think, Fred?' Tom asked.

Fred was about to take a shot, and he paused and looked at Tom.

'About what? The break?'

'No, Miss Ashton!' he laughed. 'If I wasn't already taken...'

Fred had been thinking about Mr Seagrave and wondering how much money he might make as an insurance agent. As for Miss Ashton, without thinking about it too much, he thought he might look out for her in the library. She was older than him – twenty at least, Fred thought – but she was the first person he'd met here who showed interest in something other than sport and work. He took his shot and hit the red ball into a pocket.

'Miss Ashton sounds as if she might have more to talk about than the next dance and her new hat.'

Frank lined up his shot. 'You should be happy I persuaded you to join the Institute Fred. You might have found someone who likes Shakespeare as much as you do.'

Fred watched Frank's ball ricochet around the table without hitting anything except the sides. He smiled and rubbed chalk into the end of his cue.

'You might be right, Frank. I intend to find out,' he said.

28

Two weeks later, Tuesday, 27 April 1886

Fred turned up the wick in the lamp and went over to the wardrobe to get the old workbox his aunt had given him to keep his letters in. He took it to the desk then sat down and took out the last few letters from his mother. He glanced through the latest one, then the one before that. No, he definitely hadn't replied to either of them. What about the one before that? No. Not that one either. Could it really be that long since he'd written to her? If he didn't do something about it, his mother would be on the train up here to find out what was going on!

It wasn't that he didn't want to write. He did, but there was always something else that got in the way. But not today. This unexpected holiday was the perfect time for it, and he had a good two hours before the games started.

He read through his mother's letters, inked his pen, and started to write.

Pearce's Hotel

Waratah

27th April

Dearest Ma,

A thousand apologies for not writing before this. The truth is, I've been so busy with everything, that it's only now we have an extra day's holiday that I've found the time to sit down and put pen to paper.

I'm happy to hear of the good news from Wynyard and how well everyone is doing. Every time you write there seems to be something new happening and now you tell me that finally a drama club is to start. Our drama club here has started now too. The president is a man called Mr Harris. He told me I have a natural gift for acting and he's given me a very substantial role in the next play we're doing, so you can imagine how happy I am about that. The play is called The Golden Plough, and if the rehearsals are anything to go by, it's going to be a real hit.

Easter has been a proper holiday up here and for a change the weather has been mild and sunny. On Good Friday I went with Aunt Jane and the family to watch Uncle James in the married versus singles cricket match. The baby is still too little to go anywhere, but Mattie and Harriet came along, and Mattie decided he would be a cricket man when he grows up! Aunt Jane made a picnic just like the ones you do, and apart from the cricket being so boring, it was a nice day.

Fred put his pen in the stand and pushed himself back in the chair. He had been going to tell his mother about the ball last night, but then he wondered what she would think of him dancing on Easter Monday. It would be easier if he could talk to her, then he could make her see it his way, but the words on the page were so final. And what about his father! What if she had to read it out to him? No. Best not to say anything about it.

Fred didn't feel as if he'd changed, not deep down, but every time he wrote to his mother there was another thing he decided not to mention.

He got up and stood at the window, staring down at the lights in the valley but not really seeing them. Last night. He smiled when he remembered it. For his first ball he thought he'd done rather well. It was a good thing he'd let Frank talk him into it.

It had been a couple of weeks ago, late in the evening, and Frank asked Fred to join him for a nightcap in the hotel drawing room.

'I hope you've decided to go to the ball, Fred,' Frank said. 'You wouldn't want to miss this one – it's usually the best of the year.'

'I still haven't decided', Fred told him. 'You know I've never been to a ball.'

'Well it's about time that you did.'

'It's alright for you, but I don't know how to dance.'

'Not a problem,' Frank said. 'There are only really three steps you need to know and the rest you can make up. Watch me.' They were the only guests making use of the drawing room, and Frank went over to the empty space behind the chairs and couches that were grouped around the fireplace.

'First, the waltz'. He looked hard at Fred. 'Are you sure no one has ever taught you to waltz?' When Fred shook his head, Frank held up his arms as if he was holding an imaginary partner and went spinning around the room chanting 'one two three, one two three'.

Fred couldn't help laughing, but Frank was right. It didn't look too hard.

'Now step, step, hop,' Frank said, and he jumped lightly from one foot to the other. That was even funnier. 'Come on, have a go, Fred. I'll be the woman and you be the man.'

'Really?'

'Yes. Don't be so Methodist about it. Pretend you're in a dance class. This is the way they teach you there.'

Methodist! Frank was right. 'No child dances into Heaven' Pa would say if any of them even looked as if they might be dancing. 'You'll be going straight into the jaws of Hell.'

But that was his father. Fred didn't believe in Heaven and Hell, maybe not even God, for that matter, so what was stopping him? Nothing.

After the initial awkwardness, Fred was concentrating so hard on where to put his hands, and what to do with his feet, that he forgot how it must have looked.

'I think you get the idea,' Frank said. They were sitting back in front of the fireplace, Fred a little out of breath from the exertion. 'The quadrilles can be a bit tricky, but here's an idea. You're always teaching yourself something, so why not get *The New Ballroom Guide* and teach yourself some more steps. I would be very surprised if the library didn't have a copy.'

It was good advice and Frank was right. There were no fewer than five copies of *The New Ballroom Guide* in the library and Fred did what he was good at. He taught himself.

Fred pulled the drapes over the window and sat down at the desk again. No. There wasn't anything that he could say to his mother about learning to dance. She would read the letter to his father and hell really would break loose.

He dipped the pen into the ink and while he was thinking about what to say next a drop slid off the nib and splattered onto the page. That wouldn't do. He put the pen back in its stand again and tried to soak up the worst of the ink. It wasn't usually this hard to write to his mother.

He blew on the smudged bit of the letter to dry it more quickly and noticed the two books stacked one on top of the other at the back of the desk. Poetry books, both of them. *Lyrical Ballads* had been his choice, but Elizabeth Ashton's sister Annie had insisted that he borrow *Shakespeare's Sonnets*. He'd brought both the books home, but he wasn't sure the sonnets were his sort of thing. Because he loved the plays didn't mean he would love the poems, he'd told Annie, but she had ignored his excuses.

'Give them a try at least,' Annie had told him, staring at him with that intent gaze that she had. She was such a serious girl, not at all like Bella, as Miss Ashton preferred to be called. You would think that Bella was the younger one, and it had been a surprise to learn that she was engaged to a Mr Arnold from Burnie. The last thing Fred could imagine was wanting to be married. Would he ever feel like that? Was it something that he should think about?

Fred picked up the volume of sonnets and started leafing through it. As if of its own accord, the book opened to a page in the middle, and something fell out: a delicate sheet of soft, opalescent paper. When Fred picked it up he saw that between the folded sheet of paper were dried petals of a red rose. He lay the little package on the desk and carefully prised the paper apart. A delicate, sweet scent drifted up and he bent down and sniffed closer to the petals. The smell reminded him of something that was just eluding him, and he leaned back with his hands behind his head and tried to place it.

Bella. That was it. The perfume reminded him of last night and dancing with Bella. He'd noticed it when they were waltzing, and he asked her about it.

'You really don't mind what you say, do you Fred?' Bella had laughed. 'Well, I don't mind either – it's a relief to be able to forget about what one should and shouldn't say and do. And since you ask, it's these little roses on my gown. Annie made them for me. She put dried rose petals inside.' Bella nodded down at her dress. 'Clever, isn't she?'

Fred resisted the urge to lean down and sniff the little muslin flowers, but he did notice how perfectly the squared bodice showed off Bella's smooth white skin.

That was another thing that he couldn't write about to his mother. Bella had been right in one way. After meeting at the post office, they had kept running into each other. It hadn't been hard to contrive the meeting in the reading room and then they'd gone for coffee, Fred and the two sisters. Annie was taller than Bella and very earnest, though both the sisters were what Fred thought of as free thinkers. It was one of the things he liked about them.

No. His mother wouldn't want to hear that Fred was lounging about in the Coffee Palace with two unmarried women and sharing thoughts about Charles Darwin.

He folded the tissue paper back over the petals and put it to one side, then he started to read the sonnet. *Let me not to the marriage of true minds/ Admit impediment. Love is not love/ Which alters when it alteration finds.*

The marriage of true minds. If he did get married, and in a vague sort of way he imagined that he would have to eventually, he decided that's what he wanted. Next time he met Bella and Annie he must remember to ask them what they thought about that. Did Annie put the dried petals in there? That must be it, because he remembered now, she was planning to return the book, but gave it to him instead, so she'd probably forgotten about the flower.

Fred put the tissue back to mark the page and closed the book of sonnets. He would copy the poem into his daily book later, but now he had the letter to finish. As he put the book back in its place on the desk, he noticed that some of the documents Mr Seagrave had given him were still sitting loose on the side of the desk. Now that was something he could write about. He dipped his pen again, careful this time not to take too much ink, and started a new paragraph.

In your last letter you asked how my standing is with the company and as I have assured you, there is no cause for concern. The story you heard is more or less how it was. Mr Kayser is quite the autocrat, and the doctor you mentioned made the mistake of acting against his wishes. But you don't need to have any fears about that in my case. I know you worry that my temper will get me into trouble, but I can assure you that when it comes to Mr Kayser, I know better. In fact, I'm on good terms with Mr Kayser. So much so that I have been selected to be the representative of the National Mutual Life Association in Waratah. It's the life insurance backed by the Mt Bischoff Mining Company, so it is another way in which Mr Kayser has shown his confidence in my capabilities. By the way, did you know that Mr Seagrave, my old teacher, is the bank manager here now? He's one of Mr Kayser's trusted men and has been made a Justice of the Peace. It was through him that I got the insurance agency – he manages the fire insurance for all the Mt Bischoff buildings.

Here's something else that should put your mind at rest. Mr Hall, he's the second in charge here, has asked me to put in a tender for the position of collector of road rates. It's not certain that I'll get it, but if I do, it will mean I can further increase the money I'm sending home each month. £50 per year and 5% on the amount collected is what I'm asking for.

It's such an important position that Mr Kayser himself is the current office holder. The decision will be made by May 20th, so you can include that in your prayers for my success you say every night. I think you can be happy that so far I have succeeded beyond your expectations. You have always encouraged me to build on my talents and Mr Kayser has told me that I can look forward to a secure future with the company.

Your loving son,
Frederick

29

Ten weeks later, Wednesday, 7 July 1886

Fred pulled his scarf tighter and thrust his hands deep into the pockets of his new winter coat.

This must be what the old hands meant when they told him to 'wait until you see real snow.' What was usually a metal road slick with rain was entirely covered in a thick white blanket of snow, whiter than he imagined anything could be.

It was over everything: the corrugated roofs, the fence posts and tree stumps, the verandah railings. The long row of shops up Main Street looked like the Christmas cards that his Ramsbury relatives sent every year. There was always snow on the cards, sometimes with a robin, or a log fire. His mother had a special place for them on the mantelpiece in the parlour. 'It must be so beautiful over there,' she'd say. He'd never seen her throw a single one away. It was as if by keeping them, it might improve her chances of visiting what she always called 'the Old Country'.

Tonight it was just like those cards. She would love to see this. A few flakes drifted around him, but the snow clouds had moved on and the sky was filled with more stars than Fred had seen in a month. There was still some time before the meeting was due to start, and he walked slowly, listening to the soft squeak under his boots.

Halfway across the bridge he stopped and looked out over the lights of the sheds disappearing into the gorge, the dark hills softened by the snow on the treetops, the whole lit by a strange silvery glow. Why couldn't it always be like this? So perfect.

He felt a sudden jolt on his arm and when he reached around with his other arm to rub it he saw Frank Horne and Albie Lyle coming towards him. They were both laughing, and Albie was brushing the snow off his hands.

'Not a bad shot, hey?' Albie asked.

'It depends on what you were aiming for,' Frank said.

Fred scooped up a handful of snow, packed it into a ball and pelted it in their direction. It swung wide of Frank and buried itself in the snow.

'Batter, not a bowler, I'd say,' Albie laughed. 'Come on Fred. Enough daydreaming.'

Fred fell into step alongside them and they continued over the bridge towards the Mechanics' Institute.

'Have you thought about the next play? I'm putting my tuppence worth in for *Twelfth Night*.'

'Shakespeare? I'm not sure that we're quite up to that standard,' Frank said.

'Why not? It would be perfect for the drama club. There's the woman who disguises herself as a man and everyone falls in love with the wrong people. It's funny and there are lots of parts. For women and men both.'

They were nearing the Mechanics' Institute where members of the club were chatting on the verandah that led to the rehearsal room, waiting for Mr Harris to open the door.

Albie went over to join them, but Frank stopped and turned towards Fred.

'We're just a bunch of amateurs Fred. I can't see how we could do justice to Shakespeare, no matter how good the play is. I think I know what the others are going to say. Are you sure you want to mention it?'

'I think you'll find the Misses Ashton think it's a good idea.' Fred knew that because they'd talked about it over coffee yesterday.

Frank shrugged and put a hand on Fred's shoulder.

'Come on Fred. Let's just hope it's a play that has a part in it for both of us.'

'On that we can agree,' Fred said.

Fred waited his turn to scrape his boots and he was prising a solid chunk of packed snow off them when a cheer went up. He looked up and saw that people had started to follow each other through the door that Mr Harris had just opened. Hanging back from the rush of people were Bella and Annie.

Bella leaned over the railing.

'Come on slow coach, we're freezing out here.'

Fred looked up at them and swept his arm as if introducing them to the snowy scene.

'But don't you think it's beautiful out here tonight? All this snow.'

Annie came and stood next to Bella. She had both hands inside a red woollen cloak that she held tightly around herself, and there were patches of red in the hollow under her cheek bones. Her eyes picked up something of the shimmery night and she gave him one of the smiles that she kept for special occasions.

'Yes, it's wonderful, all this snow. Just like in Dickens. But Bella's right. It's cold. I'm going in.'

Fred took the stairs two at a time and followed Bella into the rehearsal room. She had a particular way of walking that he'd noticed before: an even, confident stride that was all from her waist down, and with each step her long skirt swayed from one side to the other. For a minute Fred was mesmerised, then he noticed Arthur Willicombe waving and pointing to an empty chair next to him. He just had time to take his seat next to Arthur before Mr Harris cleared his throat and clapped his hands. The noise of chatter gradually trailed off and they waited for him to speak.

'Welcome to the sixth meeting of the Waratah Excelsior Drama Club. First of all, I think we can congratulate ourselves on the performances last Saturday. Both the plays were well received, and Mrs Kayser came up afterwards to tell me how much she'd enjoyed *The Golden Plough*. It might seem a small thing, but it doesn't hurt to be noticed by those that matter.'

There was a polite round of applause, then Mr Harris continued.

'Now to the future,' Mr Harris continued. 'As you know, at the last meeting we decided to stage a significant production in the last week of September, the play itself to be decided tonight.' Mr Harris nodded towards his wife who was seated next to him, and she went over to the corner of the room and picked up a pile of booklets. Mrs Leonard helped her, and they handed everyone a copy while Mr Harris continued speaking over the murmur as people flicked through the pages or commented on the title.

This wasn't what Fred had been expecting. 'Come with ideas' were the exact words, 'all suggestions welcome'.

He was sure he'd heard correctly, so what was this? He took his copy from Mrs Harris and read the title: *The Ticket of Leave Man*. Australian then? But no. A quick read of the first stage direction told him Act 1 was set in the Bellevue Tea Gardens in London.

Mr Harris held up a booklet. 'Our new play,' he announced. 'A few of us put our heads together and came up with *The Ticket of Leave Man*. I thought you wouldn't mind us taking the liberty of having copies made for this evening.'

There was a ripple of laughter. No, they didn't mind at all.

'Wasn't that the play that the Launceston company put on last year?' Miss Vaughan asked. 'It was very entertaining, and with such a fine moral ending. I'm sure it's an excellent choice.'

Fred got to his feet. He didn't think about what he was going to say. In fact, it was only when he started talking that the words seemed to find themselves.

'I don't know about the rest of you, but I came to the meeting with an idea I'd like to share. The last two plays that we've put on have been very much appreciated judging by the applause. The reviewer for our last play said he'd never seen an amateur performance so close to professional level. So I came here with the idea of persuading you to consider a play by our greatest dramatist, Mr William Shakespeare, and after studying many of his plays, I'm convinced that the comedy, *Twelfth Night*, would be a perfect fit for the company.'

There was an eruption of laughter from Albie Lyle and his friends, and someone called out 'A horse, a horse, my kingdom for a horse,' and there was more sniggering.

Fred could feel his face burning, and he looked across at Bella and Annie. Surely Bella would say something? She'd been so enthusiastic about the idea when they were talking about it. But instead of meeting his look, she turned towards Annie and whispered something that made Annie smile. Were they laughing at him too?

'Give the lad a chance to speak,' Mr Harris said, and the room quietened down.

'However, now that I see better how the club works,' Fred said, and looked in the direction of the three couples who seemed to think they owned the club, 'allow me to put in a bid for such a play for our next production.' Fred sat down and Mr Willicombe came to his rescue.

'Let's thank Mr Alexander for giving us such an interesting idea. *Twelfth Night* is one of Shakespeare's best plays, in my opinion, and perhaps he's correct. Some of us in this club have been at the acting business for a good many years now. It might be time to test our mettle on something of more literary merit.'

'Yes, yes. Thank you both,' Mr Harris said. 'Mr Heaton, make a note of that in the minutes please. Now, I suggest that we go straight into a run through of *The Ticket of Leave Man*. You'll see that there are two names next to some of the characters. I suggest that we read the first two acts with the name that comes first, and then swap to the next name for the next two acts.'

People were impatient to get started and the noise level rose as they found their parts and established who was to go first. Fred ran his finger down the list of characters and found his name next to Sam Willoughby. His was the only name, so at least he had the part. Not that everyone in the club wanted to take an acting role. Quite the opposite. Mr Harris always ended up having to persuade some reluctant member to have a go. It was the memorisation that put them off. And stage fright. Annie was like that. She swore that she'd die of fright if she was pushed onto the stage. 'What about playing the violin?' Fred had asked her. 'You don't look nervous when you do that.' 'That's different,' was all she would say, so he was no closer to understanding what it might be like.

By the time they read through the whole of the play and finalised the casting, it was almost midnight. It had been painful at first – some people were so halting when they read aloud that listening to them was agonising. All credit to Mr Harris though. He changed the readers around and everyone started to get into their parts. Even Frank. Fred wasn't sure whether he'd been joking when he told him that all he was interested in was wearing a costume and being part of the fun. 'When would I find the time to learn a proper part, Fred?' he'd said. But he was so obviously the best man for the part of Mr Gibson that they'd all talked him into taking the role, and he'd agreed.

'I think I've been type cast!' Frank said to Fred. 'Mr Gibson's a bill broker, so not too far from an accountant. At least my acting skills won't be overtaxed!'

They were standing in a group outside the hall. The married couples had gone home, and freed from what sometimes seemed like supervision, the single men and women were sharing notes about the new play.

'It's the opposite for me,' Fred laughed. 'I sincerely hope that I have not a thing in common with that precocious brat Sam Willoughby. Only fifteen and we're supposed to believe he's smoking a pipe.'

Bella had been talking to Mr Willicombe and now she turned her attention to Fred.

'I think that would suit you very well Mr Alexander. I've heard that no man about town can be without a pipe these days.'

Albie Lyle took up the idea.

'Yes. An excellent point Miss Ashton. Fred, in the interests of your thespian duties, I charge you with taking up the smoking of a short pipe.'

'Well, a man must do what a man has to do,' Fred said. 'Strictly for the stage of course.'

'I don't think your idea about *Twelfth Night* was very well received.' Bella said as they were walking back through the snow to Main Road.

'No help from you, Miss Elizabeth Ashton.'

'When I saw that the demagogues had gone to the lengths of making copies of the play they'd chosen, there wasn't any point saying anything.'

'Were you laughing at me?'

'No. Of course not. I still think it's a good idea, I just didn't want to make myself look…conspicuous.' Fred turned his attention to her sister.

'What were you smiling about then Annie?'

The red came rushing back into the hollow under her cheekbones and she smiled and shook her head so that the feathers on her hat swayed from side to side.

'Bella was saying that maybe you would be Tasmania's answer to Mr Henry Irving.'

'The famous actor?' Fred flung his arms wide 'To be, or not to be.'

Annie laughed and turned to Bella.

'You were lucky to get the part of Emily, Bella. I thought Miss Vaughan read very well.'

'Better than me? You're probably right, but I think I look the part more' Bella laughed. 'And I'll have you as prompt, Annie, so I won't have to worry about my lines!'

They had crossed the bridge and were standing in front of the hotel.

'I almost forgot,' Bella said. 'Mother has invited you to tea on Sunday. She's found the violin that Annie was telling you about, and you're to come in the afternoon and try it out. There could even be some dancing!'

'That's if you're free,' Annie added.

Fred thought of all the things he'd planned for Sunday afternoon. Estelle needed some decent exercise, then there were men he needed to visit about their insurance policies, and he'd promised to take Mattie and Harriet over to the dam. But a chance to learn the violin! That didn't come every day. He was free, he told them, and so it was settled.

30

Ten weeks later, Friday, 24 September 1886

Fred gave the fire a stir, then sat back, his feet on the fender, watching the smoke from his pipe drift lazily across the light from the oil lamp and disappear into the darkness.

Then he had an idea. If ever there was a good time to treat himself, this was it. He got up and went over to his desk. Earlier in the evening he'd stacked up all the papers and made room for the new silver tray and the whisky decanter and glasses that he'd bought this afternoon. Now he poured two fingers of whisky into a glass and took it back to the fire.

It was still hard to believe. Twenty whole pounds in one day. No, not even one day. One hour. He'd been entering the London tin prices when the junior clerk from the manager's office came into the room. He was an annoying boy who thought that he was better than the rest of them just because he worked directly under Mr Kayser, so Fred took no notice of him. But the boy, unaware of how silly he looked in his checked suit that hung like a joke on his skinny frame, came and stood next to him.

'Mr Kayser requests your presence in his office at your earliest convenience,' he announced.

So pompous!

Mr Patterson was always ready for a diversion and he called across the room.

'What have you done now, Fred?'

Fred ignored Mr Patterson and looked up at the boy.

'Now is convenient,' he said. 'I'll follow you to his office.'

Nothing to worry about, he told himself, but with Mr Kayser you never knew what to expect, so it was a relief to find his boss sitting at his desk and looking relaxed, almost friendly.

'Sit down, sit down, my boy. I won't waste your time. I met with the directors of the Mt Bischoff Tin Mining Company last night and they agree with you; a life insurance policy to cover the entire work force is a sound financial decision. It will improve the conditions we can offer to compete for the best men. It will also tie our workers more securely to the company and minimise worker turn over. These are points that you include in your quotation from the Australian Assurance Company, and the board has given me permission to finalise the details of the policy.'

£2000 the policy was worth, and for Fred, 1% commission. £20!

Mr Kayser pulled out a sheet of paper and scribbled something on it, then handed it to Fred.

'Show this to Mr Horne and ask him to make out a cheque for £2000 in favour of the Australian Assurance Company, and £20 for yourself. Well done Mr Alexander.'

Fred took the piece of paper.

'Thank you, Mr Kayser, I'll draw up the formal schedule immediately.' He couldn't keep the smile from his face, and he had barely refrained from skipping out of the office like a boy.

That had been hours ago, and he still had to pinch himself. Fred put his glass of whisky on the mantelpiece. His pipe had gone out again, and he emptied it into the fire, knocking it against the side of the fire dog, then put it to one side of the hearth. Perhaps it was time to give it up.

The evenings felt dull now that *The Ticket of Leave Man* had finished. What would the club do next? Surely something even more ambitious after those reviews. He went back over to the desk and brought his folder of newspaper cuttings over to the fire. Placing it on the floor next to the chair, he pulled out the top cutting. *The Tasmanian*. That was Mr Vaughan writing. He was always stinting with praise, but even he spoke highly of their production: *Would compare favourably with such professional companies as country towns are favoured with,* he'd written. And Fred knew that top professional companies like Rignold's made it all the way up to Waratah.

He took the next cutting out of the folder. This one was from the *Daily Telegraph*, and it was even better. *The careful and finished acting took everyone by surprise, and the performers were greeted with round upon round of genuine applause. It would be invidious to name any performer and I will therefore simply say that the performance is considered by competent judges to be the best ever given at Waratah by amateurs or professionals.*

Would it be invidious, Fred wondered. Everyone said how he had stolen the show, and from when he first jumped up on the chair with his pipe clenched between his teeth, there'd been so much laughter and applause that he'd had to wait for it to die down before he went on. Why not mention that?

He put the cuttings back in the folder and sat looking at the fire, reduced to glowing embers now. There really was nothing to match the feeling of performing to a packed audience, of transforming oneself into another character. It was how he felt when he recited Shakespeare too; he felt like a different person, better, fuller. It was what he wanted to do with his life, and somehow or other, he was going to make it happen.

31

Two months later, Thursday, 25 November 1886

There was a flapping noise that came from outside, and the flame in the desk lamp fluttered then steadied itself. The window was closed, but it felt as if the wind was coming right into the room. Fred went over to the unlit fireplace and put his hand between the screen and the opening. The light didn't reach this far, so he had only touch to go by, but there was definitely a draft coming down the chimney. He pulled the screen right up against the bricks and sat back down at the desk, disturbed by the strange weather that made it hard to concentrate on the list he was compiling.

He leaned back and stretched his legs out under the desk. The wind hadn't let up all day, and when it gusted, the way it rattled the glass made it feel as if the window was going to burst. It was a gale blowing from the north-east, a hot wind, not mountain weather at all. All week reports had been coming in about fires burning in the forest. They were caused by prospectors taking advantage of the spell of dry weather to burn off the undergrowth, the men said.

That had been a near thing, those fires this afternoon.

A spark had lit Mr Leonard's woodheap and more sparks had jumped into scattered timber in front of the houses along North Road. If it hadn't been for the miners who happened to be going home from work, the houses might not have been saved. Fred couldn't spare the time to go and look, but the junior clerks from the office ran up the street to help out and brought back an account of people passing buckets from hand to hand and a huge woodheap destroyed.

What if there were embers left? The way the wind sounded, anything could happen. It wouldn't take much to start another fire. If I were in their shoes, he thought, I wouldn't be able to sleep. There were still the remains of a hotel further along Main Street that had burned down not long before his first visit here. Impossible to imagine how a building like that could be wiped out in minutes. The whole town had thrown water at it, Uncle James said, but once the fire found the dried wood it was all over. There had been a gale blowing that night too.

He pulled his chair further in and leaned back over the ledger. Concentrate, he told himself, concentrate. For the past two hours he'd been compiling and cross checking the lists of defaulting road ratepayers. It was only 1 shilling in the pound. Why was it so hard to get the money out of them? He'd written the draft of a letter to send to the defaulters, and he read back through it. Notices, notices, notices. Would he have taken on this collecting work if he knew what was involved?

There was a fierce rattle on the window, a sudden gust that made him jump. It was no use. He closed the ledger and went over and peered out through the drapes. The trees by the dam were tossing around like things possessed.

The balcony would give a better view. It was so warm there was no need for a jacket, and in his shirtsleeves, he went up the corridor and out onto the wide verandah. You could see the whole valley from up here. He looked up towards the mine. The forest fires must be the other side of the mountain because there were no signs of anything on this side.

Something caught his eye to the north, and he walked up to the other end of the verandah to get a better look. It was over the bridge, a faint orange glow in the direction of the Mechanics' Institute. Then as he was watching, the glow strengthened, and sparks shot into the sky.

He rushed back to his room, grabbed his jacket off the hook and took the stairs two at a time. There were still a few men in the public saloon and John was tidying up behind the bar.

'Fire' he called out to the room in general. 'There's a fire over the bridge.'

Then he remembered the meeting for the Specimen Reef mine

his uncle had called tonight and he ran across the hall and into the meeting room. The room was hazy with cigar smoke and it took him a second to make out Frank Horne and his uncle at the head of the table. He knocked on the open door to get their attention.

'Fire. There's a fire over the bridge, towards the Mechanics' Institute.'

Frank was the first one to act. He was on his feet and heading out the door almost as soon as Fred had spoken.

'Come on Fred, let's go,' he said, and he led the way up the hallway. 'Let's pray it's not the library,' he called over his shoulder. Fred shook his head. Surely it couldn't be the library – all those books! The least bit of flame and up they would go!

Frank had to push against the wind to open the door and when they were out in the street the gale hit them head on. Frank stopped. 'You go on,' he told Fred. 'I'll find some buckets and follow you.'

There were other men running down the street now, and ahead of him Fred recognised Mr Leonard amongst a group of men about to cross the bridge. Hadn't his house nearly burnt down this afternoon?

Half running, half walking, he followed them over the bridge, his head down to blunt the force of the wind. When he turned the corner the sight was shocking.

The Mechanics' Institute was on fire.

From the far side of the big wooden building, flames were jumping and spitting, higher than the roof. The side wall of the hall was already engulfed by fire. As he drew nearer a gust of wind rushed at the flames and in seconds the fire was feeling its way over the whole building, sending out questing, spitting flames, searching the timber walls for the weakest point.

The clanging of the mine's alarm bell echoed around the valley and Fred stopped and looked to see what he could do.

There were already half a dozen men there, black silhouettes against the orange flames. Mr Harris was calling out orders, directing men with buckets of water into a chain to keep the flow of water going. It was hard to know what to do. He looked around to see if Frank was coming with the buckets, but the smoke was so thick he couldn't see.

Men were running out of the houses up the road, bringing their buckets along. Then close by the flames, but behind them, so he didn't see them immediately, Fred saw two men trying to coax a horse along. They were coming from the police station across the road and as they got nearer he saw it was Constable Burns and someone he didn't recognise. Harnessed to the horse was the town's fire cart, the only hope against the fire that was drinking up the wind and making the chain of men with their buckets of water look small and useless.

As he watched, the horse tossed its head back and forth then reared up on its hind legs, panicked by the heat and the roaring fire. Constable Burns dropped the reins and the other man moved back a few paces.

What were they thinking! That poor horse. This he could deal with.

He approached the horse calmly, talking to it. In his pocket he found the carrot left over from this evening's ride, and he held it out with one hand and reached up to stroke its nose. The other men watched as the horse stopped pawing at the ground. Its ears relaxed forward and it snuffled the carrot from Fred's hand. He picked up the reins and spoke to the men.

'We need to take her up there first, so she's heading away from the fire,' he said, pointing towards the other side of the road. 'Then we can back her down and get the cart close to the dam.' Fred turned the horse so the wind was behind her. 'Come on girl, let's go.'

As soon as Fred coaxed the horse into position, men came over to help and Constable Burns set up the pump. He left Fred and the other men to handle it and he ran back up the slope to the back of the building.

There was a steadier flow of water, but the fire was winning. The only thing that would stop it was a change in the weather.

But the change came too late. Twenty minutes too late, and in that time the Mechanics' Institute was burned to the ground.

The only thing left was charred and smouldering remains. Idle flames still flared up and the heat was so intense it was impossible to get near it. The gale was still blowing, but now it was in the other direction, onto some vacant blocks. The house at least they had saved by saturating it with water from the hose.

Too full of adrenalin to think of sleeping, people stood around swapping what little they knew. The grand piano had miraculously been saved by Constable Burns, and it sat on the blackened grass, an incongruous reminder of all the rest that was lost. The books, the journals, the theatre sets and costumes: nothing of that was left.

Suddenly the wind dropped, and it started to rain.

Fred walked back to the hotel with Uncle James and Frank. It was more than a building they'd lost, and Uncle James put into words what Fred had been thinking.

'That's a terrible loss to the town. What will you do with your evenings now, Fred?

'And what about poor Mr Harris?' Frank asked.

'At least we saved his house,' Fred said.

'Yes. Mercifully it was upwind. But did you see his furniture?'

'Those things on the road?' Uncle James asked. 'I was wondering what they were doing there. And how did the table come to lose a leg? Just one. That wasn't a fire.'

'I think I recognised the men from the bar this evening,' Frank said. 'They probably thought they were helping. The house was saved but there's hardly a piece of furniture that's worth keeping.'

'I can't take it in,' Fred said. 'The hall and all our scenery and props and costumes. And the library. All those books, the journals, papers. Everything gone.'

'It's not just things in it either' Uncle James said. 'That place was the social and intellectual centre of Waratah. The town won't be the same without it.'

'At least the foundations of the new hall are untouched, but I wonder if it will ever be possible to replace the books,' Frank said. 'When I think about that fine collection of history books, gone forever.'

They walked on in silence.

'Did you see the Kaiser?' Uncle James asked. 'He was standing on the verandah watching from afar.'

'I can't help thinking that this doesn't bode well for Mr Harris,' Frank said. 'And maybe the drama club.'

'Why?' Fred asked. The idea was unthinkable.

'Well, you know how Mr Kayser has a vendetta against him because he stood up to him about building the new hall.'

'But that was months ago. And anyway, Mr Harris was right to stand up to him.'

'You still haven't got, have you Fred?' Uncle James softened the comment with a laugh. 'It's not where the truth lies that is the problem. The problem lies with anyone who dares to tell Mr Kayser he's in the wrong.'

'And Mr Harris did.'

'Yes. And now the most valuable thing that we have in Waratah is burnt to the ground under his watch.'

'Mr Harris was there, organising the firefighting, right from the start.'

'I know, and you know. There's going to be an inquiry and I'm quite sure that they'll find that it was sparks blown from all these fires around that started the blaze. It will make no difference. I just hope that the community isn't made to suffer on account of it,' Uncle James said.

32

The next day, Friday, 26 November 1886

Early the next morning, keeping to his training routine, Fred took Estelle for a ride out to the racecourse. On the way back through town he slowed Estelle to a walk as they passed the remains of the Mechanics' Institute. The rain that quenched the fires the night before had been the precursor of a cold front that swept into the township from the south-west, and the jagged piles of blackened timbers under the low clouds were a depressing sight. Then it started to rain again, and Fred trotted on to the stables.

Nothing was going right. It was months since he'd started training Estelle. She was fit and fast and handled well, but how was she ever going to win a race if she'd never run with other horses? Back home there were always at least two or three racehorses in the stable and they trained together. That's what he needed. Without that, should he even enter Estelle in the races? But if he didn't, what was the point of it all? When he'd talked about it to Uncle James, all he'd said was 'leave it to me.' That had been a month ago.

Fred wiped Estelle down and was cleaning out the stall when he heard a voice that he recognised, though he couldn't quite place it.

'Your uncle told me I'd find you here.'

The man had his hat pulled down against the rain and it took Fred a minute to recognise Mr Hall. The last time Fred had talked to him was when he had suggested he put in a tender for the road rate collecting job. Fred knew now it was probably because his uncle had suggested it – he and Mr Hall were close friends – but at the time Fred had felt flattered. Mr Hall was the second-in-charge to Mr Kayser, but a very different sort of man.

Friendly, relaxed, renowned for helping people. Rumours were going around that he wasn't happy in his job, that he was going to leave the Mt Bischoff company and manage a new mine that was starting up.

'Mr Hall, good morning.'

Fred finished checking Estelle's right hoof and put it on the ground, then stood next to her, stroking her flank.

Mr Hall leaned on the low stable door. The overhang from the iron roof kept off the worst of the rain, though as the drops hit the ground, cold spray ricocheted off the cobbles. The noise of the rain on the iron roof made it hard to hear and they shouted over it.

'She's a good-looking horse. What is she? Two years?'

'Two in August.' Fred ran his hand down Estelle's mane then along her straight back. He took a step back and looked her over. 'Yes. She's a beauty.'

'Your uncle tells me you've trained her yourself?'

Where was this heading? What had Uncle James hatched up now?

'Yes. I'm getting her ready for the Waratah Races.'

'Riding her yourself?'

'That's the plan.' The look Mr Hall cast over him was quick but it was obvious. Was Fred too heavy to race a two-year-old?

'That's an admirable ambition. You can't weigh much over 8 stone I'm guessing.'

So he wasn't here to criticise. Fred relaxed. He laughed.

'A little under. So long as I don't have too much Christmas dinner I should be a decent weight.'

Fred tossed the rug over Estelle's back and fastened the straps.

'Your uncle mentioned that you haven't got anyone to train with. As it turns out, I'm in the same boat.'

'You have a racehorse?'

'Yes. Come and have a look at him. My trainer just rode him up from Deloraine, and we've rented a place in the stables here.'

A fierce gust of wind swirled around them as Fred let himself through the stable gate and followed Mr Hall along the row of stalls. They stopped at the one next to the end where a black stallion came over to meet them. He was a hand or so taller than Estelle, lean, but with solid flanks and legs.

Mr Hall held out his hand and the horse snuffled around looking for a treat.

'Meet Dashing Bob. I've tried him out in the autumn series of races and he's done quite well. He could run as favourite for a couple of races.'

Fred leaned his elbows against the low stable door and had a closer look.

'He's a strong looking horse. Good disposition too, by the look of him.'

Mr Hall reached up and tickled Dashing Bob behind his ears, ruffling the dark mane. 'Yes. Dashing Bob has a very even temperament. Even so, he had a bit of an awkward moment at the May races in Deloraine. Running with a stablemate might be just the thing for him.'

'What happened?'

'It was at the Deloraine autumn meeting at the finishing line. People were all crowding around, urging on their favourites and Bob went straight into them. Young Will – that's my jockey – was knocked off and Dashing Bob bowled over a few of the men. The amazing thing was that no one was hurt. Will was pretty shaken up, but that was all.'

'I've been riding Estelle out to the track here whenever I can for the last few weeks. She seems to get around the course pretty well. Even that sharp corner coming into the straight.'

'That's settled then. Shall we say 5.30 tomorrow morning? I'll tell Will to wait for you. I'm sure Dashing Bob will be only too happy to race against such a pretty mare!'

33

The sound of the steam whistle carried over the noise of the brass band and all the way to the stable where Fred was checking his saddle.

That would be the special train from Waratah. The whole family had come up from Wynyard for the races and he wanted to be there to meet them. Fred leaned over the railing of the stall next to him where Will Keating was brushing Dashing Bob.

'I'm going to meet the family Will, can you keep an eye on Estelle?'

Will leaned against his horse and gave Fred the thumbs up.

'No need to worry. I'll be right here.'

'Thanks.'

Fred made his way past the marquee where the band was playing, and through the crowd that was milling around the refreshment tents. He got to the siding as the special train bringing people out from Waratah came to a squeaky halt.

Doors were flung open, and men started jumping down onto the grass. There'd been talk of building a siding but so far all there was at Forty-Mile Camp was a signal box and the racecourse. Fred walked along the side of the train, peering in the windows and doors, then he saw Albert running towards him, pointing to the front of the train.

'We're up there.'

Through the jostling crowd of racegoers Fred spotted his father reaching up for a picnic basket that was being handed down from someone inside the train. It must have been Aunt Jane, because she was next to be handed down, then his mother, then Agnes. He barely had a chance to greet them when he heard Mattie and Harriet calling out to him.

'They've been waiting for you,' Aunt Jane told him. He lifted them down onto the grass and they competed to tell him about the train ride and how they'd nearly run over a cow that was on the tracks.

'Look out,' Amy yelled, and she took her skirt in one hand and jumped down, then grabbed Fred's hand and looked up at him, jumping from one foot to the other.

'Are you going to win today? Ma says you will.'

'Well then, I must,' Fred laughed.

'Harriet, Mattie, come over here,' his aunt called out. 'Leave your cousin alone.'

'Thanks Aunt Jane. I really had better get back to the stables – there's less than an hour to go before the first race.'

His father had his back to them and was talking to one of his racing friends, but he turned around when he heard Fred.

'I'll come with you. It was so dark last night I didn't get a proper look at this filly of yours. Albert! Get Richard to help you with that basket. You can help too Amy.'

Fred led his father back through the crowd, past the saddling yard and into the stables. Estelle was looking content, her neck stretched over the stable door, a piece of straw dangling from her mouth. She nudged his father and whinnied as he went into the stable, but soon she settled down and he ran an expert hand down her legs and along her flanks. Then he lifted each hoof in turn.

'Not bad. Not bad at all', he said. 'You're right son. She's a good-looking filly and those shoes do the job. So, you're riding her yourself, you said.'

'Yes. I bought her, I trained her and I'm riding her.'

'Are you sure that's the best choice? Your weight with a young filly like this…Albert would be only too happy to ride her for you. He's young, but he's a fine jockey already.'

Of course this was what his father had been leading up to. Probably why Albert had been so quiet since he'd arrived in

Waratah. It took him by surprise, and Fred was momentarily speechless.

'You've never been tested on a racetrack, Frederick. It's not like riding around Table Cape.'

'I haven't ridden in a race because Ma thought I wasn't strong enough,' Fred shouted, finding his voice. 'And anyway, you always chose Arthur.'

Estelle threw her head up and down and then shook it so her mane was tossed from side to side, and Fred reached up and steadied her.

'She doesn't like that temper of yours,' his father said. 'There's no shame in a trainer taking on a rider.'

Fred stroked Estelle's nose. Why was it always like this?

'Nevertheless, I've made up my mind to ride her myself in these races. I'm sure I can give her a good run.'

'Still as stubborn as ever.'

Fred said nothing, but he stopped stroking Estelle and turned towards his father, waiting, ready for a fight.

But his father surprised him. He put his hand on the crown of his hat and pushed at it, something he did when he was making up his mind. Then he looked at Fred. Could that be the faintest hint of a smile?

'I see the mountain air up here has put some iron in those bones of yours,' he said. 'I would have done the same at your age. Just remember to get off to a good start then watch for the chance to break clear. You've done a good job with her head; I can see that.'

Fred nodded and pulled the reins so that Estelle's head went up and down in a perfectly straight line.

'Just like training Titania.'

'Yes. Good. I'm going to put some bets on now, but I'll send Albert over.' Fred stared at him, and his father went on. 'Don't get on your high horse! Albert can walk you around the mounting yard. You've got enough on your mind without bothering about the crowd. You'll be surprised how stupid people can be around horses. And if you're not nervous before a race, you're not prepared.'

His father was right about both those things. Albert led Estelle around the saddling yard with the other three horses and Fred tried to calm his nerves. He had a thing like a butter churner in his stomach. To take his mind off it he called down to Albert.

'Have you really ridden in a proper race, Albie?'

Albert looked up at him.

'Only at the beach. I've never ridden on a racecourse. Is it different?'

'Very. The horse prefers to go straight. There's a problem with this course on the turn into the home straight. There's no fence there, just a pile of logs, and you have to be careful to make sure the horse goes around it.'

'Are you worried about it?'

'No. Yes. Well, I was, but she's used to the turn now, aren't you Estelle?'

Talking about it helped, and when they filed out of the mounting yard and onto the track, all that Fred was thinking about was how to win.

That turned out to be harder than he'd imagined.

In quick succession he lost one race and came second in the other. Albert and his father came to meet him after the second race. Fred dismounted and walked next to his father, and they followed Albert as he led Estelle through the swarm of people and back to the stable.

'You've got a good horse there son,' his father said. 'Give her another year and she could be a winner.'

'I'm not giving up yet. I could feel Estelle had a lot left in her in that last race and we were closing on Dasher.'

'That's as may be, but you came second by two lengths.'

'I was slow starting, but I think I'm getting the hang of it now.'

'That's exactly where Albert has the magic touch. With him in the saddle, I'd put money on your horse for a win.'

What was the point in saying anything? It used to be all about Arthur. Arthur could ride, Arthur could play cricket, Arthur could hammer out a horseshoe. Now it was Albert.

Fred walked ahead of his father, past Albert who was holding Estelle, and into the stall, where he picked up a bucket. He ignored them both and took his time filling the bucket from the pump behind the shed. When he came back his father had gone. The rain that had been threatening all day turned from a few drops to a shower, and Albert had taken Estelle under the big corrugated iron roof and tied her to the stable rail.

'Pa said he had business with the totaliser.'

Fred shrugged. He lifted the saddle off and hung it over the railing, then he brought some sponges out of the stable and gave one to Albert. The two of them started sponging down the sweating horse with water from the bucket.

'He said he'd bet on Estelle tomorrow if you rode her,' Fred said.

'I don't want to ride her, Fred, even if you wanted me to. And I know you don't.'

'I think I can win tomorrow, Albie. I just need to get off to a better start.'

'Take the weight off her back, lean forward more, use your legs. That's all I do.'

Fred looked at his young brother. He was shorter by a good many inches. Albie had always been short, so he had a way of leaning over the neck of the horse to keep control. Maybe that was it. Worth trying, Fred thought. Definitely worth trying.

Albert was coming back with a fresh bucket of water when Will Keating joined them, a mug of beer in one hand, shaking the rain off his hat with the other.

'One down, two to go.'

'You nearly won the Cup, Will. Bob fairly jumped out at the start, then when Stella ran off the course it seemed you had it made.'

Will shook his head and took a swig of beer.

'I thought so too. But you know Bob.'

Fred knew what he meant. Dashing Bob was six years old and wily. The finishing line meant nothing to him. His race ended where he wanted it to, and Will often struggled to keep him hard at it over those last few yards.

'How about that last race of yours Fred! Another turn around the course and you might have won.'

'That's what I think. After that last turn I could feel her pick up the pace and she had plenty left in her.'

Will swallowed the last of the beer in a few gulps, then tipped the dregs onto the grass and wiped his mouth.

'I'll leave you to it. Duty calls.'

Fred hardly noticed anything around him on the ride from the racecourse back into town. Will had suggested they ride together, but Fred wanted to be by himself, to clear his head. His time wouldn't be his own back at the hotel, not with the whole family there. His father wasn't the only one who didn't understand. Ma too, Agnes and her pretty friend, Frank Horne and Mr Hall, all of them seemed to think that second place was good enough. But it wasn't, not for Fred.

He let Estelle pick her own way along the railway tracks. She deserved a nibble of fresh grass, and the slow walk was good for her after the two races. She'd done well. It wasn't Estelle who needed to run faster, it was up to him to show her how to win.

Should he get Pa to take another look at the shoes? People said it could make all the difference, and Johnny Alexander was the best farrier around. But what if he did that? What if his father adjusted Estelle's shoes and then she won? Half the credit would go to his father. He didn't need that sort of help. If he won, it was going to be between him and Estelle. No one else!

Yes, he wasn't used to racing. They were right about that. So what could he do? What had he learned from today? He knew he'd trained her well. Estelle was ready to race. She liked to race, and she didn't seem to mind the crowds and the other horses. On the other hand, he had to get her off to a better start. The way Dasher had shot out in front, that's what he needed to do. He could try what Albert suggested.

He bent forward so that his chin was buried in Estelle's mane and squeezed his thighs against her flanks. She started to surge forward, and he leaned back and pulled on the reins. That seemed to work, and it might just make the difference between winning and losing.

34

The next day, Tuesday, 28 December 1886

'Whoa there,' Fred whispered to Estelle.

He'd drawn the outside position, next to the rail. The horses were all behind the line and the rope was pulled to one side. Fred leaned forward. The flag came down. He went even further forward and lifted his weight to the front of the horse. Estelle went flying along the track.

Fred could hear the noise of hooves behind him, but Estelle was maintaining her lead as they approached the home turn. 'Steady,' Fred murmured and eased her back.

Estelle ignored the command.

She took the line of least resistance, and without breaking stride went soaring over the logs that marked the edge of the racetrack. Fred kept his saddle, but Estelle was running her own race and kept going straight ahead, scattering spectators. They were almost at the railway tracks when he finally got her under control.

There was nothing for it, but to take her back to the stables. When he neared the beer tent he dismounted and walked Estelle through the crowd of people.

Men he didn't know patted him on the shoulder and said, 'Bad luck son' and one man with a frothing mug of beer in each hand waved one of them towards the finishing line where Dashing Bob had just been beaten into second place again.

'The racetrack's over there mate,' he said, and laughed as if it was the funniest joke ever.

Fred tried to smile and show that he was a good sport. After all, other horses were coming unstuck on that corner too. It was too tight, everyone said so. But he'd been so sure that it wouldn't happen to him!

It seemed to take an eternity to get back into the roped off area around the stables. He tied Estelle to the railing and removed all the tackle. She was none the worse for her one-horse race, in fact from the way she was snorting and nudging him, it was more as if she'd enjoyed the run.

'It's alright for you, Estelle,' he told her. 'You're not the one who looked like a silly idiot.'

'Giving her a talking to then?' Will Keating looked down at Fred from where he was sitting on Dashing Bob. He didn't wait for an answer but dismounted and let his strapper continue on to the stable with the sweating horse. He leaned against the rail of Estelle's stall and watched Fred wiping her down. 'Looks like we'll be racing each other for the Consolation Stakes after all. That's if you're up to it.'

'Try and stop me!'

'You did well to stick to her. That jump must have been a bit of a surprise.'

'It happened so fast I couldn't do anything.'

'It's that outside lane. Look at the other horses that've done the same. You'll be right next time. Don't let it bother you.'

'Thanks Will.'

'I'll leave you to it. Looks like you've got company.'

Sure enough. His father was heading towards the stables. His mother was a few steps behind with Albert on one side, Richard on the other.

There was something about the way they were walking that made Fred think he might have a battle on his hands. They could say what they liked! The first thing he had to do was to make Estelle comfortable. He dipped the cloth in the bucket of water, wrung it out, then started on her hind legs.

'That was bad luck,' his mother said.

Fred looked up from where he was wiping around the lower leg. He nodded but finished what he was doing. They all stood there watching him. What was there to say?

'You looked funny,' Richard said and although he tried to stifle it, he couldn't help giggling.

Fred stood up and threw the cloth into the bucket of water. It felt good that some of it splashed onto Richard. Then he saw Albert biting his lip and trying not to laugh, failing, and letting out a strangled snort instead. Richard was just a little kid, and Fred ignored him. But Albie!

'I suppose the miracle boy would never let that happen. You try racing on that track!'

'Calm down.' His mother made a waving sort of gesture, as if to dispel the bad feeling. 'We've come to make sure there was no harm done.'

'None at all. Estelle is fine, aren't you girl?'

His mother glanced at his father, who was standing with his arms folded.

'I hope you're not thinking of going in the Consolation Race,' she said.

'Of course I'm going in the race. It's my last chance to win.'

'Winning isn't everything. That's a dangerous corner and it's just lucky that no one's been injured. Your father agrees with me.'

His father threw his hands up in the air, ridding himself of the whole conversation.

'What are you trying to prove, son? You've done well, run a good second. Why isn't that enough?'

It's not enough because I want to prove to you that you're wrong. That Estelle can win and that I'm as good a rider as your other sons. That you should recognise what I can do instead of treating me like a failure. That's what Fred wanted to say.

Instead, he lifted Estelle's reins off the railing post and turned her around, so that the others had to move backwards.

'Because I want to do better and I know I can win,' he said.

He took his time settling Estelle into the stall. Fresh hay, but not too much. Clean water in the trough.

When he came back out, only his mother and Albert were still there. The crowd had thinned out now, because of the rain, and he could see his father making his way over to the totaliser, Richard running after him.

'Your father's decided to put money on you for a win,' his mother told him.

Did his father have confidence in him after all? People could be so complicated! But there was no point thinking about it. No, he just had to think about how to win.

'He knows a winner when he sees one! Come on Ma, I'll walk back to the marquee with you and then go and sign in. You stay here with Estelle, Albert. I'll be back in a few minutes.'

As soon as Fred and his mother left the shelter of the stable roof, the rain started falling in earnest. It had barely let up all day. His mother opened her umbrella and held it as high as she could, trying to cover both of them. Fred reached for the handle.

'Here. I'll take that.' He put a hand across her back to keep them both under the shelter of the umbrella and gave her shoulder a squeeze. 'Come on Ma. Stop worrying about me. You can see how well I'm doing up here.'

His mother smiled up at him.

'It's amazing what you've done in a year. Three jobs and one of Mr Kayser's favourites, Jane tells me. You don't need to win this race to prove anything to me, Frederick.'

'I know. And you don't need to worry about me. Here's the sign-in tent.'

Fred handed back the umbrella and he pulled his jacket tight. 'Wish me luck,' he said and ducked out from the shelter of the umbrella.

★

'Ladies and gentlemen. I give you the Consolation Stakes.'

Fred steadied Estelle on the starting line. This time they had the middle lane, and Dashing Bob was next to them on the inside. After two false starts they were all under pressure, horses and riders, but on the third flag fall, Fred got her off to a good start. He could feel Estelle's energy, and when Dashing Bob drew out in front, Fred had to pull her in. It was tempting to let her go, but he'd learned his lesson. Keep something in reserve for the end of the race and look for a chance to break clear. That's what his father had told him.

On the second time around, Dashing Bob was in front, but only by a length or so. Then they were around the sharp turn and on the home straight. The mud was flying and Estelle was closing the gap. There was one length between them. Will was whipping the side of Dashing Bob, and Fred did the same to Estelle. A hundred yards to go and Estelle drew level. Then she pulled away, and they were over the line, a good length in front of Dashing Bob.

He let her run on a bit and then reined her in and walked her back alongside Dashing Bob. Will Keating was as relaxed as ever. He smiled at Fred.

'Bob thought he should let you win,' he said.

Fred laughed.

'How very nice of him!'

Standing around the judge's box he saw Amy waving to him. The whole family was there, Albert with a grin from ear to ear, and his father was brandishing a betting slip in the air.

'How does it feel?' Will asked him.

It felt like success. It felt like a settling of scores. It felt as if he could do anything if he put his mind to it.

'Good,' he said, 'very good.'

35

Five months later, Saturday, 28 May 1887

It was after two o'clock on Saturday afternoon and officially the men were on their own time. But half an hour ago a message from Mr Kayser had gone around, requiring that they attend a special meeting. The company's meeting room was packed. Chairs had been placed in rows on either side of a central aisle and most of them were already taken, so Fred joined Frank Horne and Tom Patterson, who were standing against the wall at the back of the room. Everyone was talking at once.

Was Mr Kayser going to announce another bonus? An extension to the mine? A change in the working hours? Whatever it was, Fred hoped it wouldn't take too long. He was meeting Annie at the Coffee Palace at three o'clock and it was after two already.

'Did you hear the rumour?' Tom asked him, and without waiting for an answer he went on, 'they said there's been a big find of silver down on the Pieman.'

'Don't believe everything you hear,' Frank told him. 'I wouldn't be so sure we're going to hear good news.'

The door at the front of the meeting room opened and the room fell silent as Mr Kayser strode into the room and stood in front of them.

'Look at his face,' Fred whispered to Tom and Frank. 'I think he's going to fire us all.'

Tom smiled as Fred meant him to, but Frank frowned and put a finger to his lips.

Ferdinand Kayser looked as if he'd swallowed something bitter and he was looking for someone to blame for it.

'I von't beat in the bush,' he said. 'Let it be known that the Mt Bischoff company is declining to support the new hall whilst it is in the hands of the current management. I'm told there is to be a night of theatrical entertainment to mark the opening of the hall. Let me make clear that if you value your job with the company, you will decline to participate.'

Suddenly everyone was talking at once. Mr Kayser, the man who held their livelihoods in his hands, turned and made for the door. There were shouts from several of the men calling him back.

'Mr Kayser, Mr Kayser.'

Fred couldn't believe what he'd just heard, and he turned to Frank.

'He can't mean *The Lancashire Lass*, can he? There's less than two weeks before opening night.'

'I'd say that's exactly what he means,' Frank told him.

Then one voice made itself heard over the uproar and caused Mr Kayser to turn back to face them. It was Mr Richards, the bandmaster.

'With respect, Mr Kayser,' he called out. 'Does that include the brass band?'

'If the band is intending to play on the opening night, yes. The company would see it as cause for instant dismissal.'

The other men stopped talking and Mr Richards continued.

'I can't help but think this is a misunderstanding of some kind, Mr Kayser. The band has no connection with the management of the new hall. It's a strongly held tenet of the band's constitution that we play when requested for all sectors of the community, without fear or favour.'

'The band exists only because the company allows it to. You, Mr Richards, will tell your members from me, that if they want to go against my orders, they vill, as you say, get the sack. Do I make myself clear?'

And without waiting for an answer, he strode out the door, not bothering to close it behind him.

For most of the men it was just another example of the mine manager's erratic behaviour, and those who had no connections with the Mechanics' Institute or the drama club, only had a vague idea what he was talking about. But the extraordinarily rude way he had shouted at them was shocking, even for Mr Kayser, and they left the room shaking their heads and exchanging looks. No one wanted to stand out as being against him.

Fred felt too stunned to move, and he watched the room emptying. For three months he'd been learning the part of Spotty in *The Lancashire Lass*, in the past few weeks rehearsing three times a week, sometimes four. It was another comic role, but more complex than his last one, and Fred was sure he was going to make a name for himself in the part. He couldn't give it up. And even if he did, who could possibly step in with only two weeks until opening night?

'What do you think Fred?'

It was Mr St Clair. He had one of the biggest parts in the play and, like Frank Horne, was one of Mr Kayser's right hand men. Of course they couldn't all just walk out on the play.

'We can't possibly quit now,' Fred told him. 'If you and Frank have a word to Mr Kayser, surely he'll understand.'

'You still don't get it, do you Fred!' Frank Horne was famous for his good humour, but at that moment there was no sign of it.

'Get what? We can't be told what to do in our own time!'

'That's what I think.' Mr Richards and a couple of other members of the brass band had come over to join them.

'And do you both want to be sent packing from Waratah? Because that's what will happen.'

Mr Richards shook his head disbelievingly.

'Can he really do that?'

Frank and Mr St Clair both started talking at the same time, and Frank gestured to Mr St Clair to continue.

'The way I see it,' he said, 'the only people who can safely defy Mr Kayser are the men who don't work for the company, like the shopkeepers, bankers, tradesmen and so on. Even the clergy aren't always safe, and we've all seen what's happening to Dr Kennedy. There may be some who don't mind losing their jobs, but I doubt it.'

'Exactly,' Frank said. 'I hate to do it to Mr Harris and the others in the drama club, but I'm going to see him right now and tell him I'm withdrawing. He won't like it, but he'll understand.'

'I'll come with you,' Mr St Clair said. 'Mrs St Clair will have to withdraw as well.'

Fred couldn't believe what he was hearing. If they all stuck together, surely Mr Kayser would see reason. How could they give in so easily?

'How can you do that?' he shouted. 'Just give up without a fight. I'm going to see Mr Kayser by myself if I have to!'

Frank put a hand on Fred's arm, who shook it off angrily.

Now the men were all looking at Fred. It was Mr Richards who spoke.

'Look Fred, I feel exactly like you do, but I'm going to give myself time to think about it. You could see how worked up Mr Kayser was, and he's the sort of man to carry out his threat. Give yourself time to cool down, talk it over with your uncle, and then make up your mind.'

Fred nodded. He could see the wisdom in what Mr Richards was saying, and the fury left him suddenly as it always did. He looked at the anxious faces of the other men.

'It's alright. Mr Kayser is safe for now,' he said.

It was a relief for them all to have something to laugh at, and they made their way out of the meeting room and into the sunny Saturday afternoon.

It was a few minutes after three o'clock and Fred found Annie sitting at a window seat in the Coffee Palace, a cup of coffee and a scone with jam and cream on the table in front of her.

He took the seat opposite and gave his order to the waiter, then he explained what had just happened.

'What would you do in my position Annie?' he asked her. 'I like Mr Harris and I can only imagine what he will think of me if I pull out of the play with only two weeks to go. You know Spotty's in just about every scene, and it's not an easy role.'

The waiter arrived with a pot of tea and a plate of sandwiches and Annie waited until he left before answering.

'I don't know Fred. I suppose if it affected my father's work, I would have to pull out, but if it meant giving up my teaching job, then I think I would keep my part in the play and see what happened. What would you do if you lost your position with the company? Would you go back to teaching? Go to Melbourne?'

Trust Annie to put her finger on the most practical thing. Fred was surprised how the question made him feel. It wasn't that he had bad memories of teaching, no, that wasn't it. But it would be going backwards. And after all the hours he'd put in to get this far in the mining company! It made him sick to think he could lose it all. But then having to give up the drama club and his role in the play, that made him sick too. He put his cup back on the saucer with more force than it needed.

'Why can't people just get on?' he complained to Annie, as if she might have been the cause of it all.

But Annie took no notice. She put a daub of cream on the second half of her scone, then topped it with a teaspoon of strawberry jam and took a bite.

'Acting is important to you in a way it isn't to most people, Fred. You'll have to make up your own mind. As for me, I'm glad I'm not the one who has to decide.'

Fred picked up the last sandwich, but he'd lost his appetite, and he put it back on the plate. He pushed his chair back.

'I'm going for a ride,' he told Annie. 'Then I'll sleep on it and see how things look tomorrow. Ma always says that things look better in the morning.'

'I'm sure you'll do what's right for you, Fred. You can tell me tomorrow when you come for your lesson.'

36

The next day, Sunday, 29 May 1887

But when Fred woke up the next morning the same thoughts were still chasing each other around in his head.

After church he took Mattie and Harriet to the park by the dam. An old gum tree had blown down in the big winds they'd had last month, and Fred sat on the stump that was left and watched them arranging the smaller branches against the trunk of a pepper tree.

'You sit there,' Mattie had ordered Fred, pointing to the stump. 'You have to be our lookout.'

'What am I looking out for?'

'Robbers.'

'Why?'

'They might come and steal things.'

It was their favourite game, playing miners. In the hotel, Mattie would go into the specimen room that was set up next to the saloon bar and stare at the clumps of rock, each with different streaks and specks. 'What's this one?' he'd ask. 'And this one?' Now he could point to most of the specimens and tell whoever would listen what they were.

Fred watched them climb into their shack. It was just a pile of branches stacked against the tree, but that isn't what they saw. It reminded him of when he was little – six? seven? – and how he used to climb into the pepper tree in the horse yard and pretend he was on a ship.

Isn't that what they were doing when they put on plays? Acting the part of someone else, some imaginary character? When you carried it off, the people watching got carried away too. If that's all it was, how could it become so complicated?

He should have known better than to think that Reverend Jackson might be of some help, provide guidance. What he said was so far off the mark that Fred allowed himself a grim sort of smile when he thought of the difference between what he was hoping for and reality. Reverend Jackson's sermon told them all a great deal about the sin of pride, but nothing about the nuances of obligations and loyalty.

It had been awkward after the service, the way Mr Thorne and Mr Lyle had been standing in a tight circle with the Leonards, talking in such an intense way that Fred was sure it was about the play. He couldn't go up and talk to them as he usually would, not when he hadn't made up his mind, and the fact that he didn't would probably be enough to make them suspicious. What a mess. Across the dam in the paddock beyond the platypus pool he could see Estelle grazing with the other horses by the water trough.

That was another thing he had to decide. What was he going to do with Estelle? He couldn't keep putting it off. Apart from weekends, when he took her for a long ride, she wasn't being properly exercised. There was no point training her for races that didn't happen. There was only one race a year up here, and he'd promised his mother he'd spend a week with them in Wynyard over Christmas, so he would miss his one chance.

Estelle was already losing condition. He'd spent the best part of last year turning her into a racehorse, and what was the point if all he did was ride her at weekends, and not even then when the weather was really bad? He didn't have the time to keep up the training routine. Nor, if he was honest, the inclination. It had been exciting, training her, winning that last race, being a jockey: things he'd never done before. But once the excitement had worn off, he had to face the fact that being a horse trainer didn't fit into his long-term plans. Or his short-term ones, for that matter. He could see now there was something odd about training up a racehorse the way he'd done. All the other owners had trainers and jockeys and a stable of horses. What he had done wasn't what men did, it was what a boy would do, and he was eighteen now. He'd proved he could do it, that was enough.

Mr King was right. Fred knew it at the time, but he hadn't wanted to admit it. It had been at the hotel a couple of days after the races. There were a few speeches, and the cheques were handed out to the winners. Afterwards, Mr King had come up to Fred and offered to buy Estelle. At that time, so soon after the races, selling Estelle was the last thing on Fred's mind. But the offer was good, and if he did have to part with Estelle, there was no better place for her to go. The Kings' property on Table Cape was right next to Uncle Martin's farm, and Fred had known the family all his life.

'She'll lose her form hidden away up here,' Mr King had told Fred. 'She's a fine filly and just what I need in my stables.'

Now Fred had to face the inevitable. Mr King was coming on the train on Wednesday, and he planned to take a string of horses down to the coast. He should do it; he would do it. Estelle would be well looked after and cared for, and she'd be better off on the coast, away from the mountain winters where she had to spend half the time in the stable. He could go and see her when he was back down that way.

His mind made up, Fred felt better. Of course it would be sad, but when it came to horses, you had to think about what was best for them.

On the other hand, when it came to the drama club, the thing to do was to make the right decision for himself. Whatever he did, there would be consequences, and he would have to live with them. It was his own future he had to look out for.

The bell at St James' interrupted his thoughts. Midday already.

He got up and wiped the back of his trousers then went over and pretended to knock at the open entrance to the makeshift cubby house.

'Come on. Time to eat.'

Once grace was said, Uncle James got straight to the point.

'I was talking to Dr Kennedy after church this morning,' he told Fred. 'It seems that your boss is throwing his weight around again.'

'About the opening of the new hall?'

'Yes. He's trying to get rid of Dr Kennedy too.'

'Mrs Kennedy is furious,' his aunt said.

Fred poured some more gravy on his potatoes and passed it over to his aunt.

'It's as if Mr Kayser is two different people,' Fred said.

His uncle nodded.

'Yes. It's like Ferdinand Kayser has a devil and an angel fighting over his soul. The very man who has made such a success of the mine and brought all of us together, is the same one who does his best to tear the place apart.'

They ate in silence for a minute then his aunt looked across at Fred.

'The other thing Mrs Kennedy told me is that she's going to take over a role in that play you're putting on for the opening of the new hall. Apparently Mrs St Clair has pulled out at the last minute. Her husband too.'

'And Frank Horne,' Fred said.

'You've got some starring role in it haven't you?'

'Yes. I've got one of the main parts. I play a young engineer who's in love with Miss Kirby. It's a comic role – the whole play is a bit of a farce. Melodrama anyway.'

'Is it true what Mrs Kennedy said? Mr Kayser said he'd dismiss anyone who appeared in the hall on its opening night.'

'Yes. I was at the meeting and heard it myself.'

'That makes it hard for you, Fred. What are you going to do?'

'I can't make up my mind. I've been thinking about it all morning and half the night. What would you do Aunt Jane?'

His aunt didn't answer immediately.

'I'd like to think,' she said finally, 'I'd make a stand.' Then she went on more confidently, 'If enough people did that, he'd have to see reason.'

'What about you, Uncle James?'

'For what it's worth, Fred, here's what I think. I know Mr Kayser's been very good to you, but if you do decide to take Mr Kayser's side, and I think you will, remember it's your loyalty he's buying, and this might not be the only hard choice you have to make.'

Later that evening, after he'd finished his violin practice and set his clothes out for the next morning, Fred sat in front of the fire and weighed up what he should do. Was he wasting his time here? One day he did want to make a name for himself in the theatre, but the accounting he'd learned, the money he was earning, the roles he took in the drama club, all of that was already a world away from working as a blacksmith in Wynyard.

And more than that, for the first time in his life both his parents approved of what he was doing. They'd been here, seen how successful he was, and were proud of him. Imagine if he were to turn up on their doorstep back in Wynyard, unemployed, and all because of some play he was acting in.

Even the thought of it made him sick in the stomach, and he pulled his feet off the fender and sat on the edge of the chair. Now he wondered why he thought he had a choice. It was obvious. There was no point keeping his obligation to the drama club, because if he was dismissed from his position in the company, he would be forced to leave Waratah anyway.

He knocked the bowl of his pipe against the bricks on the edge of the fireplace and put it on the mantelpiece, then he went over and sat down at the desk.

The floor was littered with screwed up paper by the time he wrote something that he could send. In the end, he made it short and to the point.

Dear Mr Harris,

Owing to circumstances beyond my control, I will no longer be able to continue in the role of Spotty in The Lancashire Lass.

Please accept my sincerest apologies.

Yours sincerely,
Frederick M Alexander.

It would have to do. Tomorrow morning, first thing, he would give it to the messenger boy and that would be that. Fred thought about what Frank said as they were walking back to the hotel the night of the fire. 'It doesn't bode well for Mr Harris.' At the time it didn't make sense, but it was all too clear to him now. And his uncle was right too. Nothing had been the same since the fire. No library, no proper reading room.

And now the one remaining thing, the most important to him, was gone too. There would be other opportunities, he told himself. It wasn't the end of the club. But as he lay in bed, waiting for sleep to come, he couldn't shake a heavy feeling of loss.

37

Five months later, Monday, 24 October 1887

After spending his whole life building and running hotels, Uncle James was making a complete change, moving the family to Melbourne, and trying his hand in the auction business. It shouldn't have been a surprise to Fred; he knew Aunt Jane wanted to be close to her mother, who lived in Camperdown, and there'd been talk of it for a few months now, but he had been too absorbed in his own affairs to take much notice. Then a month ago, Mr Lawson from the general store had bought Pearce's Hotel and given Fred notice that when his uncle left, he would have to pay the same for his room as the other guests. It had seemed to Fred a good time to try living somewhere different, and he'd taken a room in the place where his friend Arthur Willicombe boarded.

Now the family were leaving, and everybody wanted to shake Uncle James' hand. Little grey clouds were puffing out of the smokestack on the train, and the whistle had almost deafened them. Fred said a final goodbye to Aunt Jane and the children, jumped back on to the platform and joined Frank. Some men from the cricket club were still crowding around Uncle James, but when he saw the conductor raising the red flag, he took hold of the brass rail and pulled himself into the carriage, closing the door behind him.

Mattie and Harriet were leaning out the window of their compartment, waving both their hands, fingers outstretched, and Fred could hear their excited giggling over the puffing of the engine. There was a final long shrill burst from the whistle and the train slowly pulled away from the station.

'Goodbye cousin Fred,' Mattie yelled.

'Be good,' Fred called back, and waved until the train rounded the bend and was no longer in sight.

With it went the excitement of the leave-taking and it felt as if something had been sucked out of the air, leaving it stale and flat. He had rather looked forward to the change and he'd already moved into Mrs. Wilson's boarding house, thinking to save some money, and inspired by the idea of being truly independent.

'It's a lot more fun being the one to leave than the one who stays,' he said to Frank as they followed the rest of the crowd back into town.

'I daresay you'll miss having your family around, Fred. For my part, the place won't be the same without having your uncle here to get things done. Not to mention keeping people honest.'

Frank was right. Fred had got used to the way his uncle juggled so many things and never gave up trying to improve the town for everyone. But what thanks did he get?

'I know what you mean Frank, but in the end, he was tired of all the conflict it caused.'

'I daresay. But I know he was proud of what he did here. And look at all those people there to see him off. Anyway, speaking of change, how's that boarding house working out for you?'

'It's not Pearce's Hotel quality,' Fred told Frank. 'But it's comfortable enough.'

That was half true. Once you knew where the lumps were in the bed, it was possible to avoid them. The fireplace was half the size of his old one, but if you got close enough it did the job. The desk was much the same, and the wardrobe, but the window was no bigger than the ones in the cottage in Wynyard. Fred wasn't sure what was worse: the smell of a room insufficiently aired, or the smell of the mothballs intended to cover it up. Still, it was cheap. And it was an adventure of sorts, an experiment, though privately he wondered how his friend Arthur Willicombe could have stayed there for three years.

They'd covered the short distance from the station to the company offices and Fred was glad to have work to take his mind off things. Even so, he sat in front of the open ledger, seeing again

Mattie and Harriet waving both hands out the window, half obscured by billows of smoke as the train pulled into the distance. Yes, he would miss the family. But even more, he wished that he could have been on that train with them, heading to Melbourne.

Fred sighed, dipped his pen in the inkwell, pulled the top sheet off the pile of invoices and began to enter the figures in the receipt book.

38

Once the amounts were entered, the task of reconciling the books took Fred's mind off everything else, and by the time he left the office his buoyant mood had returned. Walking back to the boarding house took him past the temporary reading room and he stopped there as usual to check the newspapers. As was often the case, Arthur Willicombe was there too, and the two of them left at the same time.

The road to Mrs Wilson's took them past the Alford Hotel and Arthur suggested having a drink or two. Usually, Fred found a reason not to join him, but a solitary night with his violin had no appeal, nor did he feel like following up some leads he had of men wanting to buy insurance.

'Count me in,' he told Arthur, and followed him into the hotel.

The lounge bar at The Alford had big leather armchairs and a generous fireplace that made you feel at home, and by midnight Fred had drunk more than usual. Arthur was an easy man to talk to and Fred found himself sharing his regret that he didn't take the chance to move to Melbourne with his uncle.

'I know it will please father if I stay here and make a career with the company,' he told Arthur. 'Ma too. I'm close to home, sending back good money. But acting in those plays last year, I began to think that I could really be an actor. Or a reciter. Or both. People tell me Melbourne's the place for that.'

'So, what's keeping you here?'

'Money. I'm saving as much as I can. When I do make the move, I want to have enough so I can see for myself all the things I read about.'

'Plays?'

'Yes, the theatre. All the theatres. Every play. And not just that. Music, and art. I want to be part of that world.'

'You could work in the day and do those things at night. Surely you could get a job without too much trouble.'

'The thing is, Arthur, that's just the start. What I aim to do is to make a name for myself. I want to be the one people go to watch.' He leaned towards Arthur, as if what he was saying was a secret. 'It's father, you see. If he thinks my aim is to recite, let alone be an actor, I can only imagine what a rage that would put him in.'

'I'm used to my father ranting about my poor choices in life.'

'Fathers!' Fred said, and he tossed down the rest of his brandy and stood up. 'Time to go.'

What he didn't want to share with Arthur was his fear that if he followed his interest in the theatre, his father might use it as an excuse to get back on the drink, and how in turn that would affect his mother. His father's angry moodiness made life hard enough without the other things that came with the drink.

Arthur planted his empty beer mug on the table and followed Fred onto the street. They sauntered down the middle of the deserted road, oblivious to the misty rain that was falling.

'It's not a bad life up here,' Arthur said. 'And you seem to have made some good friends.'

'Like Frank?' Fred asked.

'I was thinking of Miss Annie Ashton.'

'Oh, Annie! She's such a serious girl. But an excellent violin teacher.' Arthur nudged him with his elbow and raised an eyebrow. 'No, it's not like that,' Fred said, catching on. 'I'm only eighteen, Arthur! But how about you? Are you a bachelor like Frank?'

Arthur said quickly, 'No, not like Frank at all. I have a fiancée in Launceston. We're only waiting for my next promotion, then we're planning to marry.'

Fred wasn't sure what he meant by 'not like Frank at all'. He was about to ask, when he recognised a heavy set, dark-suited man coming down the road towards them.

'See that man, Arthur. I'll give him one more chance to pay his road tax, otherwise his name is going on the list.'

'What list?'

'The list of men going before the court for non-payment of their road tax.'

'Is that what being a rate collector is about? I'm sure I wouldn't want to be doing it.'

Privately, Fred agreed with him, but Arthur didn't need to know that.

'The more rates I collect, the more money I get,' Fred told him.

'Are you sure this is a good time?'

'The man's not short of money. I'm doing him a favour, keeping him out of the courts. Where's the harm in that?'

Arthur still looked doubtful, but he took the road to the left that led to the boarding house and Fred continued by himself.

As he drew close to the man, Fred removed his hat and greeted him.

'Good evening Mr Braithwaite.'

Mr Braithwaite stopped in front of Fred, but he made no attempt to remove, or even touch his hat in a return greeting. He was a tall man with thick dark hair that covered most of his face, and the buttons on his jacket strained across his barrel chest.

'How dare you,' he shouted. 'Allow me to pass.'

This was not how things were meant to go! A friendly reminder was all Fred had in mind.

Fred didn't move.

'How dare I what, Mr Braithwaite? It's you who owes money.'

'I know what you're up to, you and that uncle of yours, feathering your nests with other people's money.'

'That's a lie.'

'Call me a liar, do you?' As he shouted this, Mr Braithwaite took a swing at Fred and landed a blow on the side of his head.

Fred felt a sharp pain around his ear and was knocked off balance, but he recovered quickly and launched himself at the man, throwing punches with both hands. They made barely any impact on the man's broad chest and Fred struck out harder and lower.

That was all he remembered. When he came to, he was lying on the ground. He reached out with his fingers and felt gravel and rough tarmac, then he caught the stink of night soil, and with some effort he propped himself on his elbow, then slowly stood up.

His head throbbed and he rubbed behind his right ear where he could feel a lump starting to swell. There was no sign of Mr Braithwaite or anyone else. Grateful for the dark night, the late hour and the empty street, Fred inspected himself for damage and brushed the gravel off the back of his elbows and behind his knees. There was probably stuff on his back too, and he slapped his hands over his shoulders to remove what he could.

It could have been worse, he decided. There was some comfort in the thick black clouds that cushioned the valley, and he felt steadier as he set off in the darkness for the short walk to the boarding house. Despite the pain in his head, his thoughts were clear and there was no trace of the fuzz of alcohol. Arthur Willicombe was right! This tax collecting really was a thankless job! Nothing about it was working out as he'd been told it would. The humiliation of asking for money from men reluctant to pay was degrading, and worth much less than he'd been promised.

Braithwaite and men like him were not worth lowering himself for. From here on, he vowed to himself, he would never put himself in such a position again. He would earn money on his own terms, through his own efforts and talents, never at the behest of another. It felt important, this decision, and he had a strong feeling of a significant milestone passed.

39

1888 was proving to be a quiet year. Fred had moved back into Pearce's Hotel, now called Lawson's Hotel, about a month ago, and life fell into the old routine: breakfast with Frank Horne, work, more often than not a game or two of billiards in the evening.

Arthur Willicombe had left Waratah at the beginning of January. He'd taken up a teaching position in Launceston, married his fiancée, joined the drama club there, and wrote glowingly about it to Fred. Without his company, living in the boarding house had been depressing, and when Frank told him his old room at the hotel was vacant, Fred jumped at the chance to move back. The rooms were bigger, the food was better, the people were friendly; it was the sort of place one would choose to be, whereas the boarding house had the feel of a place to stay when there was no other choice.

With no drama club, no library, no rate collection, there was plenty of time to work on his violin, and the hotel was better for that too, the rooms so much bigger and the walls thicker than at the boarding house.

Today had been a rare day without rain. Not only that, but the sky was a sharp, clear blue. Fred had worked until after seven, and when he left the office the sun was setting over the mountain, the sky was deep blue, and light rose in golden rays. The air was sharp with the promise of frost, and it felt good to be alive. He made a detour to stand on the bridge and watched the fading light, then he retraced his steps to the hotel. On the way to his room, he stopped off in the guest lounge to check for mail and smiled to himself when he saw the handwriting of Mr Robertson.

There was no one else in the guest lounge so instead of going straight up to his room, he removed the fireguard and stoked the fire, then settled back on the leather couch and opened the letter.

Hamilton Academy,
Hamilton-on-Clyde
December 15th, 1887

My dear Fred,

Thank you as always for your letter. I feel as if I could find my way about the streets of Waratah and recognise the people I meet. Mr Seagrave of course I knew quite well, and he never struck me as the tyrannical teacher you used to describe when you were a youngster. I did hear him sing once at a musical evening, and he certainly has a fine voice. It's no wonder you don't recall that, because you used to be rather dismissive of 'old peoples' concerts', and I'm happy to hear that you have now embraced music along with literature. The two are inseparable in my mind.

The violin is an ambitious instrument to choose, but knowing what a determined, hard worker you are, I have no doubt that you will master it. The Ashton family must be like a haven of sanity in the midst of the less salubrious types. It seems that Miss Ashton is a strict taskmaster, just what one needs in such an endeavour.

The business with your Mr Kayser and the drama club is a very poor affair, the club and your success with them being such a fine opportunity for you to build on your talents for recitation, not to mention a chance to make your mark on the community. I think I know how angry you must be, and what a set-back it is. (It reminds me of the day you didn't recite for the Governor!) However, if you could take some advice from a friend, here's something I've learned about life. It's not what goes wrong that matters, it's what you do about it.

Have you considered starting a Shakespeare Club? I'm mentioning that because the club I started here at the Academy has been a splendid success. It has been a great comfort to me, and I continue to find there is always hope and wisdom to be found in exploring Shakespeare's works. I should also mention that the boys in the club are a fine group of young men, though none have the single-minded enthusiasm or the power of delivery to equal yours.

I'm sorry to report that Emma has still not recovered fully from the sad loss of our son. She has gone back to stay with her family in Stirling, where the company of her mother and her sisters should help her recovery. I will have to make the best of the company here at the school and hope that the winter passes without incident. My old problem has been back with me since my return to Scotland and I think with great fondness of the sunny days in Wynyard.

Yours affectionately,
Robert Robertson

P.S. There has been a delay in posting this letter, in which time I further considered your situation. Here is another suggestion. I recently came across a published (1885) anthology of recital pieces and have been using it with success. It's called Brandram's Speaker. Samuel Brandram himself is a popular performer, so he knows something about what works with an audience. I'm sure it should be available from that excellent bookshop in Launceston. Was it Birches? The collection is replete with material that has literary worth as well as entertainment value, and as you know, great literature feeds our moral and intellectual beings. RR

A Shakespeare Club? No, that would never take off in Waratah. Fred knew that for certain. In his two years in Waratah, there had not been a single production of Shakespeare, and look how they'd reacted when he suggested it to the drama club!

Fred re-read the postscript more carefully and smiled to himself. It must be Walch Bros. and Birchalls that Mr Robertson meant. Yes, he would write to them tonight. To have some new pieces would be stimulating, and Mr Robertson wouldn't recommend something that was second rate. That last sentence stirred an excitement that Fred hadn't been feeling since the collapse of the drama club and Mr Harris' forced resignation. *'Great literature feeds our moral and intellectual beings.'* It was why he had wanted the drama club to perform Shakespeare; to use elevated material that would instruct as well as entertain. It was what he aspired to, and all he was doing here in Waratah was marking time until he could make it happen.

Fred folded the letter and put it back in the envelope. He sat staring at the fire, remembering those evenings with Mr Robertson, the way he made Shakespeare come alive like a special, different world. Learning all those monologues. What a time that was.

The door opened and Frank Horne came in carrying a mug of beer in one hand and a telegram in the other.

'I thought I might find you here,' he said and sat down in the chair next to Fred. 'This is for you – the telegram boy and I arrived at the same time.' He handed Fred a folded piece of yellow paper. 'I hope it's not bad news.'

Fred took the telegram. He read it, then read it again. How could it possibly be true? In one hand Fred held the letter from his friend, in the other the telegram. It was too much to take in. Wordlessly, Fred showed the telegram to Frank.

I regret to inform you that my husband died on March 10th after a short illness. I know how close you were, and that we share the same sadness of his loss. Emma Robertson

'I was just reading a letter from him. It arrived today.'

Fred held the letter up, as if that might prove the telegram wrong. But the letter had been written months ago, he knew that. Still, it was so odd, so coincidental, that he might be reading one and receive the other.

'Was he ill?' Frank asked him.

Fred looked back over the letter. 'There's a bit here where he says his old problem is back. He was more worried about Mrs Robertson.'

'His old problem?'

'It was a pulmonary condition. He only got it in winter when it rained. He said the climate in Wynyard had made a new man of him.' He looked at Frank, startled by his own confusion. 'I can't believe I'll never hear from him again.'

'I'm not very good with words for this sort of thing Fred. It seems to me that whatever one says is never enough.'

'That's how I feel. I remember when Horrie died, and my auntie told us he'd gone to a better place. It just made me angry. To think I was complaining to Mr Robertson about the drama club! Now that seems such a small thing.'

'What did he say about it.'

Fred found the place in the letter. 'He said it's not what goes wrong that matters, it's what you do about it.'

'Well there you are, Fred. That's probably the best advice that anyone could give you. I'm sure he was a very special person, your Mr Robertson.'

Fred's voice was choked off by a pain in his throat and he could only nod in agreement.

40

Over a year later, Wednesday, 8 May 1889

There had been an early snowfall in Waratah and the hotel breakfast room was cold. The logs in the fireplace were burning well enough, but from where he was sitting, Fred was getting none of the heat. A pair of visiting clergymen had been given his usual table by the side of the fire, and Fred had no choice but to take a seat by himself at the only table left. He poured a second cup of tea; at least that was hot.

Nothing had been the same since Frank Horne had left. Things that Fred had taken for granted – like always having the best table –didn't happen anymore. Frank had been as much a part of Waratah as the mountain and the mining works, and it was only now he was gone that Fred realised just how much Frank had done for him. Not only that. Frank had a way of making things happen, of turning them into fun, and life was rather dull without him.

Fred drank down the rest of his tea, took his hat and coat off the stand, and made his way to the office. The snow had turned to slush but the clouds had lifted, and the rain had stopped. It was still early, and Fred took his time, avoiding the worst of the puddles. The one good thing about Frank Horne's sudden departure, he thought, was work. Fred wasn't officially the chief accountant. Not yet. But he was acting in that position, working hard to show Mr Kayser there was no need to look outside the office for a replacement. He had his own office, Frank's old office, and a new challenge.

He let himself into the office and sat at the desk. Last night he'd worked late and the things to be done were neatly arranged in order of importance. The junior clerk had lit the kerosene heater and a shaft of sunlight lit up the leather-bound company reports on the shelves. Fred leaned back, his hands behind his head. Not bad, he thought. Not bad for a twenty-year-old. All he had to do was keep on the good side of Mr Kayser.

There was a knock on the door.

'Enter,' Fred called out.

It was Mr Kayser's clerk. He stood just inside the door, one hand on the knob.

'The boss wants to see you,' he announced.

'Now?'

'Yes. "Tell Mr Alexander I need to see him straight away" is what he said.'

'Let's not keep him waiting then.' Fred followed the boy the short distance to Mr Kayser's office.

'Ah. Mr Alexander. Come in, come in. Take a seat.'

Fred did so and Mr Kayser handed him a telegram. 'Read that.'

Orpheus Players resp. request tour of mine etc. afternoon Wednesday May 8th. Arriving train on same. Group of 30. Mr G Hodge, Manager

'Look at the date.'

'It was sent on Monday.'

'Precisely. Two days ago, and it's only now that the wretched clerk has seen fit to show it to me.' There was nothing to say to that and Fred waited until Mr Kayser continued. 'I would do it myself, but I have a Board meeting in Launceston, so I leave it with you.'

Fred knew who the Orpheus Players were — a bunch of amateur musicians from Hobart who, according to Annie, were sure to be worth seeing. They'd bought tickets for one of the nights. Thursday? Yes, that was it. Thursday. The prospect of taking such a large group for a tour of the mine wasn't one he looked forward to, but his job was to keep Mr Kayser happy.

'Consider it done.'

'They're just musicians, so the short tour should do it.'

Mr Kayser handed Fred the telegram then waved his hand in a gesture of dismissal and went back to reading the financial statements Fred had stayed late to complete. Not a word of thanks, but that was Mr Kayser.

Back at his desk, Fred opened the payroll ledger. The salaries had to be done by Friday and now this! He couldn't concentrate and pushed them aside.

It was all very vague. He picked up the telegram. No mention of where they'd be staying. Had anyone replied? No, Fred decided. The only thing to do was to meet them at the station.

Fred thought about the last time he'd done the tour of the mine. He'd helped Frank Horne with the Rignold Theatre group, and that's when he'd met Mr James Cathcart. If only it was another theatre group! A few amateur musicians weren't likely to be of much use to him.

The theatre group had been here a week or so before Frank left, a couple of months ago now. He and Frank had picked the group up at the Bischoff Hotel. Fred had known that Mr James Cathcart would be in the party, and he recognised the famous actor immediately from a sketch he'd seen in *Punch*. Older than the others, Cathcart carried himself as if he was on the stage, a little larger than life. He was quite tall and very upright, wearing a jacket and vest that was fashionable before Fred was born, although his brown hair was swept back in the latest style.

Once he found out about Fred's love of Shakespeare Mr Cathcart claimed Fred as his personal escort. They had trailed along behind the others and Fred listened to Mr Cathcart's stories about playing with the Charles Keane Company in England. He'd even played for Queen Victoria herself! It fired Fred with new determination. That evening the performance was the best Fred had ever seen, James Cathcart a magnetic presence on the stage, every gesture deliberate and apt, his voice rich and clear.

When the play finished Fred was the last to stop applauding, and when the curtain came down for the last time he did as Mr Cathcart had suggested and went backstage to find him. The smell of the grease paint, the elation of the actors; it all made Fred acutely aware of where he felt he belonged. The dressing room was a confusion of actors removing make up and changing out of costumes, but Mr Cathcart saw him at the door and came over.

'How did you like that?' Mr Cathcart asked him.

'Splendid,' Fred told him. 'Better than anything I've seen.'

'Well in that case my boy, it's time to get yourself over to Melbourne to see some real theatre. The Shakespearean season starts in June at the Bijou Theatre and runs through winter.'

'What roles do you play?'

'All of them!' Mr Cathcart stepped aside to make room for a woman carrying a huge bunch of waratahs, then he put an arm over Fred's shoulder and moved him away from the door. 'Anyway, I must get out of this.' He held his arms to the side to show off the ill-fitting checked suit he'd worn in the last act, then patted Fred on the shoulder. 'When you decide to make the move, you must look me up. Wait here.'

Fred watched him go back into the room and search through the pockets of his jacket that was hanging over the back of a chair, then he came back and handed Fred his calling card.

'When I'm not at the Bijou, this is where I reside. If I'm not too busy, I can give you some lessons. Not elocution, mind you. Strictly interpretation and voice production.'

★

Three days later, Frank Horne had taken Fred by surprise. 'I'm handing in my resignation today,' he'd told Fred at breakfast. 'If I stay here, I'll be forced to pay part of that money still owing on the new hall. Money that had nothing to do with me, but Mr Kayser refuses to help. After all I've done for him, this is how he treats me.'

Fred had followed the litigation the builder had taken against the old Mechanics' Institute committee, and right until the court hearing, he, like Frank and the others who had been on the committee, had been sure that Mr Kayser and the Mt Bischoff Tin Mining Company would bear the cost. But Mr Kayser employed his own counsel to make sure that didn't happen, and Frank handed in his notice. Too disgusted to stay a minute longer than he had to, he took the train to Burnie the very next day, leaving a vacuum in the mining town that no one could fill.

Fred sighed and put the telegram to one side. He pulled his chair closer to the desk and dipped his pen in the ink then looked at the clock. There might be enough time to get the salaries done if he worked through lunch.

★

As it turned out, Fred wasn't the only one at the station to meet the Orpheus Players. Standing in a patch of sun at the end of the platform were Bella and her mother. Of course! Annie had mentioned that Bella, Mrs Arnold now, would be here for the Easter holiday.

Fred made his way through the scattering of people waiting to meet the train and Bella spotted him and waved.

'Mr Alexander. You look surprised to see me,' she said as he came up to them.

'Bella dear,' Mrs Ashton said.

'Fred doesn't mind me, do you Fred?'

It was true. Fred liked the way Bella was so outspoken.

'Mrs Arnold, how do you do. Annie did mention you were to pay us a visit, but it slipped my mind.'

'Fred is always so busy at work,' Mrs Ashton told Bella, 'especially now dear Frank Horne has left.'

'Did I tell you mother? I ran into Mr Horne in Hobart. He won first prize at the costume ball, dressed as a Valkyrie.'

'That would be Frank,' Fred said. 'How was he?'

'We didn't speak for long, but he said he has a job with some accountants in Campbelltown. He was in Hobart for the football.'

'And what brings you to the station Fred? 'Mrs Ashton asked.

'Work.' Fred told them, and he explained about the Orpheus Players and how he was going to show them over the mine.

'That's why we're here too,' Bella exclaimed. 'To meet my friends the Youngs. Mr Young works with my husband.'

'Are they with the players?'

'Yes. At least Mr Young is. Did you know they're all amateurs?'

'That's why we're giving them a reception tonight,' Mrs Ashton told Fred. 'If they're good enough to come all the way to

Waratah to entertain us in their holidays, the least we can do is make them welcome.'

What reception, Fred wondered. He and Annie had booked seats for tomorrow night's performance, but that was all.

'Didn't Annie tell you?' Bella asked him.

'How could she Bella?' Mrs Ashton scolded. 'We only knew ourselves last night.'

'How silly of me,' Bella laughed. 'It was my idea, but you agree that it's the proper thing to do, don't you mother?'

'We wanted to invite Bella's friends,' Mrs Ashton explained to Fred,' but it would have been awkward inviting just the two of them, so we're giving a reception for the whole group.'

'Wait until you meet Mr and Mrs Young, Fred. Mr Young is just the most interesting person. His father's from Belgium and his mother's English but he grew up in Mauritius. Imagine that!'

'And Mrs Young?' Fred asked.

'She's lovely too. Always the life of the party. I think you'll have a lot in common. She told me she wants to be an actress.'

'Do you mean a professional actress?'

'Yes. She's very serious about it.'

They were interrupted by the loud shrilling of the steam whistle and the train puffed and creaked its way to a halt at the station. From the front carriage an energetic man jumped onto the platform and started giving a hand to the other passengers. Many of them had odd-shaped cases that they handed to the man, before lowering themselves onto the platform. The Orpheus Players, obviously, and Fred guessed the man was Mr Hodge of the telegram.

Fred was about to go over and introduce himself when Bella exclaimed 'There they are' and pointed to a couple who were in the process of alighting from the train.

A handsome, clean-shaven man in a well-cut suit had swung himself on to the platform. He was reaching up with one hand to assist a pretty woman, his wife no doubt, and with the other hand made a sweeping gesture and said something that made Mr Hodge laugh.

'Come on,' Bella said. Fred offered Mrs Ashton his arm and they followed Bella over to where the Youngs were now standing side by side, watching them approach.

Up close, Fred saw that Mrs Young was a very handsome woman. Her hair was dark and thick, and some curls had escaped from under her hat. Along with her lively dark eyes, they gave her a restless sort of look. Mr Young was quite the opposite; he had a calm, measured manner that reminded Fred of Mr Robertson.

The energetic man was indeed Mr Hodge. Mr Young introduced them, and then put a hand over Mr Hodge's shoulders.

'Without Mr Hodge we'd be nothing but an excited bunch of musicians,' he said. 'Look at us.' Mr Young waved hand to indicate the chattering groups who filled the platform and were laughing and exclaiming to one another.

Mr Hodge looked pleased. He clapped his hands and the noise gradually died down.

'This is Mr Alexander,' he told them. Fred made a slight bow. 'He will show us to our hotel and then take those who are interested on a tour of the mine and its workings. All this,' Mr Hodge pointed to the untidy rows of luggage and instruments, 'will be taken care of. Those who are interested in the tour, find your rooms, and then assemble at the entrance to the hotel where Mr Alexander will be waiting for you.'

'Looks like I'm needed,' Fred said to Mrs Ashton and Bella. 'I'll see you tonight at the reception,'

But the Youngs stuck close to Fred, and the three of them pushed their way through the crowd to the far side of the platform.

Fred turned to face the group. 'This way,' he said, and rest of the players fell in behind them, straggling along the road. To the Youngs he pointed out the waterfall that turned the giant waterwheels, the rows of battery sheds, the way the land fell away into the gorge, and the familiar Waratah landmarks took on a significance for him that they'd not had before.

★

At the reception that night, Annie played a minuet by Bach and Bella accompanied her on the piano, Annie frowning with concentration, Bella playing as if the notes were her plaything. The visitors' applause was warm and sincere, and Annie caught Fred's eye and smiled. Then a few voices called out for Mr Young to do a humourous piece for them. But instead of obliging, he said he'd done enough for one night and he would rather hear some more of the local talent.

'Come on Fred, give us one of your recitations,' someone called out and others joined in. Always happy to oblige, and half expecting to be asked, Fred decided to give them a new ballad he'd learned: *Kissing Cup's Race*. Encouraged by the laughs he got, he entered into the character of the old jockey so completely it felt as if he really was Bob Doon.

When he finished reciting, there was a spontaneous burst of applause, and Mr Young came up to him and shook his hand.

'Nicely done, Mr Alexander. I can see that your talent is wasted here.'

Mrs Young had come over with her husband and she gave Fred an admiring look, so direct that he had to look away.

'Yes,' she said, 'my husband is right. You must come to Hobart.'

It was only then that Fred noticed Annie. She was standing to one side, waiting for the conversation with the Youngs to finish. Mr Young saw her too, and he took a step back to include her.

'Well played, Miss Ashton. You have a fine ear for the violin.'

Annie considered his compliment with her usual gravity before she thanked him. It seemed that she might say something to Fred, but then she thought better of it and he watched her go over to where Bella was collecting her music from the piano. For one night, why couldn't Annie be a bit less serious?

Soon after, the party broke up and Fred led the group of Orpheus Players through the dark back streets, back to the hotel. It felt natural that the Youngs walked with him, one on either side, chatting to him as if they were old friends. It was fun, and once back in the hotel, Fred was disappointed when Mr Young turned down his offer of a night cap by the fire in the guest lounge.

'Sorry, we have to get our beauty sleep, don't we Edith?' Mr Young said to his wife.

Fred thought she would have preferred to stay, but she thanked him, then followed her husband up the stairs to their room.

41

The following day, Thursday, 9 May 1889

The next morning Fred was woken by heavy rain driving against the window. It kept up all day, the sort of rain Waratah was notorious for, that filled the dams and the watercourse for the mine but made life a misery for people. It was hard to imagine that the Orpheus Club would go ahead with tonight's performance, and when he got back to the hotel after work, a message was waiting for him from Annie:

Dear Fred, I hear tonight's concert is cancelled, and quite right too. The rain just won't stop, and the roads around our place are so muddy that I scarcely made it back from school. Annie.

Fred had taken advantage of a break in the weather and left work earlier than usual, so there was a good two hours before tea. The rain hadn't stopped for more than a few minutes, and now it was coming down heavier than before, making the room feel cold, despite the fire that Emily had set for him. Things had been quiet downstairs, only a couple of the older members of the Orpheus Club reading newspapers in the guest lounge.

He wasn't in the mood to work on the insurance documents that were waiting to be finalised, but there was that new violin piece that Annie had given him. It needed a lot more work if he was to play it for her parents next Sunday. They had invited him to an informal 'at home' and that gave him six days to practise. To his ears, it didn't sound too bad, but last Sunday, when he'd played the first movement for Annie, it was obvious that she thought there was a lot of work to do. She talked a lot about tuning and getting the timing right. 'It's a gavotte,' she kept reminding him.

Fred played it through a couple of times, but he was still struggling with the timing when there was a knock on the door.

'Come in!' Fred stopped playing, the violin hanging loosely in one hand, the bow in the other. With the exertion of playing, Fred had taken off his jacket and rolled up his sleeves. His shirt had come loose and was untucked in places, and expecting to see John with a load of wood, he didn't trouble to tuck it in.

But it wasn't John, it was Mr Young, who took a step back when he saw Fred.

'I'm sorry. It looks like I've interrupted your practice.'

Fred put the violin and bow in the case on the bed.

'Not at all. Come in. It's as cold as the grave in that corridor.'

Taking care to close the door behind him, Mr Young looked around for a moment, then gestured towards the violin. 'You play as well as recite?'

Fred looked at the instrument sitting in its nest of purple velvet. In the presence of a musician as accomplished as Robert Young was reputed to be, he thought it best to be honest.

'A little. I'm still learning.' He pointed at the violin. 'I don't seem to be making much headway.'

Robert took two graceful strides and stood looking down at the violin.

'May I?'

'Be my guest.' Fred watched as Robert picked up the violin with easy familiarity, tucked it under his chin and then smiled at Fred and with a flourish took the bow in his right hand.

With musical embellishments he played a familiar rhyme, making up his own words as he went along.

'Twinkle, twinkle, little star, What's up here in Waratah?

Robert lifted his eyebrows theatrically, his chin sunk into the violin, and looked at Fred with laughing eyes. 'Tin mines and a German tsar, Let's drown our sorrows in the bar.'

He smiled at Fred as he put the violin and the bow back in the case, then walked over and stood to one side of the fire, an elbow resting on the mantelpiece. 'Poor Mr Kayser. I'm sure I'm not the only one to make the Kaiser/Kayser connection.'

'No. And he does have his own tsardom here. But don't let him hear your jokes – he doesn't appreciate the humour.'

Fred took a couple of pieces of yellow gum out of the wood-basket and added them to the fire. Flames danced and shot out tiny sparks as he gave it a good stir with the poker. The room was ill-equipped for visitors, and there was just the one armchair, placed squarely in front of the fireplace. Fred moved it to one side and stood facing Mr Young, waiting to hear what the reason might be for this visit.

'I was warned,' Mr Young said. 'But luckily only his wife and daughters were there and they came and thanked us personally.'

'It seems that I'm going to miss your show altogether. I'm told tonight's performance has been cancelled due to the weather.'

'Well, I'm afraid whoever told you that is mistaken.'

'It's what usually happens here. The road between Main Street and the Athenaeum is tarred, so those of us who live on Main Street are less affected. But most people live in the streets further back or across the gorge, and the roads aren't paved. The mud gets so bad you could sink up to your knees in it.'

'I see. Well, we'll just have to make the best of it. It's a beast of a night to be out. Does this happen often?'

'It's not uncommon,' Fred admitted. 'Concerts quite often have to be cancelled. That would be why my friend assumed you wouldn't be performing.'

'No offence intended, but I don't think I could endure this climate for more than a brief visit.'

Fred could see what he meant. If it wasn't raining, it was snowing and they were lucky to get a week of fine days in a year. But it was only weather. He shrugged.

'You get used to it. I'm glad you haven't cancelled. I'll certainly be there.' Fred pointed to the bed. 'Does a violin form part of your act?'

'Heavens no! I loved the violin when I was a child, then when I found the piano, I forgot all about it. I play and sing and make people laugh. Try to, at least.'

'Can I assist you with anything, Mr Young?'

'Oh, call me Robert please. I'm sorry, I should have said. I came to ask a favour. It occurred to Did...' He must have noticed Fred's confusion because he went on 'Sorry. That's Edith, Mrs Young. You'll find I have a bad habit of shortening people's names.' Robert laughed in a way that suggested that it really wasn't such a bad habit. He laughed a lot, Fred had noticed, and it was impossible not to be drawn in by his good humour, to feel that they might become friends. In fact, it felt as if they already were. 'Anyway,' Robert continued, 'Did thought that you might be able to help her rehearse some lines she's learning for an audition. But maybe you're too busy...' Robert looked at the violin, his head to one side, smiling.

'No. Of course. I'd be happy to help.' Fred felt his cheeks flush, and he leaned forward and stirred the fire. Robert watched Fred hang the poker back on the brass stand, then he held out his hand.

'That's settled then. We've been given the use of the music room downstairs. Shall we say in ten minutes?'

They shook hands and Fred walked with him to the door. He watched Robert disappear along the dark hallway then closed the door and went over to pack away his violin, humming to himself. He reached up to put the violin back on the top shelf of the wardrobe and as he did so, he caught a glimpse of himself in the mirror. What must Robert Young have thought of him? He rolled down his sleeves and started to tuck his shirt in, then thought better of it and took a clean shirt from the cupboard and changed into it. Next he re-buttoned his vest and put on the jacket he'd picked up from the tailors last week. Much better. He used his hands to tidy his hair, then he adjusted the fireguard and let himself out of the room.

★

In the music room an upright piano took up most of the side wall, a safe distance from the logs burning in the fireplace opposite. Robert was playing something lively and Edith was leaning against the end of the piano watching him, her head resting on her elbows. She waved to Fred when she saw him at the door and came to meet him. Robert kept playing, but he glanced over his shoulder at Fred and grinned, his head to one side, not missing a note, at least not that Fred could detect, then he struck some dramatic chords, stood up, closed the lid of the piano and joined Edith.

'I'm tinkering with a new song for tonight. The weather should be a safe enough subject to have a laugh about. What do you think?'

'Perfectly safe.' Fred assured him. 'That's if you get anyone turning up to listen.'

'But you'll be there, won't you?' Edith asked him.

'Try to stop me! Are you performing?'

'No. The Orpheus Club is men only. I'm rehearsing for an audition that I have when we get back to Hobart. This is a big chance for me to get a leading role and Bobba thought you could give me some coaching.'

Before Fred could answer, Robert interrupted.

'Exactly. I see this is going to be thirsty work. Why don't I fetch us some drinks from the bar and let you two get started. What do you think my chances are of purchasing a bottle of champagne?'

'Reasonably good,' Fred told him. 'It's one of the things about Waratah that might surprise you.'

'Wish me luck then,' and Robert was gone.

Apart from the piano, the music room was sparsely furnished, except for some chairs lined up against the back wall, the type that could be arranged for a meeting, or a performance. Fred wasn't sure what Edith had in mind, and for a moment it felt awkward, but Edith turned to him with an easy smile.

'It's very good of you to do this for me, Mr Alexander.'

'My pleasure Mrs Young. An audition I understand.'

'Oh, Mrs Young sounds so formal. Edith will do. And yes, an audition for the Hobart Repertory Company. It would be a big chance for me.'

'Then you must call me Fred. Is there a particular role you're trying out for?'

'I'm auditioning for Mrs Teazle in *The School for Scandal.*' Edith hurried across to the piano and picked up a bulky manuscript that had been lying on the top of it. She waved it in the air. 'Look, I have the script for the whole play.' Then she sat down on the piano stool and patted the space next to her.

The stool was designed to seat two people close to each other: a teacher and a student, or two pianists playing a duet. The legs were elegantly curved and the top was upholstered in brocade. To Fred it looked rather unsuitable for rehearsing lines, but he went over and sat next to her.

She handed him the manuscript. 'Act 2, scene 1, she said. 'It's the quarrel scene. First I need to check my lines, then I thought you could help me with interpretation.'

Fred looked at the title page: *The School for Scandal.* There'd been some talk about doing a production in the early days of the dramatic society, but it hadn't come to anything. Sheridan, he remembered. A comedy. He quickly leafed through the pages and found the scene.

'Ready when you are,' he told her.

'I know most of it, but you might have to help me out.' Edith stood up and walked over to the fireplace, then she turned and stood in front of it, her hands behind her back. 'Sir Peter, you may scold or smile according to your humour...' she began. After the first couple of runs she was more or less word perfect and she started to add movements to her part, but they were to Fred's eyes too forced, and he stood up and showed her his own ideas about timing and expression, things he'd learned from his time with the drama club; ways to get laughs from the audience.

When Robert came into the room carrying champagne in an ice bucket in one hand, and three glasses in the other, Fred was facing Edith, the script in one hand, the other arm stretched out in a gesture of comic despair. 'What have I not done for you?' he was asking, improvising from the script, 'I have made you my wife.'

'Bravo,' Robert told them, walking past. 'Don't let me interrupt.' He put the ice bucket and the glasses on top of the piano and went back to where Edith and Fred stood waiting for him.

'We've done enough,' Edith told him. ' But I'll show you how much better I am.'

Edith went back over some of the lines, while Robert looked on, and Fred put the script back on the top of the piano and sat on the stool, watching.

With one of her quick movements, Edith suddenly was on the stool next to him.

'Thank you, Mr Fred Alexander,' she said, and put an arm around his shoulders and gave him a hug. Fred was conscious of a softness against his arm and the feel of her hair against the side of his face, and for a moment he leaned his head against hers. Then she dropped her arm and leaned back against the closed lid of the piano. 'You were right, Bobba, Fred has helped, just like you said he would.'

★

Later that night, after the Orpheus Club's performance – a triumph despite there being just twenty-two members in the audience and rain that battered on the roof so hard that at times it drowned out voices – and after the impromptu party in the guests' lounge, Fred stood at the window in his room, watching the rain swirl around the lights in the battery sheds.

When he first started working in Waratah, the power of all that machinery had excited him. He remembered feeling as if he were part of a futuristic world where nothing ever stopped, and he was proud of being part of the team that kept the machines running, indirect though his role was. At dusk he would watch the electric lights come on in the sheds as if it was a theatrical display.

Now he was seeing these familiar things through different eyes. It was something that Robert Young had said. Fred had walked back with him after the performance, and they'd stopped on the road in front of the hotel to watch the tramcars with their load of rocks taken from the mountain. The rain had momentarily stopped, and in the quiet dark street the noise of the machines was like an assault, or at least Fred was conscious that it must seem like that to Robert.

'Dehumanising, don't you think?' Robert mused. 'You could get scooped up, carried along and spat out, and no one would notice.'

Wasn't that what had happened to Frank Horne?

He pulled the drapes across the window and went over to check the fireplace. What a night. He didn't feel like the same person he'd been this morning. For a year now, even longer, he'd been waiting for the right time to leave Waratah, to take the necessary steps towards earning his living on the stage. Reciting, acting, maybe both. He could decide later. Twice he'd told Mr Kayser he planned to leave, and each time he'd been persuaded to stay.

But tonight there was no room for doubt. Now was the right time to leave. Tomorrow if he could.

He went across to the desk, took his passbook from the top drawer and opened it to the last entry. £489. Not that he needed to check. The money he was owed for wages and his last insurance sale would bring it up to £495. Call it £500. Enough to live on for months, enough to see every play, hear every concert, sample every indulgence that Melbourne had to offer.

This time he would put his resignation in writing. That way Mr Kayser would simply have to accept the fact that he was leaving. He put the passbook back in the drawer and pulled out a piece of paper from the slot at the back of the desk. He wrote quickly, the words forming themselves: *'To: Mr H.W.F. Kayser esq. I hereby give one week's notice of my resignation from the Mount Bischoff Tin Mining Company.'* Then he signed it and left it to dry.

As he changed into his nightshirt and hung his suit in the wardrobe he glanced over at the letter and imagined handing it to Mr Kayser. Or he could add it to the mail bag. No, better to do it in person. Whatever Mr Kayser said, no matter how he shouted, Fred knew he was doing the right thing for himself. If he were to pursue his ambition to perform, then a break had to be made from Waratah, and there would be no better time than now.

Lying in bed, waiting for sleep, he went back over the evening. Half asleep, he thought of the way Edith had leaned into him, the softness, and the feeling of her head against his.

42

A couple of weeks later, Friday, 31 May 1889

It was a perfect day for sailing. The sun turned the water to a shimmer of light and Fred leaned over the railing of *The Pateena* and waved until the wharf and the people on it were swallowed by distance. Only then did he turn away and take the companionway down to his cabin.

His mother, Agnes and Amy had come to see him off. Albert had already left for Kalgoorlie, Richard stayed home to help look after May, and Arthur as usual was working with his father. Fred couldn't imagine his father coming to see him off, and it wasn't only that he was busy. When Fred told him of his Melbourne plans, there had been a scene. 'Nothing's ever good enough for you,' his father had shouted. 'The trouble with you is you think you're better than everyone else. One good thing about Melbourne is you might learn that you're nobody special. Don't expect to come back looking for a roof over your head if things don't work out.' Fred had shouted something back then stormed out of the house. No, it was just as Fred had feared, even worse; his father could see nothing but flippancy and moral decay in the move to Melbourne.

Fred opened his trunk and took out *The Collected Works of Shakespeare*. From inside the front of the bulky volume, he took out a cutting from a newspaper. Carefully, he unfolded it and spread it on his knees, then put the book on the bunk next to where he was sitting.

A man in evening dress was taking a bow to an applauding audience that filled the tiers and galleries of a London theatre. Fred wanted to be that man, and he sat looking at the picture, wondering how he would make it happen, what he would need to do. First he would contact Mr James Cathcart, he decided, take some lessons, do some performances, and start to get noticed. Mr Cathcart would have contacts, lots of them, so it shouldn't take long. And he'd find a drama club to join as well and get noticed that way. But before all of that, he would do as Robert Young suggested and immerse himself in the world of the arts: theatre, galleries, music. See everything that Melbourne had to offer. He put the cutting back into the book and sat gazing out the porthole.

His mother had looked so small, standing on the dock and waving her handkerchief. It wasn't only his own ambition he had to think of. He had to do it for her, and for Mr Robertson too. That last day in Wynyard, he'd roamed all over the Cape, visiting his Uncle Martin, and his favourite places. All of them reminded him of Mr Robertson. When he got back to the house, his mother was in the kitchen, mixing a cake in a bowl.

'I ran into Mrs Harris and we were talking about Mr Robertson,' Fred told her. 'I feel so close to him when I'm back here.'

His mother put the spoon down and gave him her full attention.

'He was a fine man, Mr Robertson,' she said. 'We were lucky that God gave us that time with him.'

Fred wished that God had kept a closer eye on Mr Robertson, but he kept that thought to himself.

'I know I can be a success in Melbourne, Ma. Just wait and see.'

'I believe you. No matter what your father says, you've made the right choice, and don't worry about me. You could never achieve the things you're meant to do if you stayed in Waratah. You're special Frederick. Never forget that.'

His mother gave Fred a hug, then picked up the wooden spoon and beat fiercely at the gooey mixture.

Fred turned back to the bunk and picked up the volume of Shakespeare's plays. He opened it at random, closed his eyes, and let his finger fall on the page. It was another thing he used to do with Mr Robertson, and it had become a habit. He looked down to see where his finger had landed and laughed out loud.

There is a tide in the affairs of men,
Which taken at the flood,
leads on to fortune.

'I can do it,' he said to the empty cabin. 'I will make it happen.'

Part 3

Melbourne

1889 to 1894

43

Three months later, Monday, 9 September 1889

Fred leaned against the railing of the gallery in the Melbourne Exhibition Building. On one side of him was Robert Young, elegantly dressed as Brutus in a long white toga. On his other side was Edith, unmistakably Ophelia, with a little wreath of fresh daisies on her dark hair and a diaphanous gown that followed her curves and showed off her soft white shoulders. The crowd on the gallery pressed around them and Fred could feel the warmth from her arm.

Below him, from the four corners of the great ballroom, costumed men, singing in unison, filled the hall with the sounds of a rousing German song. The occasion was the Bal Masque, organised by the German Gymnastics Club. The choice of entertainment was rather puzzling. Why were the men dressed as miners? Why were they pulling a coal cart? Robert had said something vague about supporting a cause, but it didn't explain why it might be the Gippsland miners. It reminded Fred of Waratah and the little carriages loaded with ore that ran night and day past his hotel room. That seemed a long time ago, more like three years than three months, and Waratah a distant, rather curious sort of place, impossible to describe to Melburnians.

In Waratah, the massive mining works had accustomed him to things being done on a grand scale, but the loftiness of this building, the extravagance of the architecture, was grandeur of a different order. He gazed up at the soaring vaults of the richly decorated ceilings of the Exhibition ballroom. The vast space, the huge crowd of people, all like himself in fancy costumes, made him feel important, though he was just one in a crowd of hundreds.

He knew he looked smart in the red hunting costume he'd hired for the occasion. The black velvet trim on the lapels, the red trim on the knee-length boots, the riding breeches, they were all a cut above the ordinary. 'The Duke of Westminster' was his explanation when people asked who he was dressed as. Racing aficionados all knew to whom he referred; the duke's horses had won the famous English derby not once, but three times, and his horse Ormonde was argued to be the greatest thoroughbred of all time. Fred had an ambition that one day he would be there to watch the derby, but that thought he didn't share with anyone, not even Robert and Edith.

The pageant below them finished and the three of them followed the crowd down the ornate staircase to the ballroom, where the band was tuning up for a waltz.

Edith reached her hand out to Fred.

'Hurry Fred. I don't want to miss the waltz. They're about to start.'

Fred hesitated before taking her hand, and caught Robert's eye, who winked and put an arm around each of their shoulders.

'You two have fun. I'm going to find my friends from the gymnasium. If I know them, they won't be far from the Hofbrau beer stand.'

Robert disappeared into the crowd and Fred and Edith found a place on the dance floor. Just in time, because the band launched into a waltz, and they began circling the ballroom. The space was enormous, so was the crowd, and it was easy to chat as they shuffled around the dance floor. Fred was out of practice, and when they started off, he narrowly missed stamping on Edith's foot.

'I haven't been to a dance since last year in Waratah,' he told Edith, 'but I'll get the hang of it in a minute.'

'Do you miss Waratah?' she asked him. 'Your friends?'

'I haven't had time. I only told you and Robert half of what I've been doing here.'

'You can't imagine how envious I am. All those plays! But what about acting? Have you found a good theatre company yet.?

Or a teacher? There was someone you met in Waratah – a Mr Cat-something.'

'Cathcart. James Cathcart. No, but he wrote to me. Too busy, he said, but he'll take me on later. Experience on the stage is what you need, he told me. Any stage. I'm considering the Richmond Dramatic Society.'

Fred pulled her closer and steered them in a double turn to avoid a couple who weren't watching where they were going.

Edith laughed and through the soft material of her dress, Fred felt her pulse quicken.

'Lately,' he told her, 'I've been thinking more about solo recitation. A one man show, that sort of thing.'

'Is that because you want to be the star of every show?'

'Of course! How did you know, Mrs Young?'

In a way, she was right, but it was more than that. There was the challenge of holding the attention of the audience for all that time, and even more of creating a show from beginning to end, being able to choose one's own material, to get the tone of it right. But the dance floor was hardly the place to try to explain that.

Edith looked directly into Fred's eyes in that way she had, and it was hard to meet her gaze. 'I understand more than you think,' she said. 'To be an actress, a real actress, is more important to me than anything in the world.'

It was the thing he liked most about her, and he *was* about to tell her that, but just then the music stopped, and Edith and Fred were caught up with the other couples leaving the dance floor. Fred offered his arm to Edith. She tucked in her hand so it nestled on the soft part of his own arm, just below the elbow, and gave him a comfortable, warm feeling.

A man in an evening suit came alongside Fred and tapped him on the shoulder.

'Excuse me sir, madame. I'm from the *Melbourne Punch*. Those are splendid costumes you're both wearing. Are you happy to be mentioned in the social pages?'

Edith looked at Fred and he nodded.

The man took out his pencil and looked at Fred.
'You're...
'Mr F.M. Alexander and Mrs...'
Edith interrupted him.
'Edith Tasco-Page.'
'And the costumes are...'
'Hugh Grosvenor, Duke of Westminster and Ophelia.'
The reporter looked around for his next target and Fred turned towards Edith. She'd left her hand there and now he gave it a squeeze.
'Edith Tasco-Page?'
'It's my stage name. Robert thought of it. You won't get far under the name of Mrs Robert Young, he told me.'
'He's right as usual. Edith Tasco-Page is a name headed for the spotlights.'
When they joined Robert and his friends, Edith released Fred's arm, and he thanked her for the dance. For some time afterwards, even as he chatted and laughed with the other men, Fred was conscious of where her hand had been.

44

Almost two years later, Tuesday, 12 May 1891

The Bal Masque, as it turned out, was the end of those exciting first months in Melbourne, not the beginning of something great. Not just for him, but for the city itself. Last year one building society had collapsed after the other, and now the Anglo-Australian Bank looked set to fail as well. When he left work, Fred had been forced to take the long way round to Flinders Street Station to avoid the line of unemployed men that stretched around Collins and Swanston streets.

He was telling the others from the drama club about that as they walked to the Richmond tram stop. It was no surprise to them – everyone had similar stories. They jointly examined the tram timetable and groaned. Half an hour before the next tram!

'There's no point waiting,' he told them, 'Not for me. If I walk, by the time it gets here, I'll be almost home.'

Fred made his farewells and walked fast along Riversdale Road, glad of the exercise after sitting all day. The night was cloudless, and the moon lit up the bare branches of the elm trees that lined the road. A gust of wind swooped on a pile of fallen leaves and swirled them around, along with dust and grit from the road. He squinted his eyes and lowered his head against the wind.

Was it time to leave the Richmond club and look for a more suitable one? It wasn't the club itself; it was one of the best in Melbourne, and the plays they produced were usually reviewed in *The Age* and *The Argus*. But of what use was that if he kept being given the sort of roles that anyone could do, that didn't rate a mention? A year since he'd joined and he was still waiting for a decent part.

A small frog in a big pond. That's what Mr Kayser had told him he would be, and that's how he felt. In one way the club here was like the one in Waratah. There were a handful of men and women who ran the Richmond club, chose the plays, and took the lead roles. The difference was, he now realised, in that first year in Waratah he'd been young enough to play the juvenile parts, and although he complained about being typecast, they were good parts, meaty roles, where he was on stage for the whole time. Now he was overlooked for the leading roles and the younger men got the sort of parts that he'd played back then.

Horses' hooves sounded behind him, and he stopped and watched the crowded tram pass. He was right about that at least; Uncle James' house was only a block away. And that was another thing. He was still living with his aunt and uncle. Not even that had changed; it was exactly the same as in his first year away from home, and that had been five years ago.

He didn't mind, not really, and it made his mother happy. When he had time, he helped Mattie and Harriet with their homework; they were competing against each other for the prize of best exercise book, so he tried to be even handed. Spelling and mapping were Harriet's strong points, maths Mattie's. On Saturday afternoons there were usually the races with Uncle James. There was nothing wrong with any of that, but every month he felt as if he was moving further and further away from where he wanted to be. On the stage! The real stage in the city, not the church hall at Hawthorn, or waiting in the wings at the Richmond Hall. And what did he have to show for all the rehearsals and play readings?

Fred let himself into the dark house and felt his way up the stairs to his room. His chest felt heavy and hurt when he breathed. Rest, Dr Bage had told him. But how could he do that when he had work tomorrow? And the next day, and the next. He went over to the dark fireplace, and held his hand over the coals, but there was no heat left. Still dressed, he removed his shoes and jacket and crawled under the quilt, pulling it tightly around himself.

If not the Richmond Club, then what? It wasn't only that the pond was big and he was small. No, it was more about who you knew in the pond, and in the world of the theatre only one name came to mind. Cathcart. James Cathcart. That had been a serious disappointment. Fred had written to him several times, and once he managed to talk to him, but it was always the same reply. Mr Cathcart was busy. And it was true. Fred could see in the theatre notes that he was performing all the time, if not in Melbourne, then in Sydney, or Adelaide, or Tasmania.

But it was his only chance and he couldn't give up now.

Tomorrow he'd write again. No. That wasn't enough. James Cathcart was playing in a comedy at the Bijou, Fred had read the review this morning. He'd go to the play and find a way to talk to Mr Cathcart afterwards. Backstage. That was it. The last time he did that, Mr Cathcart hadn't minded at all. If you acted as if you had the right to be there, then no one took any notice. Yes. That's what he'd do.

Fred rolled onto his back and gave his legs a good stretch. He pulled the quilt up to his chin and closed his eyes. Now he felt more himself; even his chest felt lighter. He'd noticed it before. No matter how low things got, once he had a plan, all he thought about was putting it into action. Now he was impatient for tomorrow to come. Change. He had to make things change.

45

A week or so later, Thursday, 21 May 1891

Fred handed his ticket to the collector then followed the crowd of passengers out of St Kilda Station and into the forecourt that fronted onto Fitzroy Street. He wasn't in a hurry, and he stood to one side and let the other passengers go past, fascinated by the sight of the elaborate white facades of the hotels across the street. An enormous tier of electric lights had been installed in front of the station and it lit up the grand buildings as if it was daylight.

The last time he'd been to St Kilda it was, in fact, in the daytime. It had been in summer, and he'd caught the new tram out with some friends from work, and they'd swum in the baths. The others had enjoyed it, but to Fred it had been disappointing, nothing like swimming in the sea back in Wynyard.

This time, instead of turning right and taking the road down to the pier as he'd done before, his instructions were to turn left at George's Hotel and follow the road up the hill until he came to Charnwood Road. *'Look out for the Italian mansion with the fountain'*, the note had said.

He crossed the street in front of the George and, as instructed, walked up the incline, away from the sea. From behind him he heard the shrill whistle of the train, and he turned to watch it pull out of the station for the trip back to Flinders Street, the smoke billowing over the roof of the station. It didn't matter how many times he heard it, a train whistle always reminded him of that first trip up to Waratah, a feeling of sheer exhilaration. He turned away from the station and kept walking up the street. He couldn't have imagined then that he would be taking the train every day. Nor that he would be rubbing shoulders with the wealthy men of St Kilda on his way to meet James Cathcart, Australia's finest Shakespearian actor, some said.

'That's a lucky break,' Aunt Jane had said to him when he showed her the message from Cathcart. 'You deserve it.' He'd made his own luck, he wanted to tell her, but he wasn't sure she would approve of how he'd talked his way backstage, not that there was anything wrong with it, nothing at all.

Up this end of Fitzroy Street, once he was past the hotels, some of the buildings were so grand that 'house' seemed quite the wrong word. Even so the Italian mansion stood out, the imposing marble fountain in the formal gardens impossible to miss. He turned right and walked past a row of solid looking two-storey terrace houses, then stopped as directed. That surely must be 'Wilcannia'. The house was set back from the street behind a low stone wall, a two-storey, stand-alone building, with a colonnaded porch that rose into a tower. A curved sweep of stone steps led to the porch and Fred took them two at a time, then gave a few raps on the door with the heavy brass knocker.

There was the sound of a door closing and low voices, then light footsteps and the door was opened by Cathcart himself. It was the first time Fred had seen him without costumes and make-up, but there was no mistaking the swept back, light brown hair that would never be allowed to turn grey, or the energy that gave him a presence, as if he was perpetually sweeping onto the stage. He must be sixty at least Fred had calculated, and there was an old-fashioned courtesy in his manner, as if was playing the part of a gentleman, though Fred had found him to be sincere, and that's what the journalists said too.

Now Cathcart held the open door with one hand and made a sweeping gesture with his free arm.

'Ah. The miner. Come in, come in, my boy.'

Fred laughed. It was a joke they'd shared in Waratah, when Fred had introduced himself as Frederick Alexander of the Mt Bischoff Mining Company and Cathcart had taken a step back and said, 'You've scrubbed up very well.' When Fred pointed out that he was an accountant from the company, they'd both found it funny, especially Cathcart.

'The same.' Fred was holding the calling card that he'd had ready, expecting a servant of some sort to open the door, and Cathcart glanced at it.

'Still working at the coal face, I see'.

The domed entry hall had doors on either side, and through the one on the left came a slender, graceful man, dressed in a well-cut jacket and tapered trousers. His fair hair was thick and wavy and fell just short of his starched collar. He had the same sort of good looks as Robert Young. European, Fred guessed, and his thought was confirmed when Mr Cathcart said. 'Ah. Louis. Meet Mr Frederick Alexander.' Then to Fred he said 'My valet. He'll take your things and we'll get on with this lesson.'

Fred handed over his hat and umbrella to Louis and followed Mr Cathcart into a large parlour that looked rather like the set for a drawing room comedy.

'Take a seat my boy, make yourself comfortable,' Cathcart said, and made for the sideboard on the other side of the room, leaving Fred standing in the doorway. He liked what he saw. The orange and green peacocks and curling vines on the wallpaper gave the room an exotic feel, though the comfortable looking wing chairs and the two settees showed obvious signs of use. Fred sat himself on the settee that faced the drinks cabinet where Mr Cathcart was holding up a bottle of brandy and waving it in his direction.

'A brandy? It's my experience that there's nothing like a sip of brandy to loosen up the vocal cords.'

Fred thought of the guinea he was paying. If the brandy came with it, what was the harm?

'Thank you.'

There was a low round table between the settees and Cathcart put the two glasses on it, then sat opposite Fred and leaned back with a sigh.

'My health isn't what it used to be,' he explained. 'It's this damned carbuncle that's draining all my energy. Now. Here's what I can do for you. Acting I know about. I was practically born on the stage, and the great Mr Keane taught me everything he knew. That I can pass on to you. Interpretation. Understanding of character. Making yourself heard. Creating presence. Outdated I might be, but they're all things that still count on the stage today.'

Mr Cathcart picked up his tumbler and waved it in the direction of Fred.

'If my memory serves me correctly, you have a particular interest in the bard.'

Fred left his own brandy untouched and sat on the edge of the settee.

'Yes, you're right. My plan is to become a professional performer. Recitals or plays, I haven't decided yet, but I do have a special understanding of Shakespeare.'

'Excellent, excellent. Let me hear what you can do, Mr Alexander.'

Mr Cathcart stood up with surprising vigour and took a few paces to the fireplace at the end of the room where he positioned himself, then he waved a hand indicating a point behind Fred. 'Yes, yes. Over there by the door,' he said, when Fred stood looking around, not sure exactly where he meant. 'The space is yours. Now. Entertain me.'

Fred stood where he was instructed and began. 'Friends, Romans, Countrymen, lend me your ears...' He hadn't got halfway through the monologue before Cathcart waved his arm and walked towards him.

'Very good, very good, my boy. I see you lean towards the natural style. Nothing wrong with that, but I couldn't hear every word. I'm going to tell you what Mr Keane told me. What you must always keep in mind is that little boy in the very top of the gallery who has paid sixpence, not to see a dumb show, but to hear the words. Remember that each vowel has its own distinct sounds. "Let", not "lut" and so forth.'

Cathcart recited the first few lines of the play. 'Like that,' he said, then he walked back and took up his stance in front of the fireplace. 'Continue.'

Fred had been practising his vowels, working from his new book by T.P. Hill, but hearing Cathcart's voice up close like that was the first time he really understood. There were those who criticised James Cathcart for being old fashioned, he'd said it himself, but he could still carry an audience with his purity of tone, and his presence.

Fred took up from where he had left off. This time he imagined that little boy in the gallery. It wasn't hard. Not that he was a boy, but since he moved to Melbourne, he'd often sat in the cheap seats in the top row of the gallery, straining to hear.

'Better, definitely better,' Mr Cathcart told him. 'Now, think about the way you move. Imagine you're entering the stage. The audience are sitting there. They fall silent as the curtain rises. There's Caesar's coffin mounted on a marble plinth, the Roman crowds are yelling and jeering and in you come...'

Fred raised his arms and imagined the noisy crowd.

'Friends, Romans...'

There was Mr Cathcart again, coming to stand next to him.

'There's something about your movement that's not right. We'll have to work on that.'

'I thought the arms like that,' Fred spread them again, as if subduing a rowdy throng, 'would suggest the crowd of Romans to the audience.'

'Yes. Keep that. It's not the arms. It's the way you stand and move. You're a slighter build than me, I see that, but it shouldn't matter. Think of yourself as a giant who takes control of the stage even before the audience can see you. When you begin to speak take hold of the stage with your feet. Make your presence felt.'

'I think I see. Should I try again?'

'Yes, yes. Let's see how you go with the rest of it.'

By the time Fred reached the end of the monologue he could feel the difference; before he'd been doing what he knew he should, now he was getting the idea of what it felt like to be fully immersed in the character.

'That's enough for one day,' Mr Cathcart said when the entire monologue had been critiqued. 'Let's attack our brandies and get to know each other a little.'

They sat back on the settees and Cathcart raised his glass. 'Your future'.

'Thank you. I'll drink to that.'

'You have the potential, my boy. The promise is there, you just need to work on it. But to be blunt, if you want to turn professional, what you need as well are contacts.'

Wasn't that why he was here?

'Since you mention it,' Fred said. 'I was thinking that you must know everyone who matters in the theatre world, Mr Cathcart.'

Cathcart leaned back on the settee and gave his genial laugh, the kind that suggested that in life one may as well see the funny side.

'Well said, my boy. I can see that we're going to get along famously. I'll certainly see what I can do, though of course the London stage is where I had my glory days.'

'You told me you even performed for Queen Victoria.'

'Ah yes! Many times. And how she loved us!' Mr Cathcart leaned forward and tapped Fred on the knee. 'You know, if you could spare the time, I could show you my memorabilia from those days.'

There was a light knock on the door and Louis opened it just wide enough to poke his head into the room.

'Supper in ten minutes, Jimmy,' he said. 'I hope I'm not interrupting your lesson,' he added, looking rather pointedly at the brandy glass in Fred's hand.

'We have a new friend, Louis. Would you say our supper could stretch to three? This young man is rather curious about my royal performances.'

Louis nodded and was gone, leaving the door ajar. 'Take no notice,' Mr Cathcart told Fred, 'Louis is a man of few words, but his cooking is excellent. Supper first, then.'

46

Seven weeks later, Tuesday, 14 July 1891

Mr Cathcart had warned Fred not to expect regular lessons. 'I take whatever scraps they throw to me these days,' he'd told Fred. 'Occasionally I land a meaty role, but I'm not the one making the decisions. The best thing you can do is to keep on with your Richmond club and I'll let you know if something comes along.'

That had been almost two months ago. Yesterday Fred thought he would have to cancel the lesson. There'd been nothing but rain for days; the parts of Melbourne near the river were flooded, people being rescued in boats, roads closed. But today the rain had eased off, and when Fred had left work it was little more than a drizzle, hardly worth putting up his umbrella, though going over Prince's Bridge in the train, he could see the river was still swollen and angry looking.

Louis answered the door this time and took Fred's overcoat and hat, then showed him into the parlour where he found Mr Cathcart in a chair in front of the fire, engrossed in a newspaper that he was holding in front of him.

'Mr Alexander,' Louis announced when he opened the door, but Mr Cathcart barely glanced up.

'He's been worried about the floods,' Louis explained to Fred. 'Some good friends live in South Yarra.'

Fred understood why that might be; he'd read about villas along the Yarra River being swallowed up by the water. Camperdown, where his uncle and aunt lived, was far enough away from the river to be safe, but the hall where the Richmond club had its meetings looked as if it might go under at one point, and Fred had spent the night when they should have been rehearsing, stacking chairs and putting them up in the loft along with the costumes and sets.

Fred walked across to the fireplace. 'Pull up a chair, my boy,' Mr Cathcart told him, glancing over his shoulder.

It felt good to sit down in front of the crackling fire. The rain outside was light, but the dampness made the wintry night feel even colder, and Fred rubbed his hands together in front of the fire, then held them to his face and let the warmth soak in.

A minute later there was a loud rustling as Mr Cathcart held the paper at arms-length and folded it back and then in half. He leaned across to Fred, holding the paper in one hand and pointing to something with the other.

'I think we might have found something for you Mr Alexander. Read that.'

Fred took the paper and quickly scanned the part that Mr Cathcart had pointed to.

'Here you mean?' he asked, holding out the newspaper so Mr Cathcart could see where he was reading. There was a short article on Messrs Brough and Boucicault, about how they were raising money for the relief fund for flood victims by donating all proceeds of Friday night's performance. Could there be a part for him, Fred wondered? Is that what Mr Cathcart meant? 'That's the Bijou theatre, isn't it?' he asked Mr Cathcart. 'Will you be taking part in it?'

'Yes, no doubt I'll be playing a crotchety old man in one or other of the plays. And happy to do it. I've never seen anything like these floods. But read on. The next column, where it mentions Mr Dampier.'

'I have it!'

Not a part in a play, then, but this. Almost as good. Maybe better. Fred was too excited to stay in his seat, and he took the paper with him and stood to one side of the fire, reading and exclaiming. 'The Olympians! A new dramatic society! That's a good name. Classical. And Alfred Dampier as president! Isn't he the owner of the Alexandra Theatre? Where they do the Shakespearian productions?'

'The same. It was Alfred Dampier's name that caught my eye. And I've heard good things about Freddy Hill.'

'I've just bought his father's book, *The Oratorical Trainer*. Do you know it?' As soon as Fred asked the question, he realised how silly it must have sounded. Of course someone like Mr Cathcart wouldn't need to follow a book on elocution.

Mr Cathcart laughed. 'I've never had an e–lo–cu–tion lesson in my life.' He pronounced each syllable of elocution separately, thereby showing exactly what he thought of such nonsense. 'But Alfred tells me that T.P.'s son is the genuine article.'

'Did you know T.P. Hill?'

'I was introduced to him once at a lecture he gave on Hamlet. The whole thing was all about one word. One word! He was a very fine orator, though not to my taste. He died a few months after that and according to Alfred it was his wife who sent him to an early grave.'

'Literally?'

'No. Poor T.P. was caught up in a scandal that ruined his last few years. Young Freddy Hill was caught right in the middle of it and Alfred kept an eye out for him. Still does. Freddy's mother's a force to be reckoned with; rather an ill wind.'

Fred looked back at the paper. It was what he'd been waiting for. 'The club may be expected to attain a high standard, both socially and artistically,' the article said. 'F. Wyndham Hill, esteemed elocutionist.' A protegee of no other than Mr Alfred Dampier! And goodness knows what other men in the world of theatre he might have as contacts.

But what was this scandal?

'Do tell,' he said, and Mr Cathcart needed no further prompting.

'It happened a year or two before I arrived in Melbourne. There was a French play on at the Theatre Royal – I'm not sure if you know it. *The Two Sergeants*. All about family, faithfulness, and honour. Trouble was that apparently T.P. had reason to suspect his wife was too fond of a certain doctor, and all steamed up with the sentiments of the play, and a drink or two during the interval, T.P. spotted said doctor coming out of the dress circle at the end of the play and in a very non-Shakespearian way, punched him in the mouth.'

'No. In Shakespeare it's words or blades.'

'The thing is, T.P. lost his work and his reputation. His wife's novel was published not long after and they say that was the final nail in the coffin.'

'Mrs Hill wrote a novel?'

'Oh yes. She's a well-known writer. The name always stayed with me for some reason. *Checkmated*, her book was called. A year later her husband was dead.'

Mr Cathcart picked up the brandy bottle that was on the nest of tables between them.

'Drink?'

Fred held out his glass.

'Who am I to resist?'

Mr Cathcart poured two fingers of whisky into Fred's glass and settled back in his chair. 'Marriage. What a can of worms that can be.' Mr Cathcart leaned across and touched Fred's arm with a theatrical flourish. 'The secret to a happy marriage, my boy, is not to take it too seriously.'

'You're married?' Married? There was something very single, very unmarried about James Cathcart. Fred must have looked as surprised as he felt, because Mr Cathcart laughed and shook his finger at Fred in mock admonishment.

'Never take things for granted! Yes indeed. I gave my wife five children and in return she lives a life completely independent from me. She's a wonderful woman. Wonderful children. And all of them wonderfully back in England.'

Fred laughed, but he could see the sense in it. The life of an actor was hardly conducive to being a family man. The only wonder was that James Cathcart had ever committed himself to marriage. But what choice was there? It's what men must do.

Fred took up the paper again. What he needed to find out was how to become part of these Olympians, and the sooner the better.

47

The following week, Monday, 20 July 1891

Freddy Hill held the knob of the studio door he'd just closed, shaking his head in disappointment. On paper the man had looked promising but when he delivered the lines from the play he'd rehearsed, it was all Freddy could do to hear him to the end. It was the worst kind of overblown elocution, the sort that was all too prevalent. No, he was not at all the type of actor Freddy wanted for The Olympians.

The heavy footsteps became inaudible as the man descended the stairs, and Freddy went across to the desk and checked his diary. There were almost fifteen minutes before the next appointment, a Mr Frederick Matthias Alexander, recommended by Alfred Dampier himself. Freddy closed the diary and sat down in the visitor's chair at the side of the desk. He picked up the *Melbourne Herald*, already folded to show his report of Saturday's races at Williamstown. It was lucky they'd been held at all, what with all that rain, but in the end the waters had receded, and it had been a good day's racing.

It always paid to check his newspaper reports – there was one occasion when they'd left out two whole races – but today everything was as it should be. He put the paper back on the desk and leaned back in the chair, his hands clasped behind his head. In the fireplace opposite him, logs from the new delivery of wood were throwing out a good heat, and already the studio had a comfortable feel to it. It had taken a whole day of moving furniture from one end of the room to the other, but he was pleased with the result.

He'd been in two minds about hanging the photo of his father over the fireplace, but it gave the right gravitas to the room, and there could hardly be anything more appropriate in an elocution studio than a photo of T.P. Hill holding his famous book. It was a studio portrait of his father, taken to celebrate the third re-printing of *The Oratorical Trainer*. T.P. was sitting on the old piano stool, looking rather distinguished. The stool had been wound up to its full height, so that he was as much resting on it as sitting, one leg stretched out in front of him, the other folded under him. In both hands he was holding a copy of *The Oratorical Trainer*, carefully positioned in front of his chest so the title was easy to read. Behind him was a collection of Shakespeare's plays, the same ones that now filled the bookshelves in Freddy's own studio, occupying the space between the large bay window and the walls on either side.

The photo was a reminder of the happy times of his childhood. He must have been about ten years old when it was taken; his brother was still alive, his mother and father living together in the lovely house in Victoria Parade, and his father the talk of Melbourne for his splendid oratory and learning.

Even though he'd been dead for more than ten years, Thomas Padmore Hill was still a name that carried weight in the world of voice production and elocution. Without his claim to fame as the son of T.P. Hill, Freddy feared he would be just another elocution teacher. But next year he'd be turning thirty, and Freddy very much wanted to come out from that shadow and make a name for himself as F. Wyndham Hill. He'd tried it once or twice, but without adding 'son of T.P. Hill' his advertisements had born little fruit.

Would The Olympians be the catalyst he needed? It was what he hoped, and people who mattered agreed with him; something needed to be done to elevate the level of public speaking and performance. It wouldn't be just any amateur drama club, the sort that pandered to popular taste. No, The Olympians would aspire to real artistic standards.

There was a tap on the door. Freddy got to his feet and stood beside the desk.

'Enter,' he called, and the maid opened the door then stood to one side to let the man behind her come in.

'Mr Alexander,' she announced. The man said something to the maid that Freddy didn't hear, and her face lit up with a pleased smile. Mr Alexander was smiling too, and he walked straight up to Freddy, extending his hand.

'Frederick Matthias Alexander,' he said.

Freddy shook the offered hand.

'F. Wyndham Hill,' he said. 'Pleased to meet you Mr Alexander. Please, have a seat.'

Freddy led the way to the desk and waved an arm at the chair he'd just vacated, then sat himself at the desk, his back to the fire.

As he was sitting down he realised he'd left the racing guide on the desk. He was about to put it back in the slot with the other newspapers, but Mr Alexander had already spotted it and was pointing to the headline.

"Williamstown Racing Club, he said. 'The punters' racecourse.'

'Are you a racing man, Mr Alexander?'

'Always have been. My mother would tell you I'm obsessed with racing, but I wouldn't go so far as that.'

Mr Alexander didn't exactly smile, but his striking blue eyes glinted with amusement. and Freddy had the impression that the man enjoyed surprising people with this sort of direct speaking. Freddy liked the look of him. The fine wavy hair, fair rather than red, was fashionably long, and his barely contained energy gave a presence to his otherwise unremarkable stature.

Freddy smiled obligingly.

'I'm not sure my mother has an opinion,' he said, 'but I admit to the obsession. I was checking over my report while I was waiting for you.' Freddy picked up the newspaper and put it back with the other papers.

'Your report did you say? Do you write for *The Herald*?'

'Guilty as charged. For the Williamstown Racing Club, and the Moonee Valley Club as well.'

Freddy could see that Mr Alexander was impressed. Not like his mother who, in fact, did have an opinion about his interest in racing. 'In my family, we own racehorses, we don't write about them,' she'd told him.

'How do you rate Little Bob for a win at Moonee Valley on Saturday?' Mr Alexander asked him.

Freddy shook his head.

'It's not his race, not on the heavy track. This infernal rain has affected all the courses, not just the ones that were flooded.' A racing enthusiast, Freddy thought. Here was a man after his own heart. Would it be too much to ask that he could also act?

'Can I ask you about your acting experience, Mr Alexander? You may have gathered from my advertisement that Mr Dampier and I are intent on making our dramatic club as close as possible to professional standards.'

Mr Alexander had come in carrying a leather document case which he'd rested on the desk. Now he reached into it and produced three newspaper cuttings.

'Reviews from my time in Tasmania,' he explained. 'I had some success in leading roles in various dramatic productions when I was working with the Mt Bischoff Tin Mining Company.'

Freddy scanned the reviews. They were undoubtedly fulsome. *Near professional level* one of them said of the production. But Waratah? What sort of a place was that? From the cut of Mr Alexander's waistcoat, and the tasteful cloth of his suit, he looked every inch a city man, but there was something underlying the carefully cultivated accent. Tasmania. That would explain the man's open manner, which Freddy found a refreshing change from the posturing of some of his Melbourne associates.

Mr Alexander continued, 'The biggest tin mining company in the world,' he explained, 'you would be surprised I'm sure at the calibre of people working there. But here in Melbourne, I'm still looking for a similar sort of dramatic society. The club I'm with at Richmond is energetic but somewhat limited in scope.'

'I understand what you're saying, Mr Alexander. I gather you have some ambitions in that regard.'

'My aim is to take up acting and recitation as a profession, so you can see why your advertisement caught my eye.'

'Excellent. My plan is to combine elocution with performance to ensure the highest standards are reached. Now, I suggest we move on to the next part of the audition. Perhaps you'd be so kind as to recite something for me.'

'Anything?'

'I have some material here, but if you have something of your own, please feel free to use it. To start with, something that shows your dramatic powers would be ideal.'

Mr Alexander rose to his feet. After a quick look around the room, and without waiting to be told, he went over and stood next to the lectern set up in front of the bookshelves. He took nothing with him, not even a little card with prompts. Freddy took his usual place by the side of the fireplace, one arm resting on the mantelpiece. He liked the man's confidence. It was all very promising.

There was a deliberate pause, then with a certain panache Mr Alexander launched into the opening of Hamlet's famous soliloquy. The text was delivered with individuality and some good modulation. The gestures were somewhat contrived, but there was no hint of stumbling over a word and Freddy found himself interested in Hamlet's dilemma, familiar though it was.

'Thank you. That was excellent. To be frank with you, Mr Alexander, there is an abundance of so-called elocution teachers in Melbourne who have given the word a bad name, but I'm relieved to find that you have contrived to stay clear of them.'

'I know what you mean. I see the results of that in my little drama club in Richmond. My own approach is to study the best in the field and to learn from them. Miss Sarah Bernhardt, for example.'

'What a great actress she is, and how fortunate we were to enjoy her performances here in Melbourne. May I ask which performances you attended?'

'All of them.' That amused look again.

'Really!'

'Yes. Every night for an entire month.'

'Astounding.' Freddy was genuinely impressed. 'And did you have a favourite role? For my part, I couldn't go past Marguerite. The scene at the end was quite sublime.'

'Yes. One of the things that kept me going back was exactly that. The way she could say so much with barely a whisper.'

'Her modulation is extraordinary; so subtle. You'll find it's one of the main things I work on: the use of modulation rather than volume, to convey feeling. No one does it better than Sarah Bernhardt.'

'I read one review that described her as art being nature, and it was always like that, night after night. So natural.'

This man surely had more than a passing interest in the theatre. 'You know Mr Alexander, you're exactly the sort of person we need. Without standing on ceremony, let me welcome you to The Olympians.' Freddy gestured to the desk. 'Now, shall we seat ourselves, and I'll take you through some of my ideas for the coming year.'

Mr Alexander followed him over to the desk and took a seat, then he packed the newspaper clippings back into his leather satchel, talking as he did so.

'You might like to make use of my experience in stage management as well. I've had some experience in the Richmond club, and it interests me to be involved in both sides of production.'

'I must confess that's an aspect of theatre of which I have little experience.' Now that he'd said it, Freddy wondered what else he might not have thought of. In the field of elocution and oratory, he knew he was the best in Melbourne, thanks to his father, but when had he ever produced an actual play? Why not bring Mr Alexander in as a sort of senior member, almost a partner, someone with whom he could consult and who could take on responsibility for those sorts of things? The very idea of having someone with whom he could share gave him a feeling of relief.

'You'll find that I like to be busy,' Mr Alexander was saying. 'My work as an accountant ties me up during the day, but the evenings I dedicate to the theatre.'

Freddy studied the man's face again. There was something special about him, a spark, something out of the ordinary; he seemed so sure of who he was and what he could do.

'You've given me an idea, Mr Alexander. If you are interested, I suggest that you join the company as stage manager and senior member. It would give The Olympians a solid foundation, and I have to say that I rather like the idea of sharing the load.'

And just like that it was decided. Not only the matters concerning The Olympians, but somehow, the talk circled back to the Williamstown races and now Freddy had a racing companion for next Saturday. He hoped that he was right about Little Bob.

48

Four months later, Sunday, 29 November 1891

Fred opened the casement windows and looked down onto the back garden. The white roses were already blooming, and the geraniums were spilling over the fence that marked off the vegetable patch. It reminded him of the garden in Wynyard and he wondered if the weather was as good over there. In two days it would be summer, and here in Melbourne, the sun was almost hot enough to think about swimming. He'd promised to take Mattie and Harriet to Williamstown on the train this afternoon, and maybe they could have a paddle in Hobsons Bay.

For now, the family were all at church and Fred had the house to himself for the whole morning. He pegged the windows open and went over to the desk. From the bottom drawer he took out a small key and unlocked the roller top, then he pushed it all the way back and picked up the letter that was open on the desk.

It was the third letter from Robert Young, and this time there was a note from Edith as well. Fred went over to the window, and leaned with his back against it, skimming through the neatly written pages and imagining what it must be like for Robert and Edith in wintry London. Whoever the specialist was that Robert was seeing over there, he must have made a difference, because it sounded as if he was entertaining half of London. Not that Robert let his illness get in the way of enjoying himself, or the enjoyment of other people, but he hadn't been his usual lively self that last time in Melbourne.

From this letter, it was clear that whatever the treatment was, it had worked.

I feel like a new man, Zan. You know how much I believe

in physical exercise as a means of keeping healthy, well to that I've added swimming in the splendid St George's Baths here. I thought of you the other night when I was invited to the annual dinner of the Otter Club (they also swim in the St George's Baths). The event was held in the Café Royal in Regent Street, a place you would love. Sumptuous is the only word to describe it. You couldn't imagine the ornate decoration, all lacquered green with wreaths of gold, mirrors and columns everywhere, and the best wine cellar in London. I composed one of my silly songs for them and you'd think I'd written an opera, they loved it so much. I couldn't get away from the piano and they ended up voting me in as an honorary member.

So far I'm finding the audiences here ready to be amused, and a little nonsense now and then is relished, not like in Hobart, where the audiences have the attitude of 'make me laugh if you can' and I've found that many things go down in London that wouldn't in Tasmania.

What a difference. When he farewelled them back in early June, Robert was wondering if his illness might force him to resign from his position with the government, and Fred was going to see Sara Bernhardt every night and beginning to wonder if he would ever get the break he needed.

Well if things had changed for Robert, they had changed for Fred too. Joining The Olympians and his lessons with Freddy Hill had made the difference Fred was hoping for; by the time Robert and Enid got back in February, he might even be ready to try his hand as a professional performer.

Fred rearranged the pages and read the note from Edith.

Dear FM,

You will see from his letter that Bobba has made quite a hit here. He has quite quickly attracted what he calls a jolly band of chaps who he goes about with, and much as I'm

happy to see his health so improved, I haven't found London to be quite as lively as I was expecting. You'll see what I mean when I tell you I've spent a great deal of time strolling through parks and shops with Bobba's cousin Amelia, and sometimes with his mother or both. That's during the day, but on the nights when Bobba isn't performing, we go to the theatre. I so wish you were here so we could go together. Apart from Bobba, you're the only one who can understand how I feel about becoming an actress and how completely I'm captivated by the theatre. As you can imagine, the plays here are simply dazzling, such large audiences and all the big names, night after night. It's my dream now to perform on the stage in London and I won't rest until it comes true. Now that you're on the way to becoming known, I'm relying on you to help me get there.
With fondest wishes,
Edith

Fred turned away from the window and sat down at the desk. He put the letters to one side, then took out his pen and paper.

Dear Robert,

I'm pleased you're so much improved and making your mark on London. The good news keeps going here too, and finally the people who matter are taking notice of me. Just this month I've had more good reviews, this time in The Age and The Herald, and Mr Wyndham Hill and I are talking about staging a full production of Hamlet next year (with me as the Prince of Denmark). As the senior member of The Olympians I have some say in the matter. It's Mr Hill who has a name in Melbourne, and he is an excellent elocution teacher, but between you and me, I wonder where The Olympians would be without me!

I've been reciting the new poems I was telling you about and can't tell you how well they've been received. It makes me feel that the time is right for me to strike out on my own as a professional reciter. As you know, I've built up a considerable repertoire, and Mr Hill has rounded it out with those sublime pieces, all of which makes me feel almost ready to resign from my job and see if I can make a living from performance (and I would need to do some teaching as well). It's never going to be easy, but now might be as good a time as any to try.

Mr Cathcart suggested that once I'm ready, a tour of Tasmania would be a good idea. He's played all over the colony and talks warmly about the audiences and the reviewers over there. His experience in Melbourne is that once reviewers are paying money to see you, they can be hard to please, even savage, and there is one man who writes under the name of Tahite who sets out to destroy people's careers.

With that in mind, I'm determined to take Mr Cathcart's advice and my first step is to get myself noticed in Tasmania. My uncle has a friend who's an occasional correspondent with The Wellington Times in Burnie. Ma says everyone in the north-west reads that paper, so I've started to get a piece ready to send in about my successes in Melbourne, and it wouldn't hurt either for certain people over there to get the idea that I'm planning to turn professional.

It's interesting what you say about things going down in London that wouldn't go down in Tasmania. It made me think that the opposite might apply, and what doesn't go down in Melbourne might go down very well in my home state.

I've been trying my luck at the Williamstown races of late. Mr Hill sends reports to The Herald for the race club, and apart from the races, I've been meeting some of his friends from there. There's a Young Man's Literary and Scientific Association that I now belong to and a dramatic society that I might join next year. They both produce entertainment of the sort that interests me and it's another way in which I can get noticed, not to mention the experience performing to large audiences.

Thank Edith for her note and tell her I'll write soon. Wishing both of you the best of everything.

Affectionately,
FM

49

Six months later, Tuesday, 10 May 1892

'You're not ready. I would be putting my reputation on the line if I went ahead with Hamlet. And yours too. It's for your own good.'

Freddy Hill wondered in how many different ways he could say the same thing. He felt as close as a brother to Fred Alexander, but on this point, they couldn't seem to agree.

'There was nothing wrong with my voice last night!' Fred snapped at him.

'No. That's not what I'm saying. With a short piece like that, your voice holds up. But listen to yourself! An hour-long lesson and I can hear the strain in your voice.'

'Another month resting it and I'll be back to normal. Look at how well I am after those two months in Geelong. It's just that wretched illness that set me back.'

'What you need to focus on is the competition I told you about. I know you think otherwise, but an amateur production of Hamlet won't make your name. On the other hand, if you win against entrants from the whole of Victoria, that will make people take notice!'

They'd finished their lesson and were downstairs in the living room, having a nightcap. Freddy was hoping it hadn't been a mistake, offering Fred Alexander his mother's old quarters. Freddy was getting used to his star pupil's outbursts, but he could be rather wearing at times.

As quickly as it had come, the frown disappeared, and Fred took his whisky and stood in his favourite place by the side of the fireplace, resting an arm on the mantelpiece. He was definitely looking better, Freddy thought. The colour was back in his cheeks and his eyes had lost that dull look. Fred could be right. Now he'd recovered his health, his voice would recover too.

'From the whole of Victoria? Who's running the competition?' Fred asked him.

'A group of the old guard in the theatre here. Some of them were friends of my fathers. They've formed an organisation called the Victorian Amateur Competitors Association. They're worried that standards of performances are declining, so the aim is to promote the arts in Melbourne. I put in a word for some elocution prizes. In fact, I'm awarding a prize myself, for an essay on drama.'

'I still can't see why we should drop Hamlet completely, but I see your point. A win in the competition could be just what I need. Should I recite Parhassius do you think? Or take on a new piece?'

'What I have in mind...' Freddy hesitated. Fred Alexander might not like his plan. Not at first, anyway. He had to be very careful. Freddy picked up the bottle of whisky and got to his feet. 'Another drop?' He held the bottle poised over Fred's almost empty glass.

The glass replenished, he put the bottle on the sideboard and walked back to stand in front of the fire, swirling his glass to give the whisky warmth from his hand.

'I've noticed you have excellent rapport with a talented student of mine.' Fred looked at him and waved the hand holding his whisky as if both to agree and to suggest that it was self-evident, that he had a rapport with the whole company. And Freddy had to admit it was true. Even when Fred yelled at them when they were slow to change a scene, or worse, when they failed to put something critical on the stage. His temper was an idiosyncrasy, a habitual gesture, that one came to accept. The first few times it caught all of them by surprise, but usually his outburst was mercifully short, and the next minute he'd be telling a joke, or a story, as if nothing had happened.

'I'm thinking of Miss Malingren.' Freddy said. There was a slight pause before Fred answered.

'Ah yes! Connie Malingren,' he said carefully. 'Ophelia. I've been helping her with the Shakespearian rhythm. She's a quick learner.'

'I've been thinking that the Macbeth scene would be a perfect vehicle for the two of you to show what you can do.'

'In the competition?'

'Yes. There's a section for dialogue. It's my belief that you and Miss Malingren can beat off all comers with Macbeth.'

Fred took his elbow off the mantelpiece and Freddy noticed the telltale reddening of his cheeks. He was still holding his whisky and from the way he was standing it looked more like a missile that he was about to launch.

'As the senior member of the company I rather thought that I would be giving a solo recitation in...' Fred had raised his voice again, and before he could finish, he broke into a hoarse cough and had to clear his throat several times before continuing. '...in the men's section.'

Freddy walked over to the sideboard and poured a glass of water for Fred, then he sat down again.

'That is precisely my point. A dialogue will give you more control over your voice, take the strain off it. And you know yourself, with the...'Freddy paused, searching for the right word...'energy between you and Miss Malingren, you're bound to win.'

Fred took the other chair and sat staring into the fire for a minute, then he turned towards Freddy.

'The truth is, Freddy, I'm worried. Nothing is working with my voice. Without that, where am I?'

'What does Dr Bage say?'

'It's always the same thing. He tells me to rest. Leave two weeks before reciting. As you know, I did what he suggested and spent the last three months in Geelong. My health has recovered – you can see that for yourself – but my voice hasn't. I'm not sure it ever will.'

'You were telling me about some treatments...'

'They're useless!'

Freddy was careful not to show it, but it worried him. He needed the Fred Alexander from that first audition: confident, talented, energetic. The Olympians would be only half as good without him.

'Have you worked on your breathing?'

It was proving difficult to train Fred in nostril breathing. In the elocution classes, Fred would start the way Freddy showed him, letting the air fill his chest then releasing it slowly, using pauses to take in more air through the nostrils and into the chest, but sooner rather than later, he would be so caught up in the drama of what he was reciting that he'd start pulling air in through his mouth. It would go some way to towards helping him overcome his voice problem, Freddy was sure, if Fred could master the nostril breathing. Maybe he's going to discover it for himself, Freddy thought. That seemed to be the only way Fred Alexander could be convinced of anything.

Fred frowned, and Freddy thought he might be about to take issue with his comment about breathing, but instead he sighed, picked up his glass of water and went back to where he'd been standing before.

'When Dr Bage told me there was nothing more he could do, I felt as if the world had collapsed on me. But then I pulled myself together and determined that if he couldn't do anything, then I would just have to do it myself. I haven't only been resting and writing poetry down in Geelong. I've been working with mirrors.'

'Mirrors?'

'Yes. Mirrors. When I first went there, I was too ill to do much, and I spent a lot of time thinking about what I could do about my voice. Where to start.'

'So where did you start?'

'Well, I thought of Shakespeare. "It is not in the stars to hold our destiny but in ourselves".'

'Go on.'

'Then I thought about how my father was always telling me to look closer at things. "There's always something more to learn", he used to say, so I had the idea of looking closely at myself.'

'And what did you see?'

Fred suddenly launched into a few lines from Hamlet, then just as suddenly he went back to his normal voice.

'That.'

'That what?'

'My head. Did you see how I threw it back when I was reciting?'

'Recite those lines again.'

This time Freddy took notice and just as Fred had said, he did throw his head back. In fact, now that it was pointed out, Freddy noticed that his friend's entire posture changed, as if he was trying to pull his whole body into his voice.

'Now that you mention it...'

'That's it. That's what is causing my voice to go hoarse.' Fred pulled his head back and put his hand on his throat and said 'Ah'. Then he dropped his head forward and did the same.

'Can you hear the difference?'

'There's a bit of roughness when your head is back.'

'Exactly. And I can feel my larynx being squashed.'

'Show me again. Give me the first few lines of Parhassius.'

Freddy watched more carefully this time and wondered that he hadn't noticed it before, the way Fred threw his head back. Surely it had grown worse.

'You're still throwing your head back. And did you realise you were gulping in air through your mouth?'

'Yes. it's ugly and annoying, but I can't seem to stop myself. I've tried to bring my head forward deliberately, but as soon as I start reciting, I can't hold it there.'

'Perhaps the long illness you've had has made it difficult for you to breathe, so you've developed the habit of breathing through your mouth to get enough air. It wasn't a problem when you joined The Olympians.'

'You might be right. I've got so used to that respiratory problem, I didn't think of that.'

Fred took a couple of deep breaths in through his nostrils.

'That does feel better. When I breathe like that, I can feel my head in the right position, and when my head is in the right position, I breathe naturally. But as soon as I start to recite, my head goes back. All I'm thinking about are the words and how I'm going to say them. The expression, the audience. All of that.'

'I wonder that I don't do the same thing. Like you say, once on the stage, you have to trust your instincts and your training. It's like being in a different world.'

'Try it,' Fred suggested. 'Stand up and recite something and I'll watch you.'

Freddy did as he suggested. It felt awkward declaiming lines in his own sitting room, but he tried to throw himself into Hamlet's dilemma as he recited from the monologue.

'Well?' he asked, as he sat back down. 'What's the verdict?'

'Your head barely moved, and I couldn't hear your breath.'

'I'm sure it must be my father's training. You know, he taught me his methods. "Breath must be effortless", he used to say. "Fill your chest with air and use it wisely". This is what he used to have me do.' Freddy put his hands on each side of his chest and took a deep breath in through his nostrils. 'You can feel your whole chest expand.'

'I see what you mean. I'll work on it in front of the mirror,' Fred told him. 'If it's a habit I've developed then it shouldn't be too hard to unlearn it. Now, about this dialogue with Miss Malingren.'

50

Five months later, Thursday, 20 October 1892

'The prize for the best tragic dialogue in the senior section goes to...'Miss H. and Miss E. Moses for their presentation of the scene from *Much Ado About Nothing*.'

Fred's mouth went dry and a hollow feeling that was almost painful gripped his chest and stomach. It had to be a mistake.

There was enthusiastic applause and some whoops and catcalls. The audience had been highly entertained by the sisters' performance. He'd seen that, but the tricks the girls used, the cheeky whistle and crude gestures, were more like vaudeville than Shakespeare. There was nothing tragic about it.

'A close second in the dialogue section goes to Miss Constance Malingren and Mr Frederick Alexander for their portrayal of the murder scene from *Macbeth*.'

Of what good was that! Look at their win in the first round of the competition. None of the other competitors came close. Freddy Hill had considered today's win a foregone conclusion and was already planning a public performance to capitalise on the win, to get publicity for both of them. And F. Wyndham Hill wasn't just anybody!

Why they would have a different judge this time was beyond Fred's understanding. He'd had a bad feeling about the grey-haired, shortish man as soon as he saw him. There was something about the way he was dressed, rather too nattily, and he had a manner that suggested he was arrogant and disdainful.

Freddy Hill was sitting on one side of Fred, Connie Malingren on the other. Around them the audience were applauding too enthusiastically for Fred's liking. He didn't join in and wondered how Connie and Freddy could clap politely the way they were doing.

'The judges haven't heard the last of this,' he said to Connie, loud enough so that people around them looked in his direction. 'They should have been disqualified.'

Freddy continued clapping and leaned over so he could speak to Connie and Fred.

'We'll put in a protest,' he told them. 'I would have done it before, but I didn't imagine anyone would consider their selection tragic.' Then he whispered so only Fred could hear, 'there's no point letting everyone see how disappointed you are.'

Why not? Fred could not see the point of pretending. Fools, idiots. As soon as he could, he would go right up to the judge and demand to know why a humorous dialogue could win first prize for a tragic recital.

It took an eternity for the rest of the awards to be announced but finally it was over. The applause petered out and Fred and the others stood up and joined the crowd of people shuffling up the aisle. The judges were sitting at a table on an elevated dais at the back, and Fred pointed to the man who had so mistakenly awarded the prize to the sisters.

'There he is,' Fred said. He knew what he was going to say, he'd been going over it in his head.

But Freddy gripped his shoulder. 'Just keep walking,' he muttered, 'I'll tell you more later.'

51

By the time they left the hall the moon had risen and the evening was mild and still. Freddy suggested they walk back by the river and Fred agreed readily. It was one of the many things he liked about living with Freddy Hill in South Yarra; it was less than an hour's walk into the city, and on the tram no time at all. The financial depression had finally forced Uncle James out of business and Fred had waved the family off for a second time. They'd left a few months after Fred had joined The Olympians and with all the lessons and rehearsals, he'd had been too busy to look for somewhere else to stay. However, with his usual luck things had fallen into place.

'Come and stay with me,' Freddy Hill had suggested when Fred passed on the news. 'This place is far too big for one person. I had it decorated so mother and I could have separate living quarters and now she's living in England I don't know what to do with myself. I only use half of it.'

For the most part it worked out well, but there were times when Freddy became withdrawn, almost secretive. He'd go off to meetings with his well-placed friends and when Fred asked him about it, all he would get as an answer would be something so non-committal it sounded evasive. Fred wondered if they were planning something else behind his back, like the competition. If he had been part of the planning committee he would have made sure that there were at least two, if not three, judges, so the decision was fair. The sisters' humorous dialogue should never have been accepted. Not in a category titled 'Tragic Recital'! No, he could have done a better job organising it singlehandedly.

Between the Hibernian Hall and Flinders Street Station, Swanston Street was busy with people hurrying to catch trains and trams, and the two men walked in silence. Freddy had his hands deep in his pockets and his head down and Fred was smarting with the way his teacher had pushed him out of the hall, as if he was a youngster who had to be controlled.

When Fred had asked him what he meant by, 'I'll tell you more later,' all Freddy had said was, 'I need to think,' and then suggested they walk back home.

After the station the crowd thinned out and as they were crossing Princes Bridge Freddy stopped by a lamppost and leaned against the railing, looking out over the river. Fred did the same. Behind was the busy noise of trams and horses taking people home after an evening out, but in front of them the moon floated on the Yarra, making a silver path on the dark water.

'What would Shakespeare make of this, do you think?' Freddy Hill asked.

'He might say "The moon shines bright on such a night as this," Fred suggested, 'like he did in *The Merchant of Venice.*'

Freddy smiled and looked across at Fred.

'Shakespeare! What my father didn't know about Shakespeare!'

'A good thing, surely,' Fred suggested.

'Look Fred, you have to trust me that we will overturn tonight's decision, but there's more to it than you understand, and we're going to have to tread carefully.'

Freddy pushed himself back from the railing and the two of them continued across the bridge.

'You'll have to tell me now,' Fred told him. 'Otherwise of course I won't understand!' Sometimes Freddy could be so exasperating.

They were walking on the path under the trees that bordered St Kilda Road, and the Botanic Gardens on their left was a brooding dark mass. Freddy spoke quietly.

'It's possible there was something personal in the judging tonight'.

'Against me?'

'No. Well that's possible too. Dr Neild can take against people on a whim. But no, I have, you might say, history with him.'

'I don't understand.'

'There was something that occurred many years ago – when I was no more than a lad – and Dr Neild took against my family.'

It was coming back to Fred now, what Mr Cathcart had told him. Something about a fight in the Theatre Royal between T.P. Hill and a doctor. Was that it? And Dr Neild, the theatre critic and judge of the elocution tonight, was the doctor Freddy was talking about.

'Are you saying that he may have deliberately chosen the sisters over us because of something that happened years ago? To spite you?'

'He's capable of doing that. Otherwise, I can't see why an erudite man, as he certainly is, could award first prize in a tragic recital to a dialogue that was clearly intended to make the audience laugh!'

'I didn't like the arrogance of the man. And in my opinion, we should have had the same judge as in the preliminaries. Even so...Was it your father? What did he do to make such an enemy of him?'

'I was too young to understand what was going on, and I still don't know the truth of it. My brother...'

Freddy broke off suddenly, and for a minute there was only the noise of the gravel crunching under their feet. Fred glanced across at him, but the dense leaves of the elms hid the moon, and in the darkness he couldn't see the expression on Freddy's face. Finally, Freddy continued.

'My brother died suddenly when I was thirteen – a bad case of scarlet fever – and my mother came to rely on Dr Neild to help her recover. My father believed that Dr Neild behaved... inappropriately, and somehow it all got out of hand.'

At the mention of the dead brother, Fred was suddenly back on the beach at Wynyard, watching little Horrie laughing and playing with his fingers. How old would he be now...?

Freddy cleared his throat and Fred realised he'd lost track of the rest of what Freddy had been saying.

'There may be nothing in it,' Freddy was saying, 'but it will be best if we deal only with the organisers of the elocution competition, and I'm of a mind to accompany our protest with a letter of support from someone who carries weight in that area.'

'Like Mr Cathcart.'

'Yes, yes. Why not? Mr Cathcart's name still matters. And I was thinking of Mr James Smith. He'll be as shocked as we are when I tell him.'

Of course, Fred thought, James Smith, famed lecturer and critic. The man been gracious enough about the poem Fred had dedicated to him, though less enthusiastic than he would have liked. If Mr F. Wyndham Hill, son of T.P. Hill, asked for Mr Smith's support, then of course he would throw his weight behind their cause. Fred would have liked to have the same standing in the eyes of Mr James Smith, but for now, he couldn't argue against the proposal. At all costs, he had to take out first prize.

*

Two weeks passed with no news. It was Fred's opinion that Freddy Hill should make enquiries, push the committee to do the obvious; it shouldn't take more than a minute's thought to realise the travesty that had been committed. He was tempted to go behind Freddy's back and contact the committee himself, but Mr Cathcart cautioned him to have patience.

Finally, on a warm November evening, Fred arrived home from work and the letter was in the pile of mail on the floor of the hallway. Freddy was still working with a student up in his studio, so Fred gathered up the letters and put them on the hallstand, holding on to the envelope with Victorian Amateur Competitors Association stamped in one corner. It was addressed to Mr F.Wyndham Hill, but Fred knew what it was about and slit it open with the paper knife.

Dear Mr Hill,

We wish to inform you that after due consideration, the winners of the senior dialogue in the VACA competition are ratified as your students Miss C. Malingren and Mr F.M. Alexander. The previously declared winners, the Misses Moses, were disqualified on the grounds that their

dialogue from Much Ado About Nothing is a humorous selection and hence does not meet the entry requirements.
Yours Sincerely,
Mr G.H. Crozier
Secretary

The sisters wouldn't be happy but what could they do?

Fred took the letter with him, continuing along the corridor and into the back parlour. It was his favourite room in the house, especially now that summer was almost here, and the evenings stayed light for so long. The curtains were pulled back from the French doors, and the room was aglow with the light from the setting sun. In one corner of the room a deep green velvet chaise longue sat in front of a palm tree that drooped exotic fronds over a little round marquetry table. In the other corner was the rosewood writing table Fred had brought with him from his uncle's place, and he sat down and read through the letter again.

Now it was official, there was nothing to stop him using his win in the competition to his advantage. Not as the pupil of F. Wyndham Hill, but to further his own career. Where would he start?

Fred leaned back and clasped his hands behind his head. The year hadn't turned out the way he'd been expecting it to. There were those lost months getting his health back in Geelong, and then more months using every spare moment to improve his voice. To think he'd almost given up! But he didn't, and now look what he'd done. The hours in front of the mirror, struggling to break his own habits, that and the breathing, it had all paid off. It had taken the best part of a year but despite that, he'd won first prize against all comers. It was nothing less than a triumph.

That was it! He'd ask his uncle's friend to send another piece off to the *Wellington Times*. A triumph. He said the word out loud, feeling the sound of it. There was no better title than that. He opened the top drawer of the writing table and took out paper, pen, and ink, then he started writing, the words spilling on to the page.

A triumph

The friends of Mr F.M. Alexander will be delighted to learn that at a recent competition held in Melbourne under the auspices of the Victorian Amateur Competitors Association, he impersonated the character of Macbeth in the winning dialogue, supported by a lady member of "The Olympians." As Macbeth is one of Shakespeare's greatest and most difficult characters, one in which many professionals have failed, there can be no doubt that Mr Alexander must possess wonderful ability, to enable him to successfully pass through such a trying ordeal, and should he adopt the stage as a profession, he has a brilliant future before him. It is only a little over 15 months since he commenced his studies in the elocutionary art, and at this competition he met amateurs of from 6 to 8 years' experience, and in one case competed against a gentleman who has been on the professional stage for three years, and who has since been disqualified in another class. These facts speak for themselves.

How to finish? Then he thought of the review in *The Herald*, the one published after they'd won their section in the preliminaries. There was no need to look for a copy – he knew it by heart.

The following account from The Herald gives an idea of how the performance was received. "The winning dialogue was chosen from Macbeth (the letter and murder scenes) and was listened to with rapt and silent attention. Mr Alexander and Miss Malingren, who played Lady Macbeth, received a most enthusiastic ovation at its conclusion, the applause continuing even as they walked down the hall after leaving the platform."

He was reading back over it, making corrections, when he heard the door open and the familiar squeak of Freddy's patent leather boots. Fred swung around, resting his right arm over the back of the chair.

'The letter came,' he said.

Fred picked up the letter and held it out to Freddy, who took it over to the chaise longue and started to read. Then he sat up abruptly and flourished the letter in Fred's direction.

'But it's addressed to me!'

'I know. I opened it. I thought you wouldn't mind.'

Freddy frowned and shook his head. He started to say something but stopped, so Fred took the opportunity to continue. He didn't want Freddy in one of his moods. Not tonight.

'I wouldn't normally open your mail Freddy, you know that. It's just that I've been so desperate for that letter to come.' Fred stood up and walked towards the drinks cabinet. 'Come on Freddy. This is something to celebrate, it's good for both of us. How about a sherry? Or whisky?'

Freddy relented and went over to join Fred.

'You're right. We worked hard for that prize, and I, for one, am going to make good use of it!'

'Hear, hear,' Fred said, raising his glass. 'I already have,' and he went and picked up the article he'd just written. 'What do you think of that?' he asked, and handed it to Freddy to read.

52

Three weeks later, Wednesday, 14 December 1892

At the hall in Williamstown the applause was polite, but no more than that. Fred took his bow with the rest of the cast, and there were some calls of bravo for Kitty, but the clapping died away after only two curtain calls. The heavy velvet drapes stuck part way across as they always did, then came together hesitantly, in a series of jerks, as if reluctant to close. Before they finally came together, Fred hurried off the stage, coughing in proportion to the effort he'd made to hold it back. He grabbed at the glass of water the stagehand held out to him and gulped it down.

The last scene had seemed to go on forever. Three times he had to be prompted and each time he said a line he wondered if any sound would come out.

He headed straight for the dressing room and changed out of his costume. The others weren't far behind him, and there was the usual excited chat that marked the end of a production. He was bending down pulling his boots on when Jasper came and sat next to him. He gave Fred a hearty slap on the back.

'Not our finest performance, but we got through it!'

Fred tugged at his trousers so they covered his boots and looked at Jasper. How could he be so pleased with himself? But then Jasper was always like that. He'd joined the dramatic society to meet women, he'd confided in Fred, and anything else was a bonus.

'No,' Fred agreed. His throat was raw and he wrapped his hand lightly around his neck and took a breath before he continued. 'It's this wretched throat of mine.'

'Is that what the problem was? I thought there must be something. You sounded so earnest.'

Earnest? Surely not. He turned to tell Jasper that, but his friend was absorbed in taking off his grease paint, so Fred checked his own face then patted down the sides of his hair and left the room.

The hall had been hot and stuffy, the stage lights making it even hotter, and it was a relief to step outside, although a thick layer of clouds had trapped in the heat of the day and the night was still warm. Freddy Hill and two of their friends from the club were waiting for him at the front of the hall and the three of them watched him as he approached. Fred pulled his shoulders back and tried not to show how exhausted he felt, but it seemed he wasn't fooling anyone, because his friend James came to meet him and put a hand on his shoulder.

'You look like you need a drink after that, Fred. We're thinking of walking to the Steampacket for a pot.'

It was what they did sometimes after rehearsals, and the Steampacket was close to the train station. But that would mean going over and over the performance tonight, and all Fred wanted was to be by himself, to have time to think. Before he could decide what excuse to give, Freddy came to the rescue.

'I have that early start tomorrow morning, Fred.' He pointed to the hansom cabs that were lined up in front of the hall. 'I'm of a mind to catch a cab back home and thought we could split the fare.'

'There you have it,' Fred told his friends. 'Another time.'

He left Freddy to negotiate the fare back to South Yarra and climbed up into the cab. The leather and the carpet smelled new, and Fred sank back into the well-padded seat. The horse flicked its tail and looked back at him as if to check on its latest passenger. Fred made a clucking sound from the corner of his mouth, the universal language of horses, and the horse tossed its head and whinnied. The cab rocked as Freddy climbed in beside him, then the cabby pulled the lever and the bottom half of the door locked in place.

'I told him we didn't need the full door,' Freddy said. 'It's such a warm night.'

'Good. Some fresh air is what I need. Did you get a decent price?'

'The cabby pointed out that the cab was new and added sixpence. "It's so well sprung you'll think you're riding on velvet", he told me. 'Rather poetic for a cabby, I thought.'

'It's a good fare for him. After this, he can go home to bed.'

At first they jolted along in fits and starts as the cabby negotiated his horse amongst the other cabs and wagonettes, but once they were past the station and running beside the river, he gave the horse its head and they trotted along at a good pace.

'Do you want to talk about the performance?' Freddy asked cautiously.

'No.'

Freddy glanced in his direction then he sighed and folded his arms, looking straight ahead. Met with silence, Fred realised that after all he did want to discuss it.

'Could you tell I was having trouble with my voice?' he asked. 'I thought I might lose it entirely.'

Freddy unfolded his arms and looked at Fred.

'Do you really want to know?'

'Yes. Tell me the worst. It seems that I can't trust my own instincts. What I think I'm doing turns out to be not what I'm doing at all.'

Fred had been so sure. Tonight was his chance to prove that all that his hours and hours of work hadn't been for nothing; that through sheer determination he'd done what the doctors couldn't do. He'd found the problem and fixed it. He could hold the stage for a full performance, he could have played Hamlet, and Freddy was wrong to doubt him.

Now he wasn't sure at all. For the first time he wondered if he should admit defeat, give up his grand ideas of a stage career. But without those dreams and hopes, who was he? What would he become? His whole being rebelled against defeat. He'd come so far; how could he give it up now? There had to be something more that he could do and for that he had to know where he was going wrong.

Freddy spoke slowly, choosing his words. 'As we both know *Randall's Thumb* is a light-hearted entertainment, a comedy, but the way you played Buckthorpe...well it felt more like a burial scene towards the end. I heard someone around me ask who the wet blanket was. We know that's not like you.'

'I couldn't find the rhythm of the lines. I tried to remember to pull my head forward, thinking it would help my voice, but that turned out to be even worse than when I throw my head back. I was so hoarse by the end I felt drained of energy.'

'Is that what you were trying to do? I was wondering why you looked so stiff. And you won't want to hear this,' Freddy continued, 'but even from where I was sitting in the middle of the hall, I could hear you gulping in air.'

'And you know how much I detest that!'

Of course Fred knew that he'd been breathing through his mouth; his throat was raw, and he could barely speak. That much he'd worked out. But to be heard so far back in the hall! It was even worse than he imagined.

He'd improved so much over the last few months, that he had dared to hope he'd found the problem and corrected it. For thirty or forty minutes, even an hour, he could keep conscious control over what he was doing with his breathing and his head, but tonight had shown that at some point he had lost that control, and with it his voice. There was some critical thing he was missing. What was it?

'I don't know what more to suggest,' Freddy said. 'Your work with the mirrors is paying off up to a point, and you're right about the need to keep your larynx free, but it seems to me that sometimes the more you try, the further you get from the natural elocutionist you want to be. You have a think about it Fred. I've had quite a day and might grab forty winks.'

Freddy leaned back in the corner of the cab, rested his head against his arm and closed his eyes.

Once they left the river and turned north the road was almost deserted, and apart from an occasional crack of the whip from the cabby, the night was quiet. Fred stretched out his legs, folded his arms, and leaned his head against the padded seat. It magnified the sound of the horse's hooves, and the steady rhythm was a familiar, comforting sound. The frustrated anger that had been burning into him receded and he started to think more methodically.

He went back over his performance another time. What more could he do? Where was he still going wrong? He knew from the months and months of studying himself in the mirror that throwing his head back put too much pressure on his larynx. Tonight, he had consciously tried to keep his head forward. He could see himself in that scene with Kitty, the way he stood, holding the floor with his feet, his head pulled forward.

A rank smell interrupted his thoughts. Faint at first, then so strong that Fred took his handkerchief out and held it to his nose, the stench of the tannery invaded the cab. They must be coming up to Footscray, he thought, and at the same time, the square frame of the Hopetoun Bridge loomed in front of them.

Holding the handkerchief over his nose, Fred glanced across at Freddy, but the smell wasn't enough to jolt him out of his nap. As they approached the bridge the cabby slowed the horse and the sound of its hooves changed as the timbers of the bridge replaced the harder surface of the road. Then they were across, and Fred put his handkerchief back in his pocket and sat up, idly watching the alert ears of the horse, its head forward and relaxed, barely moving as it trotted along the road with an easy gait. He could see the ripple of muscles along its back, changing from side to side with every stride. The movement was fluid and natural, every part working in effortless coordination.

Fred listened to the sound of the hooves and let his mind wander. If only he could be like that on the stage; fluid, rhythmic. Like he used to be. He saw himself in breeches and waistcoat, his pipe in hand, playing the part of Sam Willoughby, leaping around the stage, the laughing audience, the feeling of belonging, the sheer joy of it. Is that what his training had done? Turned him into an actor who was stiff, so conscious of how he should hold himself that he turned a comedy into a burial scene? It couldn't be Freddy's teaching; his whole method was about naturalism: the nostril breathing, the clever use of pauses, the subtle modulations of voice production.

Mr Cathcart then? Fred thought back to his first lesson, and all his lessons since. Cathcart's two mantras: think of the boy in the back of the theatre, hold the floor with your feet. Could there be a connection? There'd been no sign of Fred's voice problem before he started those lessons with Mr Cathcart. Not in Waratah, and not when he was with the Richmond club.

Did Freddy have a point? Fred knew that the secret to recovery was in whatever it was he was doing to his head and neck, but perhaps he was trying too hard to throw his voice into those back stalls, trying too hard to 'hold the floor'.

Fred looked down at his feet. They were resting on the floor of the cab, and as he looked at them, he wondered what there could possibly be to discover. He curled his toes inside his boots, then let them go. Three times he did the same thing, and each time he released them he could feel other parts of his body releasing as well: ankles, thighs, buttocks.

Then he thought about letting his feet sink into the floor and felt a pleasant shiver up his spine. Each time he let go, he had the feeling that he was sitting taller. Finally he came to his shoulders and as he let his weight sink all the way down to his feet, his shoulders dropped so emphatically he realised that he'd been clenching his whole body, as if it would fall to pieces were he to let go. But when he did let go, the opposite happened. Everything fell into place, and as he consciously relaxed his neck and jaw, he felt an inch taller. Not only that, but the rawness in his throat had lessened and he had a feeling of wellbeing, as if his body was lighter than usual.

Ahead Fred could see the lights on Flagstaff Hill. Before long they'd be crossing the bridge and then it wasn't far to Caroline Street and home. Freddy must have sensed a change because he sat up, adjusted his hat, and looked around him.

'Sorry Fred,' he said. 'I haven't been very good company.'

'You've been the best sort,' Fred assured him. 'I've been watching this fine horse and doing some thinking. If I'm right, and I think I am, I've discovered the mistake I've been making, and maybe more besides.'

Freddy looked closely at him, then shook his head and smiled.

'I must say that considering the night you've had, you're looking very pleased with yourself.' He gave Fred an encouraging pat on the knee. 'Let's hope you're right.'

53

A year later, Saturday, 9 December 1893

Fred sat on the side of his bed and read through his mother's letter again. He had glanced through it before going to the races, but now that he read it more carefully, he realised that in between her statements of unwavering support, was an unusual expression of uncertainty and worry. *'You say that your voice is better than ever, and you are ready to resign your position with Acherley and Dawson and become a professional elocutionist, but twice I've been ready for your triumphant return, and now I wonder if it will be the same this time.'*

It would make no difference were he to write to her tomorrow, because there was no postal collection on Sundays, but it was not like her to have such doubts, and he felt an urgent need to write immediately. The afternoon was still hot, and he changed out of his suit then settled himself at the desk.

Dearest Ma,

I received your letter this morning and read it with some dismay, so I'm writing post-haste to put your mind at rest. Please be reassured that this time there is nothing to stand in the way of my decision to embark on my chosen career, and I have already started to put in place steps towards my departure from Melbourne, which will be early in the new year.

On Monday night at the concert I was telling you about, I received the greatest affirmation of my readiness to take the next step. I performed to a packed audience at the Hibernian Hall and was called back several times. I wish you could have heard the applause. The following day I was given one of the best reviews so far, and I think you'll be happy and reassured by it. This is what one reviewer wrote: 'Mr Alexander is able to convey complex passions with fidelity and distinction.' Now I think you see what I mean, when I say that I would be wasting my time to continue as an amateur performer.

Speaking of which, the concert in Wynyard is now likely to be some time in February. Do you think it would be too much if I charged an entrance fee? Or would it be a better idea to stage the concert as a money raiser for a worthy cause? I'm thinking the latter, even as I write, because I want the hall to be full, and the concert can be like a dress rehearsal for when I start to charge for my performances in the other towns. I thought that a concert to raise money for the brass band might be the best idea. The advantage of that is the band plays for no charge, and some lively numbers will give the concert a sense of occasion. There could even be a street parade to commence with. Do you, or any of the relatives, have a connection with the band that I could use?

There, you see now that I am in earnest. If, as you say, some people think that I am already a professional actor, then that will do no harm at all.

I'm impatient to start this new adventure, but I have one more commitment before I leave Melbourne. An important figure in the theatre scene here has recently announced his retirement and I have been asked to assist Mr James Cathcart and Mr Walter Bentley in a tribute concert to celebrate the man's career. Mr Bentley is the actor who inspired my poem about the burgomaster, and you can see how far I've come, when these two famous actors deem me worthy to perform alongside them.

As to your other concern, I feel certain that the discovery I've made about curing the problems with my voice can be taught to others. Mr Hill is still sceptical and insists that it's all to do with the breathing techniques he's taught me, but a few weeks ago I shared my ideas with Mr Walter Bentley and he was more open-minded, and very encouraging. There is a lot about what I'm doing that I find difficult to explain to others, but I have seen my own health improve steadily since I've been working on overcoming my bad habits and allowing my body to align itself. I know it's something to do with letting go of my shoulders and the position of my head. Even my feet. I'll show you when I'm back home, and you'll be surprised. If I can remember to stop pulling myself in all directions and let go, I feel taller, and my larynx and throat and chest open, and everything feels better. As I said, I've noticed a big improvement in my general health since I made my discovery and that's why you can be absolutely certain that this time I am in the best position to follow my ambitions, and why you can be sure that I will be back in Tasmania in the new year.

By the way, I did as you suggested and presented Mr Hill with a rather fine silver tray, and I gave him a framed testimonial as well. I thought he would reciprocate and offer to do a testimonial for my work with The Olympians, but so far he hasn't done so. However, with all the good reviews and my first place in the elocution competition, I have ample testament to my ability, and I can still use Mr Hill's name (and his father's!).

I always told you I'd make you proud and everything I do is with that in mind, so you mustn't worry.

Your loving son,
Frederick

Down in the garden Freddy was using a pair of scissors to snip off the dead roses from the arbour. It was late afternoon and the shadows were long, but there was still some heat in the sun and Freddy was wearing his straw hat tilted to one side to protect his face. It reminded Fred of a painting he'd seen in the gallery the other day, a light-filled scene of abundance and tranquillity.

There were certainly things he would miss, and this was high on the list. The last fifteen months in Freddy Hill's lovely house, his generous hospitality, had given Fred a taste of a style of life different from the one he was used to, and one that appealed very much.

But he couldn't afford to be complacent, not if wanted real success. It was like he'd told his mother; he'd outgrown his teachers. They were content to go over and over the same ground, and they'd taught him well, James Cathcart and Freddy Hill. They'd also brought him into the circle of people who mattered in the world of the theatre, and from there he wanted to go beyond the tried and tested, to develop his own methods, make his own way, find his own fame, and to start that journey there would be no better testing ground than his home state of Tasmania.

Part 4

Tasmania

1894 to 1895

54

A couple of months later, Thursday, 22 February 1894

The tide was out on Fossil Beach, and Fred walked over the exposed flat black rocks and around to the boulder strewn inlet where the sandstone cliffs were most accessible. Behind him he could hear Amy and Albie laughing. They'd taken off their boots and socks and were acting like children, running back and forth on the hard packed sand, following the waves as they surged up the beach then receded.

'You go ahead' he'd told them, 'I'm going to look for fossils.'

Fossil Bluff. It had been Amy's idea to ride over here for a picnic lunch. After the success of the concert last night there was a feeling in the household that a celebration of some sort was in order. Fred wished his mother could have come with them. She'd been as excited as Amy was about the packed hall, and the way the audience had applauded and laughed and enjoyed themselves. 'Oh Fred,' she'd told him as they walked back home afterwards, 'You were even better than those reviews said.' As it turned out, though, Agnes was travelling to Burnie to stay with Aunt Jane and couldn't look after the littlies, Arthur was working at the Smithy, and on top of that little Beaufort was down with a fever, so it was just the three of them: Fred, Albert, and Amy.

He stepped around and over the boulders until he found a big chunk of sandstone that had fallen from the cliff. It was flat on one end, making a convenient seat, and Fred used his arms to pull himself up onto it. When he'd first been taken out of school, Mr Robertson had brought him here on a fossil-hunting expedition, and over the years they'd been back together many times. The surface of one part of the rock he was sitting on was dense with fossils of broken shells and bits of grey stones. If he remembered correctly, there should be an almost complete turritella amongst the other gastropods, shaped like a cone and embedded in the sandstone. He searched for it amongst the cluster of fossils, running his fingertips over the pitted surface, and thinking about what Mr Robertson had told him: the layers of exposed rock were like a story, the fossilised remains in the rock strata a record of millions of years ago.

'Found something?'

Fred was startled to hear Albie's voice right next to him.

'Just the usual gastropods. They're everywhere.'

'Can I see?' Amy leaned against the rock, supporting herself with her hands, and followed where Fred was pointing.

'Oh that!' she said, 'we learned about them at school.' She pushed herself back off the rock and brushed her hands together to get rid of the coarse sand. 'Anyway Fred, we're hungry.'

'Yes,' Albie said, 'It's already past midday. Let's eat.'

'I'll go and start unpacking the food,' Amy said, and she held her skirt with both hands and nimbly dodged between the boulders, then when she was clear of the rocks, lifted her dress up to her knees and broke into an exuberant run.

Fred and Albie followed her across the wide expanse of sand to where they'd tethered the horses on the grassy bank that lined the beach. With his trousers rolled up and carrying his boots in one hand, Albie looked less than his twenty years, and it was hard to think of him going off to Kalgoorlie the way he did.

'Tell me about Kalgoorlie, Albie. There must be more than you told me in your letter.'

Albert looked across at Fred and shrugged.

'I was hoping to make the family's fortune. You know how we were told over and over about great uncle John, and how he came back rich from the diggings in California. I wanted to be like that.'

'And Grandpa Matthias too.'

'Yes. When the stories about Kalgoorlie started, I felt like I had to go, just like them.' Albie gave a bitter laugh. 'But I didn't have their luck.'

'I got the impression that Pa supported you.'

'He understood what I was trying to do. Not Ma of course. But I wanted to get away from Wynyard, see a bit of the world. And you can't imagine how bad things are here. We're all putting on a show because you're here, but that's not the truth of it. That's why you're staying with Aunty Jo.'

'Yes. Ma can't hide the fact that things are bad.'

'I'm sure she doesn't tell you half of it.'

'Did you find anything? Any gold?

'Nothing. Bits of gold dust occasionally. It was rough and filthy and backbreaking and all I got was typhoid.'

Fred put his hand on Albie's shoulder.

'I'm glad you made it back.'

In the short time it took them to get back to the horses, Amy had opened the saddle bags and she pulled out a rug and unfolded it.

'Where do you want to sit?' she asked Fred.

He chose a flat grassy patch next to a white-flowering grove of paper bark trees, and soon they were eating ham and pickles on buttered bread. Melbourne felt a long way away. The reception he'd got last night was just what Fred had been hoping for. He'd put together the sort of programme that Freddy Hill had been afraid to do. Tragic excerpts from *Mark Antony* and *Henry V*, *Parhassius* and *The Midnight Charge*, his own poem *Matthias the Burgomaster*, some humorous pieces, a very full programme, and it had all gone down splendidly. Today there was no trace of hoarseness or soreness in his throat. Really it had been a triumph, and he wished that Freddy Hill could have seen the way the audience responded. It was what Fred had been saying: people would rise to the occasion if they were given the chance to hear elevated material.

Amy brushed the crumbs from the front of her frock and pulled her hat down, then leaned back on her elbows, looking out over the wave-patterned sand and the turquoise sea.

'This is my favourite place in the world,' she announced.

'And how much of the world have you seen?'

Albie tossed a twig in her direction. It missed its mark and Amy took no notice.

'Not much. Where are you going next?' she asked Fred. 'That was such fun last night. I want you to stay here and keep doing concerts.'

'And give all his money to the brass band again? I think our brother has bigger things in mind.'

'You're right about that Albie. My plan is to give a concert in Burnie in a couple of weeks, charging for entry.' Fred sat hugging his knees, letting himself relax. 'I'm not planning any more concerts in Wynyard, Amy, but while I'm here I'd like to give you some voice lessons. You sang very well last night, but I think I can help you to be even better.'

Amy looked up at him.

'I'd like that. I can recite, too, and I want to be as good as you. Ma's so proud of you. You should have heard her before you came.'

'I could make horses fly and she wouldn't take any notice,' Albie said. 'All she ever talks about is how clever you are. Nothing I do is good enough for her.'

'And nothing I do is good enough for Pa,' Fred said. 'Do you know what he said to me? When I asked him if he was coming to my concert?'

Fred hadn't meant to tell anyone. He was a twenty-five-year-old man, and he didn't want to care what his father said. Albie and Amy were both looking at him, waiting. He had to tell them now. 'That he was ashamed of having a son who was a strolling player, no better than a vagabond. And other things I can't tell you.'

There was silence for a few seconds then Amy sat up and put her arm around his shoulders.

Albert looked across at them. 'It's no secret that father's getting worse. You've seen it too, Amy.'

Amy nodded.

'Drinking?' Fred asked.

'He thinks we don't know,' Albert told him. 'And no one can do anything about it. I don't like the way Ma's always singing your praises, Fred, but she's right. You are clever, and everyone likes you, especially important people. Whatever you decide to do, I'm sure you'll make it work.' He looked out over the sea, started to say something. Stopped. Took a breath, then turned to Fred. 'You have to make it work. I don't know how much more Ma can take. After Kalgoorlie I don't know what else to try and Arthur's just like father. They work together and now they drink together. I have to stay at home to keep an eye on Ma and the others. If I wasn't there...' he looked back out over the sea and Fred could barely hear what he said '...sometimes it gets really bad.'

Fred stood up and held out the other hand to help Amy up.

'You're right Albie. I have to succeed, and I will. When I do, I promise that I'll get you away from here. Both of you, and Ma too of course. '

55

Three months later, Tuesday, 29 May 1894

It was a crisp late autumn day in Launceston, and on his way from the Mechanics' Institute to the hotel, Fred took a long detour through City Park. He'd spent the morning in the splendid library at the institute, taking notes from C.S. Hartley's book on natural elocution. It had been quite a find. Some of Hartley's ideas accorded closely to Fred's own, especially his emphasis on using one's natural voice, and his recognition of the importance of keeping the muscles of the neck free. Fred was still searching for a way to articulate his ideas about voice production, and this could be the help he needed.

In that way, the morning wasn't wasted, but it wasn't what Fred had been hoping for. In his last advertisement for students, he'd used the Launceston Mechanics' Institute as his address, and he'd been hoping that finally there would be mail there from people who wanted to take up his offer of elocution classes. But still there was nothing.

As he passed the Jubilee Fountain he stopped for a minute, watching the cascades of sunlit water. It reminded him of the way the water glittered on a sunny day in Wynyard, and he thought about the promise he'd made to Albert and Amy. If he was to honour that promise, things would need to improve dramatically, and for that to happen, there was a great deal more he had to do, though exactly what, he wasn't sure.

The thought caused him to quicken his pace, and in five minutes he was back in his hotel room. It was well-appointed, with large bay windows that looked over Brisbane Street, leather armchairs, an elegant walnut writing desk and a four-poster bed, but the Brisbane Hotel was more than he could afford, and he couldn't stay here for long, not without students.

He'd learned in Melbourne that giving the appearance of success leads to actual success, and tomorrow he would place another ad, giving the hotel as his address; maybe that would make a difference. It was a week since he'd started placing his advertisements in the local newspapers, and so far he'd not had a single reply. Nor had there been any enquiries following the announcement made at the end of his concert, and none of the promising contacts through his friends' connections with the Mechanics' Institute had come to anything.

He sat down at the desk and picked up Saturday's *Tasmanian*. He'd left it folded to show Touchstone's Dramatic and Amusement section, and he re-read the short paragraph: *'Clever young elocutionist has determined to sojourn in Launceston for a time to give instruction in voice culture.'*

Now that he looked at it, why did he use 'clever'? Perhaps 'clever' wasn't the problem, it could be the word 'young'. But without 'young', 'clever' changed its meaning somewhat. A clever old elocutionist sounded a bit sly, as if he was out to deceive. It was one thing to be a clever young elocutionist in a review, another when soliciting students. 'Determined to sojourn in Launceston for a time and give instruction in voice culture'. At least that suggested that he was intending to stay.

He put the paper down and from the stack of newspapers on the side of the desk, found the first advertisement he'd placed, the one he'd paid for in the *Daily Telegraph*. This one he liked; it said a lot in a few words. The heading caught the eye: 'ELOCUTION AND VOICE PRODUCTION. Talented elocutionist prepared to give lessons in the above. Improved system.' The ad was to the point and much better than 'clever' and 'young'. 'Improved system' suggested he had more than the routine to offer. Were the prices too high? Not high enough? Two guineas a quarter for a private lesson, one guinea for a class should be about right. It's a shame he hadn't thought to use the hotel as his address for that ad. 'Mechanics' Institute' as an address made it obvious that he wasn't established.

He looked through the other pieces that he'd sent into Touchstone. As he'd now discovered, no one in Launceston recognised the names of Mr F. Wyndham Hill, or even T.P. Hill, so that had been a wasted opportunity. Their names only counted in Melbourne where they were so well known.

Should he place another advertisement? Organise another concert? Did he want to stay in Launceston? He had to become known, and if he couldn't do it here, there was still Hobart. Hobart, where he'd never been before, where Robert and Edith Young were his only contacts. It wasn't like Launceston, which was such a familiar little city. But his friends at the Institute, his family connections, neither had made the difference he'd expected.

It was Tuesday today. He'd give himself until the end of the week and if he still had no students, he would take the train to Hobart and set about organising a concert there. Fred took a sheet of paper and started to list all the pieces he had in his repertoire. He wrote headings in four columns: dramatic, pathetic, humorous, dialogue, then started to fill in titles in the appropriate column.

When he finished, he read back through the list he'd written and added a tick next to the pieces that had worked the best with audiences, but halfway through he stopped and sat looking at the list. Where was this going to get him? He knew already what people liked; he didn't have to make yet another list! It wasn't what entertained the audiences that was the problem. The problem was the size of those audiences.

The packed hall in Wynyard was the first and only large crowd he'd been able to attract, and none of that money had been for himself. In all the other places, the halls were depressingly empty, and in some there were so few people that his voice bounced off the walls. The most disappointing was in Waratah. Thirty people, he'd counted, most of them Annie's family and friends. After all the work he'd done for Mr Kayser, there was no sign of him, or his family and associates. And in the end, not even Mr

Seagrave had been there to support him. Some problem with his eye, he'd said. Lefroy was much the same. Even the attendance in Launceston was half what he was expecting. The review in the *Examiner* pointed out that the size of the audience was to be regretted, because his concert deserved a packed house, but that's what all the reviews said and yet he couldn't attract students, and the money from the concerts was barely enough to cover costs.

He was startled by a loud rap on the door, and when he opened it he found the bell boy standing there, an envelope in his hand.

'Special delivery for Mr F.M. Alexander.'

'F.M. Alexander. That's me.' Fred took the envelope and thanked the boy, then he turned back into the room and closed the door.

Robert Young's handwriting. Fred tore open the envelope and unfolded the single sheet of paper. He was too curious to sit down and he started reading while he walked over to stand against the window where the light was better.

Dear Zan,

You're going to want to kiss my feet when you hear what I've done for you. While you're casting your pearls to the people of Launceston, I've been doing what you asked, sniffing around for openings for you. Here's what I've done.

I have volunteered your services as a talented artiste for a big concert that's being held in the hall of the new Exhibition Centre on the Domain. It's on Friday, in three days' time. I suggest you do a couple of shortish, exciting offerings. Nothing too highbrow. Mr Mills (he's the Musical Director) was impressed when I told him of your Melbourne triumphs, so it wasn't hard persuading him to add you to the programme, even though the rest of it had already been decided. He's expecting well over 2,000 people to attend and it will be the first event to take place in the new hall.

The long and short of it, is that you need to take the train to Hobart tomorrow. Of course you must stay with us. Did is counting the hours and has already instructed the maid to make up our guest room for you.

> Your affectionate friend,
> Robert

Fred skimmed back through the letter and punched the air. This was the break he needed. He threw open the casement and looked down on the almost empty street. A woman dressed in dark colours and carrying an umbrella was coming out of Fox's dispensing chemist; two men in ill-fitting suits were walking slowly, heads down, as if they had no desire to get to where they were headed. Suddenly Launceston seemed dreary, and without promise.

He pulled the windows shut and stoked the fire, then stood with his back to it, going over his repertoire in his mind. What would work for a crowd that size? The telegram office would be closing soon. He turned towards the fire and warmed his hands, then he went back and sat at the desk and opened his leather folder of concert programs. *Kissing Cup*. That was always a favourite. Yes. That would do nicely. And why not *The Progress of Madness*? That had gone down very well with the audience in Lefroy. It was clever and funny, and people of Hobart should appreciate political satire.

He took a telegram from the stationery provided by the hotel and wrote *I'll be on the train tomorrow. The pieces for the concert are 'Dialogue from The Progress of Madness' and 'The Kissing Cup Race'.* He added Robert's address, blotted it impatiently and left it to dry while he changed his jacket and fixed his hat in front of the mirror. He would check about the train at the same time as sending off the telegram, then he would treat himself to dinner in the hotel and after that pack for tomorrow. Hobart couldn't come soon enough.

56

The next day, Wednesday, 30 May 1894

Fred paid the cabby, then called the porter to help him take his trunk through to the platform. There was a bench that ran part of the length of the station, too high for a seat, but comfortable enough as a support to lean against, and he chose a spot in the sun and settled in to wait. No matter that he had to stand. He preferred to be out here in the autumn sun, rather than in the crowded waiting room with the other passengers. There were still twenty minutes before the train was due to depart, but he was leaving nothing to chance. It was a good thing he'd checked with the concierge. There was only one train to Hobart, the man had told Fred. The express. Eleven sharp every morning. 'You'll be in Hobart by 5.00pm,' he'd added, clearly impressed by the speed of the journey, though Fred thought it didn't sound much like an express train.

But after four busy years in Melbourne, the slower pace here suited him. In Wynyard, working with Amy on her voice, teaching her what he'd taught himself and, in the process, learning more about his method, that was not something that he could have done in Melbourne. Not just because he was holding down his accounting job over there and fitting his other interests in around that. It was also because, with the time and space to work by himself, Fred knew he was right in thinking that he'd outgrown his teachers.

No, he didn't want to be in Melbourne, not until he'd made a name for himself. Here he could set his own agenda, and the fresh, sharp air made it a pleasure just to breathe. It was doing him good; he could feel his voice getting even stronger, and with that his constitution. It still surprised him, how the problems with his health, things he'd grappled with all his life, had almost vanished since he'd been working on his voice. Amy said it made her feel better too. He couldn't put it into words, not yet, not in a way he could use in advertising his lessons, but it was more than just voice production and elocution that he could teach.

He'd bought an *Examiner* from the lad outside the hotel, and he turned the pages until he found the theatre notes, then folded it into four and skimmed down the two columns.

The only thing of interest was the piece on the Bijou Theatre. So, Mr Cathcart had persuaded Walter Bentley to take on a role in the production of 'Friends' after all. Fred lowered the paper and stopped reading for a minute, his thoughts back in Melbourne. These legends of the theatre were his friends. He'd performed alongside Mr Cathcart in the tribute concert to one of Melbourne's most respected actors. The night before he left Melbourne for Tasmania it was Cathcart and Bentley who had treated him to a fine dinner at the Café Denat.

Standing here at the Launceston railway station, a plain, unadorned building from where he could see tree covered hills to his left and an open field and straggling houses in front of him, it was hard to put these things together. It wasn't the first time since he'd been back in Tasmania that he felt he could burst with wanting people to understand who he was, what he'd done, the people he knew! At least he could make good use of winning the competition. Freddy Hill had been right about that – it meant something, even for those who had no connection with Melbourne or the world of the theatre.

He looked back at the article on Bentley. 'As in almost everything else he performed in an artistic and effective manner.' Why 'almost'? When had Bentley ever been less than outstanding?

A shadow blocked the sun for a second and Fred was conscious of someone walking past him. He lowered the newspaper and looked to his left. A well dressed, lively looking, older man had come to enjoy the sun as well, and was standing just along from him. He had an intelligent, open face and an air of geniality. A businessman perhaps.

The man was reaching into the inside coat pocket for something, and Fred tucked the newspaper under his arm and caught the man's eye as he produced a pair of glasses from his pocket.

'Shouldn't be long now,' Fred said. 'I'm told it's usually on time.'

The man smiled, acknowledging the utility of Fred's comment.

'And you've been told correctly. I haven't seen you around here before. Paying a visit?' Then he saw Fred's trunk. 'Or moving to Hobart?'

He spoke with a rounded accent that must have originated somewhere in the south of England and Fred took an instant liking to him. Fred looked at his trunk. It was rather large, but then he had all his books in it, and his suits, and so much else.

He laughed. 'It looks like that, doesn't it? The truth is, I'm not altogether sure. My immediate goal is to perform in the concert in Hobart on Friday night.'

'Then you can't be from Launceston.'

'No. From Melbourne.'

'All the way from Melbourne just to perform in our new Exhibition Hall? By the way, I'm Henry Nicholls.'

Something in his manner suggested that Fred might recognise the name, but he didn't. 'Frederick Alexander. Fred,' he said. Then prompted by the way the man looked at him as if expecting more, he added. 'I'm from Wynyard originally. I've been doing some concerts in the northern towns.'

'Beautiful part of the country. Anything interesting in that paper? I didn't get a chance to buy one.'

Fred produced the paper from under his arm and pointed to the column about the Bijou Theatre.

'I was reading about someone I've given a bit of coaching to – Mr Walter Bentley. He's playing in a comedy at the Bijou.'

'Ah. Mr Bentley. He's the best actor I've seen in a long time. He gave us Hamlet in Hobart last year, and he'll be back in July with a comedy. But I guess you know that.'

'He was telling me about the Theatre Royal in Hobart. Perfect acoustics and a splendid audience, Mr Bentley said.'

'Ah yes. The Theatre Royal is much loved by our thespians, but I'm a newspaper man myself.'

Was Mr Nicholls a journalist then? He was dressed too well to be a reporter, and he didn't sound like one either. There was an air of authority about him, but it was worn lightly. Who was he?

'You don't strike me as a journalist,' Fred said. 'Let me guess. A business correspondent of some sort?'

Mr Nicholls laughed. 'You don't beat around the bush, Mr Alexander, and you're partly correct. I am indeed a newspaper correspondent, have been for years, but that's just a sideline. Most people here know me better as the editor of the Hobart *Mercury*.'

What were the chances of running into the editor himself? Here was a man who must surely have influence in the community, the sort of man Fred needed.

Fred laughed. 'The *Mercury* of course! I should have recognised your name. That's why it seemed familiar.'

Mr Nicholls gestured with his hand, as if to say let's not worry about that. He looked up at the clock that hung from the crossbeam behind Fred.

'Five minutes before the train is due. Now then Mr Alexander. Tell me how a young man like yourself came to give lessons to Mr Walter Bentley.'

It had only been one time, and more a discussion than a lesson, but Bentley had definitely been interested, and there had been talk about meeting up in Hobart, and perhaps in New Zealand.

'It's rather a long story,' Fred began. 'I was starting to become a recognised performer in Melbourne, and then my voice went...'

The train arrived and Mr Nicholls put a hand on Fred's shoulder. 'I can see I must have the rest of your story. Let's see if we can find a seat together.' He led the way into the forward carriage and helped Fred on with his trunk. 'With luck we'll have this compartment to ourselves. Now, you were telling me about how you lost your voice.'

Five hours later when they pulled into the Hobart station, Mr Nicholls had invited Fred to dine with him at his club and had persuaded him to write an article for the *Mercury* on his new approach to teaching.

They shook hands. 'Fascinating stuff,' Mr Nicholls said. 'It sounds as if you've made quite a discovery, and I couldn't agree more about the importance of voice training. Put all that in writing, and I'll publish it for you. And good luck for Friday night.'

Fred waited for a porter and watched Mr Nicholls walk along the platform to the exit. What a discerning man, and how extraordinary meeting him like this. The train journey had done a great deal more than simply cover the distance between two cities.

57

The following Monday, 4 June 1894

Fred could hardly believe he'd only been in Hobart for three days. The concert in the Domain had been extraordinary. Never had he been in front of such a crowd, and he knew, even as he was reciting, that he was giving the performance of his life. Overnight, his name meant something in the town, and people he'd never met recognised him, including two of the men he'd just dined with.

It was after three o'clock in the afternoon when he left the Tasmanian Club. The meal had been an elaborate three-course affair of soup, meat, and pudding, served with great solemnity and more silver than he'd ever seen. Mr Nicholls and his friends had retired to the smoking room and were finishing the bottle of port, but Fred had made his excuses and left them to it. These were influential men, of that he had no doubt, and Mr Nicholls had been at pains to show Fred off to them.

The men competed with their invitations and offers to help and they all had suggestions as to how he could make a success of his stay in Hobart. There were any number of 'at homes' where he would be more than welcome to recite, and there he would meet 'the right people'. The standards of spoken English were lower than ever, they all agreed, and schools like Hutchins would pay well for an elocution teacher like himself. Connections were no problem; a word would be said in his favour.

To capitalise on his appearance on Friday night, Fred explained, he was already planning a concert, and his friend Mr Robert Young of the Orpheus Club had booked the Town Hall for the end of the month. By showing what he could do in the way of recitation and acting, he aimed to attract professional men, barristers, and such like, or singers, actors, people who misused their vocal cords. Teaching these people was his specialty; elocution for young people was not his area at all. It was voice production and natural speech that concerned him.

One man who showed a discerning interest in Fred's ambitions was Dr Agnew. He was the president of the Art Society and he had a practical suggestion for the concert. 'Royal patronage is a must,' he told Fred. 'I could put in a word for you there. Let me know the details and I'll approach the Governor in the usual way.' It was to be held on June 25 Fred told him, but the details of the program were yet to be worked out.

Mr Nicholls' parting words were, 'I'm waiting for that article, Mr Alexander,' and Fred thanked him for the dinner and promised to get it done in the next week.

The sun was getting low in the winter sky, and the imposing stone buildings in Macquarie Street blocked it entirely. After the roaring fire in the club's dining room, the street felt cold and dark and Fred walked past Walch's bookstore and continued briskly along the street, looking for a tailor's shop that had been recommended to him. He walked almost as far as the Post Office until he realised he must be in the wrong street, and he decided to leave that mission for another day. On the other side of the street, leafy Franklin Square was still bathed in the afternoon sun, and having no particular deadline to meet, Fred crossed the road, curious to have a closer look at the famous statue and fishpond.

The effect was not dissimilar to the fountain in City Park in Launceston, he thought. Certainly there were similarities between the two cities, but Hobart was proving to offer what he hadn't found in Launceston. From the minute Fred had taken the train to Hobart it was as if a curtain had been lifted, the spectre of empty country halls and the futile wait for students transformed to a scene of success and action. Where else would he have had the chance to be cheered and applauded by an audience of thousands? Who else but Robert Young could understand exactly what he was trying to achieve and know how to make it happen? And with all his contacts in Launceston, he had met no one with the influence and status of Mr Henry Nicholls.

Already Fred had two students and that, he decided, was the thing he must do first: find a place suitable for giving lessons to Edith and her friend Miss Miller. It had seemed too good to be true that the Hobart Mechanics' Institute was just along the road from the Young's house. On the way home, he could get off the tram early and enquire about a suitable room. He could, of course, give lessons in the piano room at the Youngs' house, and it wasn't used while Robert was at work, but while Fred was talking to Mr Nicholls and his friends about his concert, he had come up with an ambitious idea.

Edith already knew the part of Lady Teazle in *The School for Scandal,* so it wouldn't take much to bring her performance up to concert standard by June 25th when the Town Hall was booked for his concert. From the meeting he'd had with Miss Miller, Fred had learned that she wasn't new to performing. She sang solo parts with the amateur opera company here, and he could help overcome the problems she was having with her voice, and at the same time prepare both of them to perform with him at the concert. Miss Miller looked the part for Miss Malaprop in Sheridan's *The Rivals.* With both of them used to being on a stage, they were sure to do well under his tuition, and what an advertisement for his teaching that would be!

His head clearer now, Fred crossed back to the other side of Macquarie Street. He checked his watch: three thirty. There would be time before the next tram to call into Walch's bookshop and look for a copy of Hartley's little book and other things he could use to help him make a start on his article for the *Mercury.*

★

A parcel of books under his arm, Fred ran towards the tram stop, waving to the driver, who saw him and stopped just long enough for him to jump on the running board. The double decker trams were quite a novelty – so different from the low-slung Melbourne trams – and he paid the conductor then climbed up the stairs to the top deck. There were no windows on this level, and the warmth had already gone out of the day, but the view from up here was worth putting up with a bit of cold air.

The tram gradually climbed the length of Liverpool and Little Goulburn Streets, then more steeply up to Princes Street, where it swung around and faced in the direction in which they'd come. Fred turned his head sideways so he could see the wide expanse of river and the ships moored alongside Princes Wharf. Hobart's hills were a pain to walk up, but the views over Hobart were splendid, and he could see why Robert had chosen to live up here, especially now that the trams provided such a good service. And that was another thing he had to do. Robert had told him that the Orpheus Club always had special trams put on for their concerts, and with Royal patronage for his concert, Fred had been told that he could expect the same service. All he had to do was ask.

Moving at a snail's pace, the tram climbed even more steeply until they turned from Hill Street into Lansdowne Crescent, and when Fred pulled the cord, the tram stopped directly in front of the Mechanics' Institute.

The secretary was very obliging and only too happy to show him around and answer his questions. Compared to the Launceston Institute with its excellent library and imposing stone façade, this one was a more modest timber building, but there was a reading room with a decent collection of newspapers and a meeting room that would work perfectly well for lessons and rehearsals until he had made enough money to rent his own premises.

He reserved the room for three o'clock on Mondays, Wednesdays, and Fridays, starting the day after tomorrow. The secretary told him he could use the stage for rehearsals at no extra charge, and with less than three weeks to prepare his two students for the concert, the sooner he started, the better.

58

A month or so later, Wednesday, 18 July 1894

When the meeting of the Shakespeare Club finished, Fred walked the three new members to the top of the steps.

'Until next week then,' he said. The hallway was dark, lit only by a single oil lamp, so he watched them safely negotiate the stairs before he turned around and went back to his rooms. Next door the photography exhibition was still open and he could hear voices as he walked past. Mr Hodgman and Mr McCreary had proved to be gracious landlords and patrons of the arts, and the empty rooms over their dispensary were being put to good use.

He closed the door and stood looking around, allowing himself a quiet moment of satisfaction. The wine-coloured rug, the large mirror over the dark wood mantelpiece and the buttoned green leather bucket chairs gave the room an elevated appearance that was exactly the effect Fred had been looking for. An internal door on the left opened into a smaller room, equally well-appointed, and perfect for private lessons. The Mechanics' Institute had served its purpose – in fact the lessons with Edith and her friend had gone exceptionally well – but this was how he had imagined his rooms would look.

It had all happened in the past couple of days and in a rush; the message from Dr Agnew about the rooms, his offer to leave some of the furnishings that the Art Society no longer needed, letters sent to the men and women who had expressed interest in the Shakespeare classes, and this was the result: the first meeting of his own Shakespeare Club. If only Mr Robertson could see him now!

Not surprisingly the numbers had been small, since not everyone could come at such short notice, and it wasn't a bad thing. For his first meeting, having only three people to think about made it easier to choose suitable readings. The scenes from *Much Ado about Nothing* had been perfect for tonight; in fact the night had been perfect. There was something very special about sharing Shakespeare's words. It wasn't like just any play reading, and Fred understood more acutely now what Mr Robertson had meant when he wrote about what a comfort his Shakespeare Club meetings were, and how one could always find hope and wisdom in the bard.

And the night wasn't over; Walter Bentley was expecting him at Hadley's, and it was time for him to go. Fred tidied up the chairs, switched off the kerosene heaters and the gas light, then locked the door behind him.

It was a short walk from his rooms to Hadley's, and ten minutes later Fred was about to push the brass handle of the heavy glass door of Hadley's Orient Hotel when the door was opened from inside and a doorman in a smart black and gold uniform greeted him.

'Evening sir, can I assist you?'

'I'm here to see Mr Walter Bentley,' Fred told him. 'He's expecting me.'

'You'll be the gentleman he told me to watch out for then. He's through there in the bar. "Tell him to go through" is what he said.'

'Thank you. I know my way,' Fred told him. He hung his coat, hat and scarf on the hallstand and checked his hair in the mirror, then went through the deserted lounge room and up a couple of stairs into the back bar.

A group of five or six men and women were sitting around a table, talking and drinking. Apart from the barman, they were the only ones in the room, not surprising at eleven o'clock on a Sunday night.

One of the women he recognised as Miss Graham in *The Silence of Dean Maitland*. 'It was a near thing,' she was telling the others. 'I sneezed just as I got to the wings and the front of my costume ripped straight down the middle.'

There were shrieks of laughter and Fred let it die down before he made his presence known. 'Laugh now,' he said with mock gravity, 'for tomorrow the fates will have their way.'

He had walked around to where Walter Bentley was leaning back on his chair, holding a glass of champagne.

'Ah, Fred. You've come. Everybody, meet Mr Alexander, protégé of Jimmy Cathcart, poet, performer, and teacher.' Bentley didn't bother with the names of his companions, but surprised Fred by telling them, 'Mr Alexander was so impressed by my role as Matthias in *The Bells* that he composed his own ballad about the poor man. Give them a taste of it, Fred.'

Fred wasn't sure how to take the request, but judging by the empty bottles on the table, the mood was one of hilarity, so he took two of the most macabre lines, and delivered them with an exaggerated menace designed to make them laugh. 'He tried to sleep but all in vain, his eyes were hot and red/ The vision was before him now, it hovered round his head,' he recited. Then in his normal voice he added, 'And so on.'

Walter Bentley stood up and put a hand on Fred's shoulder.

'I'll leave you to it,' he told the others. 'I'm hoping Mr Alexander is going to give me some good advice to help with this throat problem I've been having.' Bentley put his glass on the table and added. 'Alas, champagne, as it turns out, is not the cure for everything.'

They all laughed and Bentley ushered Fred back through the lounge room and over to the wide carpeted staircase that led to the upper floors.

'Just one flight,' he said, 'my room is on the first floor.'

Away from the others, Walter Bentley was the same thoughtful, supportive man Fred had got to know in Melbourne. Like Fred, Walter Bentley's father had disapproved of his acting ambitions. So vicious was his opposition, that as a young man, Walter had taken a ship from Scotland to Australia and then New Zealand where he'd become renowned as an actor. Now he was determined to help others who had the same ambitions, and his success was an inspiration to Fred. In many ways, Mr Bentley reminded Fred of Mr Robertson and it wasn't just the Scottish background; he was much the same age as Mr Robertson would have been had he lived, and they both had the same passion for Shakespeare.

'It's good of you to come at such short notice, Fred,' Mr Bentley called over his shoulder. 'Nearly there.'

Fred followed Mr Bentley along the corridor and into a suite of rooms, the first of which had a nook with a low table between two brown leather chesterfields, a blackwood desk on the opposite wall, and through an arched alcove, a dining table and chairs.

Mr Bentley waved a hand towards the lounges. 'Have a seat, Fred. Drink?'

Fred declined the drink, and Mr Bentley sat down opposite him.

'There's not much time, so I'll get straight to the point. You probably know that we're off to New Zealand tomorrow.' Fred nodded, and Mr Bentley continued. 'The thing is, since I've been in Hobart, I've been troubled by hoarseness in my throat. So far it's not too serious, but when I got the note you sent me, I remembered that evening with Jimmy, and what you were telling us about a new method to prevent such things.'

'To be honest,' Fred said, 'I'm still finding my way, and time is not on our side. But of course I'll share what I can.'

'If you can steer me in the right direction, I can work on it during the crossing.'

Where to start? If it was anyone else, Fred would tell him to organise lessons, but this was Walter Bentley, so Fred did his best to explain about the full chest nostril breathing, and how he'd learned not to trust what seemed right just because it was what one always did.

'For me,' he told Mr Bentley, 'I could have sworn I was forward with my head, but when I checked in the mirror, it wasn't the case. The way I overcame that was by letting go of my shoulders and allowing my feet to sink into the floor. That helps the air flow over the larynx without strain.'

'I tell you what,' Mr Bentley said, 'I'll recite something, and you can tell me if I'm doing what I think I am.'

He got up from the couch and took a stance in front of the desk, one hand resting on the back of the chair, then recited the opening lines of Hamlet's monologue.

Fred stood to one side, careful not to block the light and there it was, slight enough not to be noticed unless you were looking for it, the chin slightly raised, the shoulders tensed.

'Now think about the things I mentioned,' he told Mr Bentley, 'Let go of your shoulders.'

Bentley let his hand drop from the chair and stood feet apart, rolling his head loosely from side to side, then he let his head fall naturally.

'Like that?' he asked.

'Better,' Fred told him. 'Now let your weight sink into the floor.' There was a slight but discernible forward movement of his head.

'Can you feel the difference?'

Bentley laughed, raised his shoulders and let them drop again. 'I see what you mean, Fred. It feels different and better.' He walked back over and sat down on the chesterfield, and Fred followed suit.

'You'll find you keep pulling those shoulders up when you're performing,' Fred told him. 'It takes a while to break the habit, but I'll guarantee that's the cause of your sore throat.'

'I haven't your perseverance or your youth, Fred, but I'll do what I can. Now, tell me how Hobart's been treating you.'

Fred wondered where to start. First there'd been the triumph of the Exhibition Hall recital, then there were the frantic three weeks preparing for his own concert, the disappointment when bad weather forced him to cancel at the last minute, re-organising the concert, the glowing reviews, taking on more students, publishing the article, and now his own rooms and the Shakespeare Club.

'I'm already making a name here,' Fred told Mr Bentley. 'All sorts of people have given me support in a way I haven't experienced before. Another few months and I should be able to call myself a real professional.'

'Excellent, excellent. We like it here too; they're a friendly lot, these Hobartians. But how do the numbers stack up?'

'To be honest, I need bigger audiences and more students. Even though it's a small town, there are a lot of other things to compete with. Visiting companies like yourself, for example.'

Mr Bentley laughed.

'Ah, but you're going to make your name in your own way. Anyway, the night's not getting any younger, I've kept you long enough.' Mr Bentley stood up and held out his hand. 'Thank you for coming Fred. I'll remember what you told me.' They shook hands and Mr Bentley was about to open the door when he stopped and turned to Fred.

'If you like Hobart, Fred, you might do worse than to think about a tour of New Zealand. The people there are wonderful, and they love the sort of recitation you do. I'll be over there for a year at least and you could give me some proper lessons. We could even do a bit of Shakespeare together. I think of New Zealand as my home, especially Dunedin where I started my acting career. We could meet up there, have a bit of fun. For the time being I'll continue with my acting – it's in my blood – but I've nothing more to prove in that respect, and I would like to do more lecturing, and do more to lend a hand to others in this precarious world of the theatre.'

It wasn't the first time New Zealand had been suggested. There'd been an acquaintance from Wynyard who had moved there, and Fred had gone so far as to write and ask what his reception was likely to be. 'Don't hesitate,' his friend had written in reply. 'The people here in Christchurch are avid theatregoers, and something a bit elevated would go down very well.'

But Fred wondered if he was ready. And it wasn't only that; he felt at home here in Hobart and it would be hard to leave.

'I'll keep it in mind,' Fred told Mr Bentley. 'There's more I need to do here – work on my performance and develop my teaching method. Christmas I've promised to spend with the family up north, but a tour of New Zealand early next year? Perhaps.'

'Let's keep in touch then,' Mr Bentley said. 'If you drop a line to the Post Office in Dunedin, they'll find me.'

It was a forty-minute walk from the hotel to Lansdowne Crescent, uphill all the way. The sky was full of stars and the air was biting but wrapped in his coat and scarf Fred soon warmed up. As he walked to the end of Little Goulburn Street he looked up at the mountain, the new moon hanging over the snowy cap, and for now at least, he couldn't imagine anywhere else he'd rather be.

59

Five months later, Wednesday, 12 December 1894

Downstairs Edith was holding a luncheon for Miss Miller's birthday, and Fred could hear the murmur of voices and an occasional burst of laughter. He'd taken cuttings of the reviews of Monday night's play and before he put them into his folder for Hobart, he flicked back to the review of his first concert. It was still the best one, two columns in *The Tasmanian*, with a bold heading that took up two lines: **Mr F.M. Alexander's Recital.** He placed that review by the side of the best of Monday night's reviews and noted the difference. There was no denying that the keen interest in him as a newcomer had dwindled into steady support, the articles now half a column, if that, no big headlines.

Not that he was complaining. Steady support had resulted in a growing number of students, and enthusiastic regulars in his Shakespeare Club. If he did decide to move on from Hobart, it would be hard to leave the students who were doing so well. And hard to leave some other people too, not least Edith and Robert.

Fred put the cuttings back into the folder. What he had to do right now was to write to his mother. He knew she checked the post box every day for a letter from him, and she would expect to hear how his latest, most challenging venture had gone. He took out a folded sheet of paper, dipped his pen in the inkbottle and started writing.

Dearest Ma,

It's little more than a week until I'll be home for Christmas but I know you'll be wondering how the play went on Monday night. Well you can stop worrying because it all went splendidly. You know that I had some concerns early on about Mr Webster and his stammer, but I wish you could have seen him. He played the part of the elderly, eccentric violin maker so well that you would never guess that he's a hale and hearty thirty-year-old, and there wasn't a hint of a stammer. 'Great skill' is how one reviewer described his performance. You can imagine how proud that makes me feel! The others did very well too, and all Mr Holding's anxieties vanished once he was on the stage, just as I knew they would. For my part, I thoroughly enjoyed playing the part of the hunchbacked young cripple and was deemed clever and accomplished, but that's neither here nor there. The main thing is that we gave the audience a thoroughly good night of rather instructive entertainment, and the way they applauded and called us back was a good indication of how much they enjoyed it.

As usual the size of the audience was disappointing, especially given the support I had from the Orpheus Orchestra, and of Mr Young, who is such a favourite here in Hobart. It seems that I have no luck in choosing dates for my productions. In winter I had the misfortune to have to postpone both my concerts, and now that the weather is good, I'm competing with the Exhibition and a flurry of end of year concerts. I'm not the only one; attendances are down for everyone except the really big names, and I'm beginning to think that it may be time to test myself further afield, possibly in New Zealand.

Meanwhile, I've already had several enquiries about lessons following the performance. Did I tell you that Mr Holding has a friend with a speech impediment who has already started with me? I have no intention of going anywhere until I can help him overcome his problem. I know you prefer my teaching to my acting, and it's interesting how I'm drawn more and more to that side of things, though I can't imagine turning my back on the theatre entirely. Sometimes I think about the way you can heal people, and I wonder if you haven't passed some of that on to me.

I'll let you know my exact arrival time later, but it's most likely to be the evening of December 20th.

Your affectionate and loving son,
Frederick

60

Three months later, Wednesday, 6 March 1895

It was late afternoon and Edith was busy organising the kitchen staff for tonight's supper. Fred was making the most of what remained of the sunny autumn day and had set himself up at the glass-topped table on the verandah, where he was working on an article he hoped to publish in New Zealand.

For an hour or so he read through his notes, underlining the parts that could be used, and jotting down ideas about how he might explain his new methods. He liked the words he'd used for his Hobart ads, 'ease and grace in speech', but how to expand that into an article? When he was face to face with his students, he could convey the ideas about his technique without too much trouble, especially now he'd started using his hands to help them understand, but it was no easier to write about now than it had been six months ago.

What he had written so far was depressingly similar to his other article, even though his teaching methods had evolved during his time here. Why was it so hard? He knew the work he was doing with his students was helping them, but when he tried to explain it to outsiders, he found that the words he had at his disposal were inadequate for the task. How could he describe the way he used his hands to help his students understand about lengthening the neck? The notion of stress and letting go? The need to stop and think, rather than rely on habit? The idea that we inflict ourselves with problems by poor use? Nobody else was writing about such things.

He pushed the notebook to one side. That was enough. There would be plenty of time on board the ship to work on it. When he looked up he saw that the sun was low in the sky, and over the river high banks of clouds were streaked with oranges and pinks.

He got up from the hard metal chair and walked across to the iron-lace railing. Leaning on his elbows he gazed out over the city where he'd had such good fortune. Hobart was spread below him, the dense cluster of buildings, then the wide river and the hills beyond, a familiar sight now.

Several ships were anchored close to shore, floating on water turned golden by the setting sun. The largest of them was tied up at Princes Wharf, and though it was hard to make out from way up here, Fred knew it to be *The Tarawera*. This time tomorrow he'd be well on his way to Dunedin, and in quite some luxury he realised after his visit to the boat today. In many ways he was sorry to leave Hobart, but the thought of the opportunities that lay ahead outweighed any feelings of regret.

Suddenly two soft hands covered his eyes. He took one in each of his own hands and gently separated them. Edith put an arm over his back and leaned next to him against the railing. Fred pointed down towards the harbour.

'That's my ship down there. You can just make out its masts amongst the buildings on the docks.'

'I don't want you to go.' Edith gave a little swirl then turned to face him. 'How do I look?' she asked.

She had already changed for dinner into a rose-coloured muslin gown with long sleeves puffed at the top and a wide neckline trimmed with braid. The bodice was loose and a wide satin sash sat somewhere between her waist and her hips. Her dark hair was bunched up on her head and the contrast between her strong features and the delicate dress was striking.

'Like the Fairy Queen,' Fred told her. 'Just a minute, you're a bit askew.' He took a step closer and tugged at one side of the neckline, then he pulled both corners and stood back and examined his work. 'There, that's better.'

There was a high-pitched squealing noise, and Edith and Fred turned back to the railing and watched the evening tram take the sharp turn from Hill Street into Lansdowne Crescent. The noise lessened to a rumble as the tram came along the road, there was a single sharp ding, and the tram stopped a few houses down.

Robert was the first one off the tram. They watched him turn to thank the driver, then he looked up at the house and saw them. He took his hat off and waved it in their direction and a big smile lit up his face. Edith and Fred waved back, and they watched him striding along the side of the road, trailing his hat in one hand. Tall, athletic looking despite his ill health, the cheek bones prominent and his hair swept to one side.

Edith turned towards Fred.

'Did you ever see anyone so handsome as Bobba? Admit you're going to miss us.'

For an answer he took her hand and gave it a squeeze.

'Of course I'll miss you,' he said.

Robert appeared at the top of the stairs and came over to join them.

'Don't you look a sight for sore eyes,' he told Edith. 'But it's getting cold out here. Come on F.M., let's change for dinner and celebrate your last night.'

Edith had worked hard to make the night memorable. There was crayfish with champagne sauce, a raspberry trifle with cream and brandy, champagne and wine, and whisky and cigars. Robert told funny stories about the other clerks he worked with, the way they always plotted behind each other's backs. Fred told them about the cabby who had taken his luggage to the wharf and how he'd tried to cheat him out of sixpence. Edith drank wine and laughed at everything.

After the meal was finished, Edith announced that they should go to the piano room and have some fun. It was something that they had done often over the past few months. Robert would start tinkering with a song, sometimes new, sometimes old. He'd strike some chords, sing a few improvised lines poking fun at whatever had caught his attention that day, then all three of them would add their ideas, getting more and more outlandish and funnier.

They duly adjourned to the piano room and Robert played the opening bars of a new song he was working on. Then he stopped, ran his fingers down the entire length of the keys and closed the piano lid. He looked up at Fred and Edith, who were leaning against the piano, one on either side.

'Sorry Did,' he said, 'I'm not in the mood tonight.'

Robert stood up and put one arm around Edith's shoulders and the other around Fred's. 'I suggest a night-cap before we turn in.'

Once settled in the comfortable fireside chairs, whiskies in hand, Robert raised his glass.

'Here's to you F.M. I hope you have all the success you could wish for.'

Fred raised his glass. 'To success. But there's no point in wishing,' he added. 'In the words of the bard, we hold our destiny but in ourselves.'

'Shakespeare again,' Edith said. 'Always Shakespeare.'

'And that's because he speaks so eloquently and so wisely.'

'Sometimes it makes me feel that I don't really know what you're thinking.'

'Tell me F.M.,' Robert said, 'What are you expecting from New Zealand?'

Fred didn't have a ready answer. He watched the orange flames in the fireplace, and dancing around them the almost invisible heat that formed a transparent blue flame, sometimes there, sometimes invisible. The heat that came from the flames, that's what he was searching for, how he wanted to be.

'If I knew I would tell you Bobba.'

'Let me put it another way. What has Hobart meant to you? Career-wise I mean.'

'That's easy. This is where I've become a real professional. That's why I can try my luck in New Zealand.'

'And after that?'

Edith and Robert watched him, their faces lit by the glow from the fire. Fred knew that whatever happened they would be part of it. There was no need to explain, they knew his heart's secrets. He raised an eyebrow and smiled.

'Let's wait and see,' he said.

Afterword

Fred's tour of New Zealand was more successful than he could have imagined. He traded Shakespearean monologues with Walter Bentley in Christchurch, and his other performances were rapturously received. His teaching was also sought after, and his students included some public figures, such as the Mayor of Auckland and Fred Villiers, the renowned war correspondent.

In early 1896 he returned triumphantly to Melbourne where, against the advice of his friends, he made the decision to concentrate on his teaching. Edith went to Melbourne at the same time, still counting on Fred to help her find success on the stage. During 1896 Fred brought his brother Albert to Melbourne and trained him to help in his teaching, then Amy, to whom he gave lessons to help her recover from a serious riding accident. By the end of the year, his mother and three more of his siblings had also settled in Melbourne. In 1899 Robert Young resigned from his position with the government and moved to Melbourne, and he and Edith and Fred shared a house in South Yarra.

The Olympians gave no more performances after Fred left Melbourne. Freddy Hill still taught elocution, but his main business was as a qualified teacher of shorthand.

Fred worked hard and built up a very successful practice, teaching voice cultivation and achieving health benefits beyond that.

After four years, in 1900, Fred left his brother Albert running the practice in Melbourne and moved to Sydney, where he was joined by Edith and Robert. Edith was still hoping to make a name for herself as a leading actress, and for two years Fred concentrated his energies on teaching acting and producing Shakespearean plays, with Edith and himself in the starring roles. Despite lavish productions and extensive touring, it wasn't financially viable, and Fred continued teaching his techniques of breathing and voice production.

A leading Sydney surgeon, Dr Stewart McKay, was impressed by his methods. They became good friends, and Dr McKay encouraged him to take his ideas to Great Britain. The financial problem of doing that was solved when, after a chance meeting with a bookie on a Sydney tram, he put a £5 'double bet' at 150 to 1 on two big races. Both horses won, and with the £750 he paid off some of his debts and bought a passage to Plymouth. He sailed to Great Britain in April 1904 and was followed soon after by Edith, with Robert's blessing. Robert stayed in Sydney, and helped pay off debts that were left behind. He died in 1910 at the age of 54. Edith and Fred were married in 1914.

Fred, by then known as F.M., went on to make an international name for himself and his method, first in Great Britain, then in the United States. His ideas became known as the Alexander Technique and the method is still widely taught and practiced today.

Author's Note

This novel is an imagined reconstruction of the early life of FM Alexander. However, all the characters and events in the book are firmly anchored in historical fact, and below is a list of the main resources consulted.

F Matthias Alexander, *The Use of Self*. London: Orion Spring, 2018 (originally published in 1932 by Methuen & Company); F Matthias Alexander, *Articles and Lectures: articles, published letters and lectures on the Alexander Technique*. London: Mouritz,1995; Michael Bloch, *FM: The Life of Frederick Matthias Alexander Founder of the Alexander Technique*. London: Little, Brown, 2004; J.A. Evans, *Frederick Matthias Alexander: A Family History*. Chichester: Phillimore & Co. Ltd., 2001; Goddard Binkley, *The Expanding Self: How the Alexander Technique Changed my Life*. London: STAT Books, 1993; Rosslyn McLeod, *Up from down under: the Australian origins of Frederick Matthias Alexander and the Alexander Technique*. Canterbury, Vic: R. McLeod, 1994; Nikolaas Tinbergen, *The Nobel Lecture*. Stockholm, 1973 www.nobelprize. org/prizes/medicine/1973/tinbergen/lecture/

Newspapers consulted include the following: *The Mercury* (Hobart, Tas:1860–1954); *Tasmanian News* (Hobart, Tas:1883–1911); *Launceston Examiner* (Launceston, Tas: 1842–1899); *Daily Telegraph* (Launceston, Tas: 1833–1928); *Colonist* (Launceston, Tas: 1888–1911); *Wellington Times and Agricultural and Mining Gazette* (Tas: 1890–1897); *Tasmanian* (Launceston, Tas: 1871–1879); *Table Talk* (Melbourne, Vic: 1885–1939); *Melbourne Punch* (Vic: 1855–1900); *Evelyn Observer and South East Bourke Record* (Vic: 1882–1902); *Lorgnette* (Melbourne, Vic: 1878–1898); The Argus (Melbourne, Vic: 1848–1957); The Age (Melbourne, Vic: 1854–1954); *Williamstown Advertiser* (Vic: 1875–1954); *Williamstown Chronicle* (Vic: 1856–1954); *Sportsman* (Melbourne,

Vic: 1882–1904); *The Herald* (Melbourne, Vic: 1861–1954); *The Prahan Telegraph* (Vic: 1889–1930); *Chronicle* (Adelaide, SA: 1895–1954); *The Sydney Morning Herald* (NSW: 1842–1954)

These newspapers are all available in the Australian National Library's publicly accessible database, *Trove*.